It was bad enough with all the soldiers and their demands, but she hadn't expected to face danger from a local...

He was close enough now that she could see a sprinkle of white pimples on his cheeks above the beard. "You've delivered your message. Now please allow me to pass."

"But you still think you be better'n us'ns, don't you? We risk our life to defend the Stars and Bars and the likes of you stays home and gives your favors to the Yankees." His blue eyes seemed to grow a shade darker as his voice dropped to a husky whisper. "I heerd all about you. Ain't much difference between you and a fast trick, be there?" His hand darted to grab her arm tightly. "Be there!"

"Let go of me!"

"No," he answered himself, "there ain't. First Nellie Carswell. Then a Yankee with pumpkin rinds on his shoulders. No, I reckon there be no difference at all." His other arm grasped her waist and pulled her toward him. The hard arc of his body pressed to bend her backwards. "And God damn if it ain't a long time since I had me some horizontal refreshment!"

He swept a foot behind her heels as he pushed, and, even as she fell and the limbs and gray sky swirled overhead, a small corner of her mind wondered at the practiced move of the man's foot. The heavy thud of the ground stunned her motionless. She felt a hand push into her dress, tugging and pulling the cloth as she tried to move her arms to scratch at the man's face.

"Good enough for Nellie Carswell. Good enough for a Goddamn Yankee."

Rough fingers pulled at the neck of her dress and she heard the buttons rip.

"Think you're too good for me, by God!"

His broad palm mashed her breast to hold her against the ground as he pulled his arm from around her waist and fumbled somewhere out of sight.

Young, but newly widowed, Lydia Sensabaugh struggles to make a living on her farm. Her husband had attempted to revitalize the worn-out soil with new chemicals. But he died of swamp fever before his experiment could be proven. Now, in 1861, the farm's quiet isolation is invaded—first by mysterious lights and nighttime trespassers then by rumors of secession and war. When the Union Army occupies the Delmarva Peninsula, Lydia finds herself drawn into the conflict between Rebel and Loyalist neighbors. Adding to the social complexity and tangle of emotions, she finds herself attracted to a Union officer who has classified her as "the enemy," but with whom she develops a deepening epistolary courtship. She learns hard lessons of war by following news of the bloody fighting on the Mainland, by participating in the dangerous activity of smuggling supplies to Lee's army, and by witnessing the war's effects on hospitalized soldiers in the Federal City of Washington. As the war grinds on, her world reflects the age's philosophical shift from Emerson to Social Darwinism, and promises outcomes that are both unclear and terrifying...

KUDOS for *Into Enemy Arms*

In *Into Enemy Arms* by Rex Burns, Lydia Sensabaugh is a young widow in Virginia in 1861 at the beginning of the Civil War. Struggling to survive on a worn-out farm her husband was hoping to revitalize with chemical fertilizer before he died of swamp fever, Lydia ekes out a living with the help of two hired workers—a young house girl and a male farm hand. When war comes to Virginia, Lydia's life become immensely more difficult as Union soldiers conscript her one plow horse and beat her farm hand. Now Lydia is left with only the house girl to try and raise enough food to get her through the winter. As the war drags on, Lydia forms an unlikely relationship with a Union officer. Lonely, isolated, and struggling for survival, Lydia is torn between the Southern sympathies of her neighbors and the northern man she has fallen in love with. Well written and incredibly detailed, the story paints a poignant picture of the hard life women of that era lived, even when there wasn't the added complication of war. A compelling read. ~ *Taylor Jones, The Review Team of Taylor Jones & Regan Murphy*

Into Enemy Arms by Rex Burns is the story of one woman's courage in the face greed, corruption, and war. The year is 1861 and Lydia Sensabaugh is newly widowed and left to work a farm in the marshlands of Virginia. Her husband had hoped to bring the farm back to life with brand new chemical fertilizers from DuPont that he was sure would make the land productive again. But he died before he could accomplish his mission, leaving his young wife to fend for herself. With the threat of war looming on the horizon, Lydia struggles to raise enough produce for her household and to sell for cash to obtain other necessities. Her lot in life worsens when the Union army "conquers" Virginia and starts "requisitioning" food and livestock the people need to survive. When they take her only horse, Lydia must plow her fields by hand with a shovel and a hoe, back-breaking work even for a man. Lonely for affection and compassion, Lydia is drawn to a young Union officer, and their courtship makes Lydia a traitor in the eyes of her Confederate neighbors, who make her life a living hell. A compelling and touching story, Into Enemy Arms has a ring of truth that is rare in historical novels. Burns's knowledge of the past and his vivid descriptions pull you right into the story and make you feel like you are there in the scene. This is one you will want to read again and again. ~ *Regan Murphy, The Review Team of Taylor Jones & Regan Murphy*

Into Enemy Arms

Rex Burns

A Black Opal Books Publication

Black Opal Books

BECAUSE SOME STORIES JUST HAVE TO BE TOLD

GENRE: HISTORICAL FICTION/WOMEN'S FICTION/CIVIL WAR
FICTION

INTO ENEMY ARMS
Copyright © 2017 by Rex Burns
Cover Design by Jackson Cover Designs
All cover art copyright © 2017
All Rights Reserved
Print ISBN: 978-1-626946-81-1

First Publication: JUNE 2017

Published by Black Opal Books **http://www.blackopalbooks.com**

DEDICATION

To Cynthia, Once More

Prologue

Virginia, March 1861:

In the chill, moonless night, a thick mist glided up Fowler Inlet from Chesapeake Bay toward the isolated farmhouse. Star-lit, gray tendrils slid between the spears of marsh grass, then over the old pier, and low across the lawn to reach for the shadowed porch. But that wasn't what the two women stared at through the dark parlor window. Somewhere beyond the two bare masts of the *Lydia* rising out of the blanket of mist, a pair of yellow lights hung motionless where none should be. Against the dark, wooded shore of Fowler Creek, they flickered steadily side-by-side. Then suddenly they were gone, to leave only icy stars and the pale layer of damp mist moving even closer to Marshfield Farm.

Chapter 1

Two mornings later, the lights haunted Lydia Sensabaugh's thoughts as she labored in her kitchen garden.

Her maid, before leaving on her annual long visit home, had assured Lydia that the lights must have come from a fishing boat or coon hunters. "Maybe it was some yahoos trying to frighten a widow because of all that war talk and such," she had sniffed before walking down the sandy lane that led inland through the woods. "There's some think that kind of thing's funny."

Lydia accepted that possibility, too, but nonetheless she did mention the lights to her hired hand, Roger Bradshaw, and last night she had watched again. But no more lights appeared—just mist gliding shoreward through stalks of cordgrass.

She pushed away the troubling thoughts about lights and, tucking an escaping strand of light brown hair under her sun bonnet, focused on this day's chore. The corner of her hoe scraped gently around pale, fragile sprouts lifting to the early March warmth of a clear sky. The pitted blade, freshly filed by Roger, sliced at weeds stealing life from the seedlings and worked Mr. Dupont's chemical fertilizer into the soil. Though her shoulders were tired and the small of her back ached, she found the work satisfying. It was good to be outside in the early spring air, and even better to see how well these cool-weather plants responded to the powder she had carefully measured from the kegs that Franklin, her husband, stored in the barn not long before his death. The success of this chemical would justify his faith in scientific agriculture as well as their dream of bringing new life to the old soil of this farm.

The rhythmic strokes of her hoe, the warmth of the sun, the drift of her thoughts so lulled her consciousness that she heard nothing until a near-by voice startled her: "Mrs. Sensabaugh?"

Jerking erect, she saw a horse and rider silhouetted in the glare. "Is that you, Mr. Carswell?"

"Your servant, ma'am." Carswell lifted his broad straw hat. Sunlight glinted in the gold of his heavy eyebrows. Carefully trimmed mustaches of the same tint framed his mouth and narrow goatee. "Might I interrupt your chores for a few minutes? I was riding my property and thought to stop by."

"It's no interruption, sir, but a pleasure."

"The pleasure is entirely mine." He smiled as his eyes took in the hint of her figure beneath the faded black of the widow's dress. Then he leaned forward, saddle creaking. "What's that you're putting into your garden?"

"A chemical from the Dupont mills. It brings good growth—if used judiciously."

"Ah, yes—your husband's famous chemical fertilizer! He used to speak of it often. Very often." Carswell nodded toward Roger and Star plowing in the distant field. "Do you use it on your crops as well?"

"I intend to, yes."

"Think it will keep your crop through a late frost? You're planting mighty early."

Slapping dust from her stained gardening apron, she tried to keep her voice pleasant as she leaned the hoe against a fence rail. "I believe it is worth a try." She untied the strings of her bonnet, and her hair, streaked light by the sun, fell loose around her shoulders as if her mother had never taught her to braid. No doubt her dress had unseemly dark patches of perspiration as well, but she hoped that at least the dark cloth hid from the man's eyes the fact that she wore no stays. "I'm sure you're thirsty, sir—I certainly am."

"You're most kind."

Polished boots swung down from the creaking saddle as the high-spirited horse danced under the motion. Parnell Carswell—"Nellie" to neighboring farmers who muttered behind his back—tucked his riding crop between saddle and blanket as Lydia led man and horse to the front of the house. Tying the animal to the hitching rail, he followed Lydia up worn brick steps to the wide porch that faced Fowler Creek and the Chesapeake Bay beyond.

"I hope you are well, ma'am, on this beautiful day." Even in his riding boots the man was short—scarcely two inches taller than Lydia herself—and walked with a spine held unnaturally straight to gain a fraction of height.

"I am, thank you. And Mrs. Carswell and your family?" She held open the door to the front parlor.

His answer was a curt nod. Information about him and his family was not given just for the asking. "Mrs. Carswell sends her regards."

If true, it would be the first time that Mrs. Carswell recognized Lydia's existence since a formal expression of sympathy at Franklin's funeral half a year ago. But Lydia nodded in return. "And mine to her, please."

"Certainly. Of course." He waited for her to sit in one of the two armchairs she had angled on her mother's carpet to capture the view.

"Please, sir, sit down. I'll be but a moment—Gretchen is with her family for a few days."

"My apologies, ma'am. I assumed your servants were at hand. Kindly take no trouble for me."

"It is no trouble, sir. Please be seated."

She returned with a freshly wiped face, a clean apron, and her thick hair quickly gathered down her back by a black ribbon. A small Japan ware tray held a silver pitcher of water chilled in the icehouse crock, as well as the crystal whiskey decanter and glasses—freshly wiped of dust—that had been a wedding gift from Franklin's parents. Setting the tray on the table between the chairs, she invited her guest to mix his drink to his own taste. He did—light on water, heavy on bourbon—and lifted his glass. "Your health, ma'am."

She raised her glass of water. "And to yours, sir."

He sipped and gazed through the window. The lawn, scythed last autumn and still brown from winter, led his eye to the short pier and the *Lydia* moored beside it. Its bow pointed to the creek's channel that wound through a broad stretch of dark green cordgrass dotted here and there by white egrets. On the horizon, the open waters of Chesapeake Bay glinted in the sun. "A beautiful prospect, Mrs. Sensabaugh. I have always thought it the most valuable asset of this farm."

She smiled wryly. "So far, it has been."

"I assumed your husband bought Marshfield solely for this view. I did not realize he intended to farm it. Had he asked me, I would have advised him that this land is no good. Tobacco, ma'am—like so many farms on the Eastern Shore, this soil has been leached of life by tobacco."

Again, she tried to keep defensiveness from her voice. "Mr. Sensabaugh believed the new chemical fertilizer would revivify the soil."

"Yes, but—an unproven experiment."

Lydia corrected him. "A yet-unproven experiment, Mr. Carswell."

His eyebrows bobbed upward at her tone. Then he smiled politely. "I hope it proves successful. Truly, I do."

"Thank you." Lydia, too, smiled as she wondered if Carswell had come the long half-mile down her lane merely to insult her dead husband's hopes as well as her attempts at husbandry. Seldom did anyone come to the end of her lane without a reason, even when Franklin was alive. The only regular visitor their entire first year had been the post rider, Mr. Henderson. Two Thursdays a month, the owner of Henderson's Sundries Store had turned off the high road that linked the villages of New Church and Modest Town to follow the wagon track a mile or so across Carswell property, and then the final half-mile to Marshfield. Until Franklin decided to save the cost of delivery by going himself to Henderson's store.

After that, visitors were occasional and rare, counted on one hand: Mr. Carswell, Mrs. Brown from her neighboring farm, the agricultural drummer Mr. Curtis.

The man freshened his drink. "We have missed you at church lately, Mrs. Sensabaugh."

It would not do to say that her trips to Franklin's grave were made in mid-week to avoid the Reverend Mr. Abbott's fiery sermons against abolitionists. "I apologize for being derelict. But I will attend Easter ceremonies." She spoke to what she assumed was the reason for his visit: "You may count on my subscription for the coming year—the same as last."

Carswell's grandfather had donated a quarter acre at Messongo Crossroads for the church when it had been Anglican and he had been a British subject. Carswell inherited his family's position as lay leader of what, over time and through wars against the British and Awakenings against sin, had become a Methodist congregation. "I will note your subscription with pleasure, ma'am. But it's your counsel we have missed. We debate whether to join Methodists in other Southern states in separation. The abolitionists have influence not only among Northern congregations, but also in our own corner of Accomack County." He frowned, "We, of course, allow them their beliefs, but they deny us the same courtesy."

"I trust you'll not follow the Baptist Church in separation," she murmured.

The troublesome words Separation, Division, Secession rumbled like distant thunder in conversations and appeared more and more frequently in the newspapers she found at Henderson's.

"It becomes less and less honorable to accept insults from the North. If Virginia must choose between union and self-determination, what then? Our congregation, like Virginia herself, is divided on this matter. Tempers among the brethren are running high."

Her parents' denomination had been Protestant Episcopal, as Anglicanism came to be called after the first war against Britain. If such a congregation met near Marshfield, she would be a member still. But she did not want to insult Mr. Carswell by implying that, to her, any church could be an avenue toward God. "Perhaps tempers should be cooled by love between brethren—especially brethren in the Prince of Peace."

Carswell tilted his head. "Spoken like the gentlewoman you are. But surely you have an opinion about where our congregation should stand on separation? This is a religious issue, after all, and not a thing that should be rendered unto Caesar."

"Since we are children of one God, I hope it does not come to separation. Surely a God of love is not a God of war."

The man studied her face for some hidden meaning. Then his eyes blinked. "Well said. But each must follow his own conscience." He smiled again, lean cheeks creasing beside the wings of his mustaches. Apparently, his conscience was beyond further debate. He abruptly changed subjects. "But my purpose in visiting is less ecclesiastical than worldly."

"Worldly?"

"Of this harsh and cold world, yes." His hand waved at the pier and boat and slough. "I wonder if you have noticed anything out of the ordinary in your vicinity."

"Out of the ordinary? No. Fishing boats occasionally coast along the shore, but the slough's always deserted."

"So you've seen nothing untoward?"

She hesitated. "I did see some lights."

He leaned forward. "Recently?"

"Two nights past."

"Two nights." He sipped at his glass. "And you saw boats?"

"No. Just two lights. The mist over the water hid any boats." She added, "We—Gretchen and I—assumed it was night fishermen."

He frowned at the film of dust on the toe of his boot.

"Why are you so interested, Mr. Carswell?"

"Because these are interesting times, Mrs. Sensabaugh. And promise to be more so."

She considered his meaning. "Do you suspect the presence of abolitionists?"

"Run-away slaves do come over from the western shore. They go up the peninsula to Philadelphia or to Delaware Bay and cross into Jersey. My overseer has seized several in our region, and where some have been caught, others must have escaped." He added grimly, "Misguided sympathizers in our county provide them assistance."

"I'm sure if they were escapees, there would have been no lights at all."

"Yes. Of course." He gazed out the window. "Well, the lights you speak of must have been used to lure fish into a boat's nets."

Lydia, too, studied the distant gleam of the Bay. Talk of the lights stirred the memory of another disquieting issue. "I've heard you think to raise a company of soldiers, Mr. Carswell."

"Cavalry, not infantry—and only if necessary. Should the burghers withdraw Virginia from the Union, we must be ready to defend our sacred soil. I'm proud to say that Carswells have supported Virginia in wars against the French as well as the British. Several of my immediate family served with Lighthorse Harry Lee."

"Does Sheriff Hope sanction your action?"

"We have a Constitutional guarantee of the right to as-

semble as well as the right to bear arms! Sheriff Hope has
no authority over those actions. Moreover, since his support
of abolition is well known, he will no doubt be turned out of
office—either in the next election or when Virginia se-
cedes."

"I pray that will not occur, sir."

"I truly hope Virginia will not join the secession. However, the North does not realize that a state's rights precede
federal rights. This Lincoln talks of a war to preserve the
Union. But he has rejected the Crittenden Compromise, and
his party has derided all efforts at fair and equable concilia-
tion. Massachusetts herself, madam, spoke in favor of secession not twenty years past! Now they hypocritically condemn it. The fact is, each state has a God-given right to take
back its sovereignty just as they individually declared independence from the British crown. Just as they individually
contributed their sons to the struggle. Just as they individually elected to join the Union!"

"And the issue of slavery?" She should not have said
that—Mr. Carswell was a guest.

"Abolitionists have made that an issue! You, madam, are
too young to remember that twenty-five years ago, the Virginia legislature considered an emancipation bill. But because it called for gradual and not immediate emancipation,
militant and intrusive Yankee abolitionists stirred up so
much antagonism to the bill that the vote was never called!
With me, however, slavery is not an issue. It is an historical
fact. If radicals such as William Lloyd Garrison would stop
thumping their Bibles long enough to read them, they would
discover that slavery is ordained by God! The Kings of Isra-
el had their slaves awarded by God Himself!" He caught the
anger building in his voice and stopped abruptly to cool his
tongue with a long drink and a deep breath. "I do apologize,
Mrs. Sensabaugh, for my intemperate tone. Ladies should
not be subjected to fulminous speech nor to explosive topics—especially when their sentiments may be opposed to
the speaker's. I hope you will accept my apology."

"An apology for speaking the truth as you see it is not needed." She could not help but add, "You, of course, own a number of slaves, and I understand that abolition would cost you dearly."

He slowly drained his glass then stood, hat slapping his thigh. "I do have responsibility for twenty servants. But the issue is one of personal belief, not mere lucre. I believe in states' rights. I believe in a free people's self-determination. And I believe Nigras are ordained by the Almighty to be slaves for their own good. One need only look at the poor condition of the freedmen in Jack Town—not three miles from this very room—to see their need for guidance." He paused on the porch. "You choose not to own slaves, perhaps because you do not believe in the institution." He waited to see if she would respond. "Or simply cannot afford them." Letting that barb sink in, he went on. "However, I trust that neighbors can respect each other's beliefs." His voice hardened, "as well as each other's property." And then it softened: "Certainly, I remain a friend to one who is a neighbor and a recent widow. And whose youth has limited her understanding of the world."

The best she could manage was to speak mildly and hold out her hand. "We can agree to disagree."

The coldness in his eyes told her it was not enough. But not to be outdone in manners, he accepted her gesture and forced a smile. "That's what makes horse races and politics." Squaring his hat, he tugged his steed away from the hitching rail. In the saddle, he looked at the farmhouse, the vegetable garden, the barn and outbuildings, and beyond toward Roger plowing the field, before turning back to her. "It is best to be cautious in times as restless as these, Mrs. Sensabaugh. Should abolitionists be active in the Pocomoke estuary, they could well be tempted by this landing and its isolation. Certainly you would not wish to risk loss of your farm by abetting their illegal actions, either through ignorance—or through misguided willingness. Good day."

Chapter 2

When she returned to her garden, she wielded her hoe as if the weeds resembled Nellie Carswell. After a fierce half-hour, she tired herself enough to drain away the anger and focus her attention on the labor. Despite Mr. DuPont's assurance of consistent quality, the chemical granules did vary in strength, sometimes burning, sometimes feeding a crop. Their first year at Marshfield had been a financial disaster when she and her husband lost almost every strawberry plant—the large investment that was to be their first cash crop. The initial shipment of chemicals burned the tiny roots, and Lydia and Franklin watched in dismay as the leaves shriveled in the hot Virginia sun. But certain that scientific farming would make their fortune, Franklin persisted, promising Lydia that better chemicals would double and even triple the yield from this worn-out soil. He ordered a variety of vegetable seeds and a new shipment of the chemical; recorded quantities, dates of application, amounts of water; noted the results on different plants; and then religiously posted those data to Mr. Wiggins at Dupont's Eleutherian Mills up in Delaware.

The result was a good harvest and promised that Franklin would have succeeded, had he not died.

Now Lydia followed those precise notes, and even Roger, long skeptical that this tired earth could ever be anything but pasture and wood-lot, had wagged his head and admitted there might, after all, be something to this unnatural new fertilizer.

A crow's caw sounded across the field where, softly clucking to Star, Roger guided the horse and opened rows of damp earth to the sun. Despite Franklin's dedication to science, he had not bought one of the costly new steel plows from John Deere. Those, he said, were designed to cut the unbroken land of the Western Territories, not soil that had been plowed and harrowed for a hundred years. Certainly Star seemed to have no trouble pulling the rusty and pitted old iron plow. Horse and man moved steadily across the twenty acres that, in two weeks when the soil warmed, would be sown with the wrinkled, hard kernels from last summer's crop. It would be a gambler's dare, planted in the hope that the hard frosts would be past by the time tiny spears of green dotted the field. The first crop to reach market, Roger advised, would fetch the best price, and Lydia had answered, "Then let's be the first!" She could imagine Franklin's grin as she took the risk.

Darkness fell. Lydia cleaned up after the supper she made for the hired man and herself. Roger, the farm's taciturn caretaker before they bought Marshfield, had stayed to work for the new owners. Though he took his meals at the house, he lived in the old barn with Star and Tessie, the cow. The room he occupied was built into a corner above the animal stalls, designed—Franklin explained—so that in winter the animal heat would rise and, aided by the insulation of the hayloft, keep the quarters habitable without need for a fire. In summer, Franklin grinned, the odor of animal droppings and the associated flies made the room uninhabitable unless the stalls were kept clean.

After Franklin died, Lydia had Roger build outside feed racks and a shelter for the horse, the cow, and their associated flies to use in the coming summer. Then she rummaged through the house for a small table and chair to accompany the room's sleeping bench and its straw tick. An old wool needlework carpet and some curtains made of jute sacking further eased her conscience about the hired hand's Spartan quarters.

But with Roger in the barn and Gretchen away, the house felt heavy with shadows. Adding to the gloom were lingering remnants of the afternoon's testy exchange with Parnell Carswell.

Lydia dumped dinner scraps into the hogs' slop bucket, washed the crockery plates in water from the steaming kettle, and once more mulled over the visit. She could count on one hand the number of times that man rode across the property line when her husband was alive. Each visit had the magnanimous air of an earl bestowing a call on a local freeholder. And Franklin, for all that he laughed at Carswell's pretensions, had been flattered. But those visits were casual. Their subjects had been a coming hunt, or gossip about county politics, or an issue of fence repair. This visit—the first Carswell made since her widowhood—had not been casual. Its purpose was to warn her against knowingly or unknowingly aiding abolitionists.

She pumped rinse water over the crockery and placed it in the drying rack. The man's comment about the attractiveness of the farm's landing brought to mind Franklin's pride in what he humorously called "Port Marshfield." Their inlet was the only place on this stretch of low, muddy coastline that had a channel leading from the open Bay to solid earth, and that was a principal reason Franklin bought Marshfield. Boats even as small as the *Lydia* would, for miles up and down the coast, go aground long before reaching shore. They had to anchor and send a flat-bottomed skiff through reed-choked shallows to a sedgey bank that was more swamp than soil. And at low tide, even skiffs and sailing canoes would stick in mud that could swallow a man foolish enough to try to wade through it.

The farm's isolation and the Fowler Creek channel would, indeed, make this a logical place for abolitionists to land and pick up runaways. That uneasy thought and others accompanied her to bed and she lay in the dark while her mind wandered. The white tulle which was draped around her bed kept away early mosquitoes, but it also denied every breeze, and the stuffiness increased her unease. Franklin's last words had been "the light," a whisper like silk drawn over dry leaves. Then a rattle buried deep in his pinched chest. Followed by silence. Broken by Doctor Macgregor's sigh, "He's gone ma'am. Rest in peace."

Lydia was uncertain whether the doctor's benediction had been directed at the suffering man or the exhausted wife she had become. But at Franklin's death, she had to admit a weight lifted from her weary shoulders. She loved Franklin—there was some love even after almost four years, during which the man she thought she married revealed a bitter streak she struggled to understand. And she had demonstrated that love by her care of him as the swamp sickness dominated more and more of his life. But two years after their marriage, she had been forced to ask herself if he wed her out of love or for the dowry that funded his early efforts at financial triumph or her inheritance that paid for this farm. When drink made his tongue sarcastic, he blamed her for being childless. And when he fell ill, he envied her health. Given her deeply hidden relief that she had no children to support, who could say she had not earned some blame?

This farm was his final attempt at success. Over two years ago they left Norfolk City, her parents' new tomb, sister Bonnie and her husband, and Franklin's failures. Sailing up Chesapeake Bay in the brogan bought, like Marshfield, with her inheritance, they anchored off Fowler Creek until Roger appeared through the cordgrass to guide them up a narrow channel to the farm's weathered pier. She could still recall the sense of despair as she gazed over the reedy waste toward the T-shaped home with its fading whitewash, deep porches sagging here and there, and red brick chimneys tilting at each end of a swaybacked roof.

"It stands so alone!"

"It's not Norfolk, that's for sure. But you'll love it, Lyddie! We're landed gentry, now, and—" He patted rail of the *Lydia.* "—we'll have free cartage for our produce. To Annapolis, Richmond, even to the Federal City. Cut out the middle man! When Shoemaker sees how well we do with a farm he thought worthless, why, he'll gnaw his tongue for pure envy!"

The nearest village, New Church, was eight miles away. A poor collection of clapboard buildings, it held Henderson's store and post office, the eponymous church that had been new a century ago, and a scatter of homes, most unpainted. North of Marshfield and hidden beneath a wooded ridge, was the sprawling farm of their neighbor Brown. Beyond that, into Maryland, the clearings of freemen and poor whites dotted forest and shoreline on both sides of Pocomoke Sound. Southeast, several miles of tidal marsh led to the mansion of the Carswells: Oak Hall, one of Accomack County's biggest plantations.

Marshfield itself was flat as a rug with well water that, during late summer droughts when Fowler Creek ran low, had a brackish taste. Because of its poor condition, Franklin had been able to buy house, barn, and acreage with most of her remaining money. More, it turned out, than any local buyer would pay. But that just meant Franklin alone had the vision to see what could be achieved.

The sandy soil held a barn's weight and a plow's furrow, and their hopes for the forty kegs of chemicals that promised so much more than the weed-filled barnyard fertilizer or the Chilean guano that was both expensive and unreliable in delivery. After all, Franklin reassured her, oystermen across the peninsula at Chincoteague Island found good markets as far away as Philadelphia and even New York City, and he could do as well.

Now these thirty-three acres with its hired man and hired girl was her home. With work—much work—the farm might succeed. At least it could provide subsistence and even occasional cash income if a harvest was good and the market wasn't bad. That had not happened while Franklin was alive, but she must hang on until it happened for her. And she *would* hang on—she had no other choice.

Chapter 3

It was less than a week after Parnell Carswell's visit that another horseman came slowly down the lane. Preparing the evening meal, Lydia watched through the kitchen window as the rider stopped occasionally to look toward the water and the lowering sun or at the surrounding forest. He wore the wide-brimmed hat of an outdoorsman but the plantation tie, waistcoat, and black coat of a city dweller. Pausing at the open gate leading into the barnyard, he studied the farm buildings then dismounted and led his horse toward the front porch. A moment later, she heard boot heels thump followed by a knock at the door.

"Good afternoon, miss." The unsmiling man made a stiff half-bow. "May I speak with the man of the house?" Under the hat-brim, his face was sun-browned and lean. Sharp lines at the corners of his eyes creased leathery skin, and thick mustaches arced down beside his mouth.

"My husband is deceased."

He quickly removed his hat and his gray eyes looked at her as if for the first time. "My apologies, ma'am!"

Her well-formed cheekbones and jaw spoke of permanent beauty—light brown hair with even lighter streaks contrasted with her dark eyes and the pallor of her skin. Beneath widow's weeds, her posture revealed a full bosom and slender waist.

"I am sorry for your loss."

A pale forehead showed him to be younger than Lydia had thought. "Accepted, sir." His clothing seemed new, lacking the comfortable creases and relaxed lines caused by wear. Even his collar had not yet wilted or frayed. "Is there something I may help you with?"

"I'm afraid I've lost my way. Might I ask for water for my horse?"

"Of course—the trough's around by the barn door."

"Thank you." He half-turned to look at the pier and the *Lydia*. "This is a beautiful scene. The boat is yours?"

"It was a gift from my late husband." She did not tell him that her few attempts to sail it had been clumsy and brief.

"I'm sure the vessel holds many pleasant memories for you."

Lydia wasn't sure if this rather stiff man was playing on the concept vessel. "Yes. Would you take refreshment for yourself, sir?"

"A glass of water would be most welcome!"

By the time the man had taken care of his horse and returned to the front porch, Lydia had brought out a pitcher and a small plate with a few squares of cornbread left from dinner. She set them on the board table between the bentwood chairs that had been her birthday gift to Franklin. Holding out her hand, she said, "I am Mrs. Sensabaugh. And you are…"

"Morse." He shook her hand once and dropped it. "I am honored to make your acquaintance."

"And I yours. I take it from your pronunciation you're not a Virginian."

For the first time, he smiled. "New York. I've been commissioned by the Eastern Shore Railroad to look at possible routes to Cape Charles."

"They plan to go that far!"

"They think of extending the line from Salisbury in Maryland down to the Cape." He explained, "It could serve a port at the mouth of the Chesapeake, but they need an idea of the number of bridges that might be required , sites for wood yards and water tanks, and availability of rights-of-way."

"And now you are lost?"

"I'm embarrassed to admit it: yes. Is it possible to go directly south from here?"

She shook her head. "No, we have water or marsh on three sides. The best route south is the high road."

"And which way is that?"

"East, a mile and a half. Surely you took it out of New Church?"

"I did, but I've been exploring side roads as well—the surveyors require alternate possibilities before deciding on a route." He glanced at the sky and drained his glass. "And I'd best be at that job before the sun gets much lower. I thank you for your generous hospitality, Mrs. Sensabaugh."

As horse and man cantered up the lane into the tree line, she wondered that anyone could lose their way on this part of the Eastern Shore. The peninsula, situated north-south, was but twelve or so miles wide at this point, and had the Atlantic on the east and the Chesapeake on the west. But being from so distant a state as New York, perhaps Mr. Morse's disorientation could be excused.

She set Roger's plate on the small table in the back room off the kitchen and rang the bell. He must have seen the horseman and understood why supper was late, but she nevertheless gave him a large serving of ham, sweet potatoes, cornbread, and grits as apology, and then settled to her own supper at the dining room table.

With her chickens, milk cow, plow horse, a few pigs, and a kitchen garden—fertilized by chemicals—she was proud to have managed meals like this for the past year. Even the waters that isolated the farm helped feed her: fish, crabs, oysters, mussels, ducks, geese. That bounty had been Roger's contribution. He had been raised a waterman and knew the secrets of marsh and tideland. But he preferred working on dry land, and to work as much as possible without company. As long as the farm remained free of slaves, he told Franklin, he'd work for room, board, and a dollar a week in hard specie. There were, he explained, Quakers in his mother's family, and though his father forbade him to join the Friends because they were not Christians, Roger approved of many of their beliefs. When, occasionally, he disappeared for two or three days with no explanation, Franklin had said wryly to Lydia, "I reckon his Quakerism is less spirit than spirits."

Her husband had attributed the farm hand's eccentricities to the families on Smith Island who had intermarried for almost two hundred years. But following Franklin's death, Lydia found a growing empathy with Roger's pleasure in solitude. She could still be moved by a letter from Bonnie describing the feverish stir her sister witnessed when she visited Richmond to see the Prince of Wales arrive last year. But where Lydia would once have panted to be at that event and had tears to miss it, it now seemed less interesting than the news of the Eastern Shore Railroad coming into Maryland. It was as if the isolation of Marshfield molded the personalities of those who sheltered here. As if sky and shore, woods, water, and fields narrowed the focus of daily life and gentled its pulse to blend with nature. Even Gretchen, whose youth might have led her to yearn for town, apparently found the stillness of Marshfield Farm more comforting than dull.

And on evenings like this at the verge of spring when sleep came slowly, the calm of night soothed a worried soul. Later in summer the full moon would cast shadows across fields and forests, and nature's urgent growth would make sleep seem almost a waste of life. That was when Franklin used to take his shotgun and his flask and go into the night, sometimes with Roger, sometimes with Mr. Brown and his dogs. Even occasionally with Parnell Carswell and a collection of slaves, horses, and dogs, all equally happy to enter a magical realm removed from the cares and disappointments of day. That, too, was a feeling that Marshfield led Lydia to understand: the rough world's alternative realm of moonlight, dream, and music so eloquently described by Mr. Poe. But these coming summer nights might be different. A growing restlessness was in the air. She had sensed it on her trips to Henderson's, on her occasional visits to neighboring farms, even in more recent letters from Bonnie. It had underlain her worry about those mysterious lights. And there were rumors which Gretchen began to bring back from her brief visits home: whispers about armed men gathering in hidden glades, a rash of runaway slaves, the sound of riders urgent in the night, stories of freedmen disappearing from their homes. Even Roger, habitually silent, seemed increasingly watchful. Now, the house's silence stirred that uneasy question she earlier dismissed: how could anyone, even from New York, become so readily lost?

The moon's first quarter outlined the window. Through it came a chorus of spring peepers from the marsh and night insects from the fields. A whippoorwill began whistling from somewhere beyond the cornfield, its three notes sharp and clear, despite distance. From far, far away north, even beyond the ridge that held Brown's Farm and maybe as far as Jack Town, she heard the faint, hollow report of a shotgun. Coon hunters, possibly, though she could not hear the dogs that usually accompanied them. Besides, it was too early in the year for such sport. Perhaps the hunter shot at an owl or a fox. A single, furry bang somewhere near the freedman town and nothing more—a hint that for some reason, animals and humans were prowling the surrounding woods.

Chapter 4

Roger, coming from the barn with the bucket of warm milk, told Lydia that after breakfast he would be cutting fence rails up by the creek. Star could use a rest from the plow, he said, and the pasture fence needed repair. When she finished washing dishes and had fed the poultry and hogs, Lydia took advantage of the spring morning to walk her property.

The echoing *chock* of slow ax strokes led her around the edge of the newly plowed field toward the several acres of second-growth trees that was the farm's wood lot. A century ago the original beech, pine, cedars, and massive oaks had been felled for the shipyards in Baltimore and Wilmington. The growth that followed was now as dense as the primeval forest it replaced, and it was always a surprise when she discovered, broken and unearthed by thick roots, time-pitted brick marking an old foundation. Such finds gave a haunted feel to the silent woods. Someone had made a home and then, for some reason, moved away. The remains moldered beneath trees that had been dormant seeds when those human voices echoed here. *Ubi sunt.* And the corollary to that phrase from her father's volume of Poetic Airs: *Carpe deim.*

She paused in the breeze to tug the shawl farther up her shoulders. An insect hummed past the brim of her faded black bonnet and a hint of resin drawn by the sun came from a stand of pines bordering the field. Lately she had to remind herself to seize the day. Each day seemed so quietly itself—complete, uneventful, dedicated solely to its own gently gliding sunlight and cloud shadow. The days offered themselves, not to be seized, but to be...inhaled, perhaps, or simply absorbed by eye and flesh. Indeed, time seemed to turn back on its beginnings. But 1860 had passed, Franklin had been buried, and she was a childless widow who, even if she did not feel her latest birthday, was approaching her twenty-third year. Bonnie, in her last letter from Norfolk City...four? Six weeks ago?...went on and on about how fast her babies grew and how, between the days' chores and the evenings' social duties, time just seemed to disappear. But since Franklin's death, Lydia felt that time never appeared in the first place.

Between tree trunks made shaggy by the leafing green of Virginia creeper and poison ivy, she glimpsed the silhouette of a male torso lift erect from a bent position. A moment later, the measured *chock* of the ax sounded again. Holding the hem of her black dress away from thorny vines and thick underbrush at the edge of the forest, she pushed through the prickly growth into the darker but more open space beneath the trees. Roger, the back of his shirt a damp triangle despite the breeze, swung his arms with slow, strong strokes that bit the iron blade deep into the white, sour smelling wood.

A twitch of his thick wrists to lever the ax head out of its cut, and another swing that started with a twist of lean hips and gained speed up that wide back until the ax bit again. The lithe form reminded Lydia that in fact he was not much older than she was. Like many journeymen and farm laborers, his face had been etched with permanent lines long before he was out of his teens and his manner was of a man who had supported himself for a decade.

"Good morning!"

Roger looked over his shoulder as he pried the blade free. "Morning, ma'am." He wiped his forefinger across his brow and then on the red bandanna tied loosely around his long neck. "Rails."

He nodded at the stack of thin gum saplings he had already felled and trimmed and placed near the farm wagon where Star, snorting hello, munched tufts of grass. Scattered over last winter's brown leaves were new white chips. Severed branches had been tossed onto a pile to dry for kindling. Roger's pale lank hair lay in strands over his ears and down his neck. A lipless mouth curved down at one side to give him a wry expression that, to Lydia, seemed at odds with the stolidity of his mind.

"Do we need so many?"

He shrugged. "Best to get extra now. Save time later, if need be."

"Yes. Of course." Roger's terse directness always made her feel a bit frivolous. Franklin said he was mentally deficient. Lydia thought his manners suffered the effects of solitude. But she tried, nonetheless, to engage him in some form of conversation, if not for his sake at least for hers. "Gretchen should be returning today."

"Yes'm."

She tried again. "We had a visitor yesterday afternoon."

"I seen him."

"Oh. Well, I don't think he was an abolitionist. Mr. Carswell warned me against abolitionists. He said they could be lurking about in the woods and might be dangerous."

"Yes'm."

"Have you seen anyone, Roger?" She smiled. "Any dangerous strangers lurking about?"

"No'm."

She nodded. "I told Mr. Carswell about those lights Gretchen and I saw. He said they were probably fishing boats. But I had the feeling he thought they were something else."

"Could be night fishing."

A flicker of something tiny and faint in his hazel eyes generated a brief, tense ringing in her mind. "What would they fish for at night? Especially with fog on the water?"

"Chub—for bait." After a moment, he added, "Crabs, maybe."

"Why haven't we seen them more often?"

"They wasn't there."

For good reason: bait fish, crabs, and all the other tide-water creatures could be found much closer to the fishing fleets of Tangier Island or Smith Island or Saxis or even Crisfield, across the Pocomoke Sound in Maryland. "Seems a long way to come just to catch bait fish or crabs."

"Yes'm." He scratched in the stubble of blond whiskers that covered his chin. Somewhere in the trees a mockingbird began to warble. "Maybe they was fishing in the Bay and just come in that once't."

"That's as good an explanation as any, I suppose." His eyes shifted away and she wondered if the man's inarticulateness was really the result of long habit or actually a protective mask. But if protection, then against what? What kind of threat could she be to him? "Is it not possible then, that the lights could have some other cause?"

His bristly jaw moved two or three times as if chewing a cud. "I didn't say that. I said it was most likely fishermen."

"And the least likely cause?"

"Parnell Carswell's abolitionists." Hefting the ax, he turned back to a sapling. "As for what's between most and least, I don't know. But these be troubling times, ma'am."

"You mean politics? What do politics have to do with Marshfield or with us?"

"Politics is people."

ოოო

In mid-afternoon, Lydia was happy to see Gretchen come down the lane riding on a wagon seat beside the Reverend Mr. Abbot. Following her husband's funeral, the reverend had surprised Lydia and injured her pride by offering less than half what Franklin paid for Marshfield. "I can't help what your husband laid out for it, ma'am," the preacher said. "And I'm mighty sorry to be the one to tell you the truth about its worth. But what I offer is a fair price for what the farm is." Not because he wanted to till the land—he scorned Franklin's scientific agriculture as fanciful—but because it would make pasturage. "Your land's bound on three sides by water. I'd only have to put up one fence along the east where the lane comes in. Pasture's all this soil's good for, and the creek provides sweet water for stock."

She had refused the reverend's offer more, she suspected, for her own pride than for Franklin's dream.

But today he was company and he was going out of his way to deliver Gretchen, and, for that, she was grateful. Quickly, she stirred up heat in the ashes of the stove, pumped water for the teakettle, and ran upstairs to change into formal mourning.

Originally, Franklin hired Gretchen only to help Lydia run the farm. But in the dark time of her husband's illness, the girl provided strength and companionship and became more like family than servant. Now, talking all the while, Gretchen carried her bundles from the wagon into the house while the reverend watered his horse and forked a load of hay into the manger by the barn. "The preacher gave me a ride, ma'am. Said he was going to Oak Hall to talk with Squire Carswell about church business and long's he was out this way, he should call on you as well." As she talked, the girl shook fingers through her silver blonde hair to toss the dust and quickly plait it back into two long pigtails. "I got a letter for you from your sister. And there's a lot of exciting news to tell you!"

"Later, Gretchen—I'm eager to hear, but let's be mindful of manners and hospitality first." Lydia tied a small apron around her own waist and held out another for Gretchen. "Please cut some cornbread and arrange the tray—I'll get the parlor ready."

Lydia pulled back the drapes to let sunshine warm the

parlor and Brother Abbott enjoy the view. Perhaps it would soothe the man's temper and tongue, for she had no doubt he would question her absence from the church. But the man had saved the girl a long walk, and Lydia was willing to suffer for that favor to the friend Gretchen had become.

When Lydia and Mrs. Druer worked out the terms of her daughter's employment, there had been no mention of instruction in reading or manners. The daughter of an immigrant sharecropper from Saxony, Mrs. Druer was by fifteen the wife of another Saxon sharecropper. Her only interest was in how hard Gretchen would work and how much money she would bring home. But it had been rewarding to see, over time, the changes in the girl's behavior. Not that Lydia raised an eyebrow at Gretchen's poor table manners. When Franklin was alive, her place to eat had been with Roger in the work room off the kitchen, while Lydia and her husband supped in the dining room. But the girl had the intelligence to appreciate good manners, and Lydia was careful to provide the proper model. Gretchen first silently noted, then began to copy, the way Lydia held her fork, the quiet sipping of tea, the small piece of food cut from a serving, even placing the knife on the plate and the left hand in the lap before lifting a morsel to one's mouth.

And the instruction was not all one way. Lydia's mother had told her daughters over and over that no man would marry a girl who did not have a hope chest and who could not manage a household. To have a hope chest, one must learn to sew, knit, and crochet. To properly manage servants, one learned how things were done both in the kitchen and in the drawing room. As a child, Lydia joined her older sister Bonnie in sewing, crocheting, and embroidering items for their hope chests, as well as paying attention to Sara the cook and to setting the table to properly entertain guests. But her mother had been a townswoman, not a farmer's wife.

Gretchen vastly increased Lydia's knowledge of farm life. Franklin, for all his understanding of scientific farming, knew nothing about which shoots in the garden were weeds, which weeds were valuable herbs, how to let the hoe work more than the back. Gretchen showed Lydia how her mother clipped the wing feathers of chickens to prevent them from roosting in trees and going wild. There were moon signs to learn for proper planting times, and how—without harming a shrub or tree—to burn tent caterpillars whose webs threatened to strip the leaves from their branches. Blight and scale that sapped life from wilting plants had to be identified, as well as a remedy to be mixed and painted on. She also taught Lydia the early sign of cutworms to be rooted out before they multiplied and destroyed the kitchen garden, and how to use turpentine on the nests of ants that threatened to invade the house. But it was still Gretchen who wrung the neck of any chicken selected for dinner. That, Lydia had not quite steeled herself to do.

The afternoon sun made a bright square of color on her mother's Turkish carpet as Lydia dusted and straightened the doilies that protected the plush arms of the chairs. A few moments later, she heard the preacher's boots on the iron scraper beside the front steps, and then his rap on the doorframe.

"Please sit down, sir. I have tea or something stronger, if you wish."

The preacher's weathered face had stern lines around nose and mouth, and stiff, cropped whiskers followed his jaw line. "Tea is fine, Miz Sensabaugh. In fact, for me it's total, as they say. Not that I object to others enjoying God's gifts—provided it's done in moderation." He wore his good dark coat over a collarless shirt, but his trousers had traces of old mud almost as high as his knees. "I take it you have not heard the latest news?"

"Gretchen mentioned some excitement."

"Excitement, yes. Momentous, even. The seceded states have established their own government—call it a Confederacy—down in Montgomery, Alabama. They even have a president, name of Davis."

"That's what I was going to tell you, ma'am!" Gretchen, cheeks pink, carried the tea service to the sideboard and began pouring. "It's all the ones that's seceded: South Carolina, Mississippi, Florida, Alabama, Georgia, Louisiana, and that new one with the funny name..." She thought a moment. "Texas."

The preacher accepted a cup with a touch of molasses, pinching the handle between his thumb and finger. "President Lincoln said he was going to send a supply ship to a fortress in Charleston's harbor, and they told the president if he did, they'd shoot it. It could mean war."

"War!"

Gretchen nodded. "The people in South Carolina say the fort belongs to them and they'll shoot the Yankee ship!"

"The newspapers say if the fort isn't surrendered by Lincoln it will be taken by force."

"It's like a challenge to a duel!" Gretchen's blue eyes widened.

He nodded. "A public challenge, yes."

Lydia tried to encompass the idea of a war. "Where will it all lead?"

"Only the good Lord knows that, Miz Sensabaugh."

"My brother Humphrey says if war comes, he's going to join up: Squire Carswell's calvary. Allen Rafer and Alvin Fletcher's going with him, he says, and a lot of his friends from over in Maryland. But Mr. Carswell says they got to bring their own horses, and Pa says Humphrey can't take Chloe. Says he can't make do with just one mule and no horse."

"Is Virginia to secede?"

"The burghers are meeting in Richmond now, but no one's heard anything yet." Mr. Abbot shook his head slowly and chewed at his lips for a moment. "The islanders over to Chincoteague say they're going to stay Union even if the rest of Virginia does secede. They're holding a vote on it. There's not many there want to quit the Union." He added,

"Their best markets for oysters and such are up north, you see."

From Lydia's front porch, the Maryland line was nine miles north by the high road, and several miles less on lanes and paths that cut through forests and skirted marshes and fields.

New Town, the main port on the Pocomoke River, was another four or five miles. North, some vague distance beyond Salisbury and past towns unknown to Lydia, lay Delaware, Pennsylvania, New Jersey—all of which in the last election supported the new Republican government or the even more militant Constitutional Party—both of which vowed war to prevent states from leaving the Union.

"Pa says our cousin Richard is against secession. He's going Union if war comes."

"Your cousin could become your father's enemy?" asked Lydia.

"Mine and your'n too, I guess."

The preacher wagged his head again. "A divided land and divided families."

Lydia did not want to be enemy to anyone. "I pray it does not happen. It must not happen."

"I hope it does not come. But the Lord's will must be done."

"It won't last long, they say. Soon's the North sees we mean business, they'll back off, Squire Carswell says. He told Humphrey and Allen they'd be home in sixty days, and that's what he's going to sign people up for in his calveree—sixty days." Gretchen's voice faltered, "So's the boys'll be back for harvest, he says."

"Our congregation is deeply divided, ma'am. Our people search their hearts and pray for guidance. I of course will stand with Virginia whether we secede or not, but others among us pledge to remain with the Union if Virginia does leave." The preacher frowned. "I cannot condemn them for listening to their hearts." Mr. Abbot, too, fell silent.

Lydia stared at the gleam of open water on the horizon,

still unable to grasp the extent of change that threatened. "I pray it does not happen."

Gretchen refilled their cups from the teapot wrapped in its cozy. "Squire Carswell's been telling his people there's ghosts in our slough."

"What?"

"That's what I heard in New Church. He told his Nigras we got ghosts."

"Who would believe such a thing?"

"His people, I reckon."

"We cannot deny the world of spirits, Miz Sensabaugh. Not if we believe in an all-powerful God and the imperishable soul of man." A fly, still sluggish from winter's chill, buzzed from a far distance and deepened the silence. "In other words, not to believe in ghosts would challenge the spiritual dimension of mankind. It would deny the Biblical truth that man was created in God's likeness, and that God has the power to intervene in this world. It would, in short, be atheistical."

"Your logic, sir, is...sound." Lydia bent her head to study the black lace trim on her formal dress. She feared her eyes might reveal the complete phrase that crossed her mind: "more sound than sense." Still, she could not restrain a comment. "There are those who believe that the time of God's intervention is past, that—"

"Bah! That smacks of that infidel Paine! As one of my favorite hymns has it..." His reedy and nasal voice lifted in song: "'Tom Paine and the Devil they did their best, but God protects the Methodist...'" The singing, to Lydia's relief, broke off. "Miracles do happen, ma'am. Words spoken in prayer do have their effects on this world. The spiritual world intermingles with this material world." The man's voice rose. "Surely you—with your bereavement but a year removed—do not deny the realm of the spirit!"

Lydia nodded, a strand of light brown hair swaying free beneath her cotton dust cap. When the man stopped for breath, she murmured, "I admit the human mind cannot know everything." She stifled the impulse to add support from one of her father's favorite books. The Reverend Mr. Abbot had, most likely, never heard of Herr Kant's *Critiques,* but he would be deeply opposed to it on the grounds that Herr Kant was a German and therefore alien and sinful. "I suspect it may not even perceive everything. The acute hearing of a dog demonstrates the limitations of our own hearing, sir, and who knows but the very insects and worms hear ranges of sound or see spectra of color that we can't even imagine."

"And given that, ma'am, it is arrogant to deny the world of spirits!"

"I grant the possibility—even the probability—of such a world. It's this one manifestation of the spiritual that I question."

"Humph." The minister, who relished theological argument, was disappointed in her easy surrender. He held out his cup. Gretchen, excited to hear such an exchange between her mistress and the minister, quickly poured.

"As a woman, you of course lack the skill to debate theology. However," he warned, "when you question the specific, ma'am, you question the entire class. And in this instance you come mighty close to questioning God Himself."

"There have been fraudulent claims about spirits, and even self-deception, Brother Abbot. It is an area where the unscrupulous may dupe those too eager to believe."

From somewhere a mockingbird set up a racket—the "cat squawk," Roger called it.

"You are correct, ma'am. Any spiritual manifestations should be thoroughly studied. But we are in a time of growing peril—of dire warnings of all kinds. Let us not presume to know the mind of God."

"I assure you I do not presume to know God's mind—or man's." Lydia smiled, "What I do know is my gratitude for your kindness in going so far out of your way to deliver Gretchen." It was more a reminder to herself than thanks to her guest.

"Well, I was headed this way nonetheless." The stern face tried to hide its pleasure at the woman's praise, and he accepted her change of topic. His gray eyes glanced around the parlor and its domestic treasures: daguerreotypes, the white marble of a Rogers figurine, dried zinnias under a dome of glass, two small shelves of well-used books, her late husband's desk with its collection of agricultural publications as a monument to his passing. "This is a lonely homestead, Miz Sensabaugh. One that requires much labor and upkeep. Too much, to my mind, for a single lady. My offer to buy still stands."

"Thank you. But I intend to stay and operate the farm as long as God wills." She added with delicate emphasis, "On my own."

"As God wills, Miz Sensabaugh. Always as God wills." He nodded and stood, thick farmer's hands running down the lapels of the dark coat he wore when called by his flock to pastoral duties. "But it would not be amiss to consider remarrying, ma'am. Be fruitful and multiply is the command of God. And you do share this farm with a man who is not of your family."

"Sir! He is my hired man!"

"Well. You are young enough to remarry. This property—if you don't want to sell it—is a dowry that would interest any suitable man."

She murmured tautly, "I thank you for your advice, Brother Abbot."

They watched the preacher ride away in the low sunlight, timing his trip—Gretchen opined—to reach Oak Hall in time for supper. Man, wagon, and mule became diminishing points of darkness that gave focus to the landscape until a turn in the lane took them out of sight.

Chapter 5

Showers alternated between cold rain and grains of sleet that formed white streaks in the crevices of plowed earth. It was moisture that Lydia welcomed, the kind that softened the hard kernels of corn but did not harm the cold crops—peas and cabbage and radishes—well sprouted in her garden.

One crisp morning, Roger stamped on the back stairs to knock mud from his boots and settle at the scarred table in the back room. Some weeks after Franklin's death, Lydia had asked Gretchen to join her at the main table. The girl had come first to share afternoon tea, then dinner, and finally—without either of them discussing it—supper as well, leaving Roger apparently happy to have the small table to himself. Before each meal, Lydia could hear the man murmur, "Thank you Lord for these Thy gifts which we are about to receive."

Now, knife and fork clicking and scraping, he worked through soft fried eggs on a bed of hominy, a thick slab of ham, biscuits, and coffee. Lydia and Gretchen tidied the kitchen while the girl excitedly delivered the news she'd gathered on her shopping trip to the Sundries Store in New Church. Finally, over his steaming mug, Roger said through the doorway, "They fired on Fort Sumter? There'll be fighting, sure, then."

"What will you do, Roger?" During one of the nights of
tossing worry, Lydia realized that her hired hand, like the
other men of Accomack, might join a company of the soldiers that every county in Virginia seemed to be mustering.
It would be difficult to get through the growing season
without him, but if it came to that, she and Gretchen could
survive. Up until harvest, at least.

The man was hesitant. "I don't know. Them that want to
fight, can. But I don't want no part of it, Union or Confederate."

Gretchen stood in the doorway between the kitchen and
the enclosed porch as she dried the frying pan. "No part of
it?"

Roger looked at her. "That's what I said: no part of it. I
just want to be left alone."

"That's all any of us wants! But the Yankees won't leave
us alone. That's the trouble."

"I reckon there's enough wants to fight, so they don't
need me."

The girl stared at Roger for a long moment. "I'm right
glad my brother and Allen Rafer don't feel that way about
Virginia. I'd be ashamed if they did!"

A slow redness rose under the shaggy hair at the back of
Roger's neck. "Well, Gretchen Druer, since I'm lucky
enough not to have a sister like you, I don't much care how
you feel."

Her face puckered in anger and she wrapped her hands in
the dishcloth. "I suppose you'd let Yankee soldiers march
right through Accomack County, wouldn't you—just like
the Chincoteagers would?"

He stared at the table top. "Yankees got no reason to
come down here, and I got no reason to go up there."
Frowning with the effort to put into words whatever it was
he felt, he turned his hazel eyes to Lydia. "My pa didn't get
along with my mama's Quaker relatives." He paused. "Fact
is, Pa never got on with anybody, much. He just liked to
fight. But I don't like fighting. I like the Quaker way. I'll

fight if I got to. I just don't see that I got to."

"I respect your feelings, Roger. And though it sounds selfish, we'd be hard pressed if you join either army."

"We can run this farm without him, ma'am. Pa says I plow a furrow as straight as my brothers. I reckon we'd get by."

"Let's be grateful that we won't have to, Gretchen." Lydia's vague understanding of war was born of the lithographs that had been on her father's library wall and were now stored somewhere in one of sister Bonnie's trunks: General Wolf dying in a soldier's arms as the radiance of a Canadian heaven fell on his face against a dark background spiky with the pointed implements of war; George Washington sitting tall on his prancing white horse before rigid lines of soldiers in blue and white. They were heroic scenes and stirring, but she also knew that men died in that war. One of them had been her mother's great uncle. And as a child she read stories in the *Norfolk Herald* about brave soldiers who had died in the triumph of Chapultepec in Mexico. More soldiers would die in a new war, too, even one that promised to be as brief as the coming summer. But neither Gretchen nor Roger seemed to see war as bringing death. For Roger, it threatened intrusion into his solitary life; for Gretchen it promised the same color and heroism that once captured the teenaged Lydia when she heard of distant Mexico. "We must pray that war does not come."

Neither answered. Roger sullenly dipped his face into his coffee cup. Gretchen turned back into the kitchen to loudly rattle the crockery.

୧ଠଏ

Lydia tapped straight the thin nail bent by an awkward stroke of her hammer. She was tacking short strips cut from an old flannel nightshirt to a lattice-frame the size of a small table. The frame would be set half a foot above the ground in a sheltered corner of the barn. The flannel strips would dangle to earth like a mother hen's feathers to give comfort and safety to the chicks Elizabeth Brown had bartered in return for a ham from the hog Roger was to slaughter soon.

As Lydia wrestled the frame into place, Mrs. Brown's shay squeaked and rattled down the lane under an overcast sky. The thick-bodied woman hauled herself from under the buggy's raised hood and down from its bouncing seat. Waving in return to Lydia's greeting, she called, "It do be cold!"

"Please come in and have something warm to drink, Mrs. Brown. I'm sure Gretchen has the kettle on."

"Let me take care of Angel, first." She led the plodding horse to the water trough. "Mr. Brown says always take care of the animals at the first and they'll take care of you at the last." She pumped the squealing handle and then watched as the chestnut horse, leaning forward in the shafts, sucked loudly. "Not too much, Angel—you'll get pussel-gutted, for certain."

She tugged on the reins and led him, patient, obedient, his head almost as high as the black hood that sheltered the carriage seat, toward the warmth of the barn. "Let's get the chicks out before they chill. Got eight of them, all fine Cochin stock." She hauled a light basket from its wrappings under the seat of the carriage. As it tilted, the chicks gave a scratching sound and tiny, frightened peeps. "Cochins be good for laying and for meat, both. Got a place for them?"

"Over here." Lydia pointed to the corner where Roger had built a small enclosure. Narrow slats protected the chicks from the cat, and the cat was to protect the chicks from the rats. A shallow tin of water and a v-shaped trough of finely ground cornmeal waited. The lattice-frame of flannel strips provided warmth, and more flannel covered an opening that led to the outside chicken pen. "I think they should do well here, don't you?"

"Well enough." Mrs. Brown carefully tilted the basket on its side and tapped it to slide the frightened, resisting puffs of yellow feathers through the lifted trap door and onto the dirt. They ran to the farthest corner and bunched together, fighting to burrow under each other. "Keep them away from your rooster—he'll kill them—and make sure they don't get chilled."

"I will. Roger plans to butcher the hog within the next few weeks. Either he or I will bring over the ham."

"You get to it when you can." The older woman stowed the empty basket back in the buggy and, as they rounded the house to the front porch, loosened the strings of her sunbonnet. Like Lydia, Mrs. Brown wore an everyday dress with no more than one petticoat and no stays. Lydia wondered how long it would take for her own shape to spread like the hefty woman's so that it pulled wrinkles around the buttons.

"Everything going well with you, Mrs. Sensabaugh?" Mrs. Brown glanced around as if looking for something in the greening lawn, the pier and sailboat, the gray horizon beyond. "I always worry about you being so alone out here."

"Well enough. And you and Mr. Brown?"

"Fine—fine. Mr. Brown has his aches and pains, but forty years of farming will do that for you. I see you've planted a mite early—hope no late frost gets your crop. We're still turning the ground over. Fifteenth of April, that's the time for—why, hello, Gretchen!"

The girl opened the front door with a smile and welcomed the neighbor into the warmth of the house. "Afternoon, Miz Brown. I hope all's well with you and your'n."

"It is, thank you, and I trust your folks are in good health."

"Yes'm, thank you." Gretchen had lit a fire in the hearth to take the chill off the parlor, and Lydia hung up Mrs. Brown's wrap.

"Well, I have news and I reckon I'd better tell it before I pop—our Lucy's gone and got engaged to the Rafers' middle boy, Allen."

"How wonderful!"

"Allen Rafer?" Something in Gretchen's voice drew Lydia's glance.

"Yes, Allen Rafer." Mrs. Brown settled into a chair. "I believe you and him know each other, Gretchen?"

"Yes'm." Then, softly, she added, "I truly hope they'll be happy."

"I thank you. I reckon they have as good a chance as most." Mrs. Brown added in a gentler tone, "They do make a handsome couple."

"Yes'm." Gretchen said quickly, "Excuse me, I'll fetch the tea."

Mrs. Brown's eyes followed her. "He's a nice boy and a good worker," she said to Lydia. "Be a good provider. They'll have to live with us at Blackridge Farm until he saves up enough for his own place, but I reckon that won't be too long. His pa's promised to help." She added with casual pride—as well she might, having married off two other daughters—"And Lucy has somewhat for her dowry."

When Gretchen, pale and red eyed, returned with the tea service, Mrs. Brown changed the subject. "You hear the latest noise being made over on the Western Shore?"

Lydia shook her head. "We heard that the burghers were talking about joining the Confederacy."

"Well, they're talking right hard now, I tell you. Those Republicans want to tell states how they ought to live. Abrogating state's rights, that's what they're doing." She clicked her cup into its saucer. "And all to cozy up to those abolitionists! Crazy people! That John Brown over to Harper's Ferry made me ashamed of my own name, he did!"

"Many of us have no slaves."

"Well, Mr. Brown and me, we got two servants and they're mighty happy with us, I can tell you that. A lot happier than if they was living in a shanty over in Jack Town or up north in a factory being worked to death!" Her cup and saucer rattled. "People ought to look in their own back yard before going across the street to tell their neighbors how to behave."

Lydia, following her father's beliefs, did not support slavery, and she knew that emotions in Accomack County ran strongly both for and against the institution. To her it was simply a fact of the world she had been born in. Stories of harsh masters and cruelly punished slaves had occasionally been whispered by grown-ups at the edge of hearing, and the terror of Nat Turner's rampage south of Norfolk City was often used as a bogeyman to threaten unruly children. But she had never witnessed any of the horrible things the northern newspapers accused slave-owners of doing.

Her father, quietly disapproving of slavery and against its extension into the territories, had hired freedmen as house servants and as workers in his glass factory. "Just a good business practice," he told those who questioned him. "A freedman takes more pride in his work than a bound man does."

Increasingly with each presidential election, the issue of abolition had been raised around the supper table along with cigars and whiskey. The rumble of men's voices would carry upstairs to the withdrawing room where the ladies had retired, and often further up to the third floor where Lydia, Bonnie, and the guests' children played. Her father's voice would move from his philosophical objections to slavery to detailing the material costs of owning them; another voice argued that Nigras could not survive if slavery were abolished overnight. A third admitted it was wrong, but the self-righteous Northern states had no business using the issue to elevate federal power over state's rights.

"We got a tiger by the tail," that voice said, "but, by God, it's our tiger!"

"Cotton." That voice had been Mr. Fielder, frequent guest and owner of the *Norfolk Herald.* "Cotton plantations need slave labor—that's the only place it's economically feasible."

An unfamiliar voice answered, "And since the Yankees and the British need more cotton for their industry, the growers need more slaves and more land for their cotton.

Thus, the institution must be extended into the territories to support the march of progress and civilization!"

Another voice she did not recognize snorted, "The Yankees won't shut down their mills by cutting off Southern cotton, and the South is the best market for their products. They may not want slavery up there, but down here it's money in their pockets, and don't you doubt that!"

Lydia drew her memory away from that distant parlor to return to her own. "I trust that much of the noise was generated by the heat of the election."

"No doubt," said Mrs. Brown. "And politics is a nasty business that men can keep. I want no part of it."

Gretchen, voice soft, finally joined the talk. "I hear there's militias being made up."

Mrs. Brown's eyebrows lifted. "Around here?"

"Yes'm. Squire Carswell's raising a company of volunteers. And so's a Mr. White down in Eastville, my brother says."

"Sheriff Hope hears of that, Parnell Carswell's going to be raising his face to the county judge at Accomack courthouse."

"Yes'm—maybe. But Billy Taylor says if there is a war he's going to join."

"I reckon Billy Taylor would like to play soldier! Every Taylor I know works harder to get out of work than the work calls for in the first place."

"Surely there won't be war."

"I pray not, Mrs. Sensabaugh. Mr. Brown says a rich man's war comes down to a poor man's fight, every time."

"Grampa used to say a coming war stirred up the ha'ants—that the spirits get restless when they know a war's coming."

Mrs. Brown held out her cup to be refilled. "I've heard that very same sentiment, except it was Indians was supposed to believe it."

"Well, we seen a strange thing!"

"It was a fishing boat, Gretchen."

"Well, Reverend Abbott said it might not have been."

"I recollect now—I did hear mention that you all saw some strange lights off shore." Mrs. Brown's forced surprise told Lydia what was behind the woman's earlier interest in her welfare.

"Yes'm—two that rose up out of the fog over the marsh!"

"The Reverend Abbot doesn't really think they were ghosts, Mrs. Brown. And Roger says they were lights from a fishing boat." Lydia glanced at the girl. "But they certainly were disturbing. We don't often see boats off our inlet."

"No," agreed Mrs. Brown, "it's mighty lonesome out here. Maybe it was islanders. This time of year, they like to use a bow cannon on a punt—drift up to ducks sleeping for the night and fire off nails and such and then gather up the kill."

"We haven't seen that."

"And there was no noise of shooting," said Gretchen. "No sound at all, and that made it even scarier!"

Mrs. Brown, stray curls of graying hair wagging stiffly, nodded. "They do say," she mused, "that the runaways sometimes come up the Chesapeake to the Pocomoke River."

"The river's several miles from here."

"True, true—makes no sense to land here when there's better and safer coves and guts closer to the river. Or even across in Maryland. And believe you me, our dogs would know if anybody crossed our land at night." She scratched her earlobe in thought. "Well, Edward Teach was supposed to've sailed along this coast—Blackbeard the pirate, you know—and there's stories about the people he killed. Might be some of those he killed have come back."

Lydia added quickly, "And there are stories about the many treasures he buried nearby that no one has found."

"Ha—that, too, I grant."

"I'm certain the lights Gretchen and I saw were made by fishermen."

But as they finished their tea, Lydia did not feel as certain as she tried to sound.

With a final goodbye, Mrs. Brown clucked her tall horse into an ungainly trot down the sandy lane fringed with the dark purple berries of winterkilled pokeweed. Lydia and Gretchen went into the barn to look at the chicks. Their approach frightened the tiny birds and they ran, blurs of squeaking, soft yellow, for protection under the trellis of cloth strips. Gretchen's hand chased one down and gently cupped it, cheeping in fright, in her palm. "They're so tiny and soft!"

Lydia lightly stroked the downy feathers on the head that poked nervously out of the circle of the girl's thumb and forefinger. How gigantic, how threatening, the two humans must seem to those tiny bright eyes. Gods who bound its freedom, brought its food and water, ultimately its death. And did her soul and being rest in the hand of God like this biddy in Gretchen's palm? A palm as subject to error as her own? Morbid thought—that God might be as fallible as a human. Could the world's evil and pain be less some purposeful instruction from God than an indication of His limits? It was a dark thought that had come after her parents' deaths and reemerged with Franklin's passing to haunt her mind. It was a thought she pushed away to force her attention back to the soft beauty of feathers and to a tiny life that only celebrated a Creator and never questioned His virtue.

"They're Cochins," Lydia said. "Recently from England. They're good for eggs as well as meat, Mrs. Brown told me."

"Javas is the best for laying—that's what Ma's got. But they do tend to be skinny birds. Maybe when we got enough of these I can take some eggs to Ma to brood out?"

"Certainly, Gretchen; I'll be pleased to share them."

"Thank you, ma'am."

Hesitantly, Lydia asked, "The young man Mrs. Brown's daughter is to marry—do you know him well?"

The girl set the chick down and watched it flee into the

safety of dangling flannel. "Allen Rafer—yes'm, some-what."

"You seemed surprised at the news."

The girl shrugged, face stiff. "Allen Rafer don't mean nothing to me."

"Isn't Blackridge Farm near your parents' farm?"

Another bob of her shoulder. "Used to be Pa share-cropped near there. Now we're a ways on the other side of it. Up by Wagram town."

Lydia studied the girl's sullen face. Her averted eyes, a cornflower blue, were slightly close-set on each side of a straight nose that would grow more prominent with the years. Sunshine had turned her already blonde hair almost white, and though her lips were thin, there was no meanness to them. If not pretty, Gretchen certainly was not homely. "Many disappointments are blessings in disguise."

"I ain't disappointed!"

"And I am not prying, Gretchen." But Lydia knew quite well how important it was for a girl of sixteen—Bonnie's age when she was married, and only a year younger than Lydia's wedding age—to think of becoming settled in life. And how disappointing to discover that what had been a thing of promise, no matter how vague, was now gone. "However, if sometime you wish to talk, I am willing to listen."

The spark of defensive anger disappeared and the girl's bosom rose and fell with a deep sigh. "Yes'm. I reckon it's just that I believed what I shouldn't of. It wasn't no court-ship, anyway—not really." But not all the bitterness was gone. "And her pa owns his own farm and she has a dow-ry."

"Yes," said Lydia. "A dowry is a large consideration for many men."

Chapter 6

Sleety squalls ended in days of steady rain, and the sodden earth made the plow too heavy for Star to pull. When, finally, the sky began to clear, Lydia took advantage of the horse's idleness to make the eight-mile trip to Mr. Henderson's Sundries Store. After a last scan of the shopping list with Gretchen, she wrapped herself in a heavy wool shawl and oilcloth cape against the raw wind and thanked Roger for harnessing the horse. In the wagon bed, she had the hired man store a few empty wooden crates and gunnysacks to be filled with store-bought goods, a basket of eggs carefully packed in straw for barter, and a tarp to protect it all from rain. Then, clucking to Star the way Roger did, she started up the lane to New Church.

As the wagon rattled and splashed along the shallow, seldom-used grooves, she assessed the arrival of spring on her property. If it had not been her land, the wet fields fenced by sagging wooden rails would look lonely and grim in their sad April green. But this land, sorry though it might be, was hers, and she felt what could be called an affection of ownership for it—a caring interest in the land's well-being and life. She found herself addressing the fields the same way she did the sprouting vegetables in her garden. Though the pasture was still a pale and vulnerable green rather than the darker color it would become by next month,

Roger said it would provide two harvests of silage before the November frosts. Lydia hoped that was so. The eggs and the occasional butchered hog could be used for barter at the store, but hay was one of the farm's few cash crops. Except for the labor of mowing and delivering, it cost her nothing to grow, and even made her property somewhat valuable in the eyes of the Reverend Mr. Abbott.

The wood lot closed around the lane. Branches whose tips swelled with buds shadowed her and brought out the wind's bite. This stretch of road always made her uneasy, as if alien eyes gauged her passage. The brush grew thick with closely growing poplar, beech and persimmon trees, and even at this leafless time of year she could see only a few yards into the dark woods. The mild curve that pinched off the twin ruts behind seemed suddenly to separate her from the open fields and slough, while the curve ahead obscured what lay in front. She found herself humming just to hear a human voice against the honking of long lines of geese wavering in the wind above the branches. Then she passed the weathered square post that tilted toward the lane. It marked the first half-mile of her trip and the end of her property. The next mile was a right-of-way through a neglected edge of Oak Hall, Mr. Carswell's large plantation, and it was here that she always felt something solemn and old and sentient in the air. Even Star, unsettled, snorted and twisted his head to look back at Lydia.

"Go, boy," she said softly. "Get along now, Star."

Her voice seemed to intrude into the silence of the woods, but the horse bobbed his head and settled back into his steady pace. Through the soggy-dark tree trunks, she had a glimpse of the shrubs that lined Fowler Creek, their stems yellow and red with rising sap. Then the road angled uphill away from the creek through drier forest, and for no apparent reason it wove gently this way and that between the pines. Probably, she reflected, because that's how the wildlife originally wandered, and the Indians and whites that followed merely widened the animals' paths. A faint

scent of wood smoke carried from somewhere far upwind—
somebody's cabin, possibly as far away as Bullbeggar
Creek. A landless sharecropper or a freedman, Negro or
mulatto. It would come from far beyond the boundaries of
Carswell's land. She could not imagine that man tolerating a
squatter even on this forgotten corner of his plantation. Possibly the scent came from the Beloate's farm—neighboring
yeomen whose fields were only slightly larger than hers,
and who, neighbors said, made a living by selling their corn
not to eat but to drink. Indeed, this very smoke might origi-
nate under one of the stills they were said to have hidden in
the woods. That possibility had brought Sheriff Hope, as
time and official business allowed, into this part of the
county. But the hulking Beloate twins—Arthur and Ben—
did not hide their disdain for the sheriff or his law.

Ahead, a small gap in the tree line showed where the
lane joined the high road that ran north up the peninsula
from Withams Town. When Star finally pulled the wagon
up the embankment onto the travel-packed dirt, Lydia dismounted to rest the animal as well as to stretch her limbs.
Another six and a half miles to New Church, but now the
way was smoother and the wagon easier for Star to pull.

A tall oak tree rising above the poplars and hickory that
surrounded the fields marked the Williams farm yard and
the first mile on the high road. Lydia was tempted to pull in
for something warm to drink. The door, Mrs. Williams had
told her, was always open to her or Gretchen, and on ex-
ceedingly hot days or when winter's icy cold stung tears
from Lydia's eyes and made her knuckles ache as she
gripped the reins, she had taken advantage of the offer. But
now that she was inland, she had the shelter of pines and
gum trees bordering the road, and the walking stirred her
blood. If she made good time and wasted none in New
Church, she could stop on the way back. It was always a
temptation to spend an hour sipping tea and talking with
Mrs. Williams, even though the woman could, as Franklin
used to say, talk ears onto a fence post.

But Lydia believed that a genuine affection had grown between her and Mrs. Williams, who was the age of Lydia's mother. She had even helped Lydia prepare Franklin's body for burial, talking about the weather, about the vittles, about the promising future of Marshfield even without its master as she sponged and wiped and tugged trouser legs and coat sleeves with Lydia. During that numb time when Lydia seemed unable to move or greet or even to think, Mrs. Williams, Mrs. Brown, and Gretchen filled and served the dishes, arranged the chairs, heated cider and tea, and filled the whiskey decanter from the heavy clay jug. And Mrs. Williams along with Mrs. Brown had not, as had so many who attended Franklin's funeral, forgotten the widow with the deceased.

True, Lydia visited the Williamses more often than they visited her. It was far more convenient for her to stop on trips to New Church than for Mrs. Williams to take the lonely two and a half mile ride out to Marshfield. But on occasion, the older woman made that effort, and Lydia was grateful to her. Like Gretchen, but with the better perspective of her age, the woman commented on the latest events in the lives of neighbors near and far. Her stories, interesting and often comic but not spiteful, were about the families—white, black, and mulatto—thinly scattered through the forests and fields of this northern half of Accomack County. Lydia sometimes felt that through her talk and reminiscences, Mrs. Williams had gently stitched her into the fabric of the county's life and made her feel less lonely.

Two hours later, she saw the gray wood smoke from New Church rising above the trees. In all her time on the road, she had passed only one horseman, whom she did not know. Too rushed for words, he tipped his hat as he cantered by, his horse's hooves flinging dabs of mud across the wagon bed. Two or three barefoot Negroes toting farm tools or lumpy gunnysacks over a shoulder stepped into the dead grass and weeds at the side of the road and bobbed their heads as she drove past. But the rest of the time, the road had wound cold and empty, and to accompany her thoughts she had only the rhythmic sound of Star's hooves, the wagon's steady creak, and the haunting calls of geese in the clouds overhead.

As she came down the gentle hill above the small cluster of frame and brick buildings scattered around the church, the high road began to hold more travelers. Two boys talking excitedly veered, at the rattle of the wagon coming up behind them, onto the roadside, scarcely turning from their conversation to say "Afternoon, ma'am." A farmer she did not recognize drove his wagon past in silence, eyes focused on something far down the road behind her. Nearer town, a girl leaned across a wooden gate between the road and a home's small cow pasture and shed, and Lydia did recognize her face: Sarah Kilmon, one of the large Kilmon clan who attended the Methodist church. The cloth of her cotton print dress, already too small, was thin from much laundering, and revealed hints of the woman she was becoming. She scratched in her light blonde hair and nodded a vacant hello, but her attention was focused on the settlement down the road.

New Church had come into being on the south side of a ford. Now the wide creek was bridged by stone arches. Small homes and commercial buildings, mostly unpainted wood, were sprinkled haphazardly along the high road passing the church. Its white paint had the yellowish tint of time and dust. In the fields surrounding the settlement stood two abandoned tobacco warehouses whose roofs were swaybacked with age and showed missing shingles. Freshly plowed earth cut close to their weathered and gaping walls. Just this side of the church was the brick store and an attached residence at its rear. Faded paint—"Henderson's Sundries Store"—decorated the nearest wall.

Lydia made out a cluster of figures in front of the store's covered porch. She pulled on the brake handle to ease the wagon's downhill push against Star, but the horse's ears lifted and his pace increased as he recognized the scene. For

Lydia, New Church meant the store and its post office, but for Star it meant a long drink at the mossy trough and a grain-filled feedbag to stoke up for the trip home.

As they reached the bottom of the hill, a yellow dog darted from under a home's porch boards to bark excitedly at Star's heels and cause him to wag his head nervously. A flail of the buggy whip was enough to drive the cur back, though to Lydia's relief, the whip did not strike. Carried on the breeze, a ragged cheer came from a small crowd. It was not a holiday, but something had drawn people in from the surrounding farms and plantations.

"Heyo, Mrs. Sensabaugh!" The voice came from a foot-path between unpainted slat fences that protected kitchen gardens from wandering cattle. One of Gretchen's brothers, face fuzzy with soft hairs, grinned widely at her. "You hear about it too?"

"About what, Humphrey?"

"The war's done started! Genr'l Beauregard's took Fort Sumter! Salisbury telegraph over in Maryland says the Yankees surrendered the fort to Genr'l Beauregard and Lincoln's calling for Yankees to join the Union army. He even asked us'ns in Virginia to join, and a fat chance he's got of that!"

"Why, Humphrey—"

"I'm going to enlist in the Virginia army. Infantry, not the calvary. I can't join the calvary 'cause Pa says I can't take our horse, and Mr. Carswell says you got to bring your own or buy one of his'n to join his calvary. Me and Alvin Fletcher and Arthur and Ben Beloate and Allen Rafer and Richard and Billy Taylor. We're starting down to North-ampton County this afternoon. The Eastern Shore Volun-teers are mustering in Eastville." The grin grew even wider, showing a missing bottom tooth and the others stained brown by tobacco. "By damn—pardon me, ma'am—all's you got to have to join the infantry is your feet!"

"Why, Humphrey—" She could not think of anything else to say. Somewhere in South Carolina someone had started shooting, and the heat of conflagration suddenly seemed to burn through the excited lad, through the very air that all at once felt brittle and sharp and slightly unreal.

"Yes'm. We're going to have a time of it, I tell you!"

"I—I hope you'll stop at Marshfield to say good-bye to Gretchen."

"Well." His tongue ran across his lower lip. "I don't know's we'll have that much time, ma'am. We got to get there and report in. To start learning to be soldiers, you know."

"I see. I'll tell Gretchen." A growing sense of awe at the definitive nature of the boy's decision led to a stiff phrase, "I trust all will be well with you, Humphrey." She was speaking formally to this person who had suddenly shed his childhood and foreshadowed a fast-changing and uncertain future.

Blinking, he caught something from her tone and seemed to grow an inch taller. "Yes'm. You tell Gretchen I'll be back in ninety days to tell her all about it." Then his grin brought back the boy. "I'll be wearing a uniform, then!"

"Yes—I shall."

He bound down the dirt path between wavering garden fences. His straight hair sprouted like yellow grass and wagged with his stride, elbows and knees sharp angles, legs eagerly stretching. Her heart told her that this moment and this image would be forever in her memory.

"Yeee-ha!" A high-pitched scream startled her. From the crowd, several voices howled in answer and someone fired a weapon. The crack of the firearm made her jump and yank the reins as Star heaved onto his haunches, ears back and snorting. "Steady, now, Star—steady boy—good boy!"

"Heyo, nigger! Here comes the Yankees—you better git!"

The pistol fired again and Star danced, less startled but still frightened. "Star, now, Star—"

Shouting laughter followed a figure who sprinted down the muddy street, bare black feet slipping frantically in the puddles. Another shot and the figure ducked to the side of the road to disappear behind a corner of the brick church.

On the porch of the Sundries Store, Mr. Henderson leaned out over the milling heads. "Stop that now! Stop that shooting—somebody's going to get hurt!"

"It's just a nigger—shoot him in the head, can't hurt him there!"

"You boys cut that shooting out—save it for the Yankees!" Mr. Henderson glanced up to see Lydia struggling with her horse. "There's women and children about. Now you boys step up and have a drink and put that fool pistol away before somebody gets hurt!"

A jutting, sun-reddened nose and shining black eyes suddenly peered at Lydia from a face otherwise buried in scraggly patches of gray and black hair. "That there horse is nervous, lady." A tattered coat sleeve reached out and grabbed Star's bridle. "Let me lead him for you."

"He's all right!" Lydia knew the vagabond's face but not his name. "Please, you'll frighten him even more!"

"It's all right—I talk animal talk." The man, the black cloth of his frayed coat and ragged trousers shiny with ingrained grime, muttered in Star's twitching ear. "Steady, horse. Come on, now. We go get you some water, praise the Lord."

"Looky there," a man in a brown plaid suit laughed loudly enough for Lydia to hear. "Wailin' Willie's making up to the Widder Sensabaugh!"

She recognized that man—Curtis: the agricultural drummer who traveled the New Town packet boat from Baltimore and had been a frequent visitor when they first moved to Marshfield. Smiling, advisory, he had been eager to sell more farm equipment than the inexperienced Franklin needed. He now held a half-empty bottle of whiskey and grinned, his cravat pulled aside. "Howdy, Mrs. Sensabaugh. This here's a great day for Virginia!" He lifted his bottle. "A toast to the ladies of Virginia!"

The bottle went around eager hands as narrowed eyes

and widened lips hinted at a judgment of Lydia that would not be voiced aloud in her or any woman's presence. "To the ladies, God bless them!"

"Amen—and this pretty lady especial!"

"Willy, you keep that horse settled." Mr. Henderson, stained apron swelling over his stomach, came down the board steps. "He'll look after your horse, Mrs. Sensabaugh. You come on in out of this crowd. War's been declared, you know."

She let him help her from the wagon as the faces continued to stare, and was relieved that beneath the oilcloth cape, she wore her best mourning dress and enough petticoats to look like a lady. The tall, hairy figure bobbed his head in a steady monotone whose words only he and Star could hear. Finally the horse heaved a deep sigh and let his head sag toward the water trough.

A voice from among the men standing around the wagon mumbled, "She's a looker!"

Lydia heard a muttered reply, "Yeah, well there's no reason for her to look your way, Billy Taylor, and she's a lot older'n you are!"

The voices broke into snorts of half-stifled laughter and Billy Taylor said "Gimme that bottle, damn you, Ben Beloate."

The small crowd shifted attention to the struggle for the bottle as Lydia, blood pulsing in growing anger behind her eyes, stumbled blindly up the board steps into the store.

"The boys are all excited about the news, Mrs. Sensabaugh. And a little liquored up, is all." The storeowner's face was mottled red and gray with his own excitement. "They say the burghers will certainly vote us to secede now!"

"They should vent their excitement in a civilized manner, Mr. Henderson. Surely there are some gentlemen in that mob!"

"Yes'm—in fact, Mr. Carswell's in the mob, or was. He bought the whiskey, so I reckon it's his mob." He added,

"The same mob, Mrs. Sensabaugh, that's going to protect you against the Yankees when Virginia does secede."

"In their present state, Mr. Henderson, they are incapable of protecting anyone. In fact, the Yankees may be preferable. Here is my list." She handed the storekeeper the slip of paper.

He cleared his throat and looked at the writing. "Ma'am, I'm sure you're upset and all, and rightfully so. And I'm sure you don't mean that about preferring the Yankees. But Virginia is certain to secede now—there's talk that General Beauregard fired on Fort Sumter to force us to secede. And when we do, some around here might hold those words against you." He was still eyeing the shopping slip, his spatulate fingers pressing smooth its wrinkles. "Maybe not over in Horn Town or Chincoteague, but here around New Church you'll want to be more cautious, ma'am."

But Lydia was still frightened and that made her anger sharper. "I'm certain you mean well, Mr. Henderson. However, my exercise of the English language tends to be both precise and accurate, and as far as I know, though I am a woman, nonetheless I have the right to express myself under the Constitution of the United States."

He spoke with slightly exaggerated patience. "We won't be the United States, ma'am. That's what I'm trying to tell you. And others'll be expressing themselves, too, and not all of them's going to be using only words. Nor care that you're a lady." Wagging the slip of paper for emphasis, he added, "We got neighbors ready to shoot each other over all this. It's best to be cautious in times like these." He drew a deep breath. "One sack of flour coming up. And I believe you have a letter."

Lydia struggled for self-control as she stepped into the cramped corner that was the "ladies retiring room." Behind a Franklin stove, two bentwood rocking chairs faced each other. In an attempt at domesticity, Mrs. Henderson's most likely, a small throw rug of bright quilted squares had been placed out of the way of muddy shoes close to the curved feet of the stove. Otherwise, the space was bare.

Lydia sank into one of the high-backed chairs, a sigh quivering her body, and closed her eyes as she rocked gently. In her anger, she had challenged Mr. Henderson's advice. The man was only trying to protect her against herself, but she had spurned his effort. She should have been more diplomatic. Much later, when she recalled this cramped corner smelling of a tangle of odors—dust, aging root vegetables, tobacco, floor oil, animal feed, stale meat—the memory would be of a temporary refuge whose transience had been foretold by the rumble of voices and drunken shouts outside the store.

Chapter 7

Slowly lifting out of a gray horizon of tangled branches, the tall oak tree welcomed Lydia. Brief showers now passed over occasional fields carved out of the woods to splatter on her oilcloth. Behind the wagon seat on which she sat huddled and chill, her purchases, as heavy and inert as a corpse and just as cheery, rode covered against rain by an old and tarred canvas sail from the *Lydia*. The good thing about the gloomy rain had been its cooling effect on the drunken revelers in the high street of New Church. The bad was that it intensified the mood that had been upon her since arriving at the Sundries Store.

Mr. Henderson's servant, Rufus, balked at carrying her sacks and goods out to the wagon. The sweat of fear made his face shiny as he limped backwards away from the storekeeper, his gray head shaking from side to side. "Naw, Mr. Henderson—please don't make me go out in front of them mens, sah! They likkered up—they shoot me for sport!"

"Damn it, Rufus—pardon me, Mrs. Sensabaugh—just take the goods out and put them in the wagon. They won't pay no attention to you."

"They gonna pay just enough to kill me, sah. Ain't I been worth something to your daddy? Ain't I worth something to you now? What I be worth when I be dead?"

"Rufus—"

"He's right to be afraid of those drunkards, Mr. Henderson. I'll carry out the goods myself." Lydia gripped the corner of a heavy sack of chicken meal. Planting her heels and stifling an un-ladylike grunt, she began jerking it by inches across floorboards stained dark by oiled sawdust and age.

"Now—Mrs. Sensabaugh—now you can't lift that, ma'am. Rufus, damn your black hide! Here, Mrs. Sensabaugh, I'll take it—that's all right. I can take it out." With a hot glance at Rufus, Mr. Henderson jerked the sack to his shoulder and sidled it out the door. Rufus quickly disappeared into the rear of the store, limp gone.

She waited until the last box was loaded before stepping into the drizzle. But that did not save her from the attention of the remaining dozen or so men and youths who hung like flies under the porch roof.

"Don't you worry, Mrs. Sensabaugh—we'll keep the Yankees away from you!"

"You going to move out there to keep her safe, Billy?"

"She'll need the Yankees to keep you away from her, Billy Taylor!"

"Damn your eyes—"

The stragglers shouted as the stocky, black-haired youth stumbled drunkenly down the steps after a young man who, dodging from side to side, laughed. "And you better look out for Nellie Carswell, too!"

Still gentled by Wailing Willy who, like the horse, stood as if no rain fell, Star snorted hello into his leather feed bag. Lydia offered Willy two pennies and three eggs from the remaining dozen that Mr. Henderson had no use for.

The vagabond stared at the eggs and coins as they rested in his grimy palm, then his beard parted in a snaggled grin. "The good Lord provides! And the good Lord bless you, Miz Sensabaugh!"

He scratched behind Star's ear as he removed the feed bag. Ignoring the drunks as she climbed tight-lipped onto the wagon seat, she managed to say "Thank you" to Willy.

Then, to Star's injured surprise, cracked him sharply on the rump with the whip.

℮∽℮∽

Mrs. Williams opened the door, wiping flour from her hands as she pulled off her kitchen apron. "No, I am not too busy, Mrs. Sensabaugh—just taking advantage of the cool to bake some bread. It has to rise anyway." She offered the parlor but Lydia said she would prefer the ready warmth of the kitchen. "Sure you would—you're about froze through, aren't you? Take that wet oilcloth off and let me get the tea going."

While the woman pumped water into the kettle and set it on the hottest part of the cast iron stove, Lydia told her the news.

"Well, I reckon that makes Mr. Williams a liar, then—he keeps saying there won't be a war because Lincoln promised not to end slavery in the states that already have it." When the spout began to steam, she carefully measured tea into the kettle. "Did you happen to see Clayton Boggs in town?

Clayton was their hired hand. Lydia tried to think whether his had been among the staring eyes she had tried to avoid meeting. "I can't recall."

"Well he's off somewhere. Been somewhere all day, and if it ain't to New Church, it's to chase after a runaway Nigra. He's been doing that a lot lately—we hear about a lot of runaways, lately, and that Clayton thinks he's going to get rich catching them." Mrs. Williams shook her head. "Whole county's got restless, it seems. Mr. Williams says the only nap Clayton's ever caught is when he closes his eyes. I had to do his work as well as mine this afternoon." She explained, "Mr. Williams is over to the Rayfield place near Franklin City, else Clayton wouldn't've dared go off. Took over a yearling to swap for an anvil and some smithy tools this morning, Mr. Williams did, though what in the good Lord's name we want with another anvil I don't know. But that's Mr. Williams—somebody's got something to swap, he's first in line to trade. I tell him he's more trader than farmer and he ought to swap this place for Mr. Henderson's store!" She sipped at her cup. "If that Clayton thinks Mr. Williams won't hear about him leaving me his work to do, he's got another think coming."

In return for Mrs. Williams's hospitality, Lydia sketched what she had seen in New Church.

"Well if free whiskey was to be had, you can bet Clayton Boggs was there. But pouring whiskey won't do Squire Carswell any good. That riff-raff will swig all he gives them and then poke fun at him behind his back."

"Have you heard of a man they call 'Wailing Willy'?"

"Was that poor creature there? They call him 'Wailing Willy' because he's always singing hymns. He's harmless—been wandering this county for at least ten years." She pointed a finger to the side of her head. "Tetched, you know. Works when someone will hire him, but Lord only knows how he keeps body and soul together." She thought a moment. "He does have a way with animals, though— horses and dogs. Some say it's because he lives like them in the woods."

Lydia wondered if it was because of the man's gentleness. She had heard stories of even wild beasts having patience with the occasional mental unfortunate who wandered away from an asylum. "Well, he was kind to Star and to me." She took from her reticule the envelope Mr. Henderson had handed her. "My sister Bonnie writes that war fever is rampant in Norfolk City, too, and most of the men have volunteered for the Confederate army." Unfolding the flimsy sheets with their delicate flower decorations at the corners, she read, "'Andrew—' that's her husband '—is torn between joining the army with the rest and going into the navy, which is where he thinks he can serve best. Little Richard—' He's their seven-year-old '—even has a uniform, a very sprightly light hazel blouse and trousers with gold trim, and he looks like a little general and gives very loud orders to the dogs and cats who seem more interested in avoiding his army rather than joining it. War fever, it is called, Dear Sister, but there is much more to it than that. The call for the defense of our State and our Way of Life is clear. We can have Union without Liberty or Liberty without Union. The real issue, Dear Sister, is neither slavery nor union but Virginia's right to determine her own course in accordance with the original Constitution, and were our Papa alive now, I'm certain he would agree.'"

Mrs. Williams eyed the thin sheets filled with graceful writing. "We don't get much by way of letters. But Mr. Williams did bring home a *Somerset Herald* he got up in Princess Anne last week. Said Lincoln's been moving a lot of Union troops into Maryland and Delaware—said he's ready to suspend the habeas corpus and arrest Maryland's legislators so's they can't vote to secede."

Lydia frowned. "Like you, I don't support slavery. Nor do I support secession, though you may. But an action like that seems contrary to the rule of law."

The woman agreed. "Some might say just as contrary as telling the Southern states they don't have the right to secede, which, to Mr. Williams's way of thinking, they do, even if he don't want it." Her head jiggled its tight gray curls. "Squire Carswell thinks the same, but he wants it. Now, there is one man you can trust—you can trust that everything that man does is best for Parnell Carswell."

"I hear he's raising a troop of cavalry."

She nodded. "I heard that too. And that he says volunteers got to bring their own horses or buy his'n—him with a stable bigger than our barn and house together. You tell me how many men in this county got horses to spare for fighting."

"I don't know."

"Then I'll tell you: very few. Volunteers can buy a horse from him—hard specie only, I warrant—then have the privilege of joining his cavalry troop and doing what he tells them." The gray curls danced again. "He won't get that many volunteers, and my suspicion is he don't really want them." She refilled their cups.

"But why?"

"If he goes off playing soldier, it might cost him some money, because some of those Nigras he's always chasing after might get away." She added, "It's not just his slaves, neither; it's them that come up from Northampton County and even across the Chesapeake from the Western Shore. Trying to make it to New Jersey and then on to Canada."

"Mr. Carswell's a slave catcher?"

"Wouldn't admit it—not an occupation that suits a gentleman like him, you know. But Clayton Boggs says the squire takes his prize money, gentleman or no. Claims if he don't stop them before they cross the Maryland line, nobody will, since Sheriff Hope's hand in glove with the abolitionists."

Lydia remembered the anger in Carswell's voice as he spoke of removing the sheriff from office. "Has Mr. Carswell lost any slaves?"

"Says he has. I saw his overseer, Mr. Talbot, not two weeks ago leading three poor souls back to Oak Hall. Two bucks and a wench." A wag of her head. "He'll sell them south—Mr. Talbot says that's what he does—sells any runaways he catches south. Says it makes the rest think twice about trying."

"But still he has runaways?"

"Well, I hear he does work them heavy and feed them light. And there's people in this county—free Nigras and whites—willing to help them get north, so he's got to be vigilant. Mr. Carswell says Sheriff Hope don't chase them any harder than he has to, so it's up to him to keep ahold of his own. I often see Mr. Talbot riding along the high road with his slave catchers and dogs." She added, "Did you know Carswell wanted to buy Marshfield Farm but your husband offered more for it?"

"Why, no—Franklin thought Mr. Carswell wasn't interested in the farm."

"Oh, he surely was! He just wasn't interested in paying as much as Mr. Shoemaker got from your husband. He don't want all the land in the world, just what borders his own, and I reckon if you wanted to give him your farm he'd be happy to take it." She thought a moment. "I've never figured how that plantation of his makes money. His crops are no different from anybody else's around here, just a lot more of them. And that just pushes all the prices lower."

೮ౠ೮ౠ

Despite saying several times that she should be on her way, Lydia stayed longer than she intended. The kitchen was friendly and warm, bright with yellow paint, and happy with talk that moved from politics to the more important subject of who was courting whom, what families suffered what illnesses, what weddings were planned far in advance or had not been planned far enough, and which new babies had arrived where. By the time Lydia tugged her oilcloth around her shoulders, the muddy road led into a dusk so thick that it blurred the outlines of fence and trees and merged the dark of forest with that of the sky.

"You will be cautious on the road, Mrs. Sensabaugh?"

"I will, thank you. Besides, Star knows the way—he's led us home on nights darker than this."

"Well, it'll soon be black enough, all right, as well as wet and cold. You certain you don't want a lant-horn?"

"I'm certain."

"Well, remember, this door's always open to you. And I'll be out to Marshfield one of these days soon."

Before the road curved away, Lydia looked back over her shoulder at the dots of light from the farmhouse's windows. The distant glow in the otherwise unbroken gloom made her feel more intently her isolation and chill. But, she reminded herself, it was her own fault for enjoying Mrs. Williams' hospitality longer than she should. Now she would be better served by thinking of the comfort waiting at her own home than of that she was leaving behind. She clucked again to Star and pulled the clammy oilcloth tighter about her neck as another gust of raindrops rattled on it and on the tarp behind her. Overhead, another noisy flight of geese flapped their way through the dimness.

Star sensed the turn-off before she made it out. The horse slowed and looked back in question. Then she saw, angling off the road, muddy streaks that marked the ruts her wagon had carved pulling up the wet and grassy bank this afternoon.

"Good boy, Star—up, now—let's get home."

A snort of reply and the horse turned down the lane a bit more quickly. The desolation increased, and with it, the weariness on her shoulders. An ache in the small of her back made the wagon seat even more uncomfortable. Wearily, she shifted position and strained to make out the leaning post that signaled the end of the Carswell estate and the beginning of her property. But it receded into a deepening shadow that made even the closest tree trunks only vague blackness. Gradually, she stopped anticipating it and gave herself to the sway and lurch of the wagon. But Star did not falter, and she let him have his head, grateful to Franklin for having the knowledge and generosity to purchase a horse both intelligent and gentle.

Lost in thoughts that took her mind off the cold discomfort, she sat hunched and buried in the waterproof for warmth. Where the trees closed over the road to leave the world without light or motion, the steady splash and jolt and rattle of the wagon was the only indication that she was moving. She judged that Star followed his nose more than his eyes as he led her down such dark tunnels. Relieved that no one could see the unladylike act, she tucked the lax reins under her thigh. Then she held her icy fingers to her mouth and breathed warmth on them. How on earth did the Yankee ladies endure such snow and cold as she had seen portrayed in *Godey's Illustrated*? She remembered woodcuts in the ornate gift books that showed heavily wrapped but smiling young women riding in sleds with their beaux across a snow-blanketed landscape. The breath of the high-stepping horses steamed ferociously. Certainly, the passengers dressed warmly—for them, furs were utilitarian rather than decorative—and she had heard that beaver skins, the kind that produced the fabled riches of Mr. Astor, had fur as soft as the finest silk and would keep one comfortable in the coldest regions. She had also seen illustrations of the Tartars, as well, swathed and topped in thick furs that—

Something caught at the corner of her vision and she blinked, trying to make out what it had been. She searched the darkness, eyes watering with effort, where she thought the something had flickered. Something...a brief glimmer, a wink of light...As faint and brief as those flashes of light that move behind one's eyes in the blackest of rooms. Perhaps that was what—

There! Off to the right and somewhat behind her: a quick and dim flash that disappeared even as she strained her eyes to fix it. She grabbed up the reins and pulled gently to bring Star to a halt. Bobbing his head to tug at the bit, he snorted and stamped a hoof, impatient to get to his barn. But Lydia wasn't listening to what he had to say.

"Hush, Star," she whispered sharply. "Be still!"

The only sound was the steady rustle of rain on the dead leaves covering the ground. The heavy, slower patter of large drops plummeted from limbs and twigs while the lighter, steadier drops fell directly from unseen clouds. For an instant it sounded like a thousand tiny feet scurrying closer to her, but it wasn't. It was only raindrops—a sound she'd heard all her life—it wasn't feet coming toward her from the black woods. Just raindrops.

Over the next minutes, the light glowed irregularly on and off. It varied from a dim, reflected glow to a tiny, sharp point of glare. Someone was carrying a dark-lantern. The intervals were caused by intervening tree trunks or by someone opening and closing the lantern's tiny window. The dimness of light came when the window turned from her. Its glare came when it faced toward her. From the shifting intensities, she judged that the someone was angling through the forest in her direction.

Hunched against a spasm of chill that came not only from the weather, she softly clucked Star into a slow walk, wincing as the wagon's creaks and rattles seemed suddenly magnified. She was not sure if she was on Carswell land or her own. Irrationally, she would feel safer once she entered her property, though her woods were equally deserted. The road wound from under the canopy of limbs into a less-thick grayness. Now she could make out the moving shadow that was Star and the streaks of wheel ruts through turf that ran hazily behind his rear hoofs and under the wagon's dashboard. In the woods beside her, the mysterious light flickered, dimmed, glided. Lydia gradually realized that one of the small metallic rattles was not the familiar sound of her slowly moving wagon.

"Whoa, Star. Whoa, boy," she murmured.

Then she listened more intently. Through the patter of rain came a steady rustle punctuated by a faint, repeated clink. It was a sound she recognized from girlhood: the slap of thick iron links that chained a slave's limbs together. Then that sound ceased but the steady shuffle of feet among the fallen leaves made a faint, rhythmic whisper.

Holding the reins tightly to prevent Star from pulling, she waited and watched the light in the trees draw even with her and move ahead. In a few minutes, the irregular spark of the dark-lantern's window ceased and only its glow remained. The lantern faced away and gradually faded. She loosed the reins. Relieved, the horse lurched forward, but she held him back. "Slow, now. Slowly, Star."

Ragged lines of shadow against the clouds showed where the lane cut through the woods ahead. Lydia rode slowly, paused to listen. Hearing nothing she tapped the reins against Star's haunches and they stepped forward again. Here in the open section of the lane, she could see the silhouette of Star's uplifted head and the sharp points of his ears aimed forward. The path of slightly lighter sky bent to the left, but the lantern had drifted to the right, away from her course. She again reined Star to a halt and listened. Nothing, not the brief clink, not the shuffle of feet in fallen leaves. They apparently followed some track through the woods, but where? Toward the Beloates' farm? The Browns'? Certainly, no one would take chained slaves up to the freedman's community of Jack Town?

The tilted property post welcomed her out of the dimness beside the track. The chain gang was moving across a corner of her land. But they headed nowhere she could think of, since all that lay in that direction were empty marshes and Pocomoke Sound.

Chapter 8

When, finally, Lydia glimpsed the distant glow of Marshfield's kitchen windows, she was exhausted. She had vague recollections of Roger's callused hands half-lifting her from the seat and bundling her into the warmth of Gretchen's chatty care. She did not remember eating or carrying any of the store goods into house or barn, or stumbling upstairs to bed.

The next morning, the sound of Gretchen in the kitchen woke her to a hearty breakfast of poached fish, eggs, cornbread and fresh, steaming coffee. Lydia took her meal at the kitchen table where she could tell both Gretchen and Roger the news from New Church. "The Virginia and Maryland militias are called up, and many are volunteering for the regular armies. Gretchen, I saw your brother Humphrey. He said he and some of the other young men were going down to Eastville to enlist."

"Humphrey's going to join the army?"

Lydia nodded, the image of the boy's excited grin in her mind.

"Who all's he going with?"

"I think he said the Beloate boys, Allen Rafer, Richard Taylor...He mentioned other names, but I can't recall them."

"Allen Rafer? And they're already up and gone? Just like that?"

"Humphrey was very sorry that he didn't have time to stop and say good-bye to you. They had to be in Eastville as soon as possible. But he said he'd be back in ninety days and tell you all about it. He was very proud, Gretchen. He's a very brave young man."

"He's an idjit! Him and Allen Rafer that's just got engaged to Lucy Brown and all of them!"

Roger, from his table on the back porch, said, "I thought you'd be happy they was off to shoot Yankees."

"I'd be happier if it was you, Roger Bradshaw!" The girl clattered a hot pan of biscuits on the counter and fled into the dining room, face clenched against tears.

The man shifted uncomfortably and looked at Lydia with remorse. "Well, she said she would be ashamed if I was her brother because I don't want to fight!"

"The news has her upset, Roger. It's one thing to talk about one's brother becoming a soldier, but quite another when it actually happens."

His gaze focused on the floorboards, bleached and slightly furry from much hard scrubbing. "Maybe it's not her brother's going that set her off."

"What do you mean?"

His shoulders lifted and fell in a weary gesture, and he did not look up. "She's got feelings for Allen Rafer. Everybody in this whole county knows that."

"But he's engaged—"

"Yes'm. Don't mean she wants to see him go away, though."

A thought struck her and she murmured, "Do you have feelings for Gretchen, Roger?"

Red flushed up the side of his neck even as he shook his head. "No'm!" His voice, too, was muted. "All's we do is fight and I don't reckon she's got any interest in just a farm hand." He slid his chair back and gathered up his dishes.

"But who knows what events may occur?"

"Yes'm." He carried the dishes into the kitchen and set them on the sink board. "A lot's already happened and a lot more will, but I got a good idea what won't happen." Bitterness twisted his voice, "And if it don't bother you, ma'am, I'd just as soon not talk about it."

"Of course, Roger, of course!" But her voice stopped him as he went out the back door: "Roger, I saw something in the woods last night, as I crossed onto our land."

"Yes'm?"

After a moment's hesitation, she asked, "Are there any houses or camps over on the north point?" She gestured toward the ridge that formed the northern shore of their inlet, and whose other side tapered off into Pocomoke Sound. "Does anyone except the Browns live over there?"

"Some of it belongs to the Beloates. Some's county land—reverted for taxes or whatever a long time ago, so there's probably some squatters. And there's Jack Town over by Freeschool Marsh." His eyebrows pinched together. "How come you're asking?"

"I think someone was leading slaves through my woods."

He looked at her sharply. "You sure that's what it was?"

"I heard the chains. You know that rhythmic, shuffling clink a chain gang makes."

He nodded.

"They were on my land, Roger. I think we should investigate."

He was silent for a long moment, a question forming in his eyes. But he merely said, "Yes'm."

She corrected herself. "I should investigate." Scraping the remnants of her breakfast into the hogs' slop bucket, she replaced its lid and set her dishes to soak in the pan of wash-water. "Is Star too weary to be ridden today?"

"If it ain't far nor hard. Though a good rest wouldn't hurt him."

"I don't know how far it is. But I promise to ride slowly. Would you saddle him please?"

"Yes'm."

By the time Lydia changed to her riding habit, Star was ready. So was Roger. "I reckon I better come along."

"Why?"

"People who do things so's not to be seen tend to get upset when somebody does see them."

"But we have only one horse."

"I got legs. And you said you would ride slow."

She had indeed said that. "Is that shotgun necessary?"

"Not if we don't need it."

Star's hooves thumped softly in the dirt. Beside the horse, the man easily kept pace with the stirrups. The shotgun rode on his shoulder, its downward held muzzle carefully angled away from her and the horse.

Last night's showers had thinned to a broken overcast, and drifting patches of warm sunlight made spring's green almost harsh. It wasn't until they were passing the boundary stake that Lydia reached the question that had half-formed in the back of her mind. "Do you remember those lights I told you about?"

"I remember."

She searched the side of the lane as they went, trying to feel exactly where she had been when she saw the last of the flickering dark-lantern. "Is it possible those lights and what I saw last night are somehow connected?"

"Them other lights was awhile back."

"Granted, Roger. But one's mind does tend to seek correlations between things whose explanations are vague."

"Ma'am?"

"We want to explain things we don't understand. We often do so by finding links where links may or may not be."

"Oh." His stride slowed as she reined Star to study the thick growth. "Well, if we say there's these links and there's not, then that could mess things up more than just finding out for certain."

"Of course certainty is best if certainty can be gained, and I'm not certain this is where I saw the dark-lantern."

She pointed between tree trunks, "But I believe it was in that direction."

"Yes'm." Roger took the bridle and Lydia dismounted. Then, following her, he led Star into the tangle of close growing branches.

She tried to guess the distance, glancing back occasionally to the sunlight that marked the lane, and was just about to admit error when Roger said, "Over there." She looked where he pointed. Against the brown and gray detritus of the forest floor, recently turned leaves, their wet undersides scuffed up and still dark, marked a vague trail. Roger stepped past her to examine a broken twig and she began to see the tiny pale glimmer of other freshly splintered twigs in the brush close along the path.

"Somebody was dragging leg iron, all right."

"How can you tell?"

"All this." His hand waved over the disturbed leaves. "Somebody just walking wouldn't stir up the wet leaves like this."

The faint scrape snaked among the trees, swinging around thick and impassable clumps of brush to angle again generally northwest. The underbrush thinned enough to allow Lydia back on Star while Roger, intent, strode ahead.

"One came back, anyway." He knelt to indicate the imprint of a horseshoe pointing down the trail behind them. "Horseman." Standing, he gazed at the ground ahead. "Going this way, the chain scraped over the hoof prints because the rider was leading. But this one's clean—and it's on top of the turned leaves." He held up a creased leaf to show her.

"Do you think it's abolitionists?"

He studied the leaf. "Might be. But I reckon abolitionists would cut off the chains as soon as they was in the woods. Unless they couldn't take the time or make the noise. I don't see it to be a county chain gang, neither, not sneaking along in the dark like that."

"Why would anyone be driven at night?"

"So nobody would see."

She had already figured that out and felt slightly foolish at asking the wrong question. Why would they want to be unseen, was the real question—but she gave Roger his due for being precise, if a bit mule headed, in his literalness.

Then he continued, and she had a suspicion that she had been subject to his peculiar whimsy. "As to why they didn't want to be seen, I reckon it's because somebody wearing chains was being taken away." He frowned at the leaves. "It just ain't clear if they was being taken by catchers or abolitionists." He leaned this way and that and peered ahead. "You best sit here a minute, ma'am."

"What is it?"

He put a finger to his lips and glided forward, the damp leaves silent under his boots and the branches scarcely quivering at his passage. In a moment, he had disappeared. Lydia, breath shallow in a nervous attempt at silence, tried to see something through the tangle of limbs. Star heaved a sigh, his barrel rising and falling between her knees, and seemed content to stand and rest, his tail switching occasionally.

A motion in the trees showed the passage of a squirrel, its arcs of back and tail bouncing and pausing along a limb in silent watchfulness over the invaders below.

"We're at the water." Roger's voice startled her as he stepped from behind a tree. He led Star through an opening in a curtain of growth where, suddenly, the green reeds of new cordgrass and the brown of last year's ragged cattails stretched toward the horizon. The dim path they had followed twisted off into the marsh along a spine of higher earth.

"I reckon you want to go on out there."

"Of course."

"We best tie Star here, then."

She followed Roger along the narrow trail winding between marsh and tangles of bayberry bush. Water glistened among the stems of cordgrass on each side, and rings marked the sudden dive of frogs or turtles.

At last they saw a wide patch where the reedy grass had been trampled to reveal the open channel.

"The slough. It is Marshfield property!"

"Been such for a while." He pointed toward the shore curving beyond the cordgrass. "Your farm is just there."

She could see the roofs of her house and barn just above the trees, and, closer, the two black masts of the *Lydia*. Directly across the open water and cordgrass she recognized the creek's south point.

He gestured toward a fresh gouge in the low bank. "They loaded here. Skiff, likely. Not deep enough here even for the *Lydia*." He tossed a clod of earth into the dark water and watched it fray out and disappear. "Well, we investigated. Now I reckon we better move on."

⁊⊘⊘

Virginia's long-established ban on importing new slaves from Africa had raised the value of those born to the institution. All her life Lydia had heard stories about both slave-stealing abolitionists who helped escaped slaves go north and slave-stealing traders who spirited their catch south. But it had not been until her marriage made her qualified to hear the whispered foulnesses of slave breeding and "improving the stock," that she had fully understood her father's aversion to it. What, when she was a child, had to her seemed his abstract disapproval of the system, she learned was based on an unvoiced but profound repugnance for its effects on victims and practitioners alike.

True, he had never violated the law by actively assisting a slave to escape, nor, other than making an occasional donation, had Lydia openly supported the group of southern abolitionists in Norfolk. And from the quiet isolation of Marshfield, the hot issue that excited torchlight parades and arm waving orators on the Western Shore seemed leached of intensity by distance. But when Franklin did muse about investing in a slave or two as became many other estate owners, she had surprised both of them by her vehemence against the idea. She absolutely would not, she said, ever own a slave nor would she allow any such in her life. Perhaps relieved to have an excuse for not investing their rapidly shrinking funds on slaves, Franklin had acquiesced, though not without commenting that her father's biases had corrupted her judgment.

Now, someone was using her land—and water—to transport slaves. Threat and disruption had invaded the very boundaries of Marshfield. But she did not know what, other than writing Sheriff Hope, she could do about it.

Chapter 9

The next week, when Gretchen was on a brief visit home, Lydia cleared her breakfast table and poured hot water from the kettle to soak the plates in the wash pan. From the porch, the increased pace of Roger's knife and fork worked into her thoughts.

"There's no hurry, Roger." She ate so little that she always finished before he did, and the poor man threatened to give himself indigestion in the belief that he took too long at dining.

His voice muffled by food said "Yes'm," but the pace did not slow.

Wiping dry a dish, she made up her mind and leaned through the doorway. "If it is convenient, I would like to take the *Lydia* out today."

His freckled nose lifted out of the coffee cup and he blinked at her. "Take her out?"

"To make certain she's still seaworthy."

"Well, she is that—I been tending her all winter." He went on, "But she should be hauled out one of these days to have her bottom scraped." Frowning at his plate as he dabbed a biscuit at the remains of egg yolk and spoke to what he thought was on her mind. "There's them'll buy her from you if you want to sell." A wag of his head. "But they won't offer much if they think you got to sell."

"I have no plans of selling, Roger. I want to keep her and learn to sail her."

"Ma'am?"

"To learn to sail the *Lydia*. My husband would take me out, but he did not think it seemly for a lady to sail a boat. I want you to show me how."

His jaw stubbled with a week's whiskers, hung down slightly. A bit of egg white caught at his mouth's corner. "That's a lot to learn."

She did not know whether he meant "for a woman" or "for a landlubber"—perhaps both. "I'm sure it's the labor of a lifetime, Roger. But perhaps with instruction from a waterman as talented as you, I'll be able to handle the boat on calm days."

His hazel eyes blinked. "There's better sailors than I be. And a calm day can turn foul real quick, specially on the Bay." A final wipe of biscuit at the yolk. He carefully chewed and cleared his mouth with more coffee before making a quiet statement whose perception surprised her. "But I see you're real set on learning."

It was early afternoon before the chores were completed and they finally cast off the mooring lines. Even with only one petticoat, her dress and hooded cape were clumsy wear for the narrow walkways between the low cabin and the masts' stays. But as Roger hauled up the heavy canvas, Lydia felt a lightness that echoed her childhood pleasure when she, her sister, and her parents once sailed on a packet up the Bay from Norfolk City to Baltimore. Only this time the excitement came from realizing that her role of mere passenger was over: she was to sail the *Lydia* herself!

Sail and boom swung out slowly from the foremast. The stubby mast of the aftsail jutted empty of its canvas.

"When do we put up the little sail?"

We don't." After a moment, he added, as if attempting to soften his abrupt denial. "Best to learn to handle the main-sail before adding the aftsail. A coasting canoe like this can be tippy."

"All right." The tone of her voice was meant to assure him that there were no hurt feelings on a day as fine as this.

The craft tilted as the weight of the sail and boom swung further outboard. The faint breeze, raw with late April and smelling of the salt marsh, blew the sail smooth and, almost imperceptibly, the pier moved away from the boat. Roger hauled the line taut with one hand while sculling the tiller. When they moved a bit faster, he lifted a knotted rope from its notch and, using the block and tackle mounted near the mast's top, let the centerboard swing down. Bending to peer under the sail, he measured the distance to the lee side of the channel as they swung seaward down the twisting slough.

"Wind's from the northwest—fair and light. You keep the sail taut to the wind. When you spill the wind, you can't go." He demonstrated by letting the line run hissing through his hand until the boom stopped swinging and pointed directly downwind. The stained canvas gave a heavy, muffled flop as it sagged and the boat slowed in silence. "Sometimes that's the best way to keep from going over—just let go the line." He added, "Some other times you can keep her pointed close to the wind. Then the sail catches only the little bit you need and you keep headway." He demonstrated by hauling in the boom until the sail threatened to bulge inward and sweep across the craft to the other side. "See that?"

"Yes."

"We'll get in clear water and you can try it."

"Wonderful!"

The channel widened and the gliding shadow of the broad hull on the glassy water revealed mottled patches of sand and grass that formed the floor of the slough. As Lydia's gaze took in more, she caught the shadowy dart of a fish, the scuttle of a crab, a snail leaving rows of dots on the smooth bottom. Farther from Marshfield, the wind grew stronger and the hull gave a slight gurgling song. Two small wakes spread from bow and stern to cause the cordgrass to wag gently. The reeds flanking the channel were dotted with clinging snails well out of the water with low tide, and here and there among the stems, swells of exposed mud glistened. A sandpiper rose with a squeal to fly just above the grass. An occasional swirl showed where a basking fish had plunged in fright from the tall sail. A few gentle minutes later they passed a nose of high ground where the growth seemed tangled and pushed into angles different from the rest of the reeds. A thin strip of mud, paler and drier than that revealed at low tide, was packed into a faint trail.

"Roger—is that where that boat landed? The place we saw last week?"

He looked where she pointed, studying the low mound. "Could be—good place for a landing. Could be a slide for coons or otters, too. They like to go after shellfish, and there's some around here."

"Mighty big otter."

"Some do get mighty big." His eyes swept the water ahead as the breeze pressed them on. "I'm bringing her about—we got enough open water to tack, now. Mind your head." He shoved the tiller over and the boom slowly creaked across the deck.

She felt *Lydia* tilt toward the other side and start to lift and drop on mild swells. They entered the wide estuary of the Pocomoke River where the wind-chafed water became the cold blue of springtime, and she could no longer make out the bottom. Behind them, between the two points of land that cupped the farmhouse and the roof of the barn rising behind it, the cordgrass blended into a single dark line hiding Fowler Creek's channel.

"Somebody would have to know this shore pretty well to find Fowler Creek, wouldn't they?"

Roger glanced over his shoulder and nodded.

"Especially at night."

"Yes'm."

"And most especially at night in a fog."

"True enough."

"Unless they used lamps. And maybe that was the purpose of those lights Gretchen and I saw last autumn. Someone is using Fowler Creek to transport slaves, aren't they, Roger? That's what those lamps were—guides into that landing!"

He did not respond.

"If you knew of anything, you would tell me, wouldn't you, Roger?"

Instead of grunting "yes'm" or nodding, he glanced up at the telltale fluttering at the tip of the mast.

"Roger?"

"I reckon I would if it meant harm for you or if I wanted to know much about somebody else's business. But I don't and there's no reason for you to. All I do know's that you want to learn to sail. So if that's what we're here for, you can take the tiller and mainsail now."

Lydia studied his blank face, wondering at his defensiveness. "All right, Roger," she replied mildly. "Tell me what I should do."

"Yes'm. Just hold them steady to get their feel."

In her palm, the tiller quivered with the boat's motion. As *Lydia* lifted and fell over the small waves, the hand-smoothed tiller pushed with unexpected strength against her arm. The sail, too, pulled harder than she expected, and she clamped her left hand tightly on its rough line. Pushing her attention away from Roger's evasiveness, she concentrated on guiding the craft. But the large triangle of canvas above, so steady when Roger had the helm, began to wag and spill some air.

"Hold her steady—hold your course."

"I'm trying!"

"Yes'm. And you can breathe, too, any time you want."

She took a gasping breath, unaware that she had been holding air. "Thank you, Roger."

"Yes'm."

She did not think he was laughing at her.

"Just nudge the tiller this way and that—don't overdo it—a sailing canoe's a quick boat."

Gradually, Lydia began to feel the rhythm of the small waves and the hull's rise and slight lunge down. She started to anticipate the motion and counter it with a gentle movement of the tiller: into the rise, away on the fall. The sail settled into a fixed angle and the craft ceased to challenge her. Running obedient under her touch, it gained speed. Her own breathing came more easily and she found herself even relaxing into the steady pull of the mainsheet and the rhythmic communication the tiller gave her about the life of the water. The sting of incipient argument with Roger about the lights faded in the growing realization that she alone controlled the boat, and that, like a living animal, it moved responsively to her touch. "This is glorious!"

This time she did see Roger smile. "You got a good feel for it, ma'am. You learn right fast." He glanced fore and aft. "Now let's try tacking."

After a while she could even look away from the sail and let the *Lydia* communicate through her hands. She gained a novel view of the shoreline and could even make out a few low, unmoving mounds in the quavering line of the seaward horizon.

"Are those islands?"

He peered southwest and nodded. "You got good eyes— the Fox Islands. More like sandbars than real islands, though."

She practiced tacking left, then right, swinging the boom across with more and more confidence so the sail would not die when it spilled its air. She tried letting the sail run out and drawing it back, feeling the *Lydia* slow when the sail's edge flapped loosely and, when the sail bellied taut enough to tremble her arm, speed up to leap against the waves with an eagerness that made her laugh aloud.

Finally, after what seemed a brief time but which her aching hands told her was lengthy, Roger said, "We're coming on to the Maryland shore. Keep the line tight and bring her about." She did, the craft heeling sharply enough to dip the deck to the water and make her gasp. "Steady—you're doing fine. Let the line out slowly, now."

The sail filled before the wind and they scudded even faster than the waves back across the estuary. Roger even let her bring the *Lydia* back into the channel, but he lowered the sail by himself while she used the last of the boat's momentum to steer toward the mooring.

"Head for the side of the pier, ma'am, about halfway down. Just point her in easy. When I say, push the tiller to starboard right quick."

The spindly wood framework that had seemed so small and familiar when they cast off now looked large and threatening.

"We seem to be approaching quite fast, Roger."

"She'll coast in gentle enough. Hold your course."

And the boat did slow perceptibly as Roger furled the sail and lashed it to the boom.

The bow glided closer to the barnacle-crusted pilings but Roger ignored the pier as he secured the boom, tipped the boat's fenders over the rail, and finally hauled up the centerboard. Though Lydia stifled the urge to warn him again about the on-coming pier, she felt her body tense as the open water steadily lessened. Then, when the pier came so close that it seemed the bow would ram it, Roger said, "Starboard," and, anxiously, Lydia shoved the tiller hard enough to lurch the boat. Roger grabbed a stay for balance and murmured, "Gently, ma'am—no need to break anything."

"I'm sorry—I was...nervous."

"There's times to be nervous, but this ain't one of them. A gentle touch on a gentle day, ma'am. That's what the *Lydia* wants." He hopped onto the pier and secured the forward mooring. "That was good—you handled her right well. I reckon you're a natural born sailor."

As she accepted his rough hand to step up to the dock, she tried to mask the pleasure his praise gave her. "With a lot of practice I might make a fair-weather sailor. Are you willing to take me out for more lessons?"

"Yes'm, whenever we can. Moor the aft line, ma'am, just like I done the bow line."

She did, copying his over and under loops and then standing a moment to study the craft. For the first time, really, she could appreciate the gracefulness of the hull logs' curve, the tidiness of the small cabin between the two masts, the pleasing symmetry of the stays that anchored the masts. Roger had coiled the lines on the deck in flat spirals that spoke of neatness and care, and now splashed water across the forward deck where his bare feet had tracked sand. "She is a fine vessel, isn't she?"

"Yes'm. Built by Ansel Cravey over near Crisfield. Cost your husband some money, but she's worth it—big enough to carry some cargo, yet small enough for one man to handle."

"Or woman."

"Woman. Yes'm. With practice."

Lydia promised herself to get plenty of that. "I've worked up a thirst, Roger. Would you like some tea?"

His answer was quick. "No'm—there's mending to do on the harness lines. I reckon I'll finish that before dark."

She had not planned on interrogating him further about the lights and was slightly hurt to think that might be what he feared. "I thank you for your sailing lesson, then."

He seemed surprised and somewhat embarrassed at her gratitude. "No trouble at all. You can make a good sailor." The wrinkle between his eyebrows told her he pondered something. "But I'd appreciate it, ma'am, if you didn't take her out by yourself—not for a while, anyway."

"Why?"

"You need to know more about sailing. Even on calm days, a wind can come up real fast, and a coasting canoe can be tricky to handle."

"I will wait until you tell me I'm proficient enough, Roger. I don't want anything to happen to the *Lydia* either." She smiled. "But I found this very enjoyable. And I do intend to gain that proficiency."

After a long moment during which he seemed to consider something, he finally bobbed his head in agreement.

When she mounted the stairs to the wide front porch, Gretchen, seated in one of the wicker chairs, stood to welcome Lydia. "Was that you sailed that boat in, ma'am?"

"With very much help and advice from Roger."

"Well!"

The girl's tone said more than her words. "You seem surprised."

"Well, you're a lady, ma'am. It just seems...odd. That's all."

It was Lydia's turn for surprise. Perhaps Franklin's concept of gentility was more widespread than she thought.

But running a farm entailed un-genteel duties: slopping hogs, after all, was not ladylike. Or cleaning ashes from the stove and fireplaces. Or emptying the chamber pot of a morning, or even tending the results of Franklin's illness.

Lydia had no intention of apologizing for any unladylike actions needed to survive, or for those which she enjoyed.

"Wouldn't you like to sail?"

"No, ma'am! I can't swim and the water makes me afraid. I don't even like wading in the creek."

"But you enjoy fishing, Gretchen."

"That's taking fish out of the water, not putting me in it." From the floor beside the bentwood chair, she hoisted a weighted kerchief and untied its corners. "Here's some onions and turnips Momma sent from her root cellar. She hopes you enjoy them."

"We certainly will! Please thank her for me." The globes shone white and purple with the late sunlight. "Your parents are in good health?"

"Yes'm, but they do miss Humphrey. He's the youngest, you know," she said sadly. "They send their regards." The girl gathered up the vegetables and followed Lydia into the house. "There's news, too. The Confederate capital's been moved up to Richmond."

"Richmond? Then that must mean—"

"Yes'm. Virginia's done seceded."

Chapter 10

The forest of beech and poplar and hickory beyond the tilled fields thickened into a moist blue-green. Lydia and Gretchen tested the rising swell of radish roots to harvest the first crisp vegetables. Pea pods, early formed from tiny flowers, swelled with fruit; cabbages, collards, and spinach leaves were picked along with the first asparagus to bring a welcome fresh salad to the table. In the slough, the cordgrass changed overnight from the dull gray-green of winter to the rich dark green that heralded summer, and terns, herons, and egrets joined the ducks and geese that fed among the stalks.

In the heat of a late May afternoon, Sheriff Hope—riding a tall, strong horse whose saddle bore two sets of leather bags and a gum-rubber poncho rolled thick at the back—rode into the farm's yard to hail the house. With a grunt, he dismounted heavily and lifted his wide-brimmed hat. "Miz Sensabaugh—Miss Druer. I hope I find you all in good health."

"Yes, thank you. I trust all is well with you, Sheriff?"

His lips made a flexing motion, and for a moment Lydia was afraid the man would spurt a stream of tobacco juice at her azalea blooms. But he wasn't chewing; it was, she concluded, his bovine manner of cogitation. "No'm. All ain't well. But it sure is interesting—like the business I had to tend to over to Chincoteague. And as long as I was in this part of the county, I figured I'd ride across to talk about that letter you sent me."

"That's most thoughtful, Sheriff." Lydia invited the man up into the shade of the porch for refreshment. "You've had a long ride. You're welcome to stay the night, if you've a mind to."

"Thank you, ma'am. But I told the Gilmores over on the high road that I'd stay the night with them. It'll make tomorrow's ride home to Drummond that much shorter."

Gretchen met them with a tray and the decanter from the sideboard, but the sheriff shook his head politely. "I don't imbibe, miss. Seen too much trouble caused by whiskey, but I thank you anyway."

"Why don't we all have tea, Gretchen?" Lydia sat and the sheriff's weight creaked another of the bentwood chairs. "What interesting business did you have, Sheriff?"

The girl returned with a pitcher of cool tea from the icehouse and glasses for all.

"Thank you, miss." The man drank half the glass in two gulps and sighed. "That tastes mighty good. 'What interesting business,' you ask. Y'all heard about the Great Battle of Chincoteague Sound?"

"Battle? In Chincoteague?" Gretchen gaped at the man. "No!"

"That's why I was over there. You know the Islanders voted against secession?"

"I knew they were considering it," Lydia said. "But I hadn't heard they actually voted."

"Well, they did. Two for secession, a hundred and thirty-eight against." Another long drink emptied the glass. Gretchen quickly refilled it. "Thank you, miss. So a bunch of lads from Virginia's First Families down around Wachapreak vowed to make the town secede whether it wanted to or not."

"How?"

"Well, that's a good question, Miz Sensabaugh, and I

don't know the answer. I don't think they did, either. But they come up the Broad Water loaded with powder and shot on their punts, and whiskey in their bellies." He paused to mop his face with a large blue bandanna. "I reckon they ran low on ideas and whiskey, both, because once they got to Chincoteague Inlet, they just set there doing nothing until Squire John Wealton gathered together some Union-inclined neighbors and sailed out from Franklin City to do battle."

"Oh, my!"

"Sea battles is among the worst kind, Miss Druer. The very worst—savage bad. But neither the Union patriots nor the Secessionist stalwarts gave a single flinch. The Loyalists took up their weapons, boarded ship, and braved the mighty Chincoteague Sound to vanquish their foe. And the foe, when they saw the enemy coming to vanquish them, loaded their muskets, vanquished what was left in the jug, and swore to defend the Sacred Soil—or in this case, Water—of Virginia to each other's last drop of Cavalier blood."

"Was anyone hurt?"

"Well, shots were fired, a couple, anyway, wide so's the other folks would fire wide in return. But there was horrific damage done by strong language. They exchanged some pretty hard words, you understand, and caused some deep bruises in each other's feelings. Enough, anyway, that both armadas turned around and went home with loud cheers and their flags flying, and that was the end of the Great Battle of Chincoteague Sound."

Gretchen finally broke the silence. "I reckon you need a bit more ice tea to clean that yarn out of your mouth."

"Yarn? Why, miss, I'm telling you just exactly what happened. In fact, Squire Wealton told me the fracas decided the Chincoteagers to send a delegation down to Hampton Roads and ask the Union Navy for protection so the citizens won't have to face such tribulation again."

"I pray that all the news you have for us is equally comical, Sheriff."

Something seemed to drain from the man. In his full black beard, his lips worked and the deepening lines around his eyes and mouth looked as if he woke from too short a sleep to face too great a burden.

"No'm. Some comical things do happen, but not everything happening is comical." In a quieter voice he told of armed citizens shooting at Federal soldiers marching through Baltimore and the soldiers returning a killing fire, of the Harper's Ferry arsenal burned by retreating Union troops and taken by Virginia militia, of the cannonade at Sewell's Point near Norfolk City."

"Norfolk City? Was there fighting there?"

"No'm—wasn't much by way of fighting at Gosport Navy Yard, neither. The Federals just burned everything and pulled out."

He went on to say that Maryland had been occupied by Federal troops, and that Virginia had raised an army to protect its borders.

"We are at war, then?"

"It ain't been declared by Virginia. But everybody expects the Union to invade. Lincoln's vowed to prevent secession by force. Washington City's one big military camp, they say." He drank again, his throat dry from unaccustomed talking. "That's the last I heard, ma'am: folks expect war any time and figure it to be over by September."

"What about us?" Lydia waved a hand at the sunlit lawn, the sparkling water of the estuary, the soft, slow-moving clouds drifting in from the Chesapeake. "Are we to expect war here?"

"I wish I could tell you, but I just don't know. Maryland belongs to the Union, now, so this part of Virginia's cut off from the rest of the state. What-all that means, I just don't know." He cleared his throat. "Ma'am, that's really all the news I got. Now, I would like to ask you and Miss Druer a few questions."

"Questions?"

"About your letter and what you saw in the woods."

"I don't know that I can add anything to what I've already written."

The thick torso leaned forward, the chair groaning ominously with the shift of weight. His voice rumbled earnestly, "Ma'am, the Nigra preacher over to that church near Belinda—Uncle Becket—awhile back, he told Parson Abbott about some missing free Nigras. He wondered maybe somebody took them and sold them south as runaways. Says maybe half-a-dozen in all—mostly women and children—have disappeared over the past year, even two or three from Jack Town. But aside from them being gone, I got no evidence of anything. So I need to hear from you about what-all you've seen." He leaned back to listen, his lips flexing occasionally.

After a pause, Lydia told about the lights she and Gretchen saw last winter, about Parnell Carswell's supposition that they were from a fishing boat, about her own doubts of that.

"You didn't think they were watermen?"

"I don't think they were fishing." She explained about the layer of mist thick enough on the water to prevent the light from attracting fish, and about the possible aid of the lights in navigating the slough. But this long after the event, her reasoning seemed thin and fanciful, and she apologized for boring him with hypothetical details.

"No'm, it's not boring. In fact, you make a right good witness. Not many would have the recollection you have." He frowned at his re-filled tea glass. "Now, you wrote me you saw some chained slaves going across your property at night?"

"All I saw was a dark-lantern. And I only heard the clink of chains—I didn't actually see anyone. I assumed it was slaves. Mr. Bradshaw, our hired man, said it would not be a county work gang, and he didn't think it was abolitionists, since the chains were still on."

The sheriff's lips worked silently. "We seldom have enough county prisoners for a chain gang. When we do, they work but ten hours a day like everybody else. And they're locked down nights." He gazed at the square of corn bread dwarfed by the span of his hand. "And it certainly is likely abolitionists would've cut the chains first chance so's the slaves could run for it if they had to. Anything else, ma'am?"

She told him about the trampled grass she and Roger found on the slough, and her theory of a tie between that and the earlier lights. "Unless someone were thoroughly familiar with Fowler Creek, they would require guidance at night to reach that point safely."

"That's sound reasoning."

"Is someone stealing freedmen?"

He drained his glass and stood with a sigh, a barn door of a man who seemed to take up most of the porch. "For sure, they're gone. And Uncle Becket says nobody knows where." Up on his tall horse, he asked, "Was that Roger Bradshaw I saw plowing when I rode in?"

"Yes." Lydia gestured. "The field beyond."

"You don't mind, I'll talk with him, too." He nodded to both women. "If you all see anything more, ladies, write to me. And, ma'am," he said to Lydia, "it's best you don't do more investigating on your own. There's not much legal punishment in selling a free Nigra south, but there's a lot of money to be lost if somebody proves the Nigra to be a freedman. It could be mighty dangerous for anybody who witnessed it." He tipped his hat and clucked to his horse.

Gretchen, when the sheriff had ridden out of earshot, turned to her. "You didn't tell me you and Roger done all that!"

"Since nothing came of it, I saw no need to, Gretchen." Lydia repressed a smile. "If it happens again, perhaps you and I can take the punt out to look."

"On the water? In that little boat? No thank you, ma'am!"

⁕⁂⁕

With her brother gone from home, Gretchen now took Star and the wagon to visit her parents each week. Returning through New Church for the mail and any newspapers Mr. Henderson had available, she brought back the local gossip and rumors, as well as the wider events reported in newspapers from Baltimore, the Federal City, and even Philadelphia and New York. To show their independence from the arrogant flatlanders who had always lorded it over the small freeholders in the mountains, the western counties talked of seceding from Virginia and remaining in the Union. Confederate and Union troops exchanged shots at Aquia Creek on the Potomac. Squadrons of volunteer soldiers, Union and Confederate, were mustered both north and south of the Maryland line.

Most important for Gretchen was a letter from Humphrey to her parents that told of the election of his company's officers and sergeants and of life in camp:

> ...*the chickenpox is got a lot sick but I am hunky dory and it don't keep us from reveille at four-thirty of the morning and then we march and march back and forth until breakfast at six-thirty, and then we march some more to dinner and in the afternoon have company muster and regiment muster until we muster for supper which runs to hard tack and salt horse. To my way of thinking, we waist a lot of time but drill is the word and the next word is more drill until a body starts dreaming in numbers. What we really want to do is jist get our muskets and use them to teach the Yankees a good lesson that will make them leave us alone. We got some Maryland boys who specially want to because they say their state has not even seceded but is been occupied anyway by the Union army.*

Humphrey's words seemed to define the anxiety that, even at Marshfield, intruded on the quiet pleasures of working in the garden or gazing at a flower or again taking the *Lydia* out on the Sound on a calm evening. It was as if somewhere, just out of sight and despite the ripening spring-time, Damocles' sword hung like a dark threat.

So on that hot afternoon in early June while she stood in the shade of the barn to toss corn to the chickens, she was only half-surprised to see two lines of horsemen trot from the distant tree line in a haze of dust.

"Gretchen!"

Wiping her hands in her apron, the girl came to the kitchen door and looked where Lydia gazed toward the lane. "Soldiers!" she said

Lydia asked, "Virginia? Union?"

"I don't know."

"Where's Roger?"

"Over plowing the potato field, I reckon." Gretchen, too, spoke without taking her eyes off the approaching horsemen. "What you think they're way out here for?"

Lydia shook her head, surprised at the tightness in her breast. It reminded her of the guilt that had shortened her breath when her mother found her playing with the small vials of lotions and creams on the forbidden surface of her vanity. But she could think of no guilt she deserved nor of any reason why soldiers would visit her farm.

The steady thudding became heavier, now accompanied by the jingle of equipment. One of the two men in front wore a wide-brimmed hat; the other a small cap whose brim tilted low over his eyes. The one wearing the wide hat was clad in a dark uniform jacket—navy blue or black, Lydia wasn't sure. The man with the small hat wore a pale blue jacket and matching trousers. Yellow V-shaped stripes pointed down his sleeves.

The man with the wide hat had no visible rank, but they both carried large, glossy holsters on their belts. Behind them rode six horsemen in pairs with similar small hats and pale blue jackets. They wore a variety of everyday trousers ranging from butternut tan to darkly checkered wool. A few had one or two chevrons. The last two in the column—more boys than men—held the halter ropes of half a dozen barebacked horses pulled along at the rear.

The women waited as the horsemen slowed to a walk through the open farmyard gate. The soldier with the widebrimmed hat raised his gloved hand to halt the soldiers, and Lydia stared in surprise at his face.

He said something to the man beside him...a sergeant?...and that man wagged a gloved hand toward his cap in reply. Then the sergeant ordered the column of soldiers to follow him in a trot around to the front of the house. The horse-holders remained with the officer—Lydia could now see the small straps sewn on his uniform's dark shoulders—who touched spurs to his mount and came toward the women, glancing past them to take in the farmyard, the pens and farm animals, the house behind them.

"Mr. Morse—is it you?"

"Good afternoon, Mrs. Sensabaugh." He removed his hat. The sun brought out light tints in his brown hair."

"You have joined the army!"

He hesitated. "I am a lieutenant in the Second Delaware Volunteers."

Gretchen asked, "Delaware? Are you Southern soldiers?"

"Northern."

"Yankees?" Gretchen's voice lifted in question and alarm.

A wing of the Lieutenant's mustache twitched when he saw the pretty girl's eyes widen as if Lucifer himself had reared up before her. "That term doesn't quite fit the soldiers, who are all from Delaware. I hope I find you well, Mrs. Sensabaugh."

"Yes." She was still trying to understand. "I thought you were with the railroad?"

Again that hesitation. "No. It was my duty to reconnoiter the area against the possibility of war."

Lydia finally understood. "You are a... a spy?" It was an

ugly word for a thoroughly dishonorable occupation.

"It was a necessary duty that might save the lives of my men."

"You were a guest here!"

"Virginia has declared itself an enemy of the Union, despite my wishes or yours."

Gretchen spoke up. "I don't see that you Delaware Yankees have orders to bother us! You're not wanted here—this here's Virginia!"

"We have been ordered to requisition horses and supplies."

"Well, despite it, you—"

"Gretchen, please." Lydia spoke quietly. "We are at war, then?"

The lieutenant, noting her face grow even more pale, saw alarm and sadness beneath her reserve. "Yes, ma'am. The Confederate Congress has declared a state of war between the Union and the Confederacy. Perhaps you haven't heard about the fight at Bethel Church?"

"Across from Norfolk City?" Again that catch in her breath as she shook her head. "What happened? Was anyone hurt?"

"Men were injured on both sides."

"Was anyone from Norfolk City hurt?"

"There was no report of civilians harmed." He watched as she breathed deeply with relief. "You have kin there?"

She nodded, not yet trusting her voice.

"The dispatches did not mention Norfolk. But we are, indeed, at war, and I must ask you, ma'am, do you have any men on your plantation who have joined the rebellion?"

"It is a farm, not a plantation. 'Rebellion' is a term you choose, not we. And the only man here does not fight. He shares the Quaker aversion to violence."

Lieutenant Morse nodded once. The column of soldiers came around the corner of the house and headed for the water trough. One wearing broadly checkered trousers dismounted to work the pump.

The sergeant looked at Lydia and then more closely at Gretchen.

A narrow goatee marked his long face below his shaved cheeks. His eyes under the short brim of the cap seemed distant and calculating, and his words had a brusque, hard pronunciation that Lydia had not heard before. "There's a sailboat at the pier, 'Tenant. No people. No horses. Corporal Evans says it looks like a one-horse stall in the barn, but the horse ain't there." He looked across the fields toward the trees. "I reckon this is the end of the road, ain't it? A long ride for not much."

Lieutenant Morse asked, "Where is your horse, ma'am?"

"Plowing the east field."

"We'll fetch him," said the sergeant.

"Why? What do you want with my horse?"

The sergeant grinned. "He's requisitioned, ma'am. To join the cavalry. Or the artillery, more likely, being a plow horse." He jerked his mount around and gestured to the soldiers watering their animals at the trough.

"But that's my horse—he works the farm!"

Morse's face was stiff. "Both armies need horses, Mrs. Sensabaugh. We are ordered to collect them. You will be paid for the animal."

"You can't take Star!"

"I am so ordered. I'm sorry."

Gretchen could not hold her tongue. "Sorry! You Yankee spy! You Yankee thief! You'd take a widow's plow horse? How are we going to raise our food?"

The sergeant laughed. "If the rest of you's as strong as your tongue, Missy, maybe you can pull the plow." He pointed the laughing soldiers toward the cornfield. "All right, Corporal Evans, take your squad and find what you can. And be damn quick." They spurred their horses, trampling the young stalks into avenues of bent and broken canes.

"But Star's a gentle creature!"

"We are to requisition horses to supply the Volunteers

and to prevent the animals from falling into enemy hands. Those are my orders."

The word "enemy" stunned Lydia. She had never thought of herself as enemy to anyone. Wordless, she stared at this man, seeing him from an angle of vision she had never before experienced: this stranger was, by self-definition, The Enemy. And he saw her as The Enemy. But she did not feel inimical—nor did she want to be called such.

"I am also ordered to ask what weapons you have on your farm."

"Weapons?" The question seemed to reach her form a long distance. "We have a shotgun."

"Want me to search the house, 'Tenant?"

"I don't think it will be necessary, Sergeant."

"Might be we'll find contraband."

The officer's voice tightened. "We are not looters, Sergeant Durgin. I have told you and your people that we do not enter forcibly nor search a home without specific orders to do so. Orders from General McDowell himself, Sergeant."

The sergeant's gaze went flat and lifted to some spot over the officer's head. "Sir!"

Lieutenant Morse replaced his hat and, avoiding the wide stare of the woman, felt in his vest pocket for something. Then he leaned down to hand Lydia six folded slips of paper. She looked at them without understanding. The gray and white print said "United States" and one end bore a picture of Alexander Hamilton under a large "5," the other end was filled with the engraving of a statue of America.

"These are five-dollar Demand Notes, ma'am. Thirty dollars, which is market price for your horse." He jotted something in a small notebook. "The notes will be honored in coin on demand of the bearer by the treasury of the United States and may be used as currency anywhere in the Union." The reverse side of the paper was covered with dark green fives in both numbers and spelling. White letters spelled "United States of America." Folding the notebook away into his pocket, he cleared his throat. "I further inform you, that should you give aid or assistance to any enemy forces, you will be considered as abetting the rebellion and subject to the Articles of War as administered by the Provost Marshall. Otherwise, you will be accorded all the courtesies due non-combatants." He added in a more human tone, "I am ordered to so inform all civilians."

"What about the boat, 'Tenant? Want me to scuttle her?"

The lieutenant looked at the expression on the woman's face. "We have no orders for that, Sergeant."

"But 'Tenant Morse, that boat there—"

"Is in the water, and the water is the navy's responsibility, Sergeant. We have no orders to sink civilian vessels." The sound of approaching hooves caught their attention. "We have done our duty here—let's be on our way."

The squad of soldiers came back through the cornfield. Star trailed behind them, pulled by his bridle. A soldier handed the reins to one of the horse holders and Star snorted a whinny and danced with fear as he was hauled into the collection of strange horses. Lydia, hand at her throat, watched the animal's eyes roll whitely. "Star!"

"Column of twos—at a trot!"

Gretchen and Lydia stared in silence as the soldiers rode up the lane, the captured horses tossing their heads against the tug of reins and ropes.

"Yankee thieves! I wish I was a man!"

"Oh, poor Star. What will we do, Gretchen? What will we do without Star?"

"Lord, I wish I was a man!"

Lydia tried to realize what, so suddenly, had erupted into their life as she watched Star and the other horses disappear behind the screen of trees. Then her gaze shifted to the cornfield and the ragged paths broken through the stalks. Beyond, Roger had been turning under the weeds between rows of young potato plants.

"Where's Roger?"

Gretchen shook her head. "Hiding, likely."

"Roger!" Following a trail of sandy earth torn by heavy hooves, she led Gretchen across the field. "Roger!"

Beyond the corn, they saw a figure hunched in the middle of a half-plowed field. Lydia, the freshly turned dirt heavy on her shoes, ran toward the man.

"Roger!"

As she neared, she could hear him grunt deeply with each breath and saw his body clench rhythmically.

"Roger—what's wrong!"

"They beat him up—them damn Yankees!"

"Gretchen!"

"Well, they are and I ain't sorry to say it!"

Lydia kneeled beside the curled man. "Roger! Let me help you."

The grunting shifted to a hissing breath and the lank, dark hair wagged from side to side. A strangled reply. "I'll be all right."

"Oh my Lord!"

Blood from his face dripped down his arm and stained the soil dark. Pulpy, torn flesh smeared where his nose and upper lip should have been. "Hit me. Rifle butt. Told them they couldn't take Star."

"Hush, now. Just be quiet. We must get you to the house." She hauled at his shoulders and steadied him as he rose on wobbly legs. "Gretchen, go on now. Get the water hot and soak some cloths!"

Chapter 11

She did not know how she managed to stagger with Roger through the fields to the kitchen. Somewhere along the way, sagging under the heavy arm across her shoulders, her vision narrowed to darkness. She kept in motion by willing each foot to take just one more step. Somewhere near the house, she felt Gretchen take Roger's other arm, and the two women teetered him up the back stairs to settle him at the small table on the enclosed porch. Gasping, Lydia slumped into a chair, almost nauseous from her exertion. Gretchen dabbed a wet cloth at the man's bubbling face. As Lydia's nausea eased, Gretchen, twisting bloody water out of the cloth into a basin, told her, "They broke his nose and knocked out a lot of his front teeth. He's got a big split in his lip. You want I should go for Doctor Dawson?"

He mumbled something.

"You hush, now, Roger Bradshaw," Gretchen said fiercely. "Just sit still and be quiet."

"Took Star. Can't get no doctor."

"I got feet." She glanced at Lydia and tapped a forefinger to her head.

"Let's make a pallet for him in the parlor. I'll bind his lip then we'll see how he feels before you walk all the way to New Church."

Roger may have been dazed, but he also made sense.

He mumbled in protest but the two women hauled him to the front room where Gretchen had placed a straw tick on the carpet and covered it with a clean cotton sheet.

"He's going to bleed all over that pillow, ma'am."

Lydia nodded as she gently lifted his head to rest on the down puff. "Put that cloth under him, then. We can change that easier."

"Yes'm."

Clenching her teeth against the imagined pain, Lydia bent to clean the gaping split under what had been his nose. The sides of the split glistened with seeping blood and some kind of clear liquid. Trying not to hurt Roger, she lightly dabbed the area as clean as she could, then pressed the sides of the gash together and held them in place with a pad of folded cloth. "Hold his head up, please, Gretchen."

"You want some spider web, ma'am?"

She looked up at the girl.

"Ma uses fresh spider web on cuts. It helps stop the bleeding and keeps the flesh from getting proud."

"Your mother knows better than I." Lydia waited until the girl, panting slightly, hurried back from the barn with a length of straw that had a gray swirl on one end.

"Just unroll it into the cut."

Lydia did. The blood seeping into the web congealed. Then she passed a strip of cloth over the wound and tied it behind his head to hold the bandage firm.

"Water and the bucket—he needs to rinse his mouth."

They held his shoulders while he drooled clots of blood and fragments of tooth into the metal bucket.

"Rest, now, Roger. Sleep and rest. You'll be good as new soon."

꼬꼬

But he wasn't. Three days passed before the blood

stopped making stains in the bandages they changed each morning and evening. A fever carried the man into a sweating shiver, and, for one long night, they held him down against his inarticulate howling shouts and struggles to rise from his nightmares.

Then he sank into a gray and clammy stillness, and breathed in rapid, shallow pants. Lydia felt guilty about not having sent Gretchen for Doctor Dawson.

"You think he might die, ma'am?" Gretchen, dark circles under bloodshot eyes that showed her loss of sleep, passed a damp cloth across his forehead.

"I pray not."

"Me too. But I hope he don't come out of this crazy. Crazy people scare me." Gretchen tried to repress a shiver. "That would be awful. Awful!"

On the third day, the rhythm of Roger's breathing changed and Gretchen, working in the kitchen, heard some croaked sound from the parlor. She looked and then ran to the back door to call Lydia in from the garden "He's awake, ma'am—he's talking some! And it don't sound crazy!"

Lydia tugged off her rawhide work gloves and hurried behind the girl into the shaded room. "Roger—you're back with us!"

"I'm...where?"

"In the house. The parlor. You were too heavy to carry up to a bed."

Face swollen red with soreness and dark bruises, Roger winced as he gingerly turned his head to look around. "Parlor?"

"You've been quite ill. We're so glad to see you awake at last!" Lydia pressed her hand to his forehead. It felt cool and dry. "Gretchen, warm up some soup—I'm sure he's starved."

He plucked at the quilt covering his body and then his arm disappeared and fumbled under it. "My clothes? I ain't got—"

Lydia tried not to blush. "I had to remove your clothing,

Roger. It became soiled." She gestured. "Your shirt and trousers are right there—on the sofa."

He stared at the washed and folded clothes and then at her, his hazel eyes wide over a discolored nose that was misshapen and swollen. His words lisped slightly from the missing teeth and the stiffness of his lip under the bandage. "My clothes? You…"

"It was necessary." That was all she intended to say about it

Gretchen balanced a bowl of chicken soup on a tray. "Can you lift up?"

He stared at Gretchen and the sides of his neck flushed.

Lydia, pushing the pillow under him as he stiffly raised his torso, murmured, "I'll help you."

The women watched him flinch as the heat touched his lip, and then he carefully sipped at the liquid.

"Good," smiled Gretchen. "Eating's a good sign."

It was indeed a good sign, and Lydia and Gretchen had a happy supper at the long dining room table that night. They lit the dim room with two of the remaining spermaceti tapers and, quietly so as not to disturb Roger beyond the closed parlor door, celebrated his recovery with a toast from the port bottle Franklin had kept behind the glass door of the sideboard.

෴

In the morning, Roger was gone. Lydia had rapped gently on the parlor door but heard nothing. After a louder knock, she opened the door slightly and called through the crack, "Roger? May I enter?" The answering silence had the feel of death and with a spasm of anxiety she called more loudly, "Roger!"

The straw tick was bare, its rough gray cover smoothed and the sheet and light quilt folded neatly at its foot. Roger's laundered clothes were gone from the horsehair couch, as were his cleaned boots and the chamber pot.

"Gone?" Gretchen looked up from the steaming soup she was ladling into a bowl. "Where to?"

"I don't know. I do know the man shouldn't be on his feet." Lydia went to the back door and looked out as if the empty farmyard or the fields beyond could provide answer. The chamber pot, empty and clean, sat beside the step. "His room!"

The two strode into the barn. Gretchen called "Roger— you out here?"

The girl held up the front of her dress and, with the other hand slapping awkwardly at the worn boards nailed between support studs, managed to climb up to the loft. "Roger?" She reached the top of the ladder and leaned to look across the loft into the open doorway of his small room. "He ain't here," she called down.

They stood in the barn doorway and gazed out at the lane and the wooded rise of the northern horizon. The only sounds were an occasional rusty croak from a chicken and, far off, the caw of a crow. Gretchen shook her head. "Not even a fare-thee-well!"

"I hope he wasn't delirious. I can't imagine—"

Behind them, the barn loomed like a deserted cavern. In the silence, Lydia realized that she still half-expected to hear Star's welcoming snort and the scrape of his hooves in the straw of the stall. But there was only the soft cluck of the now lanky and awkwardly adolescent Cochin pullets and, somewhere high in the dusty loft, the buzz of a wasp. Puss, the white-faced cat, strode with slow grace from the dim corner where the forty kegs of chemical fertilizer were stacked. She sat at a companionable but cautious distance and washed her face. It was an indication that the half-wild cat, which usually led a life independent of humans, also missed the familiar morning sounds of the now-vacant apartment upstairs.

"He said nothing at all to you about leaving?"

Gretchen shook her head. "No'm. He could've at least left a note."

"He can't read or write."

"Well, it's thankless behavior, anyway."

"I pray his thinking is not fevered."

She wandered around the farm yard, the animal pens, and finally to the front of the house where the *Lydia* rested. Its bare masts crossed the flat and empty line of the horizon. Gretchen trailed after her. Lydia looked for but did not expect to find any trace of Roger; indeed, the meandering tour resulted in nothing except a deepening sense of their aloneness. First Star, then Roger—it was as if members of her family had gone, as if the soldiers' invasion had torn a hole in the fabric of life at Marshfield, and, one by one, elements of that life began to slip away.

As days passed, the feeling of loss shifted from a sharp pang to an intermittent worry about the whereabouts and health of Roger and Star. Evenings sailing the *Lydia* became short and rare as she and Gretchen expanded their range of chores to include what work could be done in the fields without a draft animal and without Roger's help. One weary evening, after penciling calculations, Lydia offered a small raise in pay to Gretchen for the extra labor. The girl's satisfied nod told her that she had been mulling over the same idea, and Lydia was relieved to have made the offer before Gretchen had been forced to ask.

Among the farms that had been levied for horses— Marshfield included—hoe, shovel, and rake took the place of plow in uprooting weeds that, perversely, seemed to know it was now safe to invade the roots of corn, potatoes, and garden vegetables. What had been an often-pleasant labor for Lydia became a struggle—personal and unrelenting—against broadleaf weeds, wiry vines, and long-rooted grass that, overnight, sprouted to strangle the valuable crops. Gradually, she and Gretchen divided the labor of house and field, trading days at the kitchen, the back-yard laundry tub, the woodpile, and barnyard against hot days chopping and digging in the sun-shimmered fields. But the weeds and climbing vines conquered more and more of the crops as the mid-summer heat increased.

Gretchen suggested that they let most of the cornfield go fallow. "Let's work on the potatoes. We'll need them over winter."

And Lydia, ruefully eyeing the shreds of old blisters and the hard flesh of new calluses that made yellow bumps on her fingers and palms, agreed. The kitchen garden received first efforts, then the potatoes, then as much corn as they could defend for the poultry and themselves. At first, the sow and her three pigs had been herded out to forage the remaining corn lest it be a total loss. But Gretchen warned that even under guard, they were getting wild and harder to drive back to their pen. "Pa has a dog—Lilly—to watch his pigs don't stray. Without a dog to watch them, they get ideas—kind of like Roger Bradshaw, I reckon."

"That's unkind, Gretchen. He either had a good reason to disappear, or was bereft of reason when he did it—I do worry about which. And if he hadn't tried to protect Star for us, he wouldn't have been beaten almost to death. Remember that."

"Yes'm," she murmured. "But he still left a lot of work for us to do."

The increased labor drove both women to bed while the sky was still light and Lydia too exhausted to read other than a few pages. A clear day became a torturous labor in the fields cursed by sun and biting flies; a crashing thunderstorm became a day of rest from muddy fields but not from cleaning the house and caring for the animals.

"We're real low on salt, coffee, and flour, ma'am."

Lydia had noted the steady erosion of those staples. "Well, the work's caught up enough so you can visit your parents if you wish, Gretchen." She paused. "If you're willing, on your way back, you might stop by the Sundries Store for a few supplies and any mail." Without Star, Gretchen would have to go by foot instead of by wagon, and a stop at the store not only added the additional weight of sacks of goods, but also two miles to the girl's long walk back. But Lydia saw no other way.

Gretchen knew what the request added to her trip, but she did not wince. "Pa has a little hand wagon I bet he can let me use."

"That would be wonderful! But ladies don't bet, Gretchen."

"Yes'm."

Just after sunrise, Gretchen left. The early start would put her in the shade of the woods before the sun grew hot and allow her to arrive at her parents' farm well before supper. A kerchief carried a bit of fried bacon, cornbread, and a few vegetables from the garden. A blue patent medicine bottle—well-washed and stoppered with a cork that was only slightly crumbly with age—held cold coffee.

Lydia embraced the girl. "You will be very careful, Gretchen?"

The girl laughed. "No Delaware Yankee is going to get me, ma'am. Don't you worry about that."

First Star, then Roger. Now she feared for Gretchen. "I can't help worrying about you going alone in these times."

"Well, I'll be all right. I trust you will, too, ma'am. I'll be back in a week or so—you look after yourself, now." A final wave of the hand as she strode lightly up the lane, the low sun tinting her pale hair almost pink.

Neither woman mentioned the word "lonely," but that feeling made Lydia watch until Gretchen's figure flickered out of sight behind the tree line, and for some reason at that moment she felt a twinge of guilt for not yet giving Franklin's grave its bi-annual cleaning.

That memory of the dead, the emptiness of field and sky, the vacant wind from the Bay, combined to bring home the absence of people and things she once believed were enduring. Even this farm, seemingly anchored forever on its sandy earth, could, over time, be seen as transient—no more permanent than those vanished buildings whose brick foundations were forgotten in the forest and broken by the roots of hundred-year-old trees. Only a short time ago, she had found comfort in the belief that her farm and the people on it could be aloof from change. Now, after the soldiers, she knew the emptiness of that idea. Perhaps that was the meaning of war: permanence became an illusion, and every dawn was haunted by the anxiety of some new loss.

Even the consoling Compensations that Mr. Emerson found in nature was replaced by an awareness of struggle and change in the world. The weeds and vines choking the cornfield seemed a metaphor for the mutability and challenge brought by war. Within her soul, something new stirred; in place of the peaceful sense of stability and comfort came almost an anger. But, strangely, it was mixed with an excitement, too—it was something inchoate that she could not clearly grasp but that conflicted her fear of change with a physical stirring. It was as if the emotions numbed by her husband's death had stirred under the hooves of cavalry horses. But those old emotions were awakened to a new concept of life that was vastly different and far more challenging than the past.

Chapter 12

Busy in the kitchen, Lydia was startled by a male voice calling from the front, "Heyo the house!"

Parnell Carswell lifted his hat as Lydia opened the front door. "I came by to be certain all is well with you."

"Thank you, Mr. Carswell. Please take some refreshment."

"I hope I am no trouble, ma'am."

"I welcome the company, sir." She motioned toward one of the porch chairs. "Please rest yourself. I shall return in a moment."

Removing her apron and making her hair presentable, she came back with the decanter and a pitcher of cool water, cool tea for herself, and the remainder of the cornbread and honey that had, with some fresh vegetables, formed her light lunch.

The man toasted her health with the whiskey. "Gretchen tells me that a foray of Yankees took your horse. And that your hired man has run off."

"You've seen her?"

"Day before yesterday, on her way to her parents' home." A smile lifted his mustaches. "She mistook me at first for a Yankee soldier. I forgave her the insult and she forgave me the fright." The smile disappeared and the man leaned forward. "She told me about that Yankee patrol—

they didn't come as far as Oak Hall. I'm sorry I don't have a horse to offer you, ma'am. With the exception of Suleiman—" He nodded toward his mount. "—and a few braces of mules to work my fields, I have already delivered my animals to the Confederate Army. God willing, I will send you over a mule this October with one of my servants, so you need not worry about fall plowing."

"That's very generous, Mr. Carswell, and I'm grateful. But I understood you to be raising a troop of cavalry. I'm surprised to see you still in Accomack."

"The best I could raise was a troop of horses and too few volunteers for the cavalry. Most of the men preferred to join the infantry—the Thirty-ninth Virginia, mustered down in Northampton County. I wrote General Lee to volunteer my services in any way needed. The general's response was an interesting one." He paused to sip his drink.

Lydia leaned forward slightly to indicate the effect of his sense of the dramatic pause. "Yes?"

"He urged me to remain here."

"To remain?"

Carswell nodded. "The general begged me to curb my natural eagerness for the challenges of war, and to serve in an equally important if less glamorous manner."

"A request you could not deny."

No pause to sniff for sarcasm, just a quick, satisfied nod. "Being a lady, you will not have engrossed yourself in the mundane world of men's activities, ma'am. So allow me to explain: we in the South have, since the Settlement, developed our bountiful land as agriculturists rather than as mere tradesmen or manufacturers. But the result is that the Yankees, being more mercenary in spirit than ourselves, have far more factories and mechanics than we." Carswell sampled a pinch of cornbread, wet his throat, and continued. "Thus we are highly dependent on imports, most of which came from the North. But now we must rely on England and France, who need our cotton. All of which information, ma'am, is foundation for the Yankees' Anaconda plan."

"Anaconda plan?"

"It is reported in the Washington newspapers that General Scott plans to send an army to occupy the Mississippi River. He believes this would achieve two ends: cut the Confederacy in two and, in conjunction with a navy blockade in the Atlantic and the Gulf of Mexico, isolate our nation. He would, in short, wrap his forces about the body of the Confederacy like an anaconda snake and starve our entire population into submission to his will."

The vision had a geographical magnitude that Lydia had never considered. The pastures of Marshfield, the surrounding forests, even the Bay it touched, suddenly seemed small and insignificant against such a broad canvas. "Can he achieve that?"

"I regret to say it is possible. The Yankee navy is superior in numbers, though not in spirit, to our own. We must be ready to provide for our defense—which brings me to General Lee's request and its ramifications."

And back to the centrality of Mr. Carswell's role for the Confederacy. Lydia tilted her head with attention.

"General Lee asked that I provide supplies for our army. Foodstuffs and military goods will go much further to defeat the enemy, the general assures me, than the labors of a single officer—even myself—on the field of battle. In short, the service I am requested to give is, perhaps, less glorious than war, but equally—if not more—valuable." He helped himself to another square of cornbread

"Supply is certainly a necessity to any army."

"Very perceptive! Moreover, as our men volunteer for the army, the depletion of our population makes the ratio of people to slaves an incipient danger. I don't wish to alarm you, but the ratio in Accomack County is now one white male for every ten slaves. In Mississippi, slave owners with a ratio of one to fifteen are urged not to remove themselves from their plantations in order to insure civil stability. Like the British, the Yankees will try to foment insurrection among the slaves as a means of bringing down our country.

We must be vigilant and strong enough to prevent such from happening."

"I do not own slaves, nor have I countenanced that institution, Mr. Carswell."

"Perhaps not. But please remember that Nat Turner made no distinction between his victims who owned slaves and those who did not." He drained his glass and set it firmly on the table between the chairs. "He slaughtered anyone—man, women, child—who was white. However, I don't wish to upset you in any way, Mrs. Sensabaugh. In fact, I bring you the comfort of knowing that in lieu of my service in the army, the Virginia legislature has authorized me to form a County Home Guard for the safety of our citizens and property. Rest assured, you will not be left unprotected."

"And Sheriff Hope? Does he not bear responsibility for the welfare of the citizenry?"

Carswell frowned at a spot of dirt on his boot toe. "In times of peace," he said slowly, "certainly. But this is war, and I am not the only one of your neighbors who doubts Sheriff Hope's loyalty to the Confederacy." He refilled his glass with whiskey and splashed water into it. "The Home Guard receives its authority from the state and thereby supersedes the county authority of the sheriff. Besides, I doubt he will remain long in office."

She sighed. "I would, I suppose, be more worried if my lane led anywhere except to the Bay."

He rinsed his mouth clean of cornbread before speaking. "That brings me to one of the principal ramifications of General Lee's request." Leaning forward, he lowered his voice as if, somewhere in the silent house, listening ears might lurk. "Because of your farm's location, it is peculiarly situated to perform valuable service to the Confederacy."

"Service?"

"You have one of the few deep landings on the Virginia side of Pocomoke Sound. Moreover, it is not only distant from observation, but also close to the Pocomoke River. Should General Scott's Anaconda Plan come into effect, I have proposed that our agents import goods to Bermuda from our friends in France and England. Those goods, picked up in a neutral port, would be transported to inlets on the Atlantic side of Virginia and Maryland and transferred to this farm. Here, we would stage the goods for further shipment across the Bay to General Johnston and the Army of Northern Virginia." He sat back to watch her a moment. "Blockade runners, ma'am. Blockade runners to carry need-ed stores and munitions across the Chesapeake to our ar-my."

"The *Lydia*?"

"No, no—I would not hazard your vessel. No, I mean smaller sailing canoes less likely to be stopped by Yankee picket boats." With patience, but not without pride, he de-tailed his plan. "Small sailing canoes are difficult to detect and require only the slightest breeze for mobility. They can make up in numbers what they lack in cargo space. Your landing is almost directly across the Chesapeake from Smith Point on the Western Shore. In a good breeze at night, a sailing canoe can cross over in a few hours. If the winds are light, the Tangier Islands are just about halfway and can provide shelter during the day." He smiled. "It is your op-portunity to do a great service to Virginia, ma'am. To the Confederacy. I hope you will allow the use of your property for that patriotic service. I assure you, we will be most dis-creet."

The Yankee officer had warned that, should she in any way assist the rebel army, she would lose her protection as a noncombatant. But that man, polite though he may have been, was a spy who spoke of her as an enemy. And to prove it, his soldiers had trampled her corn, taken her horse, and beaten Roger cruelly. "I will of course help. When do you expect to commence?"

"That will depend on events, Mrs. Sensabaugh. But I shall certainly alert you. Meanwhile," he stood, "let me ex-press my gratitude and that of Generals Lee and Johnston. I was certain that we could rely on your loyalty and support."

He thought a long moment. "I'm equally certain your girl Gretchen can be relied upon. Her brother, after all, is one of our soldiers. However, I would appreciate it highly if—should your hired man return—you inform me of that fact at your earliest convenience. I don't mean to speak evilly of him, but a man who would run off and leave two defenseless women might not be reliable in an endeavor such as this. And I must caution you as well that some of our neighbors do not support our cause. I know for a fact that the Chincoteagers sailed the *Jenny Sharpley* down to Hampton Roads to ask the Yankees to send a warship up for protection against what they call 'rebel incursions.'" He shook his head in disgust. "But warship or not, they will answer for that, I assure you."

"Roger Bradshaw was badly beaten by the soldiers, sir. I'm not sure he was in his right mind when he left."

"I see. In that case he will harbor no affection for Yankees. Perhaps he can help us."

"He shares the Quaker aversion to violence."

A frown flickered across Carswell's face. "A Quaker, is he? Some Accomack Quakers have been active in helping escaped slaves. I trust, ma'am, he is not of that ilk."

"I think not." Though she would hesitate to swear to that statement in court. Roger's reserve bordered on secretiveness, and she'd noticed the ease with which he disappeared and reappeared from the woods surrounding Marshfield.

"Nonetheless, I would be obliged for the opportunity to speak with him should he return. Now, may I have leave to inspect your barn, ma'am? It will give me some idea of the amount of goods we can safely hide."

"Certainly." She led Carswell around the house and across the barnyard. "I trust Mrs. Carswell's health is good?"

"She suffers somewhat from the heat—we are forced to forego our summer retreat to Maine, and the tensions of the times wear on her patience. But despite that, she does well, thank you."

"Please give her my regards."

"Eh? Oh—yes. Certainly." He stepped into the shade of the building and let his eyes adjust. "This looks fine. That stack of kegs back there, Mrs. Sensabaugh, what might they hold?"

"Fertilizer—nine years' worth remaining, at two-hundred pounds per year."

"Good Lord! That's the famous chemical fertilizer experiment? Two-thousand-pounds of it?"

"Almost." She tried not to sound bitter. "Two hundred pounds was wasted on this year's lost crop."

He stared hard at the stack of half-barrels. "Most interesting, ma'am. Most interesting!" Another glance around the space and he tugged his hat on his head. "Thank you for the very tasty cornbread, Mrs. Sensabaugh. And again, my personal gratitude as well as that of our government for the service you offer our cause."

As she watched Carswell canter down the lane, Lydia tried to assimilate all he had told her. She struggled to recall some analogous experience, but there was none: she had never considered the subject of war except recently and only as it affected people she knew. But now, not only had "enemy" soldiers brought war to Marshfield, but she was promising to participate in one. That thought brought a sense of disjunction from the fields and trees that looked back at her. And it brought the unsettling feeling that some distant, massive door had begun to swing shut.

Chapter 13

During the isolation of the following days, Lydia's thoughts were uneasy with the sense of sounds just beyond hearing, of shapes just beyond sight. She found herself listening for a distant voice, an approaching horse, the startling creak of a porch board under weight. Working in garden or field, she often glanced toward the tree line to note tiny movements that seemed to snag at the edges of her vision. The leafy woods, the now-weedy cornfield with its stunted tassled ears, even the level, dark green of the cordgrass in the slough seemed to mask eyes that watched.

She began to wonder at her own sanity, compelled as she was at odd moments to freeze and listen and feel the approach of an ill-defined something. Even the flicker of a bird's wing against the dark of forest green caught her eye and her breath. Many evenings, she found relief in sailing the *Lydia* farther and farther out, despite Roger's warning, applying the knowledge of rudder and sail he had given her. Sometimes she went north across Pocomoke Sound under the Maryland side, or west within easy sight of the low mounds of the Fox Islands.

For some reason, she felt more isolation alone on the farm than alone on the boat where she was cushioned from troubling thoughts by the peace of a calm evening sea or by the immediate demands of the craft when the winds grew strong and the water challenging.

But when she returned, after mooring and tidying the boat, she found herself once more talking to the chickens and to Bessie and Puss, her voice a creaky, unused thing in her own ears. The recent disruptions to life, the feel of threat lurking just out of sight, the loneliness of these days, all made her behavior strange, she knew. As a girl, she had seen the old women—white and black—alone in their minds and muttering to ghosts of their own conjuring. Bent with the weight of memories, they had shuffled through the gray sand of Norfolk City's lanes. Now, in the mirror on the door of her wardrobe, she searched her face for any resemblance to those haunted old women. And for the first time, she truly understood what that Yankee writer—Mr. Hawthorne—was trying to say with his odd stories of isolated minds trapped in their own imaginings.

Late one morning, when the hot sun hung in dusty weariness, a distant shape emerged from the tree line. Lydia was unsure if she glimpsed a real figure or a creation of her anxieties. Then she recognized Gretchen and, with amazement, realized that the girl had left only twelve days ago—that the lonely days had somehow twisted the shape of time to seem without beginning or end. Quickly, happily, she kindled the stove's ashes into a fresh fire and set the teakettle on. Then she gathered together a light lunch of cold ham, collard greens, and sliced boiled egg. Humming now, she felt the warmth of reconnection with other humanity. She glanced nervously around the kitchen to repair any sign of domestic disorder, to correct any outward manifestation of the strangeness that had wrapped itself about her. Then she strode out through the heat of the lane to meet the girl.

"Gretchen," she called. "Welcome back—I trust all's well with your family?"

The girl, tugging the towrope of a small cart that lurched behind her, half-lifted a weary hand in reply. "They send their regards." She plodded nearer. "I didn't get as much coffee as we wanted because the price has gone up so. The price of everything's just about doubled, but salt's about the same so I did okay on that. I went ahead and got all the flour and sugar and grits you wanted because I figured we'd need it regardless, so we owe the difference. And Mr. Henderson would like his money soon's you can get it to him if that's all right because of the higher prices of everything and a lot more folks paying on credit and barter, which leaves him short of cash for supply." She stopped to gather a breath.

"Slowly, Gretchen—you've told me more than I can comprehend at one time. Come—you're exhausted, as well you might be. I have a meal set. Here, let me take the cart."

She led Gretchen to the house where both of them lugged sacks into the kitchen. Lydia joined her at the table, stifling comment while the girl ate in large and noisy mouthfuls that sent juice oozing from the corners of her lips, then more slowly. Finally the girl seemed replete, and Lydia finished her own plate. "Any letters, Gretchen?"

"No'm, no letters—Mr. Henderson says the Confederacy's took over all the Union post offices but can't figure out how they work. He can get mail from the North through Maryland, he said, regular, but mail from the mainland's got to come over by boat, and with the blockade, that's seldom now."

Disappointment made Lydia's shoulders droop, but there was nothing to do about it except marvel at how much she had taken for granted before war began. "Well, you rest, then. You can tell me later about your visit."

"I'm rested, ma'am. Now that my stomach knows my throat's not cut, it's not bothering me." She drank deeply of the cold tea and refilled her glass, stifling a burp. "Mr. Henderson says the price of about everything is gone up because the army's buying so much and some folks are, too—storing up, like. He don't know how much higher goods are going to go, but he says everybody in the county's planting more crops thinking the army'll buy all it can. He says that imports like coffee are getting scarce because shippers are bringing in military goods and don't have enough bottoms to carry civilian goods."

"Well, we can get by on tea instead of coffee."

"We can while we can get tea. How long that'll be, he don't know."

Lydia studied the soiled scrap of brown wrapping paper which bore sums penciled in Mr. Henderson's curly style. Their total, far more than she anticipated, gave her a hollow feeling. She had the cash to pay this time, but if prices went much higher or even stayed this high for some time, they would have to learn to do without. "I must go to town and pay him. I can go in the morning."

"I can go back."

"Of course not, Gretchen. Not after the distance you walked today." Lydia shook her head. "It was thoughtless of me to send you to the store without enough cash, and Mr. Henderson was very kind to let us have goods on credit. It's my debt, and obviously he's desperate for payment or he would not have said anything."

"Yes'm, I understand that. But it might be better if I went anyway."

Lydia heard something odd in the girl's voice. "Better? In what way?"

Gretchen frowned at her plate, lips clamped tight either against words that had already escaped or those she did not wish to speak.

"Gretchen?"

"Ma'am—"

Gretchen?"

"Aw, ma'am!"

"Gretchen!"

The words came in a rush. "Ma'am, Ben Cooper's been telling people that Parnell Carswell's been coming out here and that he's seen the squire riding out our lane early of a morning." The girl's face reddened and her eyes grew moist. "And I passed Squire Carswell in our lane when I left for home. And he said he was coming to visit with you!"

"Why, so he did—he asked to use the slough to load sailing canoes for the army. And to store the goods in our barn before shipping them."

"Yes'm. But Ben Cooper says that he's been sneaking out here for a long time."

"He's been sneaking…"

She nodded. "He says you and the squire—"

"Stop!" Lydia felt the scorch of embarrassment prickle her skin and she sat rigidly. "I understand, Gretchen. And I am certain that if Mr. Carswell heard what Ben said, he would thrash him for a slanderer and a cad."

"Well, he did. And he didn't."

"What?"

"He come riding up to the store when Ben was telling me those things and laughing. He sure enough heard what was said but just pretended not to!"

The rigidity slowly drained from Lydia's spine. "He did not deny that—that—"

"No'm. He didn't deny nothing and he didn't horsewhip Ben Cooper, neither. Just gave us a smile like he knew more than he'd say!" The heat left her voice. "And I remembered seeing him that morning when I left, coming here."

Lydia stared at the girl whose eyes were focused on her plate. "He did visit. For the purpose I have stated."

"Yes'm." Gretchen sighed. "I believe you."

There was a long silence. Somewhere over the marsh a seagull gave its plaintive, two-toned squeal. "I will go to town this afternoon and give Mr. Henderson his money."

"Ma'am?"

"I have no reason to be ashamed, Gretchen. I will walk down the high street of New Church in broad daylight and dare—dare!—Ben Cooper or anyone else to repeat that slander to my face!"

"Ma'am, you don't have to do that! Nobody believes—"

"It crossed your mind when you remembered meeting Parnell Carswell!" Lydia caught herself and spoke more gently. "If it could cross your mind, Gretchen, then it could linger in the minds of others."

"Ma'am, I really didn't believe that Ben Cooper!"

"I know, Gretchen—I spoke in anger and I'm sorry." Lydia gathered her shawl, a bag to hold her gum rain cape, and went quickly upstairs for the box that held her finest bonnet. Pausing to glare at her reflection in the dresser mirror, she snatched up the carved ivory broach that had been a gift on her fourteenth birthday and selected a bright red ribbon to lift it against her neck. It might not have been Mr. Hawthorne's scarlet letter, but it could hold just as much defiance. Gretchen, face in her hands, was still sitting at the table when Lydia came back. "Gretchen, I know you did not believe that person. But I will not have anyone think that I am afraid to show my face in public because of what that person or anyone else may be saying about me."

"But ma'am it's already afternoon now." She wiped tears from her cheek. "It'll be dark before you get home. And...and I'm sorry."

Lydia wrapped her arms around the girl's shaking shoulders and murmured in her pale hair. "Of course you are, child—I understand. Truly. But my appearance in town will at least challenge that slander, and the sooner the better. And I'm sure Mrs. Williams will give me shelter if I need it on the way back." Her voice tightened a bit. "And should I see either of those people I will call them liars to their faces!"

※ ※ ※

Perspiring heavily, Lydia was well past the leaning post that marked the boundary of her land before she eased from her angry, fast pace. As her steps slowed, she realized that the earth she trod crossed land belonging to Parnell Carswell and had the profound wish to be able to walk on air so the very dust of that man's plantation would not pollute her shoes.

She was past the Williams farm by the time the trees along the high road cast shadows that brought relief from the sun. But gnats buzzed about her ears and darted toward her perspiring face. Breaking a leafy switch from a wild azalea bush, she used it to swish away the insects. She started down the low hill above the village with the hard earth of the road now entirely in shadow. The back of her left heel had rubbed and burned and finally went numb, but she did not limp; she would not show that weakness. A dog rushed through a fence to snarl at her and she surprised herself by giving the cur a swift cut from the switch. Though her mother would not have approved, Lydia felt a bitter satisfaction at the animal's yelp.

Rufus was working behind the counter when she arrived at the store. The only customer was a young boy with a tightly clutched fist who stood before the six jars of penny candy, studying each carefully. "No'm, Mistah Henderson, he's not here. He's to home, eating supper."

"Out back?"

"Yes'm. Around this side and back."

Lydia, still marching, went along the store's painted brick wall which joined the wooden front of the Henderson home. She went up the plank steps and knocked.

Mrs. Henderson half-opened the door, her jaw dropping when she saw Lydia. "Why, Mrs. Sensabaugh!"

"Is your husband in, Mrs. Henderson? I wish to settle a matter of business with him. It should take only a moment."

The woman seemed flustered, as if a person she had been talking about suddenly materialized. "Mr. Henderson? Why, yes. Come in, please." She stood aside to let Lydia into the entryway. "Would you like some refreshment?"

"Thank you, no."

The woman bustled down the hallway as if escaping Lydia's presence. Through the parlor door, Lydia could see a dark horsehair sofa placed before an empty fireplace. Heavy red curtains hung at the sides of a window, and the light brown wallpaper was flocked with crimson *fleur de lis*.

A small table with an arrangement of peacock feathers stood near a narrow bookcase filled with gilded spines labeled "The Works of Sir Walter Scott." From the rear of the house, the sound of children's voices made a muffled noise, and then Lydia heard a heavy tread on the hallway's thick cotton runner.

"Well, Mrs. Sensabaugh. What brings you here, ma'am?"

"I wish to settle my debt, sir, for the goods you were kind enough to advance to Gretchen this morning."

"Why, you didn't have to come all that way today! Next week or so would—"

"And I was hoping to see that reprobate Ben Cooper slouching about the front of your store."

"Ben?" The man's fleshy lips sagged open with his question. Then they closed and a red flush rose up almost to his thick and wrinkled earlobes. The color told Lydia all she needed to know.

"Six dollars and sixteen cents, I believe? I trust United States treasury notes will do?"

"Mrs. Sensabaugh…" His brown eyes seemed to plead in some way.

She counted out the green paper and the copper coins into his open palm. "There. And if you see that Ben Cooper, please tell him that I call him a despicable liar!"

"Ma'am—"

"A liar, Mr. Henderson. A slanderer and a liar. Please tell that person my exact words!"

The man loomed motionless and stared at the money in his hand as she closed the door behind her. For a long moment, she stood and breathed a deep sigh, smelled the cooling dust of the street, listened absently to the bark of a dog somewhere across the creek. Mrs. Henderson's flurry, her husband's embarrassment told her they had heard Ben Cooper's lies. Well, now someone in this town had heard her call Ben Cooper a liar, and she felt better for it.

She limped down the creaking steps, walking more slowly now, and headed up the slope that led out of town. The anger that had given her strength to complete her mission was gradually replaced by a chill that was more than twilight's cool. Increasingly drained, she felt totally bereft of any acquaintance. She still had long miles to walk, and the thought of Mr.—Lieutenant—Morse and those Yankee soldiers who took Star and left her to do sixteen miles on foot brought a word to her lips that Franklin had seldom used in her presence without apology, "Damn!"

In the first miles, her weariness was buried beneath a confusion of images and emotions: Gretchen's shame and suspicion of her, that almost frightened stare of Mrs. Henderson, Mr. Henderson's revealing embarrassment. Even the knowing looks of that drunken rabble in front of the Sundries Store on the day war was declared. Those skin-crawling memories were sharpened by an overwhelming paradox: her resentment at agreeing to let Parnell Carswell—that man whose silence besmirched her reputation—use her barn, and the knowledge that Carswell's use of that barn would be compensation against the Yankees who took Star. She did not think of it as revenge. It wasn't revenge but justice. That spy had called her "enemy," as false an accusation as that filth spread by Ben Cooper. But since she was viewed as Enemy and injured because of it, she had a moral right of redress. Still, the exercise of that right called for an alliance with the likes of Parnell Carswell.

Later—miles later—even that issue failed to keep her from feeling how close she was to exhaustion. But there was no choice except to continue walking. At some time, she passed the Williams farm in the pale glow of a rising full moon. The house lights were off and even the farm dogs silent. She was tempted to turn in at their gate, to rap at their door and ask for shelter. But the temptation was overcome by the stinging thought that Mr. Williams had probably heard the slander in town and brought it home to his wife. But later, when she turned, clumsy with exhaustion, off the high road into the black shadow of trees that overhung the lane to Marshfield, she wondered if ignoring that temptation had been wise—if she had not been exercising self-pity masked as pride. With every step she stumbled over hummocks of weeds and grass, and her left heel began to throb again, this time as deep as the bone. Pausing to probe with fingers swollen and stiff from the swing of her arms, she found that her stocking was soggy with what she assumed was blood, and there was still a mile and a half to go.

The heel ached with every step. She tried to concentrate on the flow of gray and black that was moonlit sand and grass clumps passing beneath her wooden feet. Somewhere, her consciousness hovered above her, and her body moved now without volition. Her feet lunged forward, as distant from her awareness as the limbs of another being. She lost knowledge of the dark trees beside the path and of how far she had come or had to go. Forcing her attention on the stretch of moon glow in front of her stumbling feet, she caught a toe on something and fell. The sand of the lane rasped hotly on her palms and elbows, and its sting brought her back to an awareness of her body. Panting, she pushed herself back on her feet and, for another vague span strode forward with alertness. Then her mind drifted again, and again she fell, this time landing with a gasp on a knee and rolling onto her side. She lay breathing heavily for a moment and gathered herself to deny the flesh's yearning for rest, for closing her eyes. She forced herself back on her knees, then to her feet, but as she tried to stand, she tripped again on the hem of her dress, and plunged head forward. Somehow she was crying, angry at that weakness but unable to stop the tears and shuddering gasps as she struggled back to her feet and swayed in a faint, stiff-legged pace. She did not hear the rustle of leaves under heavy steps in the blackness beside the lane. Yet as she started to fall a third time into a dark that was more in her mind than in the night, she dimly sensed something—someone—grasp at her. But she had no energy left for terror and was aware only of a rushing sound like a heavy wind that blew her into emptiness.

Chapter 14

Thirst. Stifling, damp heat. A myriad of aches and twinges in almost every joint and tendon of her body, but especially her hips and knees and ankles that made her moan as she tried to pull them away from the pain.

"Ma'am?"

She recognized her bedroom. Glaring sunlight pressed hot against the curtained west window. A quilt, stifling hot, was pulled up to her chin. Even her eyeballs ached as she rolled them to take in the room.

"Ma'am, you awake?" Gretchen, frowning with worry, leaned over her to whisper.

"How did—"

The frown disappeared into a wide smile. "Glory! I was afraid you'd wake up out-of-your-head-crazy like Roger!"

Lydia squeezed her eyes shut against their throb. "Escaping this head for a new one might be an improvement." She opened them to the girl's happiness. "I remember walking—falling. How did I get here?"

"That Yankee officer brought you. The one that took Star."

"The lieutenant? Lieutenant Morse?"

"Yes'm. Said he found you just up the lane, lying by the side. Said he thought at first you was dead." The girl's head wagged as she helped Lydia hold a cup of cool water to her

dry lips. "He'll be back later today, he said. I thanked him—
I did that!—and told him it wasn't necessary, but he said he
wanted to make sure you was all right."

"Were," she said automatically.

Gretchen leaned back. "Well, I reckon you do feel all
right."

"I do not feel all right, but I am sane." Stifling a groan,
she moved her limbs against the stiff soreness that defined
them. Her heel, scraping against the sheet, stung sharply
enough to make her draw her breath. "Help me up, please. I
believe I'll feel better if I can get up." With Gretchen's assistance, she sat at the side of the bed and slowly stood
through the dizziness. As she put weight on her feet, even
the joints of her toes ached. "Please heat some water,
Gretchen. I desperately need to bathe."

After limping downstairs to the small bathing room on
the back porch, she leaned back against the high curved end
of the metal tub. The hot water worked like medicine on her
aches, and it bit like medicine on the various scratches and
scrapes that marked her hands and arms and knees. Her foot
was propped in the air across the tub's far rim, the torn skin
of her heel too tender to dip into the heat. Still drowsy, she
let half-formed thoughts float through her mind: vague pic-
tures of last night's struggle, of fighting pain, of being lifted
up as she stumbled once more.

Beneath the water, opaque with soap and dirt, her body
was a pale, slender shape. Marriage had, she knew from
sewing her clothes, thickened that body. Her failure to bear
children meant her hips had not broadened overly. But her
waist had gained a good inch.

Even so, not having seen herself in clear light for so long,
she was surprised to note that her form looked—in her own
eyes, at least—not so different from the young woman who
had married Franklin.

The months of labor spent caring for the farm seemed to
have brought back that younger figure, and in the water, her
bosom gained a fullness that, she remembered with a mix-

ture of embarrassment and some pride, Franklin had especially delighted in.

Beyond the closet door, Gretchen clattered crockery in
the kitchen. Voicing suspicion of total immersion for secu-
lar purposes, the girl had nonetheless filled the bathing tub
and laid out fresh clothing on the board shelf under the curtained window. Lydia stood gingerly to rinse, awkwardly
balanced on her good foot. Despite lingering aches and
twinges, she felt immensely better. She pulled the leather
plug from the metal tub to let the water drain into the earth
beneath the floor, then she quickly toweled dry and dressed.
The laundry boiling in the cast iron washtub outside would
soon be ready, and Lydia had already given Gretchen too
much extra labor. It took two people to adequately twist the
water from those steaming clothes—one clutching the end
of the folded cloth, the other turning the baton thrust
through the garment's fold—before hanging them to dry in
the sun. It was time to be at work.

$\infty\infty$

The day's heat began to ebb and the sun was less than an
hour above the horizon when, over the quiet sounds of preparing supper, they heard the muffled thud of hooves in the
sandy lane.

Gretchen looked out the kitchen window. "It's the Yankees—that lieutenant and another soldier."

"Invite them in, Gretchen. I'll set more plates."

"You going to ask them to eat with us?"

"It's quite possible that Lieutenant Morse saved my life.
I would hope our manners are at least equal to those of
our...enemies."

The girl gave an unconvinced, "Yes'm."

Lydia, placing silverware, heard the exchange of voices,
but not what was said. A few moments later, boots clumped
on the front porch. Gretchen came into the kitchen. "I told

them to wait in the parlor," she said. "That's mannerly enough, ain't it?"

"Yes, Gretchen, it is." Lydia gestured to the girl to collect another set of plates and limped into the parlor. "Lieutenant Morse—I believe I owe my life to your courtesy."

In uniform, the man seemed taller and brought a faint smell of perspiration, dust, and horse. The leather belts holding holster and sword gave him a bulk that made the parlor feel cramped and fragile. Behind him, a young Yankee soldier stared around the walls like a nervous cat in a new corner. The lieutenant shifted his hat to his left hand and bowed slightly as he touched her fingers. "Nothing so heroic as that, Mrs. Sensabaugh. But I am pleased to see you up and looking so well." He cleared his throat. "Healthy, that is."

"I believe I can take that as a compliment, sir."

His lips widened in the flicker of a smile. "I would be honored if you did. I've found that a number of ladies in this part of Accomack County will not accept compliments from a Yankee."

"Can you blame them, Lieutenant? First you abuse our hospitality to spy on us, then you declare yourself our enemy and invade our sovereign state, and now you go about complimenting a number of our ladies!"

The lieutenant smiled ruefully, "Well, a very small number, I must admit. And I do understand that we differ on the issue of state sovereignty over national sovereignty. I'm mighty sorry that Virginia has chosen to secede. I also deeply regret—though I do not apologize for—the necessity of scouting the terrain to insure the safety of my men. But I do apologize for my too-hasty comment about us being enemies, and I hope you will forgive that."

Lydia tried to keep her voice politely level, but it nonetheless quavered. "It's more than your beliefs or your comment, sir. It is your assault on a harmless and peaceful man who will carry scars for life."

The lieutenant noted the tightly reined tension in the

woman's voice and frowned in puzzlement. "Assault? I'm afraid I don't understand, ma'am."

"My hired hand—Mr. Bradshaw. Your soldiers assaulted him, broke his nose, knocked out his front teeth. He was bedridden and fevered for three days after, and now he has disappeared." Even in her own ears, her voice was ugly and sharp. Honoring Roger Bradshaw and his convictions, she took a deep breath and strove to put "gentle 'suasion" in her tone. "What makes it worse is that he is a peaceful man, Lieutenant. He follows the Quaker rejection of violence."

Morse looked at the private. "You were in that detail, Hines. What happened?"

The youth's right shoulder lifted in a shrug. "The secesh said we shouldn't take the horse. Told us it wasn't ourn to take. Corporal Evans said 'take this' and hit him a couple times with the butt of his carbine."

A silence that seemed to bear ice emanated from the lieutenant.

"Well, 'Tenant, don't look at me like that—it was Corporal Evans done it!"

Morse's tight jaw stifled the oath and he drew a deep breath. "This is the first I've heard of the incident, Mrs. Sensabaugh. It should not have happened—we are under strict orders from General McDowell to respect all property and persons in Virginia, and I offer my most profound apology for this violation of those orders. The incident will be looked into, I promise you."

"I trust you to do so, sir." The silence from the dining room told her that Gretchen had finished setting the table. "However, I am indebted to you for rescuing me. I hope you will join us at supper—Gretchen has laid places for you both."

"After what I've just learned, ma'am, I don't think we should impose ourselves."

"I am a Virginian, Sir, and neither deny my debts nor begrudge my hospitality. Perhaps we can call a truce whilst we dine."

He looked at her, assessing the tilt of her chin and the note of challenge in her words. Her eyes held the same level and self-contained look that had met his gaze the first time. Then, unsmiling, he nodded. "We both are very grateful to accept your offer."

It was almost a party. "Almost" because Lydia could not relax from formality. She viewed the occasion, despite her statement about ungrudging hospitality, as repayment of a debt. The lieutenant, too, was formal, maintaining a distance, Lydia assumed, from a person he still thought of as the enemy. The private was simply hungry. He did not take time away from eating to waste on conversation. Gretchen, too, remained silent, her eyes shifting between the serving dishes that emptied rapidly as the two soldiers ate. Finally Private Hines, knife upright in one hand and fork in the other, half-stifled a belch and grinned around the table over his cleaned plate. "That sure was good! I ain't ate so good since I left home!"

"Where is your home, Private?"

"Near Christiana, ma'am—it's about eleven miles from Wilmington? Up in Delaware? We been gone over a month, now. Less'n two more to go before our ninety days is up."

"And you, Lieutenant Morse? Are you equally eager to return to New York City?"

"My home is a very small village in western New York, in Allegheny County. I left it to earn a commission in the army and have little to return to."

Private Hines, now that his stomach was filled, was eager to chat. "I'm a volunteer. When Old Abe called for soldiers, I joined the Loyal New Castle Volunteers, and now they're putting us in the Second Delaware. 'Tenant Morse, he's training us." The youth, a soft shadow of beard down his cheeks and above the corners of his mouth, looked admiringly at his officer. "He's a regular—he's fought the Indians!"

Gretchen finally looked up. "Indians!"

"In the Kansas territory!"

Gretchen knew the name referred to a distant, ill-perceived area beyond the Mississippi River. "Then how come you're back here?"

Morse tried to deflect the pretty girl's animosity with a smile. "Like many others, I was recalled for the emergency, Miss."

Lydia asked, "You attended the Military Academy at West Point?"

"Yes, ma'am. Class of fifty-eight."

"Perhaps you know of my cousin, William Shirley. He also attended the Academy."

"Bill Shirley? Short Shanks?" For the first time the lieutenant's face lit with an unguarded laugh that erased his military stiffness and made him look five years younger. "Indeed I do! We were in the same company and shared...well, a number of comical adventures." He looked even more closely at Mrs. Sensabaugh for any features that echoed those of Bill Shirley. The only similarity he could note was the high cheekbones that, on Shirley, had given the man slightly slanted eyes. On Mrs. Sensabaugh's slender face, the trait contributed to a stately beauty. "I'm delighted to learn he's your relative."

She related what her sister had mentioned in her latest letter. "Are you equally delighted to learn he has resigned his commission to join our army?"

"No." The joy disappeared and the lieutenant frowned at the tablecloth. "Though I'm not surprised. A number of officers and cadets have gone south. Some willingly, but many only at the insistence of their families or the governor of their state." He absently brushed at a crumb on her mother's ivory lace tablecloth. "I know your cousin's decision was painful for him. And I still consider Short Shanks my friend." He looked up. "Now I have reason to ask you to consider me to be your friend also, Mrs. Sensabaugh. If in the future there is aught you need, please don't hesitate to ask."

"I tell you what we need," Gretchen said. "We need Star

back—you took our horse, you drove off our hired hand and left two women trying to run this farm without horse, hand, or mule. I reckon you call that friendly!"

"Gretchen—"

Private Hines, eyebrows raised, stared at the girl. "Well, we had orders! That's what armies do is follow orders. Don't you even know that?"

"You telling me you had orders to knock out Roger Bradshaw's teeth?"

"Well, I ain't talking about teeth—what I'm talking about—"

"Private!" The lieutenant's word was low but sharp. The youth clapped shut his lips and glared at the girl who glared back.

"Perhaps we should retire to the parlor, Lieutenant Morse," Lydia murmured. "Gretchen, would you be kind enough to clear the table?"

"Private Hines will assist you, miss."

"I don't need no help from him!"

"It will be a pleasure for him, not a chore. Isn't that right, Private Hines?"

The youth's breath hissed through his nose before he muttered, "Yessir."

"Fine." Lieutenant Morse, standing to hold Lydia's chair, looked at the youth and tilted his head toward Gretchen. The private quickly wiped the corners of his mouth with finger and thumb, then his finger and thumb on his trouser leg and went to her chair. He tugged it awkwardly as both women rose from the table. Gretchen stood with a graceful hauteur new to Lydia.

She led Morse into the parlor as Gretchen and Hines silently began to clear the table. "Would you care for a whiskey or a glass of port, Lieutenant?"

"Port, please." While she took the decanter and small crystal glasses from the sideboard, he glanced around the room at the dried flowers under their dome of glass, at the Rogers figurine of "Faust and Marguerite in the Garden," then closely at the small shelves of books. "Your husband was a literate man."

"Most of those books were my father's, though a few are mine. My husband preferred agricultural science." She gestured at the several books and periodicals lining the back of a desk that stood darkly against the wall. "We thought to reinvigorate the soil using modern chemicals."

"Chemicals?"

"Chemical fertilizer. Produced at the Eleutherian Mills by Mr. Dupont. You've heard of it?"

"I labored through von Leibig's treatise on agricultural chemistry to improve my Bavarian. The widow of an immigrant sold that and a dictionary to me to raise money for her return to Saxony." He smiled, "I confess it was less an act of scholarship and more an act of desperation on my part: those were the only two books I found in that corner of the prairie."

"My father had a copy of that book. That's where my husband became enamored of the idea of chemical nutrients." She did not add that she had, with her father's guidance, laboriously translated the work for Franklin. "We planned to raise a wide range of fruits and vegetables and ship them to city markets in the *Lydia.*"

"You had success?"

She shook her head. "Mr. Sensabaugh died before we could fairly undertake the project. And now..." Her voice trailed off as she poured.

"Now," said Morse, "the manufactory which created fertilizers is creating gun powder. It's a modern twist on turning plowshares into swords."

"And times have become too uncertain for peaceful trade," she said.

"Much is uncertain, now." In the silence, a short mumble of voices came from the kitchen. Lieutenant Morse read the titles on the shelves and tried for a happier topic. "I once heard Mr. Emerson speak at a lyceum in New York. He was very entertaining, though I didn't follow all he said."

This person had heard Emerson speak! "What is he like? Has he a strong voice?" For the first time, the woman's voice was warm with excitement and interest. She handed the lieutenant a glass of port and took one for herself.

To maintain that warmth, Morse made an effort at precise memory. "He struck me as a very musical speaker."

"Musical?"

"Clear and well modulated. A master at presenting the individual phrase. I came away with a few sentences in memory and the wish that I'd jotted down more: 'Our high respect for a well-read person is praise enough for literature,'" Morse explained. "He offered pellets of wisdom rather than a grand edifice of argument. He repeated his points with several different tropes to generate understanding in his hearers."

"Was he a presence?"

"Not a commanding one—more a persuasive one. He leaned forward and looked directly at individuals in the audience. But he was not an orator like Mr. Webster or Mr. Douglas." He considered a moment. "More a conversationalist—as if he were chatting over the fence rail."

"That's exactly the way he writes!"

Morse nodded. "When I read him—and it's not as often as I wish—I hear his voice lift from the page." He raised the glass, "Here's to Mr. Emerson, to your hospitality—and to peace between friends."

"As well as between enemies."

"Touché!"

Dusk settled into darkness. Lydia lit an oil lamp and tipped a splash more port into the lieutenant's glass. "I am grateful for your rescue last night, Lieutenant, but also a little curious. What were you doing in my lane at that time of night?"

"I might ask the same question."

It was her lane and she had a right to be in it at any time. But out of respect for his role as her guest, she stifled that comment. "I was returning from New Church where I was on business."

"Very late business."

Guest or no, a slight edge entered her voice. "I might make the same comment."

He laughed, teeth glinting in the lamp's soft light. "So you might. We were on patrol. Smugglers are reported bringing contraband down from Maryland to be sent across the Chesapeake to the rebel army."

"Oh?" Lydia hid her expression with a sip from her glass. "And have you discovered any?"

"No. Our force is too small to cover much ground. And this side of the peninsula has fewer loyalists than the Atlantic side, which makes it more difficult to be informed. But a Rebel privateer was seen in Chincoteague Sound, and we must do what we can to intercept goods smuggled to Jefferson Davis." A sip followed by a nudge. "Business in New Church, ma'am?" he asked pleasantly.

"With Mr. Henderson. A bill to pay." Lydia, too, was pleasant. "You may verify that with him if you wish."

"I don't need to, ma'am. You have told me."

Behind her smile, she intended to tell this spy no more—he was both persistent and perhaps dangerously perceptive. In addition, her caution was intensified by the thought that her agreement with Parnell Carswell heightened the danger this man represented. The tense silence in the parlor was accentuated by a renewed murmur of voices from the kitchen, and Lydia tried to keep from her expression the sudden worry of what Gretchen might be telling Private Hines. "You say you found me lying in the lane?"

"Yes, ma'am. Not more than a hundred yards from your gate."

"But—" She remembered cushioning arms as she fell from...someone.

"Ma'am?"

"That close to home? You are certain?"

"You had almost no need for assistance. Is something amiss?"

"Ah—no. My carved brooch. I lost my brooch somewhere that evening."

He thought back. "I can't remember if you had it when we found you."

"I stumbled several times. It could have fallen any of those times."

"And you've searched the lane?"

"Yes, but—never mind. I am grateful for your help." Lydia only half-heard his protest that it was his pleasure and honor. Her focus was still on the disjuncture between his statement and her hazy—possibly faulty—memory of someone catching her as she fainted. But it was not a subject she wanted to examine in the presence of a man searching for enemy smugglers.

She veered from that topic with the familiar ploy of asking a man about himself.

He obliged, speaking of his appointment to West Point after several years of failing to settle into his stepfather's mercantile way of life; of his posting to New Fort Kearney in the Kansas Territory; his transfer up the south branch of the Platte River to Fort St. Vrain.

"And there you found the excitement that you could not find in commerce?"

"Yes, but more than that, I found a beautiful land! A blue sky wider than any I've ever seen—air so fresh and clear that one may see the Shining Mountains a hundred miles away..." His words faded in a note of yearning, and his gray eyes seemed to gaze at some vista. "As yet, it's uncivilized. But that vast land is magnificent!"

"And filled with dangerous Indians?"

"We had only a few skirmishes with small bands— young bucks out for glory and horses so they could buy a wife. But nothing so grand as Private Hines assumes." Lydia offered the decanter and the lieutenant accepted another glass. "To tell the truth, many of our white brethren out there are far more savage than the Indians. At least those yet uncorrupted by rum and the dregs of frontier life."

"You sound nostalgic for the territories, Lieutenant."

His smile and his tone shifted to self-mockery. "I sound quite romantic. It can be very lonely and very hard." A wag of his head. "But for all that, ma'am, it is nonetheless a beautiful land."

"And you'd rather remain there than return here?"

"I have returned to a war."

"So now you round up the horses of your enemies."

"I would much prefer to round up Rebels with General McDowell and his Army of Northern Virginia, Mrs. Sensabaugh, but I must do as I am ordered."

The obvious sting of her comment gave Lydia a twinge of embarrassment; she had proposed a truce, and she just violated it. From the kitchen came the rattle of silverware and a lengthier, and worrisome, murmur of voices. She attempted to soften her words. "The army must have great respect for your abilities if they sent you to train the volunteers."

"It's nice to think so, but the truth is more prosaic. In a regular regiment, I could remain a second lieutenant for another five years. By joining a volunteer regiment, I was promoted to first lieutenant immediately."

"You are ambitious, then?"

"What man isn't? And in our new nation, what man shouldn't be? I suspect many women are, too."

She could agree with that much. "And war is a way of fulfilling your ambition?"

He carefully set his small glass on the side table as if to concentrate better on his thoughts. "It's my trade. But I'm not overeager to be at it nor to sacrifice lives to my ambition. The volunteers fear the war will be over before they can join it. From my knowledge of your Cousin Bill and other Southern officers, I believe it will be much longer—perhaps as long as one or two years, especially if the Confederacy receives recognition and support from England and France."

"Surely even after Fort Sumter it's not too late for both sides to reach some accommodation?"

That wasn't the lieutenant's belief. "Neither side wants accommodation. Dissolution versus union, slavery versus freedom: the ideas are antithetical. To settle them, one side must now force its will on the other." He gazed at her for a long moment, but she wasn't certain it was she he saw. "It's my duty—and desire—to see union and freedom win."

Lydia felt, though she was not willing to show, sympathy for both concepts. She drained the remaining port from her small glass. "So there will be no truce."

Gretchen and Lydia watched from the porch as the two soldiers mounted and rode out of the lamplight that splashed from the windows across the porch and onto the dark lawn. "You reckon they will come back like they promise?"

"As their duties allow, I do believe." The shadows blended into the night long before the sound of their horses faded. "You and Private Hines seemed to have a lengthy exchange."

"I don't know about exchange—he talked about him, mostly."

"Did you finally reconcile with him?"

"Reconcile? No, ma'am. Him and Humphrey could be shooting at each other before the month's out, is what I told him, so I don't feel called to any reconciling!" Then she said in a softer voice, "He told me he didn't want to ride way out here at first but now he's real glad he came. His first name's Joshua. Joshua Hines." She added, "He said they have to ride in pairs so's not to get ambushed so easy."

Lydia had not learned Lieutenant Morse's first name and felt an odd sense of regret. "Well, I'm sure they will visit when they can. Perhaps we will find that Yankees aren't so different, after all, from our own people."

"Yes'm. But that private also said why they was out our way when they found you: they was looking for contrabanders. And that lieutenant kept talking about doing his duty to his country. If they do come back, I hope it's not while we're doing our duty to our country with Parnell Carswell's truck stored in our barn."

That thought had also been Lydia's.

Chapter 15

Lieutenant Morse's patrols brought him near Marshfield Farm at least once a week. Often, a small squadron rode into the yard to water their horses, and the lieutenant, without dismounting, would tell Lydia and Gretchen the latest war news. Other times, when he was accompanied only by Private Hines, they had time for a cool drink in the shade of the porch. On rare occasions, they could accept the mannerly invitation to stay for dinner. If time allowed, he helped with those chores more suitable to a man's arm than a woman's. such as nailing loose boards on the barn or the pier. It was, he explained, a welcome contrast to military labors. When that happened, the lieutenant brought not only news of the fighting, but gifts that he said were from the officers' mess: tinned peaches, a ham, a bottle of port to replace what they drank, and even once, a full sack of coffee beans slung, like a hog, behind the private's saddle. "Contraband," Morse explained. "Some loyalist Virginians reported a blockade runner anchored inside Wallops Island and we boarded it. I figure a small share of the reward should go to worthy noncombatants such as yourselves." In the kitchen, Gretchen sniffed to Lydia, "At least our getting it keeps it out of blue bellies."

From her visits home, Gretchen also brought war news in the form of folded and creased copies of her father's

Richmond Examiner or *Salisbury Gazette.* Columns of small print related the verbal hostilities between Washington and Richmond; large headlines told of the movement of the Union Army into Virginia at Alexandria and Arlington. Full-page block letters trumpeted of warfare and death in places Lydia had never heard of. First came the disheartening Confederate defeats at Phillip and at Rich Mountain. Then came Bull Run.

Magnificent, elating, celebrated in cramped columns of newsprint: *Fourth Alabama...Rhode Island Battery...Sudley Ford...Stone Bridge...*

Exclamation points, italic type, and large bold-faced letters gave a sense of the magnitude of the engagement, of the noise and smoke, the heroic charges and counter charges of infantry and cavalry, the sweep of danger and death. Supreme in the description was General Beauregard who, one reporter noted, *out-generaled McDowell and forced the invaders back from Virginia's Sacred Soil.* The broken Union army had retreated past Arlington into Washington City, and the war would soon be over with the Confederacy victorious.

"That's it," said Gretchen as she read the article again, this time over Lydia's shoulder. "They say any one of our boys can whip ten of theirs, and General Beauregard can whip any Yankee general!"

But long columns of smaller print listed Confederates killed and their regiments, and Union losses were said to be four times as many.

"Oh, Gretchen, this is wonderful—but it's terrible, too. Look at all these names—hundreds. Hundreds of dead!"

"They don't mention the Thirty-Ninth Volunteers," the girl pointed out.

"I thank the good Lord your brother's name is not on that list."

എൻഎൻ

Lieutenant Morse's next visit was somber and brief, and

Lydia had to caution Gretchen twice about gloating.

"It's only one battle," the lieutenant told the girl, "and regardless of what the Richmond papers say, it won't end the war. Our soldiers were ill trained, but they came very close to winning the day. Mistakes by equally ill-trained officers led to their defeat. This war, ladies, is only beginning."

August brought a muggy thickness to the atmosphere and a haze that blanked out the horizon on the Chesapeake. Clouds built into crashing storms that made the sky almost purple. Jagged spears of lightning rent the windy darkness, and thunder rolled heavily from one side of the heavens to the other as the women struggled to harvest what ears of corn remained salvageable in the overgrown field. To Lydia, nature reflected the mood of the times, and her whimsy was reinforced when, after a particularly violent storm, a heavy knock rattled her front door.

A bearded man about her height stood with his wet hat in his hands. His gum poncho glistened and dripped from the last of the rain. "Mrs. Sensabaugh?" Both his soft voice and his manner held an easy authority.

"Yes."

"I'm Squire Carswell's overseer—name's Talbot. He sent me to tell you we'll need to use your barn and landing. He can't say exactly when, but soon."

"Oh—yes. Yes, of course." A cold feeling made her realize she had been hoping that, over the many silent weeks, Parnell Carswell had forgotten her pledge.

"Squire says to tell you his plan is to bring the goods into your barn at night, then move them out as soon's possible, no mor'n a night or two after. Says to assure you we'll be little bother."

"Of course," she repeated. And of course Parnell Carswell would hire an overseer shorter than himself. "Let me show you the barn."

The man's heavy dark beard parted in a low laugh. "No need for that, ma'am—I seen it already." He leaned toward

Lydia, voice still full of good humor. "That hired hand of yourn—he come back yet?"

"Mr. Bradshaw? No. Why do you ask?"

"Squire wanted me to. Just you and Miss Druer living here now?"

"Yes. Have you seen Mr. Bradshaw?"

"No'm. Just some talk he's up near Freeschool Marsh. Near the nigger settlement there."

"Is he all right?"

The man shrugged. "No idea, ma'am. He don't seem to want help from any white people, leastways." He fumbled under his wet cape. "You hear yet about Bull Run?"

"Yes. Gretchen brought the news."

He pulled out a tightly rolled newspaper. "Squire wanted me to be sure to give you this. Said it shows that the Confederacy will win."

Lydia unrolled the paper. Under the smudged banner of the *Richmond Daily Dispatch,* large black letters blared, *Wonderful Victory at Manassas* and a column of smaller headlines featured the now familiar events and actors.

"Some say we should rename the creek—call it Yankee Run instead of Bull Run." His teeth shone in another laugh.

The man remounted to rest his hands on the pommel and gaze down at the woman on the bottom step. His voice did not rise, but the good humor was gone and only hard authority remained. "Squire also wanted me to tell you that Yankee officer who's always coming around mustn't find any of our shipments in your barn. It wouldn't be safe for us, for you, and especially for him." He replaced his hat and showed his teeth again. "Good evening, ma'am." The horse's hooves made soft, squishing noises in the muddy earth, but Lydia scarcely heard them.

∽∾∽

A few weeks later as the September sun burned low in a

hazy western sky, a wilted Gretchen returned from home with another collection of newspapers and Humphrey's latest correspondence.

All we been doing is marching and drilling and having parades and inspections and we don't even have musket nor uniform and I must say we look pretty silly acting like soljers in the same clothes we brought with us which are getting pretty wore and rank and my boots about worn through from the sand cutting there sols. Me and every man in the reg't wishes like blazes we was at Bullrun and keep telling the capt. we want to go to the mainland but he says there ant orders yet. He says he hopes the war's not over before we can get in it but it looks like the only war we get to fite is against the cooties of which there is a number.

The Salisbury weekly, which gave the Yankee perspective, echoed Lieutenant Morse's belief that the war, despite the disaster at Bull Run, had not yet begun. Stories spoke of volunteer regiments converging on Washington from all across the Union, the Territories, and even California. Rebel mobs in Baltimore attacked Union troops marching between trains and were fired upon in return. Known secessionists were rounded up in Maryland, disarmed, and imprisoned. The First Maryland Eastern Shore Regiment under Colonel James Wallace advertised *We seek able and willing men for the purpose of putting down Rebellion in Maryland.* An accompanying report said the regiment was having difficulty getting enough uniforms, equipment and weapons to supply all those who clamored to join, *But we are secure in the belief that stocks of supplies and armaments will be forthcoming in the next weeks, sufficient to the needs of our loyalists to stifle the proponents of secession wherever in Maryland they may dare to rear their heads.*

Gretchen's finger tapped the regiment's name. "Daddy

said our cousins, the ones up in Somerset County, have joined the Eastern Shore Volunteers. Aunt Cicely's husband wanted to join up, too, because he hates Rebels so much."

"Do your father and his sister still communicate?"

"Yes'm, they write now and then. But they never did visit each other too often. I reckon they won't see each other at all, now, what with her husband hating Rebels so." The nation was a house divided, as the Union president phrased it, and now families were dividing with it.

Gretchen had also picked up a letter from Lydia's sister. It was franked with an odd "Paid 5" mark where the normal postage would be. Bonnie's welcome handwriting filled both sides of the single sheet. After opening with a greeting and an apology for the hurried quality of her letter, she told of Norfolk and family.

You may recall our Cousins James and Richard from up near Murfreesboro. I am ashamed to say they have joined a regiment from Virginia that has chosen to support the power of the Dictator instead of the rights of their native State. But they are worthless trash anyway, being from North Carolina, and the Yankees are welcome to them. The Yankees continue to hold Fortress Monroe, but our soldiers are building redoubts and trenches from Craney's Island as far as Tanner's Creek. My friend Alice Waugh sends her regards and begs you to remember her. Her husband was at the Victory at Manassas and has written a very thrilling letter in which he describes what he did and saw and how the Yankees skedaddled, as they call it. I will tell you all about it when I get time from sewing uniforms and shirts and bandages for the Army. But I am happy to tell you that he said many of the Yankees were killed with their own powder that our soldiers took from old Fort Norfolk and sent by the railroad to General Beauregard prior to the battle. There has been cannonading and shooting up and down the James River and a lot of the citizens here are worried that the Yankees, like the British in the last war, will attack and burn the town. Many are talking of closing their homes and moving elsewhere. If such occurs, you may write to us in care of Uncle Mangrum's plantation in Charlton County Georgia. Andrew has been appointed Captain of a sloop designed to run the blockade and will be sailing from our ports with cotton to trade for materials of war shipped from England to Nassau in the Bahamian islands. He is very eager for the ship to complete outfitting and to be at sea.

I am not so eager, as you might surmise, to have my husband go into danger, but I am proud of him for willingly and bravely doing his duty for Virginia and for freedom. No matter how long the war might last, everyone I know is ready to support the Confederacy in its resistance to tyranny. We may be called Rebels, my dear Lydia, but far better that appellation than one of Ignoble for allowing Lincoln to establish a despotism and call it by the sacred name of Union.

えかえか

September slid warmly into October. On the fifth day of that month, as Lydia forked the last potatoes from the earth and gleaned the vegetable garden for any late-ripening fruits, she felt rather than heard something in the still air: a mild, distant thud, then a series of thuds, as if someone far away beat heavily on a rug. Gretchen came to the kitchen door. "You hear that? Is that thunder?"

The quick thuds pulsed again, then ceased, then stuttered again.

"I don't think so." Lydia glanced around the clear sky. "It seems to be coming from inland." A small flock of birds swirled up from the distant tree line, swung in a large circle against the blue, then dove again into the sheltering limbs. Another rumble of thuds sent them in a wider flight.

The two women looked at each other. Gretchen asked, "Guns?"

"Why? Where?"

The girl shook her head. "A long ways away, I reckon."

A final rumble of thumps followed by silence. The blue sky offered no clue, the faint call of birds began again. Behind the barn, a hog grunted.

To Lydia the event was both ominous and mysterious, as if the battles and death of newspaper headlines had gained voice and, in a giant leap, arrived within reach of Marshfield.

The next week, when Gretchen returned from another long walk to home and New Church, she brought the answer: a Union warship had sunk a Confederate privateer in Chincoteague Bay.

"They say three or four were killed and twice as many hurt—the Chincoteagers told the Yankees where the sloop was hiding up Coklis Creek, they say." Gretchen set her tote bag on the kitchen table. "Here's the newspaper, but there's nothing about the fight in it. There was no mail for you, ma'am, but Humphrey wrote to Mama again." She unloaded the small packages of yeast and phosphorous matches that made up that trip's store-bought goods. "He says the regiment's going over to Norfolk City soon before the Yankees can come down the peninsula to Eastville and capture them. He didn't say nothing about Allen Rafer or Billy or any of them, but he did say everybody's healthy and in good spirits and glad to be going where they can do some good." Gretchen looked out the window at the gray evening. "Norfolk City seems a lot further off, now, don't it?" Her voice faded to a whisper, "Said he misses Mama and Papa and the boys and me, too."

そそそ

Unsettled weather and occasional squalls blown in from the Bay began to alternate with autumn days of crisp sunshine and chill winds. Lieutenant Morse and his soldiers rode into the farmyard wearing capes against the growing cold. On his longer visits he told of ambushes against Union soldiers patrolling further south on the peninsula in Northampton County, and of rumors that civilians were forming an underground Home Guard. "They have no hope of open warfare, but the army may have to send a stronger force to protect loyalists from their assaults, and that will mean fewer troops for the mainland." On two different nights, Gretchen and Lydia heard the creak of wagons move slowly down their lane to halt in the farmyard. The women waited in the black house as the sounds of heavy lifting made muffled noises. Then the wagon-creak began again, moving away quickly. In the mornings, they looked in the barn to see, half-hidden behind Star's empty stall and the barrier of fertilizer kegs, a lumpy mass of tarp. A night or two later, came the clomp of heels on the pier and lawn, soft murmurs, followed by silence. And the next morning the tarp was empty and folded.

The two women harvested the remnants of the garden to cook and seal its bounty in Mason's glass jars, scraped dried ears of corn for the seed that would be needed next spring, and hefted buckets of potatoes into the shallow root cellar for winter use and for barter at the Sundries Store. Lydia had even less time to take the boat out, and when she did, she stayed close to the shoreline and within a quick downwind reach of Fowler Creek. Gretchen's harvest of gossip reported Yankee vessels patrolling the Chesapeake from Hampton Roads to above the Potomac River. However, in the sheltered and shallow waters of Pocomoke Bay she seldom saw other boats, and those glimmering sails usually moved away, as reluctant to approach her as she was them. One distinctive mutton-leg sail with a brown stain like a half-folded wing near its peak appeared a dozen times, but it remained near the shoreline and never drew near the *Lydia*.

On an evening when the coming night chilled her face and hands, she coasted home across glassy water, surprised to see Gretchen come down to the pier to meet her.

"That lieutenant's here again." Despite numerous visits and a growing acceptance of the man's presence, Gretchen always referred to Lieutenant Morse by rank instead of name. It was, Lydia believed, a means of maintaining the man's identity as an enemy rather than possibly seeing him as a friend. "He brought us something more than his appetite, this time."

"And did he bring Private Hines as well?"

Gretchen's face flushed. "It ain't my fault he keeps coming!"

"I'm certain it's only for your cooking, Gretchen."

"If it ain't, it should be."

The two women walked through the deep grass of the unscythed lawn toward the farmhouse. The flaming sunset glowed pink across its façade as Lieutenant Morse came down from the porch to greet them. Private Hines stood behind him, looking hungrily at Gretchen.

Morse lifted his hat in greeting. The scarlet clouds of sundown tinted the air with a rosiness that heightened the expression of calm happiness on Lydia's face. Now beyond the term for mourning, her dress was no longer widow's weeds but a light blue that brought out the youth of her eyes and cheeks, and the color of her light brown hair. "Ma'am. I would guess your cruise was a pleasant one."

"Very pleasant. The water is beautifully calm this evening."

"The experience suits you very well." He held her fingers longer than necessary and looked at her with an intensity of some sort, until she felt she had to withdraw her hand.

"You sail the boat very well, Mrs. Sensabaugh."

"Thank you. This gentle breeze makes a good sailor of any landlubber. Are you on patrol again?"

"No. We come specifically to see you both. To thank you for the hospitality you've shown us. It brought great comfort to Private Hines, being away from home for the first time, and it brought to me a kind of joy that's been rare in my life." He reached the end of the speech he had rehearsed as he rode, and said simply, "So, we thank you."

"But—that sounds almost as if you are saying goodbye."

He nodded. "Private Hines returns to Delaware—his enlistment's up. And General McClellan has offered me a commission as a captain in the Army of Virginia." He added with a note of apology, "It's an advancement I can't refuse."

"Oh. I see. So it is a farewell."

"I hope not a permanent one."

"Well—yes—well, I also hope not." Curiously, his announcement had drained some of the glow from the soft evening. "When do you leave?"

"Tomorrow."

"Ah."

He cleared his throat. "I brought you a small gift. I hope it goes some distance toward repairing the harm done you earlier." He gestured toward the back of the house where three horses stood tethered at the water trough. Two were saddled but the third wore only a halter. "It's not as fine a horse as we took from you, but I offer it with sincere apologies."

"Such a gesture isn't necessary, Lieutenant Morse. I don't hold you responsible for obeying your orders."

"You're gracious. But I do this for my own pleasure." He handed her a small envelope. "The bill of sale, made out in your name, in case some future soldier questions your possession of the animal," he said. "His name's Dan."

"I scarcely know how to thank you, Lieutenant."

"I don't give it for thanks, Mrs. Sensabaugh. But out of gratitude for allowing me..." He groped for a phrase—this was the part of the speech that he had not framed to his satisfaction. "...to glimpse a type of happiness I have never known."

"I don't understand."

"A domestic happiness, ma'am. A happiness foreign to a soldier and, frankly, foreign to my life since childhood."

"Domestic?"

He rushed to apologize for the term. "'Domestic' in the sense of sharing your...parlor—" Some imp brought the word "boudoir" into his mind and his voice stumbled over the impulse. "Dining at a domestic table," he said quickly.

The delicate arcs of the woman's eyebrows lifted above those dark brown eyes, and he had the embarrassing suspicion that she had read his thought.

"Domestic, ah, in the sense—"

"In the sense of being seated in a domestic parlor having a domestic discussion of domestic topics." Lydia tried to keep the laughter from her voice as she glided over his awkwardness. "I understand, sir."

And Lieutenant Morse, within hours of leaving, perhaps forever, those dark eyes that had suddenly become merry, fell completely in love. "I am delighted you do, Mrs. Sensabaugh."

Chapter 16

Later, Lydia had many opportunities to reflect back on that evening, its farewell dinner, the candlelight soft against the green glow of late evening, the air cool and fresh through open windows. Whenever she did, it seemed as if time had, for those short hours, crystallized into a fixed scene that had the structure and emotional content of a painting. It was an instance of life capturing art, of a harmony of feeling and setting—the kind of arrangement often sought in an evening's shared friendship and dining, but, for one reason or another, seldom achieved. In addition, the evening had been made...sweet? piquant?...by a felt quivering in the air, by unspoken emotions whose possibilities conflicted with the time's impossibilities. It touched the happiness with a note of regret that made it even more intense, and, in retrospect, gave a sense of one of those rare moments that clearly marks a pivot in life's direction.

It was like one of those soirees when, as a fifteen-year-old in Norfolk City, she had first sipped a thimbleful of wine and felt as attractive and mature as sister Bonnie. She had danced and tingled to her fingertips surrounded by the luminous eyes of young men who begged her in drawling urgency to allow them one more dance, to walk with them through the perfume of moonlit gardenias, to permit them to call at her home. That kind of youthful sweetness had also been transient, fading even as she talked excitedly with Bonnie, who almost seventeen and safely promised to Andrew, offered her advice from the mature perspective of an engaged woman. How they had analyzed the words and prospects of this boy or that, and stifled giggles about others! And wouldn't Bonnie have advice for Lydia now if she had an inkling that a Yankee was being wined and dined at Marshfield!

But even as it happened, she had told herself that this wining and dining would pass, this evening's picture would fade. Even while Lieutenant Morse's eyes, deepened by candlelight, gazed into hers as he begged permission to write to her, she repeated to herself that she was too old for such romantic trappings. She was not a girl to be romanced, but a grown woman and a widow and, officially at least, a foe of this man.

Yet later memories of that evening brought back those earlier surging tides of a vague love that was ambient, embracing, pure—and unfocused. It echoed the ill-defined girlish yearning that preceded Franklin's courtship and, she reminded herself sharply, like that courtship came more from the intoxication of the moment and the place than from any person.

Nonetheless, months later, when February's damp and icy winds made every room except the kitchen almost uninhabitable, Lydia's mind would drift from the open book in her lap to a vision of that evening, and she recalled not the moment but the man. The occasional letters from Lieutenant, now Captain, Morse—stiff in phrase and precise, thoughtful, and sometimes witty—made her dissect those feelings whose re-emergence had ambushed and confused her that evening, feelings that had come from such a distant past but had so intensely pervaded the room. And they made her wonder about things left unsaid, or about caresses that, may she be forgiven, she might have allowed had they been offered on that magic evening.

When, at the Sundries Store, Lydia received Morse's letters, few and wrinkled, she retired to the heat of the Franklin stove in the ladies parlor to scan quickly words that would accompany her during the long ride home, and that she would later re-read at leisure:

Washington City, 14 November 1861

My Dear Mrs. Sensabaugh, I pray that you will excuse the haste of my writing, which by no means is an indication of the pleasure I find in penning this to you. My life is filled with the innumerable preparations for war, as I am assigned to the general staff in Washington City. This place, like the Union itself, is unfinished. The marble column that will be a monument to General Washington stands at what I am told is not half its proposed height, yet it is already impressive, and the dome that is to cover the Rotunda of the Capitol Building is likewise only partially clad. From the chunks of marble and stone lying about the grounds it is difficult to say if it is in a state of completion or destruction. I think Mr. Emerson would see it as an image for the state of our Union. Lamentably, I missed the action at Ball's Bluff...

My Dear Mrs. Sensabaugh, it is with great pleasure that I sit to respond to your letter of the seventeenth instant. Please do not apologize that you have little news to write to me. Each and every word you write is a most welcome delight to read. Indeed the picture you draw of the war-fevered rooster marshaling his pullets for parade is most comical. It has especial pertinence, since I have recently been trying to convince a company of New York clerks and tradesmen that drill and more drill is the basis for becoming a soldier. They are parlor soldiers in need of a strong dose of military discipline, believing that a soldier's life is but warlike airs and strutting about in new uniforms. The volunteers straggle into camp wearing coats of regimental gray and a variety of everyday

trousers, hats, weapons, mud, and attitudes. It is a
challenge just to have the men stand in line for roll
call. One of my fellow regular officers in the Forty-
Eighth New York laments that our occupation is not
unlike herding cats.

All the letters were signed *Your friend, S. Morse* and
Lydia pondered the "S" names: Sylvester, Seward,
Selwyn...Solomon, Stanhope...She went through "S"
names that might fit her image of the man. Stewart, Samuel.
But in the end she had to be content with "Captain Morse"
both when she thought of him and when she wrote.
   Like his, Lydia's letters were filled with the minutiae of
domestic chores—a filter, she admitted to herself, for any
expression that might be misinterpreted as going beyond
friendship and gratitude. Perhaps he felt the same way, for
he included only a sentence or two that expressed personal
feelings, and even those words seemed carefully phrased so
as not to offend: warm memories of visiting Marshfield, a
formal expression of missing her company, gratitude that
she allowed him to have someone to write to, and delight in
receiving her correspondence. When she read those sentences she felt a stir of emotion, and that was ironic, since
she avoided any intimations of affection. If she never saw
Morse again—and that could be quite possible—her life at
Marshfield would continue much as it was now. She found
sadness in that thought, a loss at that incipient possibility—
the loss of something not explored but only hinted at. And
that feeling kept nudging her during long winter evenings
when the fire flapped in the muffled roar of wind across the
chimney top, while she, wrapped in a dressing gown and the
thick cotton of her padded slippers, re-read his letters by
candlelight.

ေသေ

March blew February away. Lydia and Gretchen hitched

Dan to the plow to dig dark rows through wet soil. The mule promised by Parnell Carswell the previous year as a favor returned for the use of her barn had not appeared. Lydia did not remind the man of his promise. The earth, fallow over summer, was heavy and hard to cut. But Gretchen plowed deep and straight furrows, while Lydia took on the farm's other duties. Based on rumors of high wartime prices for crops, the spring planting was extensive.

On a raw day when the wind cut tears from her eyes, Lydia slogged across the clinging mud to bring hot coffee to Gretchen. The girl, almost lost in Franklin's old topcoat, struggled to keep the jolting plow handles upright, and Lydia had a pang of guilt and regret as she watched Gretchen's efforts. She had, Lydia noticed, begun to walk back from the fields with the rolling heaviness of a man worn by labor, and the skin of her face was growing dry and chapped from sun and wind. But Gretchen did not complain; rather she took pride in how much physical work she could achieve. Lydia, aware that the plowing had to be done and that she could not do it as well as Gretchen, tried to ease the girl's labors as much as she could. When hailed, the girl halted Dan and dabbed at her red nose with the tip of her knitted mitten.

"Oh, I thank you, ma'am—that does warm a soul's middle!" Her icy hands wrapped around the thick mug as she turned her back to the wind. Between sips she hugged it inside her coat.

"I think you've done enough for today, Gretchen. Come in to the fire and warm yourself."

Tendrils of blonde hair streamed from under the brown wool scarf knotted tightly beneath her chin. She glanced at the yet-unplowed section. "A quarter-acre more. We'll want at least another quarter acre of corn. Dan and I can finish it by tonight," she promised. "We need to get the seed in now. The trees already got leaf buds swelling."

"One day won't make a difference, Gretchen."

"Well, it might—specially if it comes rain tomorrow and I can't plow."

But Lydia wasn't listening. The sound of horses heralded the now-familiar scene of a column of blue-clad soldiers trotting down the lane, and she felt her heart lurch.

But as the riders neared, the only face she recognized was the sergeant with his narrow goatee. Sergeant Durgin, that was his name, and Lydia remembered the man's past eagerness to enter her home in search of contraband. She lifted the thick collar of her husband's hunting jacket against the wind. Beside her, Gretchen steadied Dan as the horses approached.

The Union troops all dressed alike now: dark blue jackets and lighter blue trousers. Their captain had dark trousers with a yellow stripe down the leg. Sergeant Durgin's trousers bore a red stripe and his jacket had light blue chevrons on the sleeves. Crossed sabers glinted on top of his forage cap. "That's her," he said and pointed at Lydia. "She claims she owns the place."

The captain reined his horse. The animal's nostrils steamed with hot breath. "Morning, ma'am. I'm Captain Gaines. You might remember Sergeant Major Durgin."

The sergeant grinned. "Got yourself a new horse, I see."

"I have a bill of sale for him!" Lydia stifled the urge to reach for Dan's bridle. "You can't take him."

The sergeant's grin died. "Well, ma'am, that ain't quite true. If we need him, we'll take him, and don't you forget it. Lieutenant Morse tried to get me court-martialed because of you." The grin came back. "But that bastard ain't here anymore, is he?" He touched the brim of his forage cap toward Gretchen, "I'm real glad to see you, too, missy."

The captain wiped his wet mustache on the wide cuff of his gauntlet. "We've been told there's contraband being sent from this side of the Bay over to Virginia." A wet cough and he swallowed something. "You seen any such activity in this neighborhood?"

"Who told you that?"

"Gretchen—"

"People we can trust told us, miss. Some of your loyalist neighbors. What you been seeing?"

Lydia shook her head, struggling to keep all emotion from her face. "Nothing." It was a near-truth, she told herself. They'd heard things, but they hadn't actually seen them. "We've seen nothing."

The captain, pale eyes watering in the wind, coughed again and stared at her for a long moment. "Sergeant Major, search the goddamn grounds."

"We've seen nothing!"

He snorted and spat something heavy at the ground. "And you'd be likely to tell us if you had, wouldn't you? Like maybe boats coming in to your dock."

She could not bring herself to deny that. "Gretchen, let's finish the plowing." She turned her back on the captain and started leading Dan down the field. Behind her, she heard Gretchen give a half-sob of anger and frustration as she leaned back against the plow strap.

The soldiers spread out in groups of two, some trotting toward the pier and the *Lydia*, some across the unplowed section toward the trees. Others went into the barn. As the women reached the end of a row and turned, Gretchen hissed to Lydia, "You ought to go back to the house—I seen that sergeant go into the house!"

"I'll not leave you alone here. Remember what they did to Roger."

"Yes'm, but—"

"We're safer together."

They plodded down the next row into the stinging wind. Lydia wished she had brought a wool scarf to wrap around her face as Gretchen had done, but all she had was the coat collar that she held tight across her nose. They almost reached the end of that row before the various patrols trotted back toward the farmyard and the water trough. The squawk of chickens and a shriek from the pig pen told them soldiers were busy in the barn. A moment later three men appeared, two holding the legs of a struggling shoat, the other with a brace of chickens in each hand. They tied the loot behind their saddles. Captain Gains, coughing again, walked his horse toward the women. "What's that in them barrels you got in the barn?"

"Fertilizer. One's opened—you can see for yourself."

"I did. It don't look like fertilizer. Don't smell like it, neither." His chin jerked up in dismissal. "And I don't know anybody in their right mind stores fertilizer in barrels."

"It's a chemical fertilizer."

The captain stared at her, his eyes doubting her truthfulness.

"It's from the Dupont factory. Chemical fertilizer—a new product that my late husband was testing." She struggled to keep her vice reasonable. "We bought it long before any war started—you can read the shipping date on the barrels!"

After a moment, his hat bobbed in a short nod. "I reckon I can find out how true that is." He pulled his horse around and said something to one of the soldiers. After a few moments, the soldier returned and said something to the captain, who gave another nod. Then the column trotted away down the lane. Neither the captain nor Sergeant Durgin glanced their way.

"Damn Yankee thieves!"

Lydia did not reprimand the girl's language.

In the house, she found her husband's silver flask and the bottle of whiskey gone from the sideboard. The drawers of his desk were partly open and papers had been stirred about, but there was little to steal. The kitchen pantry had been raided for a few jars of canned fruit. Apparently, Sergeant Durgin had not taken time to climb the stairs to the second floor. Neither Gretchen's nor her dresser and closet had been disturbed, and Lydia was grateful for that much: the security of those private areas, fragile though it might be, remained intact. And the few Union demand notes that she hid beneath the false bottom of the wooden box on her dresser were, thank the Lord, untouched. But Gretchen reported that the pewter serving ware had been stolen from the kitchen cupboard, along with the small silver salt bowl that had been the wedding gift from Lydia's parents.

"I hate them—I hate them!"

"It could have been worse, Gretchen. They could have found Mr. Carswell's stores in our barn or taken Dan like they took Star."

"They won't take no more horses—they got to leave them for farmers to grow crops to feed their fat blue bellies. I read that in the newspaper—they stole too many horses last year and drove crop prices too high."

"Nonetheless, we must find a place to hide our valuables where they can't get them next time."

"Next time? You think they'll be back?"

"They are looking for smugglers," Lydia said. "And they rightly suspect us."

ຕ∕ຍຕ∕ນ

Hitching Dan to the wagon, one or the other of them now rode into New Church as often as once a week. The Cochins were laying well, and, as more Yankee soldiers were sent to the Eastern Shore, Mr. Henderson bought all the eggs Lydia could supply, along with any excess from her kitchen garden. Those sales and barter brought a little welcome cash and provided an occasional loaf of sugar, a sack of wheat flower or corn meal, or even an up-to-date newspaper. Though almost all the publications were from the North, Lydia and Gretchen would spend the evening reading whatever papers, used or new, they could obtain.

Columns of newsprint told of fights and skirmishes in the rain and mud, of army troops protecting Eastern Shore loyalists from attacks by Rebel sympathizers, of Rebel defeats in western Virginia, and of the *Battle of the Ironclads* which, editors wrote, *heralds a new era of naval warfare.*

To southern sympathizers, even those writing in Northern papers, the sea battle *proves beyond dispute that the South, despite its disadvantages in meeting the power of the Northern manufactures, can match and even surpass the ingenuity so widely proclaimed to be the sole domain of the Northern industrialists.* However, the editor of the Salisbury paper saw the battle as a startling but ultimately failed attempt by the Rebels to break the blockade. Writers from both sides prophesied *the strangulation of the South should the Mississippi River be controlled by Union forces,* and a fulminating editorial copied from a Richmond paper called for a quick strike at Washington, *which will, assuredly, turn unrest in the North against this unjust invasion into outright rejection of it.* Baltimore papers reported that Lincoln relieved General McClellan of overall command of the Union army and re-assigned him to lead the Army of the Potomac against Richmond. Advertisements in papers from Philadelphia and New York touted barrels of *Loyal Chincoteague Oysters* for sale and urged Northern shoppers to support *those merchants in Virginia who are loyal to the Union.* In late April, almost stunned language in all the papers told of unbelievable thousands killed in Tennessee at a place called Shiloh Church. Nashville fell to the Union, and—a major blow to the rebels—the Union navy captured New Orleans. Fort Pulaski guarding the Savannah River was destroyed; and General McClellan's troops, moving south by foot, rail, and boat, invaded the Jamestown Peninsula between the James and York rivers on their way to attack Richmond.

The papers formed a steady chorus, while the occasional letter created a solo aria that brought personal and painful counterpoint to that roar. One awkwardly printed sheet from Humphrey to his parents somehow made its way across the lines.

I got no idea when I am to come home now since our co. is now reorganized here in Norfolk City and we every one signed on I. W. which means In for the

War. But even some whos enlistment is up will not be going home. They have something called conskripshun which means every able body between eighteen and forty-five yrs. of age is made to jine the army. Unlest you are a slave holder with twenty head or a injineer. Our eastern shore co—called The Refujees since the Yankees hold Accomak and Northampton counties—is now a unattached company here in Norfolk City. But no matter what they call us nobody is doing any fighting despite that the Yankees have moved into Newport News and Roanoke Island and a lot of towns across the James River. A lot of people in camp are sick and all we do is march and have musket drill and dig more trenches and redoubts in mud up to our asses for dam little pay and less food. I hope everything is okay with my beloved mother and father and I ask you to say Hello to Edwin and tell him not to jine the army unless he likes marching around in circkles instead of fighting. Pa do not worry about the sow since she had the same thing last yr. I think it is some weeds that comes up about now and she likes to eat. I miss youall and it would be nice to get a letter from somebody now and then but I no how hard it is to send them acrost the Lines and I hope this gets to you all. I miss you and love you. Humphrey Druer, Pvt.

The two latest letters from Captain Morse were delivered at the same time, one written near the end of March and consisting of two entries, the other letter written early in April. Like the preceding ones, both were brief, telegraphic, penned between duties.

The first said that he was still in Washington, re-assigned to McClellan's staff as one of the commissary officers preparing for the coming campaign.

This duty is increasingly demanding as our Army

of Northern Virginia builds. Nevertheless, I have applied to the Fifty-First New York Infantry Regt., which, I am assured by Col. Ferraro, will welcome a West Pointer to their roster. A few of their officers have resigned their commissions because of illness or issues in their businesses or personal lives that require their presence more than Army life allows. Their absence creates an opportunity to gain a post in a line company, which is my profound wish.

The second entry was dated several days later and thanked her for the letter of twelfth of March that had caught up with him finally at his New Posting.

I am very pleased, My Dear Mrs. Sensabaugh, to announce that my efforts to join a line company have succeeded. Please address future correspondence to Captain Morse, Company K, Fifty-First N. Y. S. V. The company sergeants have assured me there will be no trouble from the men since, in Sergeant Reilly's words, "We already know you are a regular soldier, Major Honey, and we liked you when you was drilling us earlier." How long this "honey" moon will last is another issue, but it is good to feel that the men accept my leadership and discipline. The last paragraph closed, *On these cold nights, the memories of the most pleasant evenings in my life stay with me and warm my thoughts, and I return to them often with the hope that they might soon be repeated.* He signed it, *Yours with Great Affection.*

Lydia studied the strokes of ink that, in the candlelight, revealed few of the elegant curls that her instruction in penmanship had entailed, and that even Mr. Henderson practiced. The arid formality of his phrasing seemed like one of the polite bread-and-butter notes her mother made her write as a child to thank a relative for a birthday gift.

But, she had to admit, her own letters were even more stiff and formal, and she resolved to tell him that she, too, missed his visits to Marshfield, that she, too, remembered those dinners with warmth and affection. Because it was true. The passage of months and the exchange of letters had worked an odd chemistry in her feelings toward Morse. Her mental picture of the man gradually blurred to leave only a few images: the gray-blue of his eyes whose carved lines at their corners contrasted with the youthful fullness of his lips, the whiff of sunshine and open air that emanated from his clothes, a sense of his masculine bulk carried with unconscious grace of movement. But with their exchange of letters, her sense of the man's character had grown more distinct. Clearer, she realized with a mild shock, than her sense of Franklin's character before their marriage, even though she had spent far more time speaking with her suitor and then fiancé than she had with this Yankee soldier.

Morse's voice in his letters wooed her, she realized. Though arid, his style held sincerity and an effort at precision. Even its occasional awkwardness of language, which he admitted and regretted, he let stand in his search for truth of expression. Yet, paradoxically because she recognized his truthfulness, the almost unfeeling tone of this letter depressed her with the thought that any affection he may have developed was, with time and distance, evaporating. Scolding herself, she used Gretchen's phrase about Allen Rafer— *'It wasn't no courtship anyway,'*—and tried to stifle the ache that this letter had stirred.

She opened the second letter with far more deliberation. The hand was the same—direct, scarcely ornamented, hurried. The date was April 3 and the place *Near Grove Crossing, Virginia,* described as two hovels at a cross-roads in the pines, the better one for horses, the other for people. Captain Morse trusted that the silence from Lydia was due to uncertain mail service rather than to any insult his earlier letters may have inadvertently caused, and he promised a better letter when occasion permitted.

At present, the Army of the Potomac advanced on York-town.

> *...and the men of the Fifty-First are eager to make up for the defeat at Manassas. I apologize again for brevity and haste, and beg to be excused for using pencil rather than pen. I plead for the first the press of many duties, and for the second the difficulty of maintaining a proper desk on the march as well as the effects of rain on ink. I do promise, My Dear Mrs. Sensabaugh, to write more fully soon. I recognize that in a few hours men will die, but not one in my compa-ny will be reluctant to toe the mark. Should I fall among the dead, I wish you to know that, as well as any other man, I did my duty even though that duty is opposed to your sentiments. It is the conflict of those emotions and the knowledge of impending death that makes me even more certain of my affection for you. I pray to have soon some correspondence from you.*

This time he ended with a phrase that included the word "love," and which generated an almost giddy elevation of spirit that sharpened into a stab of fear for him.

The newspapers had already reported the battle he wrote about, but without any names other than of regiments and generals. The list of fallen had not yet been published, and she felt her breath draw shallow with the thought that the words she read might be from a man now wounded or dead. She stared at the paper, noting a smudge on one corner where, apparently, his thumb had anchored it while he wrote. Even the imprint of the pencil's graphite seemed ear-nest, and she could imagine him in the field, writing by the light of a campfire, taking precious time from preparing himself and his men for battle to tell her what was in his heart. And all the while, her letters, poor and vapid as they might be, had not reached him. Perhaps would never reach him now. The swelling in her throat brought dampness to her eyes and she fumbled quickly in her writing cabinet.

Despite efforts at cheer and friendship, her words seemed dull and mundane, and she spent more time gazing at the blank page than dipping her pen in the ink well. *My Dear Captain Morse—Congratulations on your well-deserved appointment, and thank you for your letters which, I know, you write under most difficult circumstances. It is a*—She paused to weigh the adjective, then put it in—*great pleasure to receive them.* Which sounded too formal even for her. *They warm my evenings*—That sounded not quite formal enough—*and I can almost imagine that you and Private Hines*—There, a chaperone, as it were—*are joining Gretchen and myself at table for one of our pleasant dinners.*

She told him of the spring plowing and that Dan was a hard worker and gentle horse, that Gretchen had completed almost a whole field, and seed was sown and the earth greening with sprouts. The Cochin chickens had multiplied into a good stock that provided eggs, chicks, and fat pullets for market. She did not mention the visit by Sergeant Durgin, nor the occasional stir of night sounds that marked the transport of contraband through her barn.

You may be interested to learn of the depredations by Union soldiers who come ashore at night from patrol boats in Chincoteague Sound to steal pigs and chickens from those Loyalists they are supposed to protect. I'm certain that if you were in command, the malefactors would suffer punishment. Gretchen has received a letter from Private Hines who said he was going to re-enlist. She now fears that he and her brother will face each other. Here, she paused even longer, her fingertips brushing across the letter from him. *And I pray for your safety, for I have only just read brief reports of the conflict you faced and—* another problematic modifier—*deeply wish that we have the opportunity to see each other again. I think of you with affection—*

She considered adding "and friendship," but that phrase shifted the meaning of "affection" away from the direction she felt. After long thought, she simply signed her name— *Lydia Sensabaugh*—without the "Mrs."

Chapter 17

By May, Captain Morse still had not replied to her letter, but Lydia was grateful not to find his name among the list of Union dead and wounded published in the Salisbury paper. General McClellan's army was awaiting reinforcements before moving on Yorktown and Williamsburg. The editors were pleased to report that the famous anaconda had grown lengthier with the fall of Norfolk City to the Union Navy, and now the entire Chesapeake Bay was under Northern control.

That explained why there had been no recent letter from her sister. Lydia could only guess that Bonnie and the children had fled to their uncle's plantation in southern Georgia. But there was little time for Lydia to mourn that loss and less she could do about it. The kitchen garden, set back by a late frost, had to be rescued with much care, and the hoe and spade became familiar to her hands and back. In the field, the corn rose in stiff spears and the competing weeds had to be plowed under. Because Dan worked hard turning so much sandy earth, trips to the Sundries Store dropped to every other week.

On one long ride back from New Church, hot and sleepy beneath the mid-May sun, Lydia let the reins fall slack as the seat swayed and jounced along the track. By now, Dan knew the route and pulled the creaking wagon with a soporific gait and little guidance. The horse was almost as gentle as Star, though Lydia tried not to compare the two animals and seem ungrateful. Still, she did miss Star's intelligent alertness and, when woodcuts in the papers depicted war scenes with wild-eyed and broken animals trapped in artillery traces, she ached for Star's well-being.

The cawing of crows somewhere in the trees impinged on her drowsy thoughts about the dearth of mail. Once again, no letters from North or South had come for her or Gretchen. Lydia never asked how Mr. Henderson managed to get mail to and from the Confederacy, but Gretchen repeated her father's observation that on both sides, a certain amount of commerce was allowed by local authorities who had a closed eye and an open palm.

The two Maryland newspapers available this week—one from Baltimore and one from Salisbury—were full of the exploits of a Rebel general called *Stonewall Jackson who earned his sobriquet at the Battle of Manassas when he held his men against Union forces that threatened to overwhelm his position.* Somehow this general had recently avoided the armies that were to keep him at bay in the Long Valley and he now threatened Washington City. *Our forces must be used to man and supply those forts and strong points that have been built to protect our nation's Capital from depredations by the enemy. Surely the president and his advisors must recognize and confront the dangers that bear on us from this "Stonewall." Had the president listened to wiser heads last July, perhaps he would not have so hastily replaced General McDowell with General McClellan who now absents himself from the nation's capital when threat appears on the horizon.*

More important stories, to Lydia if not to the editors who seemed to know more about war than did the Yankee president, told of General McClellan's army finally taking Yorktown. But, halted at Williamsburg, they now awaited reinforcements before moving toward Richmond. In her sleepy mind's eye, Lydia traced trips with her family up the James

River from Norfolk City, past the village of Newport News, the plantation landings that dotted the muddy, wooded banks, and on to the Jamestown landing with its high road across rolling hills and among tall pines to Williamsburg.

The thought of Captain Morse encamped there among thousands of invading soldiers gave her a tangle of emotions: resentment of those whose cannon shot and fire threatened the lovely old city, the strange realization that his blue uniform was the same as that worn by Sergeant Durgin and Captain Gaines, the fright that he could even now be wounded or dead. She had ceased to think of him as "the enemy." It was as if he existed in some third category belonging to neither army but sharing the dangers of both. Her drifting thoughts were struggling to make some sense of that feeling when the crows cawed even nearer and the wagon gave a lurch. Dan snorted and swerved from the brush bordering the lane. Startled awake, she saw a shadow move beyond the tangle of leaves and, hauling back on the reins, called out, "Who's there?"

The limbs shook and a wildly bearded face appeared among the leaves. "Mrs. Sensabaugh?" asked a rusty voice. "Praise the Lord, remember me? I hope I didn't scare you none, ma'am."

"Willy? Is it you?" She recalled the ragged figure that had lunged for her horse when that drunken mob in New Church frightened poor Star. Now, as last time, Willy stroked the horse's neck and murmured to calm him.

"Yes'm." Wailing Willy, black clothes shiny with dirt and even more tattered than when she saw him months ago, craned to gaze up and down the empty lane before he edged closer along Dan's flank. "I heard your wagon and looked to see was it you," he whispered. "I wonder, ma'am, if maybe you got something to eat with you?"

She stared at the gaunt face with its prominent sunburned nose and black eyes that gazed back like a hopeful hound at the kitchen door. Then she fumbled beneath the wagon seat for the cloth that held the remains of her lunch. "Here's a little chicken and cornbread, Willy. It's all I do have."

"The good Lord provides! I thank you, ma'am." With a sound of gulping and a hissing nose, the man devoured the food almost as soon as it touched his grimy fingers.

Taken aback by the ferocity his eating, Lydia sought her bottle of tea. "Here, Willy, wash it down before you choke to death!"

"Mn." A hand webbed with dirt took the bottle. In seconds, the tea was gone and Willy's black fingernails were picking through his beard for crumbs to nibble. "I ain't et real food in so long!"

He held out the empty bottle in return. Lydia wagged her hand. "You keep it—it's yours now. Is life so harsh for you, Willy?"

Lydia tried to see the man beneath the hair and dirt and filthy clothes that had collected pine needles and dried grass along with various stains, snags, and Lord only knew what crawling things. His cheekbones poked out above the snarled gray and black whiskers that hid the lower part of his face. His lips fell in over missing teeth. Wild, straight hair wilted down to hide his ears and nape. From the frayed cuffs of his coat, red and bony wrists hinted at thin arms, and his stocking-less ankles were a mottle of unwashed patches of gray dirt on skin pink and raw from scratching.

"Oh, ma'am—first it was Squire Carswell and his Home Guard conscriptors after me. Now it's the Yankee soldiers in the days and woods-rovers in the nights. A body ain't safe staying more'n a day or two in one place. Hallelujah, I had me some plowing work over at Jack Town on Peter McFail's farm this spring, but nothing since then. And the varmints is scared so it's hard to snare anything tasty. There's snakes and turtles, praise the Lord, but I'm too scared to build a fire to cook them and they do be stringy and taste right strong, raw."

The words tumbled from the man's cracked lips as if having been stored for months, which they may have been. Lydia tried not to imagine the texture of raw turtle on her tongue. "Isn't Peter McFail a freeman? Up by Freeschool Marsh?"

"Yes'm. He put in another twenty acres this year—he got a almost sixty-acre farm, now! Says the Yankee army buys all the corn he can grow, so he give me work breaking the new ground. But ain't no work now—not till harvest, and that's a long time off. Usually I get through summer on rabbits and wild greens and such."

"Did you see Roger Bradshaw around the marsh? I was told he was up that way."

Willy nodded, his eyes shifting to some vague spot beside her.

"Is he in good health, Willy? I've been worried about him."

"Health? Well, yes'm, I reckon. He was sure busted up in the face, though—I didn't hardly know him when I first seen him. And he done grown a beard to hide it but it don't cover his nose none."

"Oh, poor man! I must do something for him!"

"I don't reckon he wants nothing from nobody. He stays mostly alone back in the marsh and don't want nobody around him. He run off from me, even. Scared me, he did, like he was crazy."

Lydia shook her head in sympathy. The heavy blow must have injured Roger's mind as well as his flesh. "You must show me where you found him, Willy."

The dark eyes shifted to stare past her other side. "I don't know—"

"I don't mean right now. In the near future."

"Oh. Yes'm."

Lydia inhaled cautiously against the man's odors and made up her mind. She could imagine Gretchen's shocked query. But Willy had come to her rescue during that drunken roistering in New Church, and plainly he was starving. "I could use some help at my place."

Behind the hair, the dark eyes blinked. "You want me to work for you?"

"Yes. I can't pay much, but it will include meals and a decent place to sleep."

"Lord be praised!"

Besides, poor Gretchen had finally complained about the pains in her back from heaving against the plow strap. Lydia told herself that she was doing this as much for Gretchen as for this unfortunate. "You may praise the Lord now, Willy. But before I let you set foot in my house or barn, I will expect you to worship a lot of hot water and soap.

"Ma'am?"

"When did you last bathe?"

"Well...Whenever it rains—mostly. Some, anyway."

ɔɔɔ

Gretchen's voice rose as Lydia had foreseen. "Him?"

Willy stood on one leg scratching his shin with his foot, and—perhaps—smiled at the girl. The gnarled hair made it hard to tell any expression, but the dark eyes looked happy and eager. Lydia had set the man as far from her as possible on the rear of the wagon, where, as Dan plodded on, his ripped shoes swung contentedly through the tall grass between the lane's tracks. Much of the trip had been accompanied by a lugubrious rendition of "Salvation's Joy"—at least that's what the words if not the nasal, wailing seemed to state. The hymn had, before she stopped counting, at least fifteen verses, and dragged to a quavering end only as they turned into the farmyard. Lydia, weary in mind, body, and ears, was in no mood to argue with Gretchen. "Heat water for a bath, please. Much water. He will eat only after he bathes."

"Ma'am, there ain't enough water in the Chesapeake to—"

"I will make certain it will be!"

"Yes'm."

They had Willy drag the laundry tub out of sight behind

the barn. By the time the fire under the wash-pot heated enough buckets of water, Lydia had rifled the storage trunk for some of her husband's clothes. But as they prepared the bath, Willy's joy slowly faded.

"Cleanliness is next to Godliness, Willy."

"Well, yes'm, but...well, Miz Sensabaugh...well..."

"You come here behind the barn, Willy. You will remove every rag of those filthy clothes. Then you will get in that tub and bathe thoroughly: hair, hide, and all—you will scrub yourself absolutely clean!"

"Well, ma'am, I never! I don't believe in—"

"You will scrub all over. Your hair and your beard until they squeak! Then you will put these on." She balanced her husband's folded clothes on a sawhorse beside the steaming tub. "When you are dressed, I will trim your hair."

"Miz Sensabaugh, I can't—" His broken shoes shuffled first one way, then another, as if the ground beneath them burned, and he looked longingly at the distant line of trees. "I don't think—"

"Gretchen," Lydia called toward the back porch. "Bring out a dinner plate: a gammon of ham with grits and lots of butter. Fresh collard greens with a boiled egg. A little extra gravy, if you please. And cornbread—hot off the stove."

"Oh, lordy!"

Disapproving and silent, Gretchen brought the heavy dish. Lydia halted her at the corner of the barn.

"You see that, Willy?"

"Oh, yes'm. I can even smell it!"

"While you smell it, know that if you intend to work for me you will bathe all over once a fortnight. And you will wash your hands and face before every meal. Now, you may leave here dirty and hungry, or you may remain here clean and well-fed. Make up your mind right now."

"Oh, Lord, help me."

"Right now! There are the woods, there's the wash tub, and there's the food. You decide, right this minute!"

The man groaned deeply and wiped a sleeve across the

beard that curled around his lips. Then his grime-blackened fingers fumbled at the buttons of his coat. The two ladies retired, taking the dish with them.

ⓔⓢⓔⓢ

"Well, that do beat all!" Gretchen stared at the man seated at the work table on the enclosed back porch. Scrubbed and shorn, he was dressed in clothes that, though hanging loosely on his thin frame, were clean. "With that skinny neck of his'n and his hair chopped off, I swear he looks just like a turkey-buzzard!"

Lydia, washing her hands once again in a pan of hot, soapy water that also soaked the scissors and comb, glanced at the man hunched over his plate. "That's unkind, Gretchen—to me for my lack of tonsorial skill and to him for suffering the results." But the image fit, and she laughed softly. "I hope he doesn't make himself ill by eating so fast."

Willy rubbed the last corner of cornbread across the plate's shiny surface and popped it in his mouth. Then he lifted his closed eyes to the glare of May sun that filled the barnyard and chewed slowly. When his Adam's apple bobbed for the last time, he looked at the farmyard, at the barn and animal pens, the fields and lane, then around the enclosed back porch with its table, shelving, cabinets, and door to the bathing closet. Then he looked down at his fresh clothes and carefully unfolded himself to stand at the back door. With slender, gentle fingers, he brushed away each crumb from his coat. Hauling up his pants, he studied the shoes Lydia had provided. He tugged at the shirt, the coat collar, the sleeves, and shrugged the clothes into a semblance of fit. When he was ready, he rapped on the kitchen doorframe. "Miz Sensabaugh?"

She pretended she had not been watching. "Yes, Willy?"

"Praise the Lord, ma'am, and you for what you give me." He handed her his dish. "I'm ready to work now."

"All right. I'll get you started."

But the man didn't move. Something formed behind his eyes and he seemed to grope for words to express it.

"What is it, Willy?"

"I reckon it's these clothes, ma'am. I never had such, and I don't want to get them dirty. Would it be all right if I put on my old ones to work in?"

She gazed at the man's worried face. "That's very commendable, Willy. But we've burned your old clothes—they were too filthy and ragged to wash. Let me find some other clothes for you to work in. Then I'll show you your room and you may change."

As they walked to the barn, her husband's oldest and most worn shirt and trousers in Willy's arms, he half-whispered to her, "Ma'am, I ain't never had two sets of clothes before." His long fingers gently stroked the worn shirt as if the frayed cloth was an animal's fur. "And now a real room with a roof and all—just for me!" He lifted his face to the sky. "Ma'am, I will raise my voice in hallelujah!"

"Please don't frighten the pigs, Willy."

Chapter 18

Life at Marshfield flowed into the lengthy days of another summer. Willy took over the fieldwork, and Gretchen and Lydia sighed with relief from that burden. Perhaps Dan as well felt relief to work with an expert plowman because he pulled much faster. Or, as Gretchen opined, he wanted to escape "The Lord watches always and ever" sung behind him in wailing monotony. It was strange to once again share only the work around house and barn; it was an almost forgotten luxury to sit for a cup of precious coffee after the noon meal, or to have the time and strength to read in the evenings, or to take a long twilight sail in the *Lydia*.

Union patrols visited almost weekly. Sergeant Durgin, with a sly smile but without dismounting, would touch his finger to his hat brim and then water the soldiers' horses with never, as Gretchen said, a "by-your-leave or a thankee."

For weeks, no goods were hidden in the barn, and as July and August passed—busy with picking the corn as it ripened and carting it to Mr. Henderson for sale—Lydia felt a growing hope that Mr. Carswell's smuggling had been halted by the patrols and the picket ships on station in the Atlantic off Chincoteague and out in the Chesapeake.

On a late August afternoon, when storm clouds piled so

high their tops were painted red by the setting sun and thunder muttered and growled in the dark over the bay, Gretchen rode the wagon back from delivering the last of the corn and visiting her home. From the kitchen, Lydia saw Willy shuffle barefoot from the barn to unhitch Dan. Gretchen sat while Willy talked, but she made no gesture in reply. Then, bending from the waist as if her stomach pained, she slowly stepped down as Willy gaped at her.

"Gretchen? Are you all right?" Lydia came down the back steps, wiping flour from her hands. "What's the matter?"

"Oh, ma'am—" The girl's red eyes welled tears. Behind her, Willy mumbled into Dan's flicking ear and led him into the barn. "Allen Rafer's dead. Killed in a battle. Over near Richmond."

"Oh, Gretchen!"

The girl stumbled into Lydia's arms. "Humphrey wrote and said they fought the Yankees over on the Jamestown Peninsula last month." Her body wrenched with a silent sob. "He said it was awful—Allen Rafer—He said—" Her voice broke into gasps.

"Gretchen—shh, now. There, now." Lydia did not know what words she spoke or for how long. She let the low sound of her voice reach for the girl lost in her pain and rocked her gently to bring a semblance of comfort until the girl could be led into the house.

Gretchen finally fell asleep on the sofa, her teacup with its drops of laudanum half-empty. While she slept in the parlor, Lydia quietly finished making supper and then served Willie on the back porch.

"They're closing in, ma'am." The cropped beard on the man's lean jaw wagged with his chewing. "They be closer and closer."

"Who, Willy?"

"All them—in the woods." He waved an arm toward the distant trees whose gray, in the gathering dusk, had thickened to black.

Lydia stared at the forest that rose on the far side of the corn stalks. A whippoorwill called through the gloom, its three notes soft and furry with distance. The slow wink of fireflies drew sparks through the air. "Who do you mean?"

"Them that do things in the woods at night—the woods rovers. The ones why I didn't make no fires. The ones I seen but didn't see me."

"What do they do in the woods?"

The jaw stopped moving and he finally found the words. "Some go here, some go there. Fast and quiet. They don't want nobody seeing what they do, but I seen." He, too, gazed across the cornfield as if eyes stared back from the tree line.

"Were any of them in chains?"

He chewed four or five times and then stopped. "Some— yes'm. Before the Yankee soldiers come." Another chew. "Used to be, I'd hear them in the dark of the moon or maybe in the fog—the chains. Going down to the slough." His head tilted toward the pier.

"This slough?"

A nod.

"Who was it, Willy?"

"Slavers. Peter McFail over to Jack Town said they caught runaway niggers and stole free niggers, too. Said they sold them way south, where they couldn't never be found. Said anybody—white or black—coming on his farm to grab him or his'n gonna be shot dead." The bristly head bobbed. "He'd do it, too—Peter McFail is a free nigger and his whole family is free and his daddy was free. Said he'd kill whoever he had to, for his children to stay free."

"Who was stealing them? From where?"

The man shrugged and took another mouthful. "Mary-landers, maybe. Peter McFail said some doing it was even from around here."

"Who?"

The man's eyes shifted away. "Don't know."

"Are you certain? Willy?"

"Don't know. I don't know nothing."

"Did they put them on a boat, Willy? Did the slave-stealers take them down to this slough and put them on a boat?"

He nodded. "Only slough around. Use a ship's small boat. It come up the slough to the lamps."

"Two lamps? To guide the boat to a landing?"

He nodded and concentrated on finishing the food.

"Who, Willy? Who was doing that?"

"They kill me if I say. Kill me dead."

The man seemed to contract inside his clothes as if trying to disappear. He said no more, but he had explained those lights if not who lofted them above the fog. "Who is going through the woods now?"

"That was mighty good, ma'am. Could I trouble you for a little more cornbread and some molasses?"

She added to his plate. "What else did you see or hear, Willy?"

"Folks going here, folks going there. In the dark. In a hurry." He bit into a square of cornbread. "They scared all the varmints. Couldn't hardly snare nothing."

"Why do you say they're coming closer?"

He considered that, his torso rocking gently back and forth. "I can feel them."

"You can feel them?"

"Yes'm." He gathered together his plate, mug, and utensils and handed them to Lydia. "I can feel them," he said again. "I hope Miss Druer's feeling better. 'Night, ma'am."

After washing the supper dishes, Lydia settled in the parlor where Gretchen slept on the horsehair couch. She rocked gently as the room darkened. On the high ridge to the north, lightning spit somewhere beyond the Brown farm and distant thunder rumbled. Despite Willy's unsettling disclosures and her thoughts about them, the rhythm of the chair carried her into a light sleep. Finally, in the blackness, she heard a faint moan from the sofa.

"I'm here, Gretchen. Just a moment, I'll light a candle."

"Oh, ma'am!"

The glow showed her propped on her elbows to look around in puzzlement.

"It's all right—you needed sleep. Now you need to eat. I'll fetch some supper, you just stay there."

"Oh."

The meal was no longer warm, but the girl ate hungrily. Lydia restrained any questions except to ask if she wanted more.

"No, ma'am, but thank you. I didn't know I was so hungry."

"Food and rest are good medicine, dear. When you feel better, I would like to hear what happened."

The girl sighed heavily, but at least there was now color in her cheeks.

"I don't know that I'll ever feel better. But I can talk about it now."

"Only if it doesn't distress you, Gretchen."

The girl stared at the candle flame reflecting in the varnish of the dinner table. "I reckon I want to talk about it, ma'am." Her body shuddered as she drew a long breath. "He was killed—Allen Rafer—in some big fight called Seven Days Battle. Over near Richmond. Humphrey wrote Mama about it. Allen Rafer was standing right beside him. The Yankees were set up on a Malvern's hill and they attacked them again and again, and a lot were shot. Humphrey said he was happy to come out of it with a whole skin and a hole in his hat, and he reckoned the whole company got all the hard knocks they been asking for."

"Anyone else killed, Gretchen?"

She wagged her head. "Said six were killed but he only named two: Allen Rafer and James Harmonson—he was elected second lieutenant just three months ago. From over near Assateague Island. Said Arthur Beloate was knocked out by a Minnie ball, whatever that is, but he's okay now, and Billy Taylor got lost when they were marching through some swamps and missed the whole fight and hasn't shown up for roll call since."

"Thank the Lord no more were killed."

"Amen." The girl stifled another tremor with a deep breath. "I went by Mr. Brown's farm on the way here. I went to tell Lucy that I was sorry for her—and I am, Miz Sensabaugh. I truly am!"

"I know, Gretchen. I know."

"Turns out nobody had told them about it yet." Gretchen shook her head. "Oh, ma'am, I had to be the one to tell them! I said 'I'm sorry' and Mrs. Brown said 'What for?' and I said 'You mean you ain't heard?' and so then they made me tell them! And Lucy just screamed and fainted dead away. I kept telling Miz Brown how sorry I was and she just said 'Lord's will be done' and 'He's gone to a better place.' And Lucy woke up and was just wild crazy—I never seen anything like it, not even Roger Bradshaw, her eyes was just as big, and looking all around and she kept saying 'He'll be back, he promised me he'll be back, he wrote me so'"

The girl broke into sobs. Lydia wrapped her arms around her. "There, now, Gretchen—"

"She said I was glad! Lucy Brown said that. Said I was glad to be the one to tell them because I was jealous, and no matter what I said, Allen would come home."

"She was out of her head with grief, Gretchen. She didn't know what she was saying."

"That's what Miz Brown said, too, but it still hurt—it hurts now just thinking on it!"

"Well, don't think on it! Lucy was striking out in pain and you were at hand."

Gretchen did not answer but only stared at the candle. A gust of wind from the dark made the flame jump, and a night insect thumped softly against its glass chimney.

Then she spoke as much to herself as to Lydia. "I guess maybe I still thought he'd change his mind when he came back."

Lydia nodded. "You suffer his death, too."

"Yes'm. I reckon Lucy Brown don't like that, neither." Her voice turned bitter, "And I don't know how not to think on that."

"There's no need to inform her. Perhaps in time she'll find some comfort in knowing that you loved him too—that her loss is shared."

"I doubt that." She looked up, her eyes sad and swollen. "There's worse."

"Worse?"

"Lucy—she's three months gone."

It took a moment for Lydia to comprehend. "Lucy Brown is going to have a baby?"

Gretchen nodded. "Somehow Allen Rafer got home on a fishing boat about the time the Yankees took Norfolk. He couldn't stay long, but he stayed long enough. To see Lucy." A forlorn wish crossed the girl's face, and Lydia read it.

"It is going to be very, very hard for Lucy," Lydia warned. "It would be hard for any girl in that situation."

"I do reckon. Miz Brown says Mr. Brown don't know anything of it. But she don't know how much longer they can keep it from him. And when he does find out, she don't know what he'll do—Lucy's the youngest and his favorite." Another slow shake of her head. "And Mr. Brown is a proud man—he fought a duel when he was younger. Killed a man."

"My lord!"

"Yes'm."

Chapter 19

"Two letters come for you! One made it up from Georgia and the other's from that lieutenant." Gretchen shook the cold October rain from her oilcloth and hung it on one of the pegs near the back door. She held her hands to the warmth of the kitchen stove. "My folks got a letter from Humphrey—it said his company's now called Company F of the Forty-Sixth Virginia, but it don't say where they're at. I stopped by your Mama's, Lucy. She's fine and sends her love and says she'll be over in the next day or two."

Lucy Brown, cheeks red from the heat of the stove where cornbread and yams baked in the oven beside the firebox, stood close to Lydia. It was, Gretchen had noted, where she often stood since Mrs. Brown, disheveled, almost babbling, had ridden into the dark farmyard with the girl wrapped and moaning on the seat beside her. "Miz Sensabaugh—in the name of God, Miz Sensabaugh—please don't turn us away!"

"Away! Of course not. Come in—get down and come in, both of you. Gretchen, make some tea. Please hurry!"

"Mr. Brown—" The older woman's voice caught and she fell against Lydia as she was helping Lucy from the bouncing wagon seat. "He drove her off—Lucy. I told him about the baby, and—"

"Hush, now. Let's get her inside where it's warm. We'll talk inside—shhhhh."

Mrs. Brown stumbled into the kitchen where Gretchen, frowning with concern, hurriedly pumped water into the kettle and stirred up the fire in the stove.

Lydia whispered to Gretchen, "Please ask Willy to take care of Mrs. Brown's horse. I'll settle them in the parlor."

"Yes'm."

Gradually, under the influence of the tea, of the quiet room, and the touches of sympathy, a coherent story came out. "We couldn't hide it no more, and Mr. Brown, he's been suspicious for a while already."

"He knows it was Allen Rafer?"

"He does now. I told him they were going to get married but he didn't care. Crazy mad," she explained. "Lucy's been his favorite. The youngest. But he just kept saying she's dead to him. She's dead to him now."

"I don't think he meant that, Mrs. Brown."

"He meant it. He might change his mind in time, but he meant it when he said it, and he meant it when he told her to leave his house. 'It's no longer your home,' he said. 'Yours and your bastard's.'"

"What is she to do?"

"Lord, I don't know!" The woman began weeping again, silently, dabbing the corners of her eyes with a small hand-kerchief. "It's not that I question the will of the Almighty, but He does sometimes make things hard to understand." Beside her, Lucy moaned and leaned her head in her hands.

"Gretchen, take Lucy up to my bed. The poor thing's exhausted."

"Yes'm."

Mrs. Brown watched the two girls disappear up the stairs before murmuring, "He told me he'd kill her if she ever came back—her and her bastard both."

"He wouldn't!"

The gray head nodded. "In his anger, yes. He's a proud man, Mrs. Sensabaugh. He fought a duel when he was younger." She said again, "And Lucy was his favorite."

"Trust me, Mrs. Brown, if there's any love at all in your husband's heart—and how could there not be for his daughter?—he will repent his harshness and welcome her back."

"I pray that's so. Oh sweet Jesus I pray that's so."

"Meanwhile, let Lucy stay with me. She'll be out of Mr. Brown's sight, but close enough for you to visit. And the girl's in no condition to travel farther."

Mrs. Brown stared at her, then her face sagged into a grimace of tears. She tried to thank Lydia, but she could only sob with a mixture of gratitude, relief, and exhaustion.

eↄeↄ

A rub of irritation made Gretchen's voice tighten. "Your pa didn't say nothing, Lucy. He didn't send you greetings, either, ma'am."

"Ohhh—"

Lydia looked up from the envelopes. "Gretchen, please! Lucy, strengthen yourself."

"Well she hates me!" Lucy shouted weakly. "She's jealous because—"

"I am not!"

"Ladies—both of you! Gretchen, will you please step into the parlor with me?"

Sullenly, the girl followed as Lydia closed the door. "I invited Lucy here, Gretchen. She is our guest and she needs our support in a very difficult situation."

"Well, I didn't invite her." Gretchen's voice rose on the edge of tears. "I wasn't even asked!"

That was true, and Lydia should not have followed her impulse to charity without at least telling Gretchen first. "I knew you would not deny her shelter, Gretchen." It was a lame explanation. "We have the extra room and you have a generous heart, and it never crossed my mind that you would not agree. Now, since we must share this roof until the baby comes, we will make the best of it, and that does not allow for bickering."

"Well, I'm not jealous of her! It's just she acts so...so mousy! She's always hanging on your skirts. I swan, Miz Sensabaugh, it's not that I don't like her for carrying Allen Rafer's baby, it's just she's got no gumption!"

"She's a child herself. It would be much different if they had been married. But her child will have no father, as may she. And the only home either one has right now is this one. Charity, Gretchen—in this imperfect world we must have charity toward each other."

A hot breath sounded in the girl's nose. "Yes'm. But it would be a lot easier to have charity if she'd just...I don't know...if she'd just stand up on her own two feet instead of hanging on to you like a pickaninny!"

It crossed Lydia's mind that Gretchen was jealous not only of Allen Rafer but also of her—that to the older girl, Lucy not only triumphed with Allen, but now invaded the home and friendship she shared with Lydia. She set the precious letters on the mantle until after the meal, and, patting the girl's arm, focused on making peace. "Come, Gretchen, let's have supper. For the short time that Lucy's here, please keep in mind that anger has no place at our table." She led the sullen girl back into the kitchen.

Later, Lydia asked the two girls to clean the dishes so she could read her letters. A full stomach eased anger, she knew, and sharing work might lead them toward some accommodation, no matter how tenuous. Stirring the fireplace logs into flame, she wrapped a quilt around her legs, then, lighting a candle, settled down to read by the gleam reflected from its pewter backplate. She opened the envelope from Georgia first, setting Captain Morse's letter aside both for the pleasure of suspense as well as for her undivided attention. She had recognized Bonnie's hand with relief, having no news since the Yankees captured Norfolk City over six months past. But the ornately patterned envelope was odd, and its corner held a scrawl that, with some effort, she made out as "Geor" and "CSA" and "10C." The return address said *Mangrum Plantation, Near Traders Hill, Charlton County, Georgia, June 13, 1862.* Her sister's words, after informing Lydia of their flight south to escape the Yankees, explained the strange envelope.

Paper, dear Lydia, is in short supply, along with coffee, salt, muslin, medicines, sugar and almost everything else you can think of or want. Although Andrew brings a few necessities and even delicacies with him when he visits, he cannot provide much since all the space aboard his vessel is devoted to those cargoes which will contribute to the welfare of our army. My writing paper, which I buy from the Postmaster already franked, is adapted from wall paper, and don't you find it stylish? Wheat flour is going for near $100 a barrel, so we of course use cornmeal and relish both the flavor and the thought of saving so much cash. The more we eat, the richer we grow! I have seen receipts for making gloves out of tanned dog skin, as well as shoe blacking concocted from molasses, soot, neat's-foot oil and vinegar. And you would be surprised at how good our coffee is. One flavor is made from dried and roasted sweet potatoes, and another more robust flavor from roasted cotton seeds. Or, if your palate is more delicate, you may have sassafras tea. If this ink appears strange, know that it is a mix of pokeberry juice and copperas from Uncle Louis' mineral spring, and it works just fine! We do without, but we do so in good spirits because everything goes to the army. Our soldiers are suffering terribly, many without shoes or enough to eat. 'Spartans,' we call them, and certainly Spartan is their life. When this terrible war is over, we will have no trouble living without Yankee luxuries. Then they can starve for want of a market for them!

It pains me to write that Cousin Edward was killed

at a battle near Seven Pines in Virginia, and Cousin Albert wounded. He is alive but in a Richmond hospital, though Uncle Louis has not yet had a letter from him. The son of a neighbor who is also in the Forty-Fourth Georgia wrote his parents and asked them to tell Uncle Louis. Both he and Aunt Julia mourn deeply and find what consolation they can in the thought that Edward is with the Savior and that his exemplary life on this earth has surely won him a place in heaven.

The pain and darkness I see in their life makes me ashamed of bewailing the mere loss of my home in Norfolk. It is a time of sacrifice and of submitting to God's Will in the trust that our Cause will triumph despite the legions of the Oppressor who threatens us. I thank God that Andrew my husband and the father of my children is safe. I received a letter from him this morning, which made me aware of my deleteriousness in writing you. He sails under a British Flag out of Nassau for those ports along the Atlantic that are still under our Flag. Sometimes it is Jacksonville and then he may have a chance to visit the plantation, and my Dear Lydia, I cannot tell you how ecstatic and precious those all too brief visits are for me. But it pains me to see the changes in him from the man who wooed and married me. Alas, so many of our ports have fallen to the enemy that now the Yankee patrols are heaviest off those few harbors of mercy that are left. Andrew writes that they pray for storms and fog to slip past the picket boats to the protection of the harbor guns, and are very grateful when the Lord provides them. He says nothing of the dangers he faces, but I am fully aware that the weather in which he is safest from the enemy is that which holds the most threat for seamen. All I can do is pray that he remains safe and that he does not change too much during those long periods he is separate from us.

*And now I see that I have crammed about as many
words as I can onto this elegant if small sheet. But I
do save room to express my hope that all is well with
you and that you have found an island of comfort and
peace in this ocean of pain and loss. Please write,
even though I know the difficulty of posting letters out
of those lands the enemy occupies. You have no idea
how precious letters have become. Waiting to hear
from you, I remain Your Loving Sister Bonnie.*

Lydia read the letter a second and a third time. Then she
sat in quiet sadness. Dampness chilled her shoulders despite
the wool shawl and the fire at her feet. Truly, her own losses
were behind her. She sat before her own fire. The harvest,
thanks to Mr. Dupont, had been very good, and she had a
favorable balance with Mr. Henderson. In comparison to the
losses suffered by Uncle Louis and Bonnie and so many
others, she was very fortunate.

In the kitchen, the girls made small, domestic noises that
promised peace at least for this evening. Upstairs, the rain
drummed steadily on the shingles, and from the puddles under the eaves came the irregular counterpoint of individual
drops. They were comforting sounds that emphasized both
the warmth and quiet of her home, as well as the shape of
life with its large harmonies and individual variations. Lydia listened and pondered the emblematic quality of nature's
music. Truly, her reading of Mr. Emerson was making her
quite transcendental, and it was an idea she would have to
remember to include in her reply to Captain Morse's letter.

She felt a twinge of guilt for her reluctance to inform
Bonnie about him, a guilt that was not assuaged by the
thought that there wasn't really anything of substance to tell
her sister. After all, she did not even know Captain Morse's
first name. A more pertinent source of her guilt should be
for enjoying, without consideration, things that were now
dreamed-of luxuries to Bonnie: coffee, sugar, salt, and even
paper to write on. And what Emersonian compensation did

nature provide her sister for those deprivations? Or her uncle and aunt for the loss of their son? That thought gave her new perspective on the contraband Parnell Carswell stored in her barn: those goods went to soldiers who needed so much and were supplied by the sacrifices of people like her kin in Georgia who had so little.

Finally, sighing deeply, she re-folded the brightly patterned fragment of brittle wallpaper into its envelope shape and turned to the letter from Captain Morse. This postal mark clearly stated "Washington" and the frank—August thirtieth—was over nine weeks old. The return address was the Fifty-First N. Y. S. V., at its location Near Fort Columbia.

It began, as had all his letters, with *My Dear Mrs. Sensabaugh,* but then, following a dash, offered an amendment that made her catch her breath.

> *...or, unless you forbid me, My Dear Lydia. I discover that in reading and re-reading your letters, and in expressing myself to you, I find my mind intimately entwined with yours. It is an intimacy that, to me at least, is not only a heretofore unexperienced delight but also a basis for the use of your name, Lydia. If you do not wish me to address you by that name, merely say so. I will of course accede. But merely writing the name Lydia brings gladness to my heart as well as an ache to say your name aloud. To say it to everyone and especially to say it to you, Lydia.*
>
> *I apologize for the shakiness of my hand. It is a very weary hand, grateful to still be attached to its arm. We have marched and fought, and marched and fought again, and my once fresh fish have "seen the elephant" of war. It is more terrible than any I witnessed in the Indian Nations, and I confess to being made sick at so many wounded and dead. Surely God must have His reasons for this slaughter, but I am*

convinced it would tax even Mr. Emerson to justify
such pain. Certainly, it is far beyond the understanding of this mere soldier.

Marching toward Richmond we entrenched ourselves atop a ridge called Turkey Hill. Late in the afternoon, regts from North Carolina and Virginia attacked. They charged through our bullets and cannon
fire to within yards of our entrenchments. But they
came no further. Those left alive turned and ran, our
grape and canister killing more. We then gathered
powder and shot from our own wounded and dead.
Those wounded who could walk I sent to the rear,
bearing those who could not walk. A few healthier
soldiers suddenly discovered much tender feeling for
the injured and begged me to allow them to carry
their friends out of harm's way. But I would not, since
they could manage without three or four solicitous
and able bodied assistants, and we would manage
much better if those able bodies stayed to fight. The
Rebels charged again with their peculiar high
screams.

But our boys held and broke their lines. When they
formed up and charged once more, we ran short of
powder and shot. They reached our line and pushed
through as far as the provost pickets. Our artillery
ceased fire for fear of killing our own, and with that
the 'running fever' infected those on both our flanks.
To the credit of my battns, we fell back in orderly
fashion. Though we lost Turkey Hill, we managed to
keep firing as we withdrew and like the Scythian cost
the enemy dearly for his victory. I counted twelve
lives lost from both battns. Twenty-three were wounded, many, I am sure, mortally.

Even now my face feels hot and dry from powder
smoke. I am still weary in body and soul and must
apologize again for this execrable penmanship. As I
hear a runner calling my name, I must continue this

letter later.

A new paragraph was headed *Harrisons Landing, August 12, 1862:*

> *Our loss of Turkey Hill is being called the reason for our retreat. We had victory at Malvern's Hill but withdrew here to the James River and the protection of our gunboats because Genl McClellan fears our army is no longer strong enough to overcome the combined Rebel armies. On To Richmond has become Leave Richmond Alone. Presently, we rest under canvas, our supply wagons have found us, and we await the transport boats that will take us back to Washington. I confess chagrin that we did not hold against the enemy at Turkey Hill. But had we stayed when those on either side of us fled we would have been made prisoners. Nonetheless, I feel shame at the loss and am determined that no lack of training nor of personal courage will ever be the cause of defeat for any regt I serve.*

Another abrupt transition was headed *Later,* and the handwriting was stronger.

> *My Dear Lydia, I have written only of those events which have filled my days, and now I must post this with the adjt. before we board our transport. Please know that other events, now seeming far distant, have made these days worthwhile. Despite the deep weariness of war and loss and the constant marches, my thoughts are steadily with you—as is my heart. I have become intensely aware that true value is neither in the so called glories of war nor the winning of riches, but in the love between a man and a woman who are united in soul and spirit. Certainly, I long for the early defeat of your country and for the victory of mine— but please believe it is not out of enmity between us,*

*but because of those convictions which you know, and
because the sooner this war ends, the fewer men, Rebel and Loyal, will die. And the sooner I can find myself riding down the lane to Marshfield and, I profoundly hope, to you.* The signature was *Yours affec-
tionately, Simon Morse.*

Simon. The "S" stood for Simon. She tried the name on
her tongue while she re-read his letter. Then, staring
through the window into the darkness, she thought how
strange it was that paper and ink stirred a deeper feeling
than had the presence of their author. It made her wonder if
her destiny was to find greater life in the abstract idea of a
suitor than in the concrete man—she knew now that it had
not been Franklin himself that she had loved so long ago,
but her private vision of him.

After months of marriage when that vision faded and reality had slowly taken its place, she discovered that, despite
her own denials, what she felt on the eve of her marriage
had been...delusional. That the love molded subsequent to
her marriage was no longer the heady excitement of courtship but an acceptance of faults. And the duties of marriage,
mysterious and frightening at first, became functional ac-
quiescence to Franklin's abrupt and even preemptory demands, demands that became biweekly, monthly, and finally, as his attempts at business ventures demanded more and
more of his energy, rare—to her secret relief. She had tried
not to show that relief. To do so would have hurt Franklin.
It was a sign of her failure as a wife—and was the reason,
no doubt, they had no children. Now she found her imagina-
tion using this man's letters to once more generate an object
of love.

She was, she chastised herself, a woman who loved
words more than the speaker of those words. And what
would happen when Simon appeared in the flesh and was no
longer masked by the aura of those words?

The girls came into the parlor and settled before the fire

to knit or page once more through the latest *Washington
Star*. Lydia opened her writing box to reply.

> *My Dear Simon—for it is true we have come to
> know each other on a basis this familiar—I have read
> and re-read your letter dated August 30 which has
> only now arrived, and will find pleasure, gratitude,
> and fear in reading it yet again. Pleasure in having
> heard from you, gratitude that you have survived a
> terrible fight, fear that you will face such again. So
> much time has passed since you have written this let-
> ter, and so many battles and deaths have been report-
> ed in the newspapers, that I pray for your safety—as
> well as the safety of my loved ones who are your "re-
> bel" enemies.*

Not that Bonnie would thank her for such a prayer.

> *Here, lingering summer has passed into a rainy
> October, and our labors are focused on Mr. Mason's
> jars and the filling thereof as sustenance through the
> coming winter.*

Lydia re-read that with dislike for its affected tone and
diction, and focused her effort on plain speech.

> *You may remember I wrote you of "Wailing Wil-
> ly." Well, he has turned into a respectable farm hand
> and, with the redoubtable Dan, contributed to the first
> profitable harvest that Marshfield has enjoyed. We
> will plant twice as much corn in the Spring, since talk
> in New Church is that grain prices will go even high-
> er. My neighbors are already calculating good profits
> for the coming Summer.*

And that sentence, Captain Morse—Simon—would find
about as interesting as the price of eggs in China.

> *We also have a new resident, a forlorn child of fif-*
> *teen who awaits the birth of her own child. The ba-*
> *by's father was killed at one of the places you name—*
> *Malvern Hill—and did not take time to wed the girl.*
> *Her father has disowned her and, for her mother's*
> *sake, I have offered refuge until the child is born.*
> *Perhaps you remember the Brown farm? The one on*
> *the north ridge above Marshfield? The girl is Lucy*
> *Brown, and I worry for the future of her and her child.*

Lydia paused, then decided not to write of Gretchen's jealousy and the cause of it.

> *I read of the Second Battle of Bull Run, as well as*
> *of General Lee moving into Western Maryland, but I*
> *have not seen your Fifty-First New York State Volun-*
> *teer regiment mentioned. I can only hope that you are*
> *not involved in those battles. I know how busy you*
> *must be, and you must know how much I appreciate*
> *the precious time you take to write to me.*

Lydia pondered the sentence that next came to mind, wondering if it would seem too forward. But Simon had written from the heart—she could feel the sincerity of his words—and his definition of true value was derived from a shocking and painful perception of the loss of so many men. Surely, she, too, could speak with as much honesty. When she had written of that honest emotion, she read the inked words over with even greater conviction.

> *When you write of riding down the lane to Marsh-*
> *field, I find myself scarcely constrained from going to*
> *the window to stand vigil for you. I pray, Simon, that*
> *my vigil may be rewarded.*

Chapter 20

Near the end of the week, the rain eased from steady drizzle to intermittent showers. In the gray of a cloudy morning, Lydia was first into the kitchen. She placed wood shavings in the warm ashes and gently blew them into a bright fire, then put the large coffee pot on the black iron stove to heat. Gretchen came down to set the table; Lucy still slept.

"Would you call Willy, please? Tell him the coffee's hot."

"Yes'm." Gretchen shrugged into her oilcloth and clumped down the stairs to the stepping-stones that led through the muddy yard to the barn.

After some time, Lucy came into the kitchen wrapped in a quilt and stood blinking sleepily in the stove's heat while Lydia finished stirring the grits. She was on the verge of going to the barn herself when she heard Gretchen return. "Ma'am—"

"What is it, Gretchen?"

"He's not there." Rain dripped from her cape onto the porch floor. "He's gone. There's stuff been put in there—" She glanced at Lucy. "—you know, they come last night, I reckon. But Willy's nowheres around."

"You called for him?"

"I called. I climbed the ladder and looked. I even knocked on the outhouse door. He's gone."

The rain had covered the sounds of contraband being unloaded last night. But in the barn, Willy would have heard the noises just below his room. "Is Dan there?"

"Yes'm. But he wasn't fed, so I took care of that."

They ate breakfast while it was hot, then Lydia shrugged into her gum cape. Dan, munching in his trough, snorted hello and she murmured compliments to him in return. But her eyes were on the tarp that formed a lumpy mound, and her mind was on the missing man.

"Willy?"

Her voice sank into the earth and the barn's damp walls. She climbed the rungs to the loft and called again, this time perfunctorily. Willy's room waited his return. His "good" suit hung on pegs placed in the wall, but his work pants and shirt were gone, as was the square of oiled sailcloth he used for a rain cape. The quilt on his straw mat was flung back as if he had just arisen. His good shoes were placed under the suit. A fringe of mud had stiffened above their soles. His washbasin and drinking mug were dry but the pitcher held water. The flannel cloth he used for a towel was dry.

Lydia tried to read signs in the wet earth around the barn. But too many boots had churned the mud, and the chickens, feathers drooping with rain, had crossed and re-crossed the soil to cover it in twiggy prints filled with water. While Gretchen milked Tessie, Lydia shook grain onto the dry floor of the barn for the scrambling birds, gave Dan a second scoop of oats, and stared across the wet fields toward the gray tree line as if it might reveal something. But there was only the drip of rain, a brief squabble of jaybirds in the trees, the melancholy croak of a crow flying overhead through the wet.

Tugging the stiff canvas, she revealed some of the boxes and hogsheads that Mr. Carswell's men had stored last night. Cryptic marks, abbreviations, and labels were inked on the rough wood of slats and staves. She could make out three

crates that said "Fortnum & Mason," and most of the hogsheads were labeled with the name of a distillery in Jamaica.
Another crate held "Willis Finest Soap," while two more
were marked "Bradley & Sons, Clothiers." She did not find
any boxes or barrels warning that they held munitions or
implements of war; rather all seemed the kind of luxuries
that Bonnie had been proud to eschew. But Carswell did not
govern which ships made it to Virginia's shore, and certainly the men in the army deserved what luxuries could be
smuggled in. Replacing the tarp, she tried to think where
Willy might have gone.

࿎࿎࿎

Like Roger Bradshaw, like Star, Willy had simply vanished. It recalled her mother's observation that stray dogs
stayed where they were cared for only as long as the call of
adventure was mute. But when it spoke—as it always did—
the wandering dog set forth again, and there was no help for
it. Perhaps Willy had answered the call of a life of unattached drifting. Perhaps Carswell's people had frightened
the timid man when they brought their shipment into the
barn. If so, he might return when the scare was over.

But as days passed, the thought nagged that Willy might
be neither safe nor warm, nor have enough to eat. That worry re-generated her concerns for Roger Bradshaw as well,
and led her on a magnificently crisp October day to heave
blanket and saddle on Dan's patient back and ride north
over the ridge and along the wide marshes that bordered
Pocomoke Sound. Seaward, the cordgrass stretched in an
autumn yellow as far as the horizons.

The breeze from the Chesapeake, clean and chill, made
the sun's warmth all the more welcome. Overhead, the sky
held that deeper blue that occurs in late fall, as if the cooling
air had rid itself of summer's dust. Only a few brushstrokes
of feathery clouds hung so high that they seemed gossamer

webs. It was a glorious day of scarlet oak and yellow beech blossoming among the dark of pines. But given the purpose of her trip, Lydia felt almost guilty about enjoying the lovely mix of cold air and warm sun, as well as the vast, clean openness of the marshes whose channels and rivulets were bright flashes in the carpet of grass.

Nonetheless, nature's beauty, she told herself, was God's medicine for a burdened spirit, and, guilt or no, it was a desperately needed balm for the worries of the latest war news. Gretchen had brought her father's well-thumbed copy of the weekly *Delaware Gazette and Peninsula Advertiser* and Lydia had read its reports collected from other newspapers about a recent battle near Sharpsburg. It was a town in Western Maryland *in which the Army of the Potomac has once again been victorious, and which exceeds in extent any battle heretofore fought on this continent.* The names of the generals—Lee and Jackson, Hooker and Sumner, Burnside and Porter—had been used by the writer instead of the numbers of regiments and brigades. When her eye lit on McClellan's name, Lydia's heart stumbled as if suddenly gripped in a fist. McClellan commanded Captain Morse and his regiment, and, as the article went on, her heart's constriction had grown tighter:

It is impossible at this time to form any correct idea of our loss or that of the enemy, but it is heavy on both sides. Ours will probably reach in killed and wounded 10,000. That of the enemy will not exceed it.

Such a number surpassed her ability to comprehend. It was as if there were not enough names or even faces for those thousands and thousands and thousands of dead and wounded. Indeed, she was ashamed to acknowledge that the absence of Roger Bradshaw and now of Willy brought a far deeper ache than the shock of those impossible numbers. But should—God forbid—Simon Morse lie among them, her feeling of loss would become sharp enough, she knew.

The soft clop of Dan's hooves and the faint whisper of wind across the cordgrass intensified the loneliness. Under the brilliant autumn sun, the view seemed a lovely painting that offered escape from thoughts of the suffering and anxiety that lay somewhere beyond the western horizon. *Carpe diem.* Enjoy this beauty and peace. Winter soon will be upon us, she told herself, and days like this will be but memories. But for this moment, in this place, this beauty is here to be relished. Seize it, for nothing is permanent, all is change, and this, too, will pass.

The admiration of nature's glory mixed with the pang of its mutability rode with her to the scattering of small houses and shanties that made up Jack Town. The exposed, sandy rise between Pocomoke Sound and Freeschool Marsh had been bought in years past by a freedman named Jack. Like Topsy, the shanties had just grown over the decades until now a dozen or so homes were scattered along the wind-blown coastal ridge. On the water side, rowboats were pulled up into sea grass above the tide; on the marsh side, reeds and hummocks bushy with autumnal bayberry stretched to a distant dark line formed by loblolly pines growing on firmer land. When Lydia reached the sandy lane, dogs set up a howling wail and Dan, uneasy at the sound, snorted.

"There, boy. Settle down, Dan." She patted his withers and clucked him toward the nearest shanty. Its walls were made of driftwood logs and varicolored boards capped by bleached shingles. A white-haired black man rose from a sun-cracked tree stump to squint toward her.

"Good morning, Uncle." Lydia drew Dan to a halt. "I'm looking for Peter McFail's farm. Can you direct me to it?"

The wrinkled black face gaped at her to show a tooth or two. At one edge of the doorway behind him, two small faces peeked out, one eye each. The roundness of the eyes testified to the rarity of visitors, especially white visitors.

"Peter McFail," she said again and wondered if the old man were hard of hearing. She spoke louder. "I wish to find the farm of Peter McFail."

"Heyo, miss!" A woman stepped around the shanty's

corner, her head wrapped in a red bandanna. "Who all you after, miss?"

"Peter McFail. I'm looking for his farm."

Her bulbous eyes, pupils almost luminous in their dark irises, stared back. "You that new lady lives over at Marshfield? The one whose husband's died?"

Later, Lydia would wonder at the woman's knowledge of her, while she herself had lived in ignorance of this black settlement. And she would wonder at how much other ignorance she bore. "Yes—Mrs. Sensabaugh. And you are…"

"Emma. Emma Crippen. *Miz* Emma Crippen."

"Well, Emma Crippen, can you direct me to the Peter McFail farm?"

"It's about a mile over yonder." A long hand flapped toward the marsh "What you want with him?"

"I want to discover if he knows the whereabouts of Mister Roger Bradshaw or the poor unfortunate called Wailing Willy."

"He that white man sometime works for him? The crazy one?"

Lydia nodded. "Have you seen either of them?"

The woman's bulging eyes blinked. "Why you want them?"

Lydia had heard stories of the secretiveness of both black and white who lived in isolated villages and islands along this coast.

The former, rumor went, because escaped slaves on their way north often found shelter near places like this; the latter because they often made their living beyond laws that governed smuggling, distilling, and—at a not too distant time— causing shipwrecks with false beacons.

"They have worked for me in the past, and I wish to discover if they are in need of assistance."

The thick toes on the woman's left foot dug absently at the gray sand speckled with broken oyster shells. Then the red turban bobbed. It wasn't uncommon for an employer to help a good worker in a time of trouble.

"Zekial'l show you." She lifted her chin to call, "Zekial! You, Zekial—come here!"

A boy of about ten or twelve stepped into view from behind the other corner. Despite the chill wind, he wore only a ragged flannel shirt and gallused pants that frayed out halfway down his skinny legs. "Yes'm?"

"This here's Miz Senzbaw. She live down on Fowler Creek—you know the place?"

"Yes'm." The boy did not look directly at the white woman, but she was visible from the corner of a dark eye that, like his mother's, bulged out.

"She want to go to Mr. McFail's farmhouse. That's where you going to take her, understand?"

"Yes'm."

"And then you come straight back here and finish your chores—you better understand that, too."

"Yes'm."

The woman turned to Lydia. "He take you."

"Thank you, Miz Emma Crippen—I'm much obliged."

Zekial glanced at her before beginning to walk quickly ahead of Dan's bobbing head. In two minutes they had cleared the packed sand that served the village as a lane and were following a path that wound along hummocks leading into Freeschool Marsh.

"Is it very far, Zekial?"

"No'm. Just over yonder." He pointed toward the treetops. Near-by, in the head-high, brown reeds, redwing blackbirds croaked and hopped and fluttered.

"Have the Yankee soldiers visited Jack Town?"

One eye looked back over a bony shoulder. "Just once't. Wasn't nothing for them to steal so they ain't been back."

"To steal! I hear they liberate Nigras from slavery."

"We free—been free. Don't need no liberation. They say they looking for contraband." A wag of his elongated head. "What's that 'contraband'?"

"Goods and food for the Confederate army—stuff people want to smuggle to the mainland to help the Confederacy."

"Oh." The trail turned boggy, and the reeds now rose almost as tall as Lydia's hat. "They say they give us a reward if we tell them about any contrabands."

Lydia hesitated before asking, "Have any of your people seen any?"

"No'm. But they axed us if we was contrabands. I don't know if we gets a reward for telling them about us—they already know about us. But I sure don't want to go over to the mainland."

"I think they were using the term loosely."

"Ma'am?"

"Perhaps they thought you were runaway slaves."

"We ain't—we free! My grandpa got papers says so!"

"I know that, Zekial." The trail twisted sharply and rose again to a mound of higher ground. "I'm grateful that you're guiding me. I would surely be lost without your help."

"Yes'm. But ain't but one good path, so it ain't all that hard."

"For you, perhaps." She studied him. "Do you know of any freemen who have disappeared?"

Again the boy glanced back, this time frowning slightly. "They say Tabitha Chesser been gone. Nobody knows where—she just didn't come home."

"Where was this, Zekial?"

"Over near Shad Landing. She went out to the field, her momma say, and she never come back."

"When?"

"Last year about this time." He added, "Her momma's been looking and looking, but nobody's never found nothing."

"How old was she?"

"Ten, maybe."

"Oh, poor child—poor mother!"

"Yes'm."

"Was Sheriff Hope told?"

"Yes'm. He looked around real hard, but says the slave

catchers likely grabbed her. They do that, you know. Boy or girl go off alone in the woods near dark, the slave-catchers grabs them." His eyes showed a ring of white. "Hear stories like that all the time!"

"Are you frightened of slave catchers?"

Zekial strode ahead without answering. Finally, "Yes'm. I reckon so."

"Have you ever seen any?"

"No'm. Don't want to, neither." His voice dropped. "But one time I seen Marse Talbot and his dogs going through the woods looking for runaway niggers."

"Mr. Carswell's overseer?"

"Yes'm. They say he's always in the woods looking for runaways. Say he make a lot of money slave catching."

"Do they say he takes free people as well?"

Zekial did not answer immediately. "One time he stopped my Auntie Hannah. He didn't know who she was and she didn't have no pass—didn't need one 'cause she free. But he made her take him to her home to prove she wasn't no runaway. She was mighty scared."

"Does that happen often?"

His eyebrows jumped at her ignorance. "Stopping strange niggers? Sho—a body don't have papers or a iron tag say who they belong to or where they live, the paterollers gets them, sure!" He puffed out his chest. "But when I gets bigger, I won't be afraid. Slave catchers don't mess with full-grown mens. They afeard to mess with them cause of the law. Sheriff Hope, he gets hot about something like that!"

"Perhaps when you are grown, slavery will have been abolished."

He studied that word. "You mean there be no more slaves?"

"Yes. Slavery may be over."

His answer came as an almost unvoiced sigh. "That be mighty good!" Then he caught himself. "Maybe."

"Why 'maybe'?"

The thin shoulders bobbed. "Some folks wants to keep their slaves."

"I am not one of them, Zekial. Neither I nor my family have ever owned slaves." Even as she spoke, she felt a flush of guilt: neither had they joined the small group in Norfolk who openly condemned the practice and worked actively to abolish it. She erased any self-righteousness from her voice. "I would be happy to see slavery ended." She said it as much to make herself feel better as to reassure the boy.

He looked at her but did not voice his thought. It was, Lydia guessed, as if he suddenly recognized danger in the direction of the conversation, and a distrust of this white woman had arisen in him. "Yes'm."

A few minutes later, the path angled upward again to become dry sand, and Lydia saw nearby treetops above the reeds. Then they were on solid earth and approaching a shotgun house whose white paint was fresh and whose windows and doors were trimmed in bright blue. "This be Mr. McFail's farm. You just holler out—Miz McFail come out."

"Thank you, Zekial." She held out a coin.

"I don't need no money for this."

"Please. You can buy a gift for your mother."

He looked at the coin in his palm. "A whole dime?"

It was an exorbitant gratuity, but it eased her conscience, and Zekial's wonder gave even greater value. "Thank you for your assistance."

"Yes'm. Thank you!"

The grinning Zekial disappeared running even as she was dismounting. As she went up the stairs to the narrow front porch, a large black woman stood waiting in the doorway.

Chapter 21

Later, as Lydia rode home, she tried to sort through a tumult of odd feelings. Foremost was awareness that she had discovered a new neighbor: a farmer's wife not unlike Mrs. Brown or Mrs. Williams, who just happened to be black. Mrs. McFail—and the woman's name came to her mind as "Mrs." Rather than "auntie" or a first name—had shown neither the obsequiousness nor defensive pride that might elicit even the most polite condescension. Nor had she shown suspicion or resentment at having her home entered by a white woman. Instead, Lydia had been made comfortable by a hostess unselfconsciously offering the finest hospitality her station in life could support.

For the first time that Lydia could remember, she saw and spoke with a Negro as her equal. And the woman spoke with the same openness to her, rather than as a white person to be obeyed or feared, or—worse—to be hated and tricked. The distance between Negro and White, pervasive and unquestioned in Lydia's world, had made the Negro world invisible to her. Because of Mrs. McFail, Lydia had stepped into an reality she had never known existed.

She had been welcomed into a simple but neat parlor with a pot of hot tea and fresh corn puffs that almost floated from the serving dish. Stifling her surprise, Lydia accepted the hospitality in the manner it was offered—as between equals. Not fifteen minutes later, she found herself and Mrs. McFail laughing together at the foolishness of men in general and of husbands in particular. By the second cup of tea, they were wondering at the war and its outcome.

"The Lord works His own will His own way," said the large woman. Her rounded shoulders rose and fell on a long sigh. "And in this war, the righteous and the unrighteous both suffer."

Lydia had to agree with that. "We seem to be the instrument of our own punishment as well as our own sins."

"Um hmm! And punishment is surely coming, Miz Sensabaugh. Mr. McFail say we get rich from all this fighting—the Yankees gonna buy food and fodder, as much as a man can raise, he say. But there be no light without the dark, and maybe we be rich and maybe we won't. But I fear hard times. I feel them coming and I fear them."

"For some, hard times are already here." She mentioned Roger Bradshaw and Willy.

The wide face nodded. "And for a lot of my people, hard times always been here. But we will get rid of slavery—Mr. Lincoln, he say emancipation coming. Then times be better, no matter how hard they be."

Both the Salisbury and the Richmond newspapers had articles on the Preliminary Emancipation Proclamation. And though, as many thought, it might have been a ploy to stir the slaves to rise up against their masters, Lydia nevertheless marveled at the simplicity of one man's order abolishing a practice that had started more than two hundred years ago and had been argued over ever since. "But I wish it could be without so much death and suffering."

Though Mrs. McFail nodded, her agreement was not very enthusiastic. Her dark eyes rested on a small wall-shelf with its Bible and five or six other books. They were so worn by use that Lydia could make out only one title among the scuffed and flaking spines, *Pilgrim's Progress*. The thought crossed her mind that perhaps the past suffering of black slaves provided Mrs. McFail justification for the present suffering of white owners. Such a feeling of retribution would be only human, but Lydia would feel some disappointment in the woman if that were the case. She led away from a topic that brought confusion and ambiguity. "Have you seen either Mr. Bradshaw or Willy lately?"

"Mr. Bradshaw, a while ago. He lives over yonder in the woods. Takes out his boat sometimes for to fish and crab." She shrugged. "He don't want to see nobody if he can help it."

"The poor man!"

Mrs. McFail agreed. "Ain't right for a soul to be so alone. But that's the way he wants it."

"Why?"

Her large head wagged slowly. "I been told he never was much for company. Not even before you all moved into Marshfield."

"Would it be possible for me to visit him?"

The woman looked at Lydia for a long moment, but she did not ask why. "I can tell you how to reach his place. But whether or not he be there..." The heavy shoulders lifted and fell.

"I would be obliged. I worry that he might not be well since the Yankee soldiers beat him so."

Mrs. McFail nodded again, and also agreed to notify Mrs. Sensabaugh should Willy show up.

As she rode down the track from the McFail homestead, Lydia found herself gaining a greater understanding of her father's belief in the burden of slavery on both servant and master. Lydia had only occasionally wondered at the justness of what many called "the peculiar institution." But after the last hour, she could not imagine someone like Mrs. McFail being deprived of the life that all humankind deserved and which the woman and her husband had worked so hard to obtain. Nor could Lydia deny the shame of knowing that her blindness had contributed to the arrogance and dehumanizing greed of those who profited from slavery. True, she had occasionally been hurt by the distrust and suspicion many Negroes held toward her simply because she was white, but given her ignorance of the true effect of chattel servitude, those hurt feelings now seemed petulant and embarrassingly selfish. Moreover, Lydia felt that in joining the new Confederate nation, Virginia was defending "property rights" in human beings and was party to a vast and terrible crime. There was, after all, justification for Mrs. McFail's ambiguous response to the idea of so much suffering among those who had tolerated the enslavement of her people. One could only pray that out of this horrible war something good could arise: the eradication of slavery. It would be an Emersonian Compensation equal to the vastness of its evil.

Those thoughts rode with her until she finally reached the big pine at the fork in the trail where the main path led right and the secondary trail's faintly worn grass went left. She guided Dan that way against his wish to stay on the better-marked route, and concentrated on keeping her heavy brown riding dress from snagging on the brush that began to wall her in. The short path widened into a clearing that held a lean-to of canvas and woven branches. A campfire's white ashes made a mound a few paces from the shelter's open wall. From a metal rod, held up at each end by forked sticks jammed into the earth, dangled a blackened pot. An equally soot-marked frying pan leaned bottom up against a thick log that served as a bench. Beyond the clearing and glimpsed through a thin screen of shrub, an arm of water twinkled with sunlight. Thirty or so feet out from a patch of muddy shore, a rowboat was tied to a float.

"Roger!" She listened to the echo of her voice fade into the surrounding trees.

Somewhere out of sight, an answering blue jay gave four short squawks.

"Roger Bradshaw!"

This time, not even the loblollies sighed answer. Lydia thought a moment. It would not do to leave a note, since the man could not read. But rustic as it was, the encampment's neat orderliness comforted her with the hope that it reflected the man's mind. Stepping down from the saddle, she undid the clip that held her riding cloak closed at her neck. She pinned the clip around the wire handle of the pot as a signal to Roger that she had visited and with her wish that he might feel obliged to return it. Then she mounted Dan and headed back toward the main trail.

The path eventually became a cart track edging around fields now empty of crops. Mrs. McFail said that Marshfield lay two, at most three miles south of her farm, and that no one could get lost. Nonetheless, when, crossing a ridge where a break in the forest allowed her to make out the familiar shape of Fowler Creek, she felt relief at knowing exactly where she was. She paused a moment to savor the view of cordgrass scalloped along the shores of the Bay and the yellows and reds of remaining leaves patching the dull green of pines. A memory of summer lingered in the resiny aroma drawn out by the sun. As she clucked her tongue for Dan to move, something odd caught her eye and she pulled back on the reins. Almost at the southern horizon, out of place above the tree tops beyond her farm, a plume of gray-black smoke began to rise. As she watched, it grew in bulging domes as if alive but ominously silent. A fire—a big fire—but not the sheet of pale smoke made by burning off a field. It seemed, and the thought chilled her, to rise out of the neighborhood of Oak Hall.

ↄↄↄ

Well over an hour later, Dan's wet flanks heaved against her knees as the horse gasped for breath. The poor beast was in no shape for the long, hard trot she had demanded, but he had valiantly lurched down the ridge and across the fields, then struggled panting up the sandy lane toward the smell of burning wood. When she broke into open pasture, she saw the pile of charred timbers, some still flickering, that had been Carswell's barn and stables. A dozen exhausted blacks sat and kneeled out of range of the heat, surrounded by a scatter of hastily rescued tack and empty buckets. Beside them, the overseer, Mr. Talbot, fanned himself with his hat and was saying something to Parnell Carswell and his wife.

"Oh, Mr. Carswell!" Lydia reined Dan to a welcome halt. "How terrible—is there any assistance I may offer?"

The man pulled his gaze from the wreckage as they noticed her for the first time. "Assistance? No. All that can be done has been. And all to no avail."

"How did this happen?"

An angry clench of his jaw made his voice strangled. "Yankee soldiers. Zouaves. Destroying civilian property— looting, burning. Vandals!"

"Soldiers? Why?"

"Because we are the conquered! Because they have the muskets! Because they are damned savages!"

Mr. Talbot coughed, a smear of ash along one sweaty cheek, and his voice still raspy from smoke. "Somebody told the Yankees that Squire was running supplies to the mainland. So they come on a raid." He coughed again. "They didn't find anything, but they burned the barn anyway."

Mrs. Carswell, her arms holding the two children tightly against her side, glared at Lydia. "They threatened to burn Oak Hall as well—our home!"

"Oh, surely not!"

"Oh, surely so!" Her harsh voice threw the words back. Rage pinched her face and her eyes tore into Lydia's "Oh surely so," she said again. "Yankee soldiers like that one you have been—been consorting with!"

"Consorting!"

"You think we don't know? You think the whole of Accomack County don't know? First you set your cap for my husband and then like a brazen—"

"Madam!" Carswell cut off his wife's words.

Lydia, stunned, looked at the angry woman and the faces

of the two children staring wide-eyed at her. "I—What—"

Carswell's voice was a hot, hoarse whisper to his wife. "You will not embarrass me, madam! Take the children into the house." He wheeled away. "Mr. Talbot!"

The overseer jerked his gaze from Lydia. "Yes sir?"

"Get these people back to the fields. Now."

The shorter man turned. "All right, there's no more to do here—let's go. Virgil, call the hands together, let's go!" The slaves stirred and re-grouped as the black boss gave orders.

Lydia, groping for understanding, watched Mrs. Carswell, back stiff with rage, march her children toward the mansion and disappear between the Doric pilasters framing the doorway.

"What—Mr. Carswell, what—"

"My wife has had a severe shock today—as we all have. She does not know what she is saying."

"I do not know her meaning, either, Mr. Carswell. But obviously, someone has said something very insulting. I must ask you to never visit Marshfield again!"

His face tightened. His eyes bulged. His head bobbed forward slightly with a burst of rage stifled behind clamped, white lips. Then he blinked two or three times and drew a heavy breath and his hand gestured toward the tangle of smoking timbers. "Mrs. Sensabaugh, your barn and landing are vital. To our cause. Now more than ever."

"I ask you not to, sir."

The hot eyes blinked again but his voice was a gentle whisper. "It has been a very difficult day for me, madam, the severity of which you do not seem to comprehend. I currently have a shipment in your barn and it must be forwarded."

"Immediately, sir. Immediately and then no more."

"As soon as is practicable." His lips moved, though nothing else about the man was flexible. "But you must understand, madam, that your property—the landing and the barn—provide vital service to the Confederacy. And will continue to."

"'Will' sir? 'Will continue to'?"

His bloodshot eyes looked through her. "If you are wise, you will not interfere. I brook no challenge on this, madam. To deny this service to our nation is nothing other than treason."

"No! I do not want you on my property or in my presence, sir! There will be no more commerce across my land. It ceases now!"

The taut silence lengthened as he glared at her. Finally, before he turned away, he said harshly, "That is treason, madam. Treason against your own people. You are warned!"

Chapter 22

Shock and disorientation rode home with Lydia. Shifting between anger, puzzlement, and mortification, it lingered through the evening. Aware of Lydia's mood, Gretchen and Lucy were quiet as they worked at their chores, ate at table, and sat in the parlor—Lucy sewing baby clothes and Gretchen reading.

Lydia's sleep was restless. She dreamed of frantically running from some vast but unclear threat that closed tighter and tighter around her like an inimical fog rising out of the slough, and the sound of her own scream startled her awake.

"Ma'am? You all right? Ma'am?"

Gretchen's voice came through the door and Lydia, panting, aware of sticky perspiration on her neck and forehead, oriented herself to her bedroom. "Yes. Just a nightmare. Please go back to sleep, Gretchen."

The floorboards creaked as the girl moved away. Lydia stared through the mosquito netting at stars framed by the black wall surrounding the window. Then she heard muffled scrapes and shuffles as men worked hastily in the dark. A few muttered words, a thump or two, heavy heels thudding across the pier followed by the gentle splash of paddles. Then the noises ceased and her mind unclenched with the knowledge that Carswell's goods were out of her barn.

A few days later when Gretchen returned from New

Church, she announced that Wailing Willy had been found.

"Where, Gretchen? Is he in good health?"

"No'm. Somebody hung him. Up near Freeschool Marsh."

"Hanged? Oh, good lord!"

Gretchen placed a week-old *Salisbury Gazette* on the table and an envelope whose familiar handwriting gave a fillip to Lydia's heart. Pumping herself a glass of water, the girl added, "He had a sign on him that said 'Death to Traitors,' but nobody's saying who done it nor what kind of traitor he was." Gretchen drank deeply and sighed, "I been about to die of thirst!" Then she looked guilty. "I reckon I shouldn't't've said that. Poor Willy—I don't think he had the brains to be any kind of traitor."

"Did anyone have any explanation at all?"

"No'm. They say Sheriff Hope's looking into it, but nobody much is talking about it. Mr. Henderson couldn't understand it at all. Winifred Mears was the one told me, and she reckoned Willy saw something in the woods that he shouldn't and told somebody or somebody thought he did. She said there's meanness in the air now. People are scared to talk, people that used to be friends now hate each other." A thought crossed her mind. "Even relatives, like our kin up in Somerset County."

"Poor Willy." Lydia, her mind lingering on the term "traitor," asked, "When will the service be?"

"Done been. They buried him just after they found him a couple days ago. Sorta had to. Preacher Abbott said words over him." She drank again. "I don't know that they sang a hymn. Should have, I guess."

An image welled out of her memory: the man's long fingers, graceful despite their dirt, gently stroking Dan's neck. "I should like to place flowers on his grave."

"Yes'm. Potters field, then. It was a county funeral," Gretchen said. "I met Mrs. Brown on the way. She asked about Lucy and you, and said to tell Lucy she'd be over in a day or two."

"Lucy will be happy to hear that. She's sleeping just now." Lydia stared at the farmyard and the field of dead cornstalks that stretched brown and tattered to the distant tree line. They would have to be cut and stacked for fodder, a chore Willy had spoken of weeks ago when the stalks were still green. Now dead. God rest his soul. He was a harmless and gentle person. Never a traitor. Indeed, the thought nagged, that label was meant to be a warning to others—such as herself. But how terrible that a human being, especially one so gentle, so harmless, would be sacrificed in order to frighten others! With so much death on the Mainland, perhaps even here on the Peninsula life was growing cheaper.

The thin Salisbury newspaper could wait. Lydia took the envelope into the parlor and tried, as she read, not to dwell on Willy. However, the image of Willy dangling from a rope kept intruding until she forced her attention on the sentences. But even those words seemed to breathe a weariness, that of their author. A brief statement said that the Fifty-First was in defensive lines near Washington for the winter, the fight at Sharpsburg, now called "Antietam," was mentioned briefly followed by a summary of current gossip in the capital of rumors that the Union victory, though costly, would prevent England and France from openly supporting the rebel government.

Simon added, *Calotypists and undertakers hang around the camps and hospitals like vultures, finding much new business among the survivors of Antietam and the relatives of those in hospital. The calotypists offer mementos for soldiers to send to loved ones. The undertakers offer free cartes de visite for soldiers to write their names on and sew in their shirts before an attack. The cartes serve for self-identification as well as naming which undertaker has claim to the corpse. I have heard of instances wherein the undertaker will not ship the deceased home until full payment is rec'd, and of some who despite being paid will hold the corpse for additional monies. The greed of those who profit from soldiers who have given their lives for their country is disheartening to one's view of human nature.*

The note of weary bitterness continued:

Whilst I admire Genl McClellan for many attributes, he is overcautious and slow to respond to such generalship as Lee has displayed. My men do their duty, of course, but not with the eagerness that inspired leadership could elicit. I overhear words of resignation from the men that no matter how well they fight, the genls do their best to lose the battles. I pretend not to hear, since there is some sad truth in their words. The final paragraph, its news kept for last perhaps because he was unsure of its reception, lifted her with a surge of excitement whose intensity surprised her and erased the tone of weariness she sensed: *My Dearest Lydia, I have earned a two-week leave which I propose to take soon. I hope you will not object if I spend that time at Marshfield.*

అలఅ

Lydia found herself, as weeks passed, often looking down the lane for a glimpse of an approaching horseman. But November became December with cold rains and a steady northwest wind that blew damp into the bones. It brought neither Simon nor a letter explaining his absence. She and Gretchen fell back into the labors they had assumed after Roger disappeared; but this late in the year the field-work was light—shocking corn stalks, feeding livestock. Lucy's morning sickness faded as her abdomen swelled and she added her effort to the household chores.

One gray afternoon Lydia silently fretted, not for the first time, that her eager replies to Simon's letter had gone astray and he might have interpreted her apparent lack of response as a rejection. Gretchen, peering through the kitchen window, said, "Somebody's riding down the lane. But it don't look like the one you've been so anxious about."

"Who?" Lucy peeked over Gretchen's shoulder into the wet. "Who've you been so anxious about, ma'am?"

Lydia did not look up from chopping vegetables for the stew pot, though she almost sliced her thumb when Gretchen first spoke. "No one, Lucy."

"I hope to smile it's a no one," said Gretchen. "Just a Yankee—the no one who's been writing all those letters." The girls glanced at Lydia. "The no one that's making her go all pink just thinking of him! Look at that, Lucy—her ears are just bright red!"

"They are not! Anyone would blush at being stared at!' Lydia dropped the knife and wiped her hands on her apron, trying to will the blush from her face. But the more she tried, the warmer her cheeks felt. "Stop staring—it's impolite!"

Gretchen laughed loudly and a moment later Lucy joined with her giggle, not quite certain what the joke was, but sharing the merriment.

"Ladies, stop—Gretchen, you have said it's not him. Please see who it is."

"I reckon a not him is a no one, for you!" Gretchen laughed again and Lydia, trying to hold a straight face, nonetheless felt a surge of girlish joy at Gretchen's teasing her for having a suitor. It was, she scolded herself, a foolish emotion, far too childish for a matronly widow, certainly too presumptive for the little she and Simon Morse knew of each other, and certainly not appropriate to her role as a veritable governess for two young women.

"Ma'am?" A worried question wrinkled the fine skin between Lucy's light brows. "Do you really have a Yankee for a beau?"

"He is an acquaintance, Lucy. He was very kind to me

when he was assigned here. But I do not think of him as a beau."

Gretchen, good humor gone, appeared in the dining room doorway. "It's Mr. Carswell's overseer, ma'am. Mister Talbot. He wants to talk with you."

The short man had placed his gum poncho over the porch rail to drip and was scraping his boots on the mat as Lydia came to the open door. "Ma'am," he lifted his hat and shook off the rain. "Might I come in?"

"Certainly, Mr. Talbot." In place of the calm authority he usually evinced, there was a quickness to his eyes, a restlessness of his hands that showed nervousness. "To what do I owe this honor?"

He gazed at her for a long moment. "Honor, it may or may not be. But might be you'll recognize friendship."

"I don't consider you to be other than a friend, sir." She did not add: perhaps not less, certainly not more.

Beneath the drooping mustaches, his mouth twisted in something like a smile. "No more, I opine, than you do the squire. But be that as it may, I come with a...proposal...you might say. One I ask you not to talk about to anybody after you hear it."

"I don't lightly accept confidences. But once accepted, they are kept."

He nodded and made three quick, silent strides across the parlor to close the door to the dining room and the kitchen beyond. "I reckon you'll accept this one. It's about your welfare."

"My welfare?"

"You've made an enemy of the squire. You're a threat to him."

"*I* threaten *him!*"

"In the worst way—his pocket book. By telling him he can't run his goods through your barn no more."

"But that's—" A jolt somewhere in her mind seemed to sharpen the face that looked at her: black gleaming hair swung lank across his forehead and over the tips of his ears, a lean jaw dark with a stubble of equally black whiskers, waiting eyes whose blackness held some feral quality and calculated something about her on a basis she did not comprehend. Perhaps the man did have the Roanoke Indian blood that rumor said found refuge in his veins. "You mean he is selling those goods to the army? For a profit?"

"Sells to whoever's got money, and for a real good profit. Mostly that's people in Richmond or Petersburg, and no Confederate shinplasters accepted, thank you." The man shrugged. "It's a business. Better than selling niggers south, now. Squire reckons this is the time to make his fortune—he's mortgaged his plantation to invest with a English merchant down in Wilmington, North Carolina. Cotton to Liverpool; silk, laces, linens, quinine—you name it—back to Nassau." He wagged his head in appreciation. "Squire knows how to turn a sow's ear into a greenback. In Nassau, they break the cargo onto smaller boats to sneak through the Yankee picket. Cuts the risk that way: if a couple get caught, it's still good money on the rest. But the boats have started coming in by Wallops and Matomkin Islands over on the Atlantic side, and after the Yankees fired his barn, he needs your'n more than ever now."

As she tried to encompass all that the overseer was saying, her attention lingered on one of his phrases. "He sells Negroes?"

"Not no more." He shrugged. "Lincoln claims he's going to set them all free, and the way the war's going, nobody in their right mind's certain he won't." Another wolfish grin. "Nigger market's plain dried up."

Her mind held a swirl of thoughts. "He—you—carried Negros across my land and loaded them on boats in the slough?"

Talbot's eyelids drooped as if masking his thoughts and he hesitated. "It was done by somebody, and that's all I will say." For a long moment, he studied the wet hat he held. "And I won't say even that much to anybody else."

"Runaways? Stolen freemen, too?"

"Niggers," he said with finality. "But that line of work is done and over, at least in this part of Virginny." Another glimpse of teeth in his grin. "Uncle Abe says slaves in Rebel states ought to go free, but them in Maryland won't because Maryland's in the Union. But you can bet nobody in Maryland's buying, neither." He wagged his head. "Squire, he wants money—sees a good chance of making it now. So he's gambled on blockade running, and I tell you, Miz Sensabaugh, he ain't about to let you or anybody else make him lose that gamble."

"I will not accede to his wishes, Mr. Talbot."

"I don't blame you for not wanting to, ma'am. But whether you will or won't might not be up to you alone."

"He cannot force his will on me!"

The man did not answer immediately. He cleared his throat and rasped his fingernails in the black stubble along his jaw. "Even a treed coon will fight. And without a barn, Squire's right now a long way up a short tree. He will fight, ma'am, and he don't care who he hurts nor how. That's one of the things I come to tell you."

Steady. Lydia repeated the caution to herself: steady— don't let your temper flare now as you did when Mr. Henderson tried to give you advice. She took a deep breath and let it out in long, silent sigh. "I thank you, Mr. Talbot, for your warning. And I do take it very seriously."

The unease came back and the man coughed softly deep in his throat. "There's something else. I don't think Squire's going to need my services as overseer much longer." Again, a wag of his head. "Don't think I mind all that much, neither, tell you the truth—he can be a hard and proud man to work for, and he squeezes a copper tight enough to make the eagle scream. But might be there's a way—Might be you and me—we—can help ourselves out some."

"I don't understand."

"I could convince him that it would be dangerous for him should he be a danger to you or your'n." The flash of teeth this time held no humor but reminded Lydia of an animal's snarl. "He knows what I can do, ma'am. He would think twice before trying to run over the likes of me."

"That's very...generous, Mr. Talbot. But—"

"But what do I want? Well, if I had some vested interest, Miz Sensabaugh—say, a reason to tell Squire that he has to pony up to keep using this barn and landing—I would have good reason to stand up to him."

"A vested interest?"

"A reason, you see, to quit taking his pay a little sooner than he intends to quit paying me—and to earn a sight more than he has paid me in the past."

She rephrased his words to be certain she understood. "You want me to hire you for protection against Mr. Carswell—to pay you with money extorted from him for use of my property."

"That ain't exactly it." His hat rotated once before he looked up to speak rapidly. "You're a handsome woman, Miz Sensabaugh, and young yet. I've thought so a long time. And right now this farm and landing's worth a lot. It'll be worth a lot as long as this war goes on. You might say you got a dowry here that is at its peak value right now. After the war, you'll need a man to farm it. It won't be worth near as much, but with the money we can make on it now, we can live right well off what it will produce then." Another of those smiles. "I'm proposing we get married, Miz Sensabaugh. Marriage is a business proposition, as being a widow I reckon you know, and this ain't any different from most marriage offers—maybe a little heavy on the business side, but the times calls for it. Like I say, you're a handsome woman, and I'd be right proud if you became Miz Talbot, and I reckon you wouldn't find me a bad husband: I don't drink nor chew nor smoke."

"I—" She tried to find the words—any words. He stood and waited, dark eyes expressionless. Somewhere in their depths she sensed a hard coldness that stifled any impulse she had to laugh at the absurdity of his offer. "You—" She could think of nothing and, to cover her mind's emptiness, blurted, "You heard that horrible accusation from Mrs. Carswell and still you offer?"

His head wagged once as if shaking away a fly. "Squire needed a reason for being seen on your land at odd hours. You know, coming back from the slough early in the mornings, and all. So he let people think what they would, just like he told his niggers there was hants here. I know full well there's nothing to what Mrs. Carswell said."

She felt as if she faced a dangerous snake whose glittering eyes calculated her worth as prey, and which could strike at any moment. "I—am at a—I thank you, Mr. Talbot. I need time." She inhaled deeply. "You surprise me, sir, with your offer. I am flattered, but I need time. As you say, marriage is a business arrangement. I need time, sir, to consider the offer."

"Fair enough. But you don't want to take too much time. Squire will act pretty soon—he can't afford not to." He ran a hand over his raven-black hair to smooth it before tugging on his hat. "I am serious about admiring you, Miz Sensabaugh. And I have been forthright about all my reasons for proposing to marry up with you. Take my word. I'll be a good husband—you could do a lot worse." He opened the door but she could not will her feet to follow him onto the porch; they wanted to stay in the safety of her parlor. "I'll call again. 'Night, ma'am."

Chapter 23

Lydia woke staring at the canopy over her bed. Her stomach twisted with anxiety and a prickle spread across her shoulders as she realized that Mr. Talbot's inevitable return was one day closer. The issue was not what her reply would be. It was what would happen when she said no to a man who combined such pride with viciousness and coldness. For the first time, she realized that she stood as isolated and vulnerable as one of the lightning rods that thrust up from the barn roof. The Brown Farm, over a mile north, was her closest neighbor, but Mr. Brown was blind to his daughter and to any who helped her. As for the Williamses, even farther away, what could they do against Yankee soldiers? Or Carswell's enmity? Or any resentment Mr. Talbot might harbor?

The worry nagged throughout the day and into the evening as she used routine chores to stifle her anxiety. The following day, when Gretchen came in from the field where she cut and shocked the last of the corn stalks, Lydia had come to a decision.

"Gretchen." She met the girl at the foot of the back stairs.

"Ma'am?" She looked up from the scraper where she balanced on one of the stepping-stones and pried clinging mud from her field boots.

Speaking low so Lucy in the kitchen would not hear, Lydia asked, "Do you think your parents would allow Lucy to stay with them?"

Gretchen's jaw dropped. "What on earth for? I mean, they would, I reckon—I know they would. But why, ma'am? I thought she was to stay here till the baby's come?"

"I would like you and Lucy to take Dan and go to your parents' farm for a while. I'm afraid if you stay here, you might be in danger."

"From who? Yankees? Ma'am, we can stand up to them fancy pants—even the Yankee Zouaves wouldn't—"

"Shh. Don't alarm Lucy. And it isn't just the Yankees."

Her voice also dropped. "Who, then?"

"Mr. Carswell. He considers me his enemy because I forbade him to use my barn anymore. Mr. Talbot informed me that I'm in danger from him. I won't have you or Lucy share that danger."

"Ma'am, I'm not about to run from that Nellie Carswell or—"

"It's Lucy, too, Gretchen. Think of her condition—each day she grows more delicate."

The girl was silent for a long moment. "Maybe you better come too, then."

"If I abandon my farm, Mr. Carswell will use it with impunity. My presence here might dissuade him from that."

"What about Sheriff Hope? We ought to write Sheriff Hope."

"I don't know what his authority is under the occupation. And if he learns that we assisted Mr. Carswell in the past, he may be bound by his office to tell the Yankees. And they said that aiding the Confederacy is punishable." She sighed and shook her head. "Remember, they burned Mr. Carswell's barn on the mere rumor that he smuggled goods to the Mainland."

Gretchen's blue eyes studied Lydia. Then she nodded. "We'd best get Lucy away. You're right on that much. But better you tell her than me."

❧❧❧

The small sounds Lydia made preparing meals echoed in rooms empty of the girls' talk and laughter and tears. Lydia had waited long days for Mr. Talbot's return, but this gray afternoon she had not heard any horse's hoofs in the rain-wet sand. In the silence, the sudden thump of boots across the front porch startled her, and before she could cross the parlor, knuckles rapped a hard three knocks on the door.

The bearded man, broad hat in hand, nodded. "Evening, ma'am. I trust you've had time to think over what I said last time."

Words that she had rehearsed rushed out. "I have, Mr. Talbot. And whilst I am very grateful for your offer, and respect the forthrightness with which it was given, I must decline." She polished the little speech every day, measuring the balance between directness and kindness of tone, trying to select phrases that would be emphatic as well as assuage the man in his disappointment.

As was his habit, he waited before he spoke. His eyes, so black that she could not tell where the pupil ended and the iris began, finally blinked. "I figured that might be your answer. It ain't a good way to start a new year for either of us, but I reckon you are stubborn or you wouldn't've lasted on this farm as long as you have. And, too, you think you can stand up to somebody like the Squire."

"Marriage to a stubborn woman would be a difficult life. You should count my answer a blessing, Mr. Talbot."

Half-hidden beneath the droop of his mustaches, his lips twisted into the smile. "If dealing with stubbornness made my life too difficult, Miz Sensabaugh, I would never have become an overseer. A good whip-arm can handle stubbornness. Ignorance, now, that's another thing altogether."

"And you believe I am ignorant of Mr. Carswell's potential for violence against me?"

"I do."

"Perhaps I am naïve, sir. But while I respect your offer and your candor, I cannot marry you."

"I reckon it's that Yankee soldier."

"It—" She caught herself before saying that it wasn't Simon, but this man himself: his core of coldness, the sense that he understood, in ways she did not wish to know, the efficient use of cruelty.

The overseer took her silence for agreement. "Well, so be it. It is your mistake to make. But I expect you to keep your word and say nothing of this offer to anyone—it would be bad for both of us should Squire hear of it." He ran one hand across his glossy black hair and with the other settled his hat on his head. Then he glanced around at the twilit yard, at the pier, at the *Lydia*. Wagging his head once, he went down the porch steps. "You'll be hearing from Squire soon enough. Or, more likely, somebody speaking for him. Squire don't like getting his hands dirty—he hires others to do that for him." Hauling himself into the saddle, he gazed down at Lydia. "It won't be me—I promise you that much. But whoever he hires will be good at the job." He touched his hat. "A lot of soldiers have been killed, and a lot more will be. If that happens, you might reconsider. Evening, ma'am."

⁊⁊⁊

The rain lasted through the next week. Heavy drops pattering on the shingles at night drove Lydia deeper beneath the flannel-covered quilt where she tried to ignore the worry that weighed even heavier after Mr. Talbot rode out of sight. At first light she waked from troubled sleep to look out across the sodden expanse of rain-bent cordgrass toward the Bay. The rooster crowed half-a-dozen times, and after that came the twitter of wrens in the leafless tangle of lilac bushes at the side of the house. With full light, the rain lessened but still ticked lightly overhead. Lydia heated water and warmed the breakfast meat in the oven, her mind returning to Mr. Talbot's parting words. Many soldiers were, indeed, being killed...and it had been such a long time since Simon's last letter.

She was drying the breakfast crockery when, through rain drops on the kitchen window, she saw a movement in the lane. A one-horse shay, its leather curtains closed against the wet, jounced and wagged across puddles and ruts. Recognizing Mrs. Williams's rawboned horse, Lydia quickly pumped water into a kettle and tossed kindling onto the stove's coals. Slipping into the low boots waiting at the top of the back stairs, she took an umbrella out to the empty barn's door.

"Mrs. Sensabaugh—Happy New Year! Is everything all right with you?" Mrs. Williams's voice carried over the shay's jingle and squeak as it halted. "Gretchen Druer rode down to see me last week. She didn't have time to get all the way out here—her ma's got the fever and needs her—but she had to go to New Church anyway for medicine so she took the time to come as far as my place. She says to tell you that as soon as she can she'll bring back your horse, and she told me about poor Lucy Brown and what-all's been going on. Is everything all right?"

"Yes—but I am so happy to see you! Please—let me help you with your horse. I have a blanket and feed for him."

The older woman thanked Lydia and grunted as she stepped down from the rocking shay. The brown horse loudly sucked water from the trough, then as the woman continued to talk, followed the tug of reins into the barn and its manger. "I've been so worried! I told Mr. Williams I just had to come over to see if you were safe—I could never forgive myself for not looking in on you. He wanted to come too, but he has to be down in Eastville on business—not an auction this time, thank the good Lord, but some kind of permit so we can sell our corn direct to the army. Union Army. Mr. Brown says we have to live no matter who's

fighting, and the army's the best market to sell to now."
They quickly dried the horse with handfuls of straw, Mrs.
Williams talking ceaselessly while they rubbed, and draped
him in Dan's blanket. Then Lydia held the umbrella over
the older woman as they picked their way across the muddy
barnyard into the shelter of the back porch.

"I swear this war is terrible, and the good Lord knows
both Mr. Williams and me would prefer to sell to our own
army. From what we read in the papers—oh, please remind
me, I have some mail for you that Gretchen brought down
from New Church—our soldiers are having a hard time, and
if there was some way to get it to them, why, we'd do so
gladly and without taking a cent for it. But there ain't, so Mr.
Williams says we ought to get what we can from the Yankees and I can't say I disagree. Could be they'd take it anyway, from what we hear about the way their army loots and
burns up and down the Long Valley."

Lydia, shaking rain from her wrap, let the woman's
voice wash over her like a soothing touch. Its sound re-
joined her to humanity and pushed back the worry that had
been her only companion in the lonely days since Gretchen
and Lucy rode away in the wagon.

"Anyway, he can't be here but I can and am, and I hope I
find you all right, because from what Gretchen told me,
Squire Carswell's just looking for the chance to drive you
out from your own home." Hanging her oilcloth to dry, she
insisted on helping Lydia gather the tea and biscuits and
jellies before they settled at the small table in the warmth of
the kitchen. "That girl Lucy—I do feel sorry for her, but it
does seem to me if her pa's so almighty upset, he should
have been around so it didn't happen in the first place. But,
then, children will get to where they can't be watched to do
things they don't want seen, won't they? And I know if it
wasn't for this terrible war such a thing wouldn't've happened, and after all, they were engaged you know, and it
wouldn't be the first time a baby was born miraculous-quick

following the wedding, except, of course, for poor Allen Rafer getting killed."

"Perhaps the Rafer family will take in Lucy and the baby. It could be a comfort for them to have Allen's child."

"My very words! Lucy told Gretchen that her ma was supposed to tell the Rafers about it, but she don't know if she did because of Mr. Brown and the hard way he feels. Such a man, to do this to his own child and his grandchild as well! He will repent of it; mark my words, Mrs. Sensabaugh—Mr. Brown will repent of his actions. But Gretchen did say her ma would tell Mrs. Rafer about Lucy, Mr. Brown or no Mr. Brown, as soon as she's up and around. If I was the Rafers, I couldn't think of a happier Christmas gift that that, I tell you..."

The woman talked through two pots of tea as well as a light lunch, and Lydia insisted that Mrs. Williams take a bite more with her for the long ride home. As she watched the black shay jounce out of sight, Lydia felt a touch of guilt at her sense of relief. The many days of silence made her unused to constant talk, and, at some moment during the visit she gained insight into Mr. Williams' frequent and long absences from home. As Mrs. Williams continued talking, weariness wrapped around Lydia's mind and she had found herself increasingly unable to respond with more than a nod or a shake of the head to the woman's unending narrative. Perhaps, Lydia feared, her discomfort under Mrs. Williams' verbal deluge was a sign that she was becoming a recluse.

But in addition to bringing her talk and the latest Salisbury and Richmond weekly newspapers, Mrs. Williams had brought three letters—one from Bonnie, another in a hand she did not recognize, and a third from Simon. That one she opened first and found it dated more than seven weeks past: November 12, 1862

Fifty-First N. Y. S. V.
Near Alexandria, Virginia

November 10, 1862
My Dearest Lydia

I am deeply disappointed to tell you my leave has been cancelled. As the newspapers will have informed you, Genl McClellan is removed by the president because of his lack of aggressiveness following the battle at Antietam Creek. The man could have—should have—pursued Lee more energetically, but McClellan has the respect and even love of this army, and his removal has cast a pall over the men who see it as another failure of command. Genl Burnside, with whom few of us have acquaintance, is set in his place to stir the army into action. He has issued orders to attack the lines at Fredericksburg, and we will be on the march in a few days. I hasten to write before we depart, and tell you that you are in my thoughts and my heart. Be assured that I will have leave, although I do not know when.

There is good reason that maneuvers are undertaken in sunnier weather because now the streams are swollen and the roads are nothing but rivers of mud themselves . However, Genl Burnside promised the president he would vigorously pursue the Rebels despite the lateness of the season, and so he is. I wonder that the supply wagons and artillery will be able to keep up. My troops do not look forward to soggy rations and wet bivouacs, but their humor sustains them and if this shortens the war it will be worth it. They tell the risible story of an infantryman who sees a cavalryman up to his ankles in mud and asks if that is as deep as the mire gets. 'Yes,' said the cavalryman. The infantryman stepped forward to cross and sank to his neck. 'You said it was a deep as it gets!' he accused the cavalryman. 'It is,' said the cavalryman—'I am standing on my horse.'

These and other jokes as well as songs and even skits lighten the long days, but beneath the levity, one may sense the feeling among thousands of men that they want this war over. Indeed, some whose enlistments are expiring refuse to bear arms, and even among my own regt some companies have voted to go home when their year's contract ends. The government is offering bonuses and promotions for reenlistments, which helps keep many veterans in the ranks. But it also causes resentments among those who enlisted for three instead of one year and who, therefore, receive no monetary or promotional favors.

But enough of those issues. I had the pleasure of receiving your letter of the first inst. yesterday and cannot express the depth of my gratitude for your words of comfort and friendship. That you look forward to seeing me, makes me both overjoyed and sad—the former as an indication of your feelings, the latter because of the cancellation of our plans. You write that the news you offer is mundane and scarcely worth mentioning. Please be assured that I value highly all you say. I want to know what your days are like, even to the smallest event. Your words bring to mind the peace and beauty of Marshfield and its mistress. It is your voice I hear in your words, your eyes I see beyond the page on which they are written, and your hand that has touched this very paper I caress.

I treasure your letters because they are yours, Dear Lydia. And though I must post this now, know, too, that whatever happens, my thoughts and my heart are ever with you. My love, Simon.

For a long while, she listened to the rain drip into the puddles under the eaves, a soft sound that deepened the silence of the house. Then she carefully refolded his letter into its envelope and turned to the one from Bonnie. This envelope, another wallpaper construction, unfolded into a small sheet filled with cramped writing:

Mangrum Plantation, Traders Hill
Charlton County, Georgia
December 7, 1862

My Dearest Sister Lydia, I trust that the goodness of the Lord will see my letter safely to you. I only now rec'd yrs mailed twelve Sept. and hasten to thank you and to reply. It is good to know you are safe, even though the enemy occupies Yr County, and my prayers are that you will continue so. Cousin Albert died in hospital at Richmond of fever after his legs were cut off. So now Uncle Louis and Aunt Julie have given both sons to the Cause, and you can imagine the grief and sadness that fills our days. Although we do without—and without and without—my children are growing and healthy, Lord be Praised, and I am determined that this Christmas will be a happy time for them. It will be if my Andrew can only be here. Our determination to repel the invader from Southern Soil is not lessened. The enemy told us we must have Union without Liberty but we place Liberty above Union, and our fight for that will never end. My husband continues his efforts in running the blockade. He is a brave man who writes laughingly of some of his adventures, but I know how dangerous his work is. We have just lost Jacksonville where Andrew would often call and from whence he could occasionally visit us. Now Wilmington and Charleston are the only ports still open. The enemy can concentrate his picket boats even more at those sites, where my Husband dares to sail.

I beg your prayers for his safety, for you must know I constantly worry and ask God for His protection of my Husband and the Father of my Children. Dear Sister Lydia know that my heart is always open to you, and I pray for the time when we have won our freedom and have the right to once again unite our family. Much Love from Yr Sister, Bonnie.

The rain fit the tone of her sister's letter. Gone was the light-hearted and even prideful dismissal of discomfort and making-do. Now, a single phrase, "Do without and without and without," told Lydia more about Bonnie's state of mind than any of the brave sentiments she voiced earlier. These latest words hinted of mindless struggle, of grim determination, of dogged persistence despite death, suffering, loss, separation from her husband, and the constant fear for his safety. Bonnie and so many others sacrificed so much that Lydia felt almost blameworthy about fretting over Parnell Carswell and his threats. There should be something she could do for her sister, some aid she could render. But little could be offered across the barrier between them except her prayers and, if fortunate, her letters. She could at least do that, and today.

She examined the third envelope with its unfamiliar hand addressing her at "Marshfield Farm, Accomack County, Eastern Virginia." It carried a due note for ten cents that she would have to repay to Gretchen or, more likely, Mr. Henderson. But it bore no return address. Opening it, she was surprised to see the familiar salutation *My Dearest Lydia* and, above the final paragraph on the single sheet, *My thoughts and my love are ever with you. Simon.* The remaining penmanship, however, was not his:

I lie wounded in the Regimental Hospital at Aquia, Virginia. Please let me assure you I am in very good care and my wounds remain clean. The surgeon tells me they are likely to heal successfully. I was wounded at Fredericksburg on December twelfth. The first wound, to my left shoulder, came from an artillery shell fired as we formed for assault. The second I received was a bullet in the side, which knocked me out of the charge. Strangely, I did not know at first I had been shot, only that for some reason I was on the ground. Corporal Held assisted me to the rear, he, himself being wounded in the arm, which was later amputated. Though he goes home with but one arm, he is in reasonable health and grateful to be alive having done his duty valiantly.

I assure you my health is as good as can be expected and although this is not how I wished to take my leave, I will travel to Marshfield as soon as I can. I trust all is well with you and hope that your letters will find their way to me in this place. You must know how dear they are to me. This is written by Mr. William Paterson, a volunteer with the Sanitary Commission. Please give my regards to your girl Gretchen and, as always, a pat on the nose for Dan."

A short paragraph followed before his signature: *Madam, Captain Morse is too weak to dictate more. His wounds are serious but as he states, the surgeons give him good hope of recovery. Let me add that he would be grateful for a few toiletry items. Should you be able to send them, they are a razor, soap, comb, etc., since his personal effects were lost in the army's retreat from Fredericksburg. His spirit is strong and his outlook cheerful, and that is one of the most important indications of recovery I have seen during my service. Your ob't serv't., Wm. Paterson, VMA.*

Chapter 24

New Church was four hours' struggle along soggy January roads. Heavy mud clung to her boots, and long before she arrived at the Sundries Store, the sack over her shoulder grew twice as heavy as when she started. She had quickly gathered Franklin's razor out of its cabinet drawer, his block of somewhat desiccated French shaving soap, and his set of horn-backed hairbrushes. She added a few items she thought Simon might need: kerchiefs, heavy wool stockings, a housewife containing needles and assorted thread, and a knitted waistcoat and scarf that Franklin had found comfortable on cold days such as this. Though she tried to believe Simon's assurances about his recovery, her thoughts kept returning to Bonnie's news of hospital deaths. The cold, light drizzle matched the chill in her heart as she envisioned him in the hospital, icy and still,.

She plodded down the high road toward town and into the welcome heat shimmering off the Sundries Store's potbellied stove. As she removed her dripping oilcloth, Mr. Henderson emerged from the back room, his hands wiping down the stained bib of his apron.

"Mrs. Sensabaugh! Happy New Year to you. It has been a while since you visited—I hope all is well with you."

"Happy New Year to you and yours, Mr. Henderson." Lydia placed her sack on the worn and polished boards of the counter and gently lifted out each item. "I hope you have a need for eggs—I've brought some. And I have need of a tin of crackers and wish to mail a package."

"Yes'm." His spatulate fingers counted out the eggs and he set them in a large basket behind the counter. A printed sign said *Fresh Eggs 3c.* Let me see what I have. Will you be sending your package to a soldier in the army?"

"Yes."

He nodded. "I see a lot of that. Have to warn you, though—it won't be easy nor cheap to get it through the lines, and no guarantees."

"This," she said defensively, "is a Union soldier."

He was neither surprised nor offended. "Oh. Well that is easier, of course. Provided nobody don't steal it." He saw her expression and went on hastily, "It'll be safe enough in Uncle Sam's mails—especially boxed up so's it can't be opened easy and pilfered. Boxes do get to the regimental mail sergeants, all right. It's just we don't have control over them once they get delivered to the military." He waved a hand. "There have been some stories about the kinds of soldiers the Yankees been putting in uniform, what with the draft and all." He disappeared down a narrow aisle and came back a moment later with a tin of ginger crackers and two sardine tins, which he held up. "These travel good, and folks say their boys like them. Your eggs will cover the cost."

It crossed her mind to say that she did not need charity, but she stifled the comment. Her pride was unimportant now. "That is a very generous barter, Mr. Henderson. I thank you."

"Oh, well, we always need fresh eggs. Army buys all I can get. Now, let's see…you want to box up a package for a soldier boy." He rifled around under the counter to come up with a roll of thick gray paper. "Package that size is about three cents to wrap and twenty cents for wood and cordage. And I'll have to know the distance, to figure the postage."

"Aquia. It's near Fredericksburg."

"Oh—that big fight over there. Papers say the Union lost a lot of soldiers at that one. Editorial in the *Baltimore Eagle* says Lincoln shouldn't have put Burnside in place of McClellan. Says Lincoln don't know what he's doing, and I'm inclined to agree there. But then, it don't seem like any of the other Yankee generals know what they're up to, neither." He thought a moment. "Not like the newspaper editors believe they should, leastways."

From the quiet of the empty, rain-soaked street came a muffled thud of hooves and jingle of equipment. Through the rippling panes of the front window, they saw a group of mounted Zouaves trot their horses to the store's hitching rail and swing out of their saddles. Heavy boots thudded across porch boards and the door jangled open. A young officer, ballooning red pants splashed with mud above his riding boots and rain dripping from his cape, shook water from the neck-guard of his forage cap. "Storekeep!"

"Yes sir?"

The officer pulled a slip of paper from the wide cuff of his glove. "Here's what we need. Be quick." He spoke over his shoulder to the man behind him, "Hutchings, you help him out and make sure he don't give us bum goods."

"Sir."

The officer returned the private's salute without looking at him. His eyes were on Lydia and he nodded. "Ma'am. You live hereabouts, do you?"

"I do."

"Within a mile?"

"A mile? No—farther than that."

"Can I see your pass?"

"What pass?"

"To travel. All civilians in occupied territories got to carry a pass signed by the provost marshal if they go a mile beyond their home."

"I've never heard of such a thing!"

"Well I have, ma'am. From the Adjutant General. To prevent smuggling of contraband to Rebel soldiers. You need a pass to travel more'n a mile from your home or you can be arrested."

"Lieutenant, not everybody's heard about that order yet. And Mrs. Sensabaugh lives on a farm so far out, she'd be the last to hear." Mr. Henderson thumped a sack of flour onto the counter. Behind him, Private Hutchings carried another. "What's more, she came in to mail a box to a Union soldier." He tapped the address that Lydia had penned on the thick paper. "A Union Captain."

The lieutenant frowned down at Captain Morse's printed name and regimental address. "What did you say your name was, ma'am?"

She repeated it.

"How come this name's not the same as yours?"

"He is a friend." The description sounded weak and she had a sudden fear that this soldier would forbid her to communicate with Simon. "He's wounded," she added quickly. "He was wounded at Fredericksburg. He's in the hospital at Aquia. I'm sending him a few things."

A spatulate finger tapped the package. "Fifty-first New York, Lieutenant. Right here. Ain't you boys New York Zouaves?"

The lieutenant did not reply. To Lydia, he seemed to be balancing some conflict between his sense of duty toward an enemy and her apparent Union sympathies. A figure stepped in from the doorway and murmured in the lieutenant's ear. Lydia recognized Sergeant Durgin.

"Oh?" said the lieutenant. "Her and this Captain?"

The sergeant's grin widened as his eyes rested on her.

The lieutenant, too, looked at her with new interest. "I reckon we'll have to ride out there, won't we Sergeant? See if we can make that pretty lady's acquaintance, too." He put his cap back on, its white neck-guard flaring behind his ears. "Okay, but you better apply for a pass, ma'am. And it's not safe for a woman who has a Yankee 'friend' to be alone on these roads right now, what with Rebel irregulars causing mischief around here." He motioned to the two soldiers to gather up the sacks, eggs, and canned goods, while he counted out Demand Notes.

Mr. Henderson looked at the small stack of papers. "Can't you pay in coin, Lieutenant? These greenbacks are down to seventy-five cents on the dollar, now."

"This is how I'm authorized to pay for supplies, and that's the cost you got marked on your goods. You don't like it, you take it up with the United States Treasurer."

"Well you can at least pay what the goods are worth in coin!"

"You can take that up with the United States Senate. I reckon they'll be interested to hear from a secesh how much they should pay for the U S Army's forage in enemy country."

Sergeant Durgin laughed. "Mr. Henderson, you are dum fortunate we pay you at all. You know that, so just shut up." He winked at Lydia. "And you keep a tight hold on that horse of your'n, ma'am. They're getting scarcer than hen's teeth in the artillery. No telling when we'll have another horse draft."

ᘓᔿᘓ

By the time Lydia plodded past the Williams farm, the tears on her cheeks had dried. She had held them back until she was alone on the road, then they came as much for the look of embarrassment and defeat on Mr. Henderson's face as for her own sense of insult in the knowing eyes of Sergeant Durgin and that lieutenant. And, she wearily told herself, perhaps the tears had also been an outburst of her stifled worry for Simon.

As she reached her turn-off, a smaller column of mounted Zouaves cantered up the high road toward her. The sergeant in the lead halted the riders to stare down at her. She felt a painful clutch at her heart as it seemed to quit beating.

"Afternoon, miss. You got a pass?"

"I—I live within a mile of here." Her fib made her flush hotly. "I didn't think I needed one if I lived within a mile."

The sergeant frowned and rubbed his hand across the bristles of his chin. "Whereabouts do you live?"

She nodded toward the weedy lane. "Down there. Marshfield farm."

"Where you been?"

Again she felt the heat of a lie, but the unjust power this man had over her made it necessary. "To visit Mrs. Williams. A little ways up the high road."

"You seen anybody along the way? Anybody at all?"

"No."

"There's Rebel guerrillas in the area, ma'am. I reckon you would tell us if you seen any."

"I haven't seen anyone."

"Uh huh." He seemed to grope for something else to say, but finally turned in the saddle. "Let's go." The squad cantered away. Lydia dipped her face to avoid mud flung by the hooves.

Taking several deep breaths, she tried to still the trembling of her hands as she pulled her gum cape tighter. She fled the soldiers, she fled the spot where she had lied, she fled the need for that lie, she fled the sense that she had just lost something of herself.

Leafless branches closed over the lane. She threaded between puddles, trying to erase the unclean feeling as she awakened to the understanding that unjust power could drive one to defile one's sense of truth, and that her lies to the soldiers were not unlike the lies of slaves toward those who had power over them.

Passing her boundary stake, she wanted to caress the weathered, square post that leaned toward her like an old friend. Home was around this last bend. She hurried through the narrow passage where little-used wheel tracks curved between close-growing tree trunks, and leafless underbrush grew thick in the fading light of early evening.

Suddenly, a figure stepped from the tangle of dark

woods to block her way. "Howdy, Miz Sensabaugh."

Startled, she almost did not recognize him. His face was covered with a black beard that curled far enough down to hide his neck, and he had gained the bulk and height of a fully-grown man. "Billy Taylor?"

A white grin opened in the beard. "Yes'm. In the flesh, which is more'n I can say for some of the boys now."

"I thought you were with the army. I heard you were at Malvern Hill."

He nodded. "Close enough to it, anyway. But I come back. Transferred, you might say, to the Home Guard." He moved toward her almost cautiously. Something in his stealth made her step back. "Whoa, now, I ain't going to hurt you." His voice was soft as if settling a nervous horse. "Nothing to be afeard of here. I been sent to give you a message."

"What message?"

"Message what says you better let your barn and dock be used to support our boys in gray."

"Parnell Carswell sent you?"

"Don't make no difference who sent me. The difference is what you do about it." Another stealthy stride.

Lydia braced her legs. She would not yield to this person's intimidation.

"Damn if you don't look even better'n you did when I left."

He was close enough now that she could see a sprinkle of white pimples on his cheeks above the beard. "You've delivered your message. Now please allow me to pass."

"But you still think you be better'n us'ns, don't you? We risk our life to defend the Stars and Bars and the likes of you stays home and gives your favors to the Yankees." His blue eyes seemed to grow a shade darker as his voice dropped to a husky whisper. "I heerd all about you. Ain't much difference between you and a fast trick, be there?" His hand darted to grab her arm tightly. "Be there!"

"Let go of me!"

"No," he answered himself, "there ain't. First Nellie Carswell. Then a Yankee with pumpkin rinds on his shoulders. No, I reckon there be no difference at all." His other arm grasped her waist and pulled her toward him. The hard arc of his body pressed to bend her backwards. "And God damn if it ain't a long time since I had me some horizontal refreshment!"

He swept a foot behind her heels as he pushed, and, even as she fell and the limbs and gray sky swirled overhead, a small corner of her mind wondered at the practiced move of the man's foot. The heavy thud of the ground stunned her motionless. She felt a hand push into her dress, tugging and pulling the cloth as she tried to move her arms to scratch at the man's face.

"Good enough for Nellie Carswell. Good enough for a Goddamn Yankee."

Rough fingers pulled at the neck of her dress and she heard the buttons rip.

"Think you're too good for me, by God!"

His broad palm mashed her breast to hold her against the ground as he pulled his arm from around her waist and fumbled somewhere out of sight.

"No, you won't be too good—"

The words cut off, and she felt more than heard a hollow, almost thumping rip of sound somewhere in his body. Taylor's angry surge suddenly went stiff and he folded backward and away from her and then fell limp. His full weight pressed the breath from her lungs. Then the weight rolled away and, gasping, she stared into the darkening sky and tangle of limbs.

"You all right, ma'am?"

The voice came from somewhere but she could not turn to see. Gulping for air, she slowly realized that Taylor's hands no longer jabbed and grasped. She groped numbly at her blouse to clutch the torn cloth together and tried to govern her breathing. "Who?"

The movement of a head and shoulders among the hazy

branches focused her eyes. She made out a face that gradually congealed into a tangle of beard, wild hair, and a distorted nose.

"Roger Bradshaw? Is it you?"

"Yes'm."

She tried to say "thank you" but the only sound she was able to make was "Ah—" Her body, sagging exhausted, followed her mind as it slid from terror to relief and she fainted into darkness.

ↇↄↇↄ

Lydia opened her eyes to a familiar dim canopy overhead. For an instant she felt she was waking from a nightmare. But the twinge of pain in her back brought the memory forward and she lurched to sit up. She was in her own bed, in her dark room. Her shoes were off but her clothes, torn and disarrayed, were not removed. She felt at the buttons of her blouse as, guarding against the stab of bruised muscles, she managed to stand and light a candle. The mirror behind her dressing table showed the paleness of her face and the tangle of loose brown hair falling over her shoulders. Her quilt had been laid over her, but her clothes had marked the coverlet with mud and her stockings were still wet. Propping herself against the wall, she washed her face at the nightstand and gingerly peeled off her dress to dab cold water at red and scratched flesh before putting on clean clothes. Then, leaning on the banister, she slowly made her way down the stairs.

"Roger? Are you here?"

A sound came from the kitchen. He had placed the teakettle on the stove. In the light of the kitchen lamp, a wisp of steam rose from its spout. "Yes'm. Out here."

She saw his shadowy figure on the porch where he used to dine. "Please, Roger, come into the kitchen. I am so grateful to you—"

He cut her off. "It were necessary."

"Nonetheless, I thank you, Roger. I—I have been worried about you—I thank you."

"No thanks needed. You feeling fit now?" He had a lisp and she studied the man's face: over the unkempt beard his nose had a sharp, white ridge of bone and an unnatural angle to one side. His lips, the upper one scarred as if it were cleft, sank in where his front teeth were missing.

"Yes. A bit bruised here and there but, yes, I'm fit, thanks to you."

"No thanks needed," he said again. "Where's Gretchen Druer?"

"I sent her home. With Lucy Brown. I didn't want them endangered by staying here."

His beard had streaks of gray that belied his age, and beneath it his jaw made the familiar chewing motion as he digested her words. "Yes'm. That be wise. But how come Lucy Brown was staying with you?"

Lydia told him about Allen Rafer's death and her words rushed on. "Why did you leave, Roger? We've been so worried about you—I visited your camp over near Jack Town, but you weren't there. And how did you happen—" A shudder went down her spine as the scene flooded back. "—Billy Taylor—How—"

"I reckon the tea water's ready. And that you could use some."

She stared at the teakettle. "Yes. Of course." Almost without thought, she took two cups and saucers from the side boy. "Please." She spooned leaves into a teapot, poured the hot water to steep, and set a jar of honey on the table. The familiar domestic motions calmed her. "You must tell me, Roger: why did you run off?"

The man scratched in the unkempt beard and looked down. "Well, you seen me. You and Gretchen Druer. Without no pants." His eyes continued to avoid hers. "I weren't comfortable staying."

"Oh, Roger! You were injured. It was necessary. You had befouled your clothes—"

"Yes'm. I thought about it a lot since. I ain't saying it were your fault."

"Nor yours. And if it makes you feel better, please know that Gretchen did not 'see' you—only me. And I avoided looking at you." Her cheeks felt the warmth of a blush. "A married woman knows how to do that, Roger."

He had to consider that.

And she did not want to. She strained their tea into cups and motioned him to join her at table. "But how did you come to be in the lane this evening? How did you happen to be there when—"

Without a word, he placed two small objects in front of her. One was the clip she had left pinned to the handle of his cooking pot when she visited his camp. The other, and she had to touch it before she believed it, was her mother's carved ivory brooch that had been lost that night so long ago when she fell exhausted in the lane.

"Where did you find this?"

"It come off that night."

"You were the one who—When I fell exhausted, it was you—"

"Seems I got a full time job in that line."

"But you left me there for Simon—Captain Morse—to find."

"Them soldiers come before I could get you home all the way. I laid you down and hid in the bushes to make sure they done the right thing."

"Oh, Roger! You have been watching over me?"

"Some. You and Miss Druer." His head wagged, "Marshfield's a lonely farm and it's bad times."

"And you were watching tonight!"

"Well, yes'm. But mostly over Billy Taylor tonight."

"Billy Taylor?"

"He's been skunking about. I seen him a couple times in the woods. Sometimes him and Parnell Carswell both, keeping an eye on what's going on here at Marshfield. Other times him and them Home Guards. Getting up to no good in other places."

It was Lydia's turn to digest news. She sipped her tea and added a dollop more of honey. "I am very obliged to you, Roger."

"No obliging needed."

So her isolation had not been complete; the guardian was not an angel but this man. "And I am very touched by your care."

"You cared for me." He shrugged and made a slurping noise in his cup. "Like I say, I been thinking about that."

"You were so badly hurt—I've been so worried about you."

"I appreciate that, ma'am." The jaw worked again. "But maybe them Yankees done me a favor after all, despite they didn't mean to."

"A favor?"

"Yes'm. Knocked out my front teeth, so the Home Guard leaves me alone. Can't be a soldier with no front teeth to bite the cartridges with, you see."

Soldier. A thought crossed Lydia's mind. "Where's Billy now?"

After a long, still moment, Roger said softly, "In hell, I reckon."

"You killed him?"

Roger bowed his head and his shoulders lifted and fell on a long breath. "I didn't aim to. I pocket knifed him to make him stop. When he was holding you down. It were necessary. That's what I tell myself and what I'll stand up and tell the Lord when the time comes: it were necessary. But I didn't mean for to kill him."

"Someone will come looking for him—"

"Won't nobody know who done it nor what for, and most won't care. Maybe Parnell Carswell might care, but not that Billy's dead or alive, just whether he give you his message." He added after a moment, "It's best you leave him guessing on that."

"You mean if he thinks I did not receive his warning he might not act?"

The shaggy head nodded. "Not so quick, anyhow. And I figure he needs you at Marshfield right now on account of that Yankee officer. If the soldiers believe you're Union-inclined you wouldn't be running contraband to the Rebels." Another nod as if reaching a conclusion. "Soldiers won't waste time watching this place as long as you're here, so what he's got to do, Parnell Carswell, is not run you off but convince you to keep helping him."

"But Billy's family—"

"They'll maybe mourn. Old woman Taylor, leastwise. Billy deserted and come home, and he's been running with some hard cases—Parnell Carswell's Home Guard people. She'll likely think one of them got drunk and killed him. Or the Yankees."

Lydia studied the man's broken face. Its nuances were hidden behind his beard, but she saw something in his eyes that made her say, "I'm sorry, Roger. I'm sorry about Billy."

"Yes'm. I reckon I am, too." Then he spoke the refrain that she had come to agree with and which profoundly deepened her sense of what this religious man had lost for her: "But it were necessary."

Chapter 25

Despite her shipment of toiletries and an accompanying letter, she heard nothing from Simon as weeks passed. The rain-soaked skies of February thinned to show streaks of washed-out blue and to hint of coming March. For a few days, the wind would blow the clouds away, then the heavens filled again with rain. Roger had remained for several days, sleeping in his old room in the barn until he was certain Lydia was recovered. This time, he had gone with an apology: "I'm just more used to living in my camp. But I'll be around."

One damp afternoon, Gretchen, riding her father's mule, led Dan into the muddy yard and returned him to his stable. "I reckon it's about time you got Dan back and I'm sorry I kept him so long, but Ma's been real sick and still needs me. Yes'm, she's getting better, and I'll tell her you asked. No'm, no letters—I stopped at Mr. Henderson's, but there wasn't nothing for you. I did save up these newspapers, though."

Gretchen remained overnight before returning. Having collected a range of neighborhood gossip, she was happy to repeat it all to Lydia. And Lydia was happy to listen as the fire fell into ticking embers. Nothing had come from Humphrey for a long time and that wore on Gretchen's mother. She gave details of her younger brothers' activities and her mother's long illness, and, privately, Lydia doubted the woman's recovery. Lucy Brown's baby was, Gretchen said with a stiff face, a girl, and they were staying at the Rafer's farm. She sent her greetings to Lydia. Roger Bradshaw had stopped by the Druer household one time to say hello to Gretchen, though he didn't say much else. Gretchen was glad to note that despite his scars he seemed as normal as he ever did, which maybe wasn't saying much, neither.

The warmth of that evening remained long after Gretchen headed home, and the newspapers gave explanation for the absence of letters from Simon: General Burnside had been replaced, condemned for mismanagement in the Fredericksburg campaign and for causing many deaths among his wounded by moving them from Aquia to Washington before they were fit to travel. Nothing said if Simon were among them or where he now lay, and Lydia kept recalling the image of turkey buzzards spiraling over the trees just beyond her unplowed field.

The image of the vultures haunted her every time she rode Dan to New Church and passed the narrow stretch where Billy Taylor had waited. She could almost see his bones bereft of a Christian burial and scattered by animals somewhere in the thick growth. No one approached Marshfield looking for the missing man, nor had there been talk of him around the Sundries Store. That made the vision of his scattered bones all the sadder and even brought, in the silence of a long evening, one of her increasingly rare and tentative prayers, this one for forgiveness for Billy, for peace for Roger's soul, and for God's pity on us all.

As the absence of letters grew heavier, her restlessness increased until, like the slowly rising sap of March's arrival, Lydia could wait no longer. She counted her small stock of coins and Union greenbacks and rode to Jack Town. In the saddlebag, she carried two books from her library for Mrs. McFail: a volume of orations by the famous Wendell Phillips, and James Fenimore Cooper's *The Last of the Mohicans*. Although none of the well-read volumes in Mrs.

McFail's parlor had been fiction—and possibly morally suspect therefore—perhaps she and her family would appreciate Cooper's fine adventure story. Certainly, its language was elevated enough to provide instruction. Besides, Wendell Phillips's moving orations should repair any damage that a made-up story might do.

In Jack Town's sandy road, she handed the books to Zekial to deliver. The boy caressed the covers as if the tips of his thin black fingers could read the contents. From inside the ramshackle home, the rustle of whispers told Lydia that Zekial's younger siblings watched with shy curiosity.

"Can I look inside?"

"Certainly, Zekial."

He gingerly folded back the cover of *The Last of the Mohicans.* "Whooee, that's a lot of writing! Must of took that man forever to write all that!"

"Can you read it?"

He squinted at an open page and moved it back and forth until the print was clear. "'The noble red man stood and...add-res-ed?...the braves who sat in a—circle, while the fire light threw its rud-dy gleam across...vis-a-ges'? I don't know what that means—'painted with the in-ven-tion of sav-age im-pulse—'" Heaving a sigh, Zekial closed the book with embarrassment. "I can read some, but that's a lot more than the some I know."

"I will find a book that you might better enjoy, if you wish me to."

"A book for me? Just for me? Yes, ma'am!"

"And in addition to taking these books to Mrs. McFail, I would like to hire you to look after Marshfield while I am away."

"Me?"

"I believe you will be trustworthy. Will fifteen cents a week do?"

His brown eyes narrowed slightly with the craftiness of a businessman. "What all you want me to do?"

"Milk the cow every day and feed the livestock."

He shifted his gaze to the beach and the waters of the sound as he thought. "That be a long walk to make every day, ma'am." He paused. "For fifteen cents, that is."

Well, Lydia admitted to herself, it was. "Twenty-five cents, then. That's the most I can offer, but I will pay four weeks in advance. If I return sooner, you keep the dollar. And you and your mother can have all the milk and eggs whilst I am gone. And one chicken when I return."

"A dollar?"

"In advance for four weeks. If I am gone longer, it will be twenty-five cents for each week or part thereof."

"And milk and a chicken, too?"

"Don't forget the eggs."

"Your farm just got a lot closer!"

The following day she rode the loaded shay to New Church where she bartered all her eggs, half-a-dozen of the chickens, and her last two shoats to Mr. Henderson for tins of meat and oysters, his last three bottles of apple brandy, and what government script he felt he could spare. Then, mind fixed on her preparations, she rode back and began to ready the *Lydia*.

ᘓᕓᘓ

She refused to dwell on how little she knew of sailing in bad weather or what might go wrong; ignorance, her father had said occasionally, was a good substitute for courage. Instead, she focused on the demands of a boat that had lain mostly idle all winter. Using the hoe weighted with a rock, she scraped the hull clean of long streamers of weedy grass along the waterline. Then, as far down as she could reach, she awkwardly scrubbed the blade over the nubble of barnacles until it ran almost smooth. The sails needed mending at many seams, and that took another two days and left her fingers stiff and sore from palming the big needle through thick canvas. Some of the lines were frayed, but they would have to do because she had no money to waste on new rope. If she did not crowd on sail, they should hold. They would have to hold. And the small cabin between the two masts needed to be stocked for the journey. After five long days of labor, she sank into bed, muscles aching, and once more went over the list of clothes and gear she would need. Zekial would come day after tomorrow. In the morning she would milk Tessie, feed the other animals, select a book to give the boy, load the *Lydia*, and make a final inspection of Marshfield. Then, in early afternoon, she would cast off and with luck be in sight of the Western Shore by dark. Mixed with the worry, she felt relief and even excitement at the idea of knocking the mud of Marshfield from her shoes.

The next afternoon that tangle of feelings returned as a raw March breeze bellied the foresail, and water gurgled along the *Lydia's* sides. She looked back once at the silent farmhouse and the three lightning rods on the barn roof rising behind it. Then she pulled her wool jacket tighter about her shoulders and clamped the tiller under her arm. As the slough gradually widened into Pocomoke Sound, she even found herself smiling.

She bore west toward the smudge of Watkins Point. She planned to enter Tangier Sound just off that finger of Maryland. From her husband's Johnson and Ward atlas, she knew that Smith's Island was due west of that and big enough so her weak navigation would not miss it. Somewhere between the southern tip of Smith's Island and the Tangier Islands, she could get her bearings. Then a course west-by-northwest should take her to the Potomac River's wide mouth, and that would lead straight to Washington.

As the boat cleared the shelter of the estuary and entered the open Bay, it began to rise and fall, and her spirit lightened even more. Adventure! She was no longer bound to the soil of Marshfield Farm. Even the *Lydia* seemed to sense freedom and heeled in a gust to tease her with a surge of cold water up to the washboards. Lydia turned into the wind to bring her back from tipping, and the seas began to thump at the hull. She paid off the large foresail to gentle the ride, tacking closer to the shelter of the Maryland Shore and the small islands that blended with the greening peninsula. Concentrating on the telltale at the foremast and on the rapidly approaching land, she did not know of the other boat until a hailing voice startled her into lurching her craft.

"Hoy! Miz Sensabaugh—hoy! Heave to!"

Behind, looming close, was a leg-of-mutton sail with a familiar v-shaped stain near the peak. She recognized it from other times when she had taken the *Lydia* into Pocomoke Sound. In the stern of the open craft, Roger Bradshaw peered under his boom.

"Heave to! I'm coming alongside."

She let the sail run downwind to flap, and the *Lydia* slowed reluctantly.

"Roger! What are you doing out here?"

"I seen you go by. Ma'am, where might you be headed?"

"Across to the Potomac and then up to the Federal City. Captain Morse—I think he's in hospital there." When she said it aloud, her reason sounded flimsy. To reduce the magnitude of what she was attempting, she added, "I should be in the Potomac by this evening."

Roger guided his smaller boat to the windward side of hers. As the gunnels pushed closer, he tossed over two bumpers of hemp. Wordless, he dropped his sail and tied the two boats together at bow and stern cleats. Then he lightly stepped across the bobbing rails, using the mainmast guys for balance.

"Ma'am," he said with quiet intensity, "it would be best if you didn't do this."

"But I haven't heard from Simon—Captain Morse—for over twelve weeks, Roger. He was badly wounded and may need help." She finally voiced her worst thought: "He may be dead. I must learn something of him."

Under the full beard, the man's jaw worked. "Yes'm. But there's Yankee patrols cruising all over looking for Confederate blockade-runners. They will stop you and search the boat or claim it as a prize. And the Potomac's got torpedoes in it—Union ships go up and down all the time cleaning out the torpedoes that the Southrons put in from the Virginia side. Not to mention the sharpshooters ashore that keep a lookout for Yankee targets on the water."

"I'm a civilian—a non-combattant!"

"You know it, and I know it. But they don't know it. Ma'am, they got a war over there. The Yankees sunk a Rebel ship right where the Wicomico joins the Potomac." He stopped to catch his breath, mouth dry from saying so many words. "So you don't want to go up the Potomac to Washington," he concluded.

"But that's where the newspaper said Simon might be."

"You will never make it."

"I must make it."

"If you do maybe make it, they won't let you in the city. There's guards at every bridge and landing. Anybody coming up the river or across from Virginia's got to have a pass."

"It is where Simon may be."

His fingers scratched in a small patch of gray in his whiskers as he studied her. "Well, I seen you look that way before." He wagged his head once. "Annapolis is safer. It's longer and I better go with you because you ain't yet the sailor to do it. Though you're getting there, all right—you're getting there. But I better go with you regardless because you're sure going to go whether I like it or not."

"Annapolis is not the Federal City."

"Close enough—a railroad goes right there. One line goes up to Annapolis Junction, and the B and O line goes from the junction to Washington. It's a lot safer than going up the Potomac, and coming in from the north on the railroad you won't need no pass."

"I can't impose on you, Roger."

"And I can't let you go alone, ma'am."

ℰℛℰℛ

Roger would not relent, and finally Lydia said, "Yes."

They tied his sailing canoe aft the *Lydia* and, governed by his skill in using both sails, went much faster than she could have with just the foresail. An hour before sunset, they nosed up a narrow gut in the cordgrass near the southern tip of Smith Island where they anchored Roger's boat and waited for darkness. "No sense giving the Yankees two prizes," Roger said. "And best we go at night."

As dusk thickened, Roger pulled the anchor from the shallow bottom and used the last gray light to steer away from the island's shoals and bars into the open Chesapeake. "You ought to go in the cabin. It's warmer there."

"I'm comfortable, thank you. And I've never sailed in the dark. It's exciting."

"Yes'm."

She could not see the top of the sails in the starless overcast, and Roger, only an arm's length across the cockpit seat, was but a shadow of thicker blackness. "Should we not light our running lamps?"

"It's best we don't. Less likely to get shot."

"Oh." She paused. "Have you sailed this way often? In the dark like this?"

"Used to, some."

She waited for him to amplify, but the only sound was the smack of water on the hull and a humming from the lines. Finally she asked, "Have you smuggled supplies to the army?"

The thicker blackness that was Roger seemed to shake its head. "Runaways. Before emancipation."

"Slaves? You helped slaves escape?"

"My uncle—the Friend—asked me once't if my conscience accepted slavery. I thought about it a long time and it didn't. And since that was the case, it didn't seem much good not to do something about it. So I did."

Lydia weighed this information, tying it to Roger's unwillingness to hire out to a slave-owner, to his dislike of Parnell Carswell, to his periodic disappearances from Marshfield—attributed by Franklin to alcohol. "There really is an Underground Railroad in Accomack County?"

"More like an overwater boatroad."

In the dark, she could not see his expression, but she felt his small smile. And she wondered at the depth of this man whose world had, earlier, seemed so narrowly circumscribed by field and marsh and bay. Truly, that eccentric disciple of Mr. Emerson—Mr. Thoreau?—had been accurate to write of the voyages one could take at one's own fireplace. But Roger had in fact gone far beyond his own hearth and far beyond her passive acceptance of slavery, and neither Franklin nor she had known of it. "Did you take them all the way to Pennsylvania?"

"Oh, no—slave catchers were right thick along the Susquehanna. And some was their own kind, too!" The voice in the dark paused as if considering that type of betrayal. "No, we'd go up the Nanticoke or the Choptank to near the Delaware line and set them ashore. They'd go either by land to Pennsylvania or boat across Delaware Bay to Jersey."

"And thence to Canada?"

"A lot, I guess."

The two figures sat both isolated and together in the darkness of the boat that bumped into a quarter-wind. Lydia's mind was on those others who had, with far more desperation, made this lightless journey. The chill breeze seemed to carry the cold of their fear, and she pulled her woolen jacket closer about her shoulders. "Where are we now?"

"Coming to Cove Point." A shadowy arm pointed off the port bow. "That's the Cove Point light there."

"Oh." She stared at the wink, like a yellow firefly low in the dark, but had no idea where Cove Point was.

The boat rocked as Roger suddenly stood and muttered, "You take the tiller, ma'am. Just hold her steady."

"What's wrong?"

"Patrol boat—listen."

He slid forward to lower the sails quietly. With a faint squeal of pulleys, their gray folds dropped into sight from the darkness above. Not knowing quite what to listen for, Lydia gradually made out a faint grunting chuff like some animal gasping for breath.

"Steam boat—just set quiet."

Steadily and inexorably, the sound grew, Lydia thought, like fate itself bearing down on them from the blackness. Now she could make out the sound of paddle wheels smacking a rapid companion rhythm to the huffing grunt of the engines.

"They won't see us. Just set still."

The noise became louder and Lydia found herself holding her breath, her eyes wide and staring into the black night.

"Will they run over us?"

"No'm. They're off the port beam and heading south."

Her eyes watered from effort as she searched the darkness.

A flash of light crossed left of where she peered and suddenly she made out the glitter of portholes. The spots of light were farther away than the sound implied, but their number made the boat seem massive. Sprays of orange sparks puffed regularly into the dark above the row of lights and gradually the gleams, then the sparks, and finally the sounds, began to fade.

Roger hauled the sails up again and took the tiller.

"We got a long ways to go yet. Best you get some sleep in the cabin, then you can spell me come daylight."

It seemed but a moment later that she heard Roger saying her name.

"Yes—I'm awake." She groped through the low cabin to the door. The cold of coming dawn nipped her cheeks as she came up the steps. A pale, almost colorless hint marked the eastern horizon, but night still covered the Bay.

"We're about four hours off the mouth of the Severn.

And well above the blockade boats. You might take the tiller for a couple hours, if you want."

"Certainly, Roger. What's our course?"

"Steady north." His gray face nodded to the port side. "Just keep the lights to port and low on the horizon. That's Plum Point light, there. A little while after it drops down, you'll pick up the Herring Point light. Maybe two hours, in this breeze."

The wind had slacked, and the *Lydia* moved over glassy water at a slow walk. "I can handle it, Roger. Please sleep."

"Yes'm. But wake me when we get to the Severn. You'll see the flag at Fort Madison on the high ground to the northwest. I'll take her in."

"Yes."

As soon as the cabin door closed behind the stiffly moving man, Lydia tied the line and rudder in place. Though Franklin had provided a chamber pot for the boat, she had been reluctant to use it when the craft tilted and bobbed under last night's wind. Hastily, she struggled with her clothing. Despite the awkwardness of even the single petticoat and undergarments, she sighed with relief as she dangled over the lee stern, rather chilled and certainly unladylike. Men had the advantage, but nature had the demands.

As dawn reddened, the mild breeze drew the sails taut enough to start a small wake. She was hungry—the clean, cool air whetted her appetite. She also found deep satisfaction in holding the *Lydia* steady under the large foresail and the smaller aftsail in the quiet emptiness of the Bay. On the smooth water gleaming with dawn, the riffle of a shoal of fish moved like a cat's-paw of wind. It brought a profound sense of contentment and made her wonder sadly at the anger and regimented death that, from this quiet spot, seemed so distant, so wasteful, so unnecessary. Would that the beauty of the world, as simple and ordinary as dawn on the Bay, be enough to satisfy everyone.

Roger came up from the cabin before she needed to call him. He said good morning, blinked, yawned and looked west toward the land that caught the rising sun, then east, shading his eyes against the glare. He cleared his throat. "Reckon you might go below, ma'am, and maybe see what's aboard for breakfast?"

"Oh, yes! Of course."

She sliced bread and ham from her stores and ladled drinking water from the crock as she tried to ignore the long tinkle off the lee side, praying that she had not been as loud. After a suitable time, she brought the tray up to the cockpit. "Would you like coffee, Roger? I can light the stove."

"No'm, this'll be fine. We're less than an hour off the Severn." He nodded at the eastern shoreline, a series of low sand hills backed by treetops. "That's Great Island over there. We'll pick up Fort Madison and Fort Severn on the Western Shore soon." He gestured to the port bow where the low coast reached out to cross their bearing.

Small fishing boats began to sail out of Annapolis harbor. Other approaching vessels were sea-going steamers whose masts were reefed in the light breeze but whose stacks pushed out black smoke that spread like a stain on the morning sky. Roger guided the *Lydia* past a man-of-war whose tall black hull had a white band marked by open gun ports. Spurts of water splashed out of them as unseen hands swabbed down the decks, and a bearded face under a navy blue cap peered down from the taffrail high above.

"That's a steam frigate. I think she's the flagship of the Annapolis squadron.

"It's gigantic!"

"She be big." Roger wagged his head in agreement. "But one of the new ironclads could sink her, easy. The *Virginia* sunk bigger off Hampton Roads, and if the *Monitor* hadn't stopped her, she would've sunk more."

"How truly wonderful," she murmured, "is human invention for destruction."

"Yes'm, ain't it."

Ahead, the points of the river mouth opened, each marked by a sturdy dark rectangle that rose out of the low land. Old Fort Severn, Roger said, was on the south point, new Fort Madison on the north. Over the latter twinkled a color that was now the flag of Virginia's enemy. Seeing the familiar banner, Lydia felt a twist of emotion whose intensity surprised her. She gripped the rail and stared at the flag and then at the rise of land that was Annapolis with its scattered church spires. Ship after ship lined the wharves on both sides of the river, and other vessels rode at anchor in the crowded harbor. The Naval Academy, its grass and young trees bright in the morning light, swung past as they tacked toward the city.

"What's that vessel, Roger?"

He squinted toward the black, three-masted ship that rode at anchor just off the Academy grounds.

"Old Ironsides. The *Constitution*. It was used as a training ship for the Navy boys; now it's used for harbor defense, I reckon."

Lydia studied the trim and graceful hull of the sailing vessel; its myriad stays and braces formed complex lines woven in air between spars swollen with furled sails. It, too, was now the property of the enemy, as was Mr. Oliver Wendell Holmes' patriotic poem that she had memorized at Miss Howarth's Seminary. And the sense that a part of her own past had been taken from her generated a hurt, empty feeling.

Intent on finding a place to moor, Roger scanned the crowded quays on both sides of the harbor as he lowered and lashed the mainsail. Lydia, holding the tiller, gazed at the boats, at the clusters of houses and tangles of unpainted picket fences that made up Eastport, then ahead and across the harbor where Annapolis rose in dark roofs toward the State House atop the city's hill. It had been years since she had seen so many buildings, and she felt both disoriented and a bit frightened by the apprehension that she had been too long at Marshfield and away from a world crowded with people.

"We'll have to moor down there." Roger threaded between two anchored ships. One was a steam boat with "New York" painted in an arc of red letters around the dome covering its side-wheels. The other was a strange craft with no masts but two smokestacks, a short one forward and a taller one aft. A large cannon was mounted in a housing in front of a central wheelhouse whose stunted bridge was only slightly taller than the sailor who wiped down its metal plates. Riding low in the water, the vessel's hull was almost awash and lacked, Lydia thought, every grace. All sense of the beauty of a ship like the *Constitution* was thrown away in its total dedication to the function of dealing out death. It was as if the mechanisms of the modern world had turned from advancing civilization to destroying it—as if in this machine the power of steam turned from servant to master.

Roger, too, gazed at the brutish contraption. "It's a Monitor," he said. "A lightdraft Monitor. I reckon that's what war ships are coming to." Then, "Stand by the bow line."

The *Lydia* angled into the weedy piles of an almost abandoned quay far upstream from the busy warehouses. Roger dropped the sail and, with a deft twist, slid the boat sideways to bump gently against the pilings. Agile despite her skirts, Lydia clambered up half-rotten rungs to wrap the bow line around a rusty cleat. Then she moved aft to catch the stern line that Roger tossed to her.

"Done right well, ma'am."

She almost blushed under the praise, but hid her pleasure behind a deep breath and a glance around. Beneath her feet, the worn, splintered planks seemed to sway like the deck of the *Lydia*, and she felt she had stepped through a secret door into a new world. The contents of that world were nothing out of the ordinary—an old weathered quay piled here and there with frayed, coiled lines and weathered pulleys, stacks of bleached wooden crab traps, lumps of bulky gear hidden under tarpaulins—but they brought a hint of the sense of adventure that sailors the world over must feel when landing on a new shore. Then she began to look more intently for a privy.

Chapter 26

Though it was only March, the train to the Federal City was hot from crowded bodies and sunlight burning through the closed windows. Roger had said it would be best if he awaited her return while guarding the *Lydia*, and it was a good thing, since all seats were taken and the aisles were choked with soldiers. Odors of unwashed wool and unclean flesh, tobacco smoke from pipes and cigars, a variety of sharp smells from hampers, soldiers' haversacks, and greased paper wraps made the air thick. She had believed, when she changed trains at Annapolis Junction, that the trip could not grow worse. But her next train was even more burdened by troops loaded with bulky, stained equipment, and most bore savage-looking muskets as tall as some of the men. Many faces, including the beardless ones of youths and even uniformed drummer boys, seemed flushed with heat and—she guessed—whiskey. Some snored loudly on their feet, others gazed dully at her, at the passing landscape, at some vision of their own somewhere beyond the varnished wooden ribs of the car's ceiling. A few found something in her face that constantly drew their yearning eyes to snag at hers, while other eyes—the ones she tried most to avoid—were almost feral in their stare.

She tried to ignore the probing looks, the talk and laugh-

ter and snores of men crammed into seats, sitting in the
aisles, leaning over seatbacks for what relief they could find
for their legs. Long before the wheels rattled and clanked
across a series of hard jolts, her neck was stiff from facing
the window as she gazed away or pretended sleep. The train
slowed as farmland and trees were interrupted more frequently by domestic gardens, small barns, animal pens, occasional shanties where black or white children waved at
the passing train. Finally, only small muddy lots framed by
sagging stick fences and decorated with outhouses crept
past. From the car's far end a voice called something and a
general stir rustled like an unfelt wind among the soldiers as
they sluggishly began to gather up their packs and knap-
sacks and weapons.

"It won't be long now." The face crowded beside her,
cheeks bright red and round as apples, grinned. The soldier
had sipped steadily at his canteen and Lydia smelled the raw
whiskey on his breath. His dark blue forage cap bore
crossed brass cannons. One of his front teeth was missing
and the rest tobacco-stained; a soft and curly attempt at a
beard fringed his jaw. "We'll have a chance, now, to show
what Pennsylvany can do!" His wide blue eyes stared at her
and through her toward something in his own mind. "We'll
have a chance now to teach Johnny Reb a lesson!"

His accent made her guess, "You are from the west?"

"I am, yes ma'am. Allegheny County. But we got a lot of
Philadelphy boys, too. We're the Hundred and Twelfth
Pennsylvany Volunteers, Second Heavy Artillery." The
youth said the phrase like one long word. "We been to Fort
Delaware. Now we're reporting to Washington—General
Doubleday. Uncle Abner, the boys calls him. I reckon we'll
see some fighting, now."

"Have you not been fighting?"

"Well, no, not yet. But not because we don't want to!
Heavy artillery, you see, mans the forts. But if the Rebs do
come at us, they'll find out what the boys can do, you bet."

"I wish you good fortune."

"Thank you, ma'am. You live here in Washington?"

"No...I'm searching for my...my fiancé. He was wounded at Fredericksburg."

"Oh." Then he shook his head. "I'm sorry, ma'am."

"Thank you."

The car lurched to crash its couplings, then moved forward over another slowly thudding stretch of rails. The men crowding the aisles jostled and stumbled with the floor's sway, teetering like a blue wave over Lydia so that she pressed against the varnished wall of the car.

"You best let me get you through these old possums, ma'am. Hey—listen up!" Startling Lydia, the youth half-stood and called into the crowded car. "Stand at rest and listen up!"

The murmur of voices paused and faces craned past shoulders, arms, weapons toward her.

"This here lady's fancy was wounded at Fredericksburg, and she's down here a-looking for him. So you boys give way and let her out first."

When the car lurched again and was finally still, the tobacco-stained teeth grinned. "Come on, ma'am. We're at the station."

He lowered Lydia's small valise from the rack and pushed through the forest of blue coats, brass buttons, and leather belts. Men pressed back to give them a tight aisle, faint puffs of breath laden with garlic, tobacco, and whiskey murmuring "What?" and answering "Wounded—Fredericksburg."

She half-stumbled, face burning and almost faint from the heat and the odors, toward the car door.

"Here you are, ma'am." The young soldier helped her down the iron steps to the planks of the crowded platform and handed her the valise. "I sure hope he's all right."

"Thank you—thank you."

౸౸

She paused under a green and white striped awning in front of a men's haberdashery that gave a spot of welcome shade to the busy plank walk. Breathing deeply to clear her nose of the train's odors, she realized she never asked the soldier his name. But then he had not asked hers, and perhaps that was what Washington was: a massive gathering of so many faces that people were like fish in schools, anonymous parts of a confusingly orchestrated whole.

Certainly, the faces pressing down both sides of dusty Pennsylvania Avenue seemed oblivious of each other. And the variety of uniforms and coats added even more heterogeneity to the throng. Gentlemen's hats varied, too: tall styles that bobbed like stove pipes above the shorter top hats, derbies, slouch hats, straw hats, even the occasional workman's bandanna.

Among them paced a few women, whose azure or beige or rich green crinoline dresses, wide with voluminous petticoats or cages and trimmed with swags of decoration, swept the dusty boards to show the twinkle of shoe tips.

Across the unpaved street and marked by rows of arched windows, brick buildings reached as high as six floors. Some windows were shaded from the sun by awnings, others were recessed in the protecting shadows of thick masonry walls. Horse car rails ran down the center of a street that was almost buried in loose dirt powdered by iron-rimmed cart wheels and broad hooves.

Thousands of gentlemen's and ladies' shoes, heavy boots, and bare feet crossed from one boardwalk to the next. Straight down the avenue, her eye—guided by converging lines of trees—traced the glinting white dome of the almost completed Capitol Building. It was, Northern newspapers boasted, a symbol that the Union would stand united and not fall to rebellion. What the papers did not report was the rumor of rented slaves in its construction even after the start of the war, providing one more indication to Lydia of the political guile of Mr. Lincoln.

Threading through crowds on the walk, she paused at F

Street and, with a slight start, recognized the famous name of the impressive building on the corner: the Willard Hotel. It, too, was one of the tallest structures, but capped in the modern French style of a tall, curved roof with inserted window dormers that gave it yet another level. Franklin boasted of staying there on one of his business trips, and had brought home a sketch of the hotel on a postal card and told her of its decorated and spacious lobby filled with sofas, plants, ornate columns, and all the conveniences of modern and sophisticated life. She had read in a magazine article by Mr. Hawthorne that it was the true center of Washington City, and if anyone could offer her advice in her search, surely one of its clerks could.

Shifting her valise to the other hand, she went up the low steps into the F Street entrance. Under the lofty gilded ceiling and glowing ornate lamps, men looked with interest at her. Despite the heat, many businessmen wore topcoats and stiff collars and even old-style, frilly stocks. Union soldiers in blue with shoulder straps—officers, she now knew—sat here and there in the wide lobby's stuffed chairs or stood talking in small groups. Like the suited men who balanced tall hats on their knees and looked important, the officers smoked and sipped iced drinks brought by gloved and smiling Negro waiters. A flowered carpet runner led from the doorway to the gleaming counter of the registration desk. Among the clerks stood one with a shaved chin and gray whiskers in the latest fashion called "side-burns" after a Union general. He looked her way with quickly masked surprise and nodded politely. Lydia, stifling the feeling of being an unfashionable country bumpkin, smiled with what, she hoped, was self-assurance as she asked directions to the hospital.

"We got at least fifteen hospitals in the city, miss, but they're for Union soldiers. Most Confederate prisoners, you see, are held in Maryland and Pennsylvania."

"He is a Union soldier."

The man's brown eyes glanced at the doors behind her. "But you came in by F Street."

"I don't understand your meaning."

"Ah." He smiled again "You are new to Washington." He leaned forward to speak confidentially, the faint aroma of a lavender pastille on his breath. "The Willard is neutral territory, Miss. We offer hospitality to advocates of both sides. But to insure peace among our guests, we humbly request that Union sympathizers use the Pennsylvania Avenue entry—a Northern state, you see—and Confederate sympathizers use the F Street entrance."

"I shall remember in the future."

"And I hope for the pleasure of serving you and your husband." He leaned even farther across the counter, glancing at the men on each side who, though turned away from her, rested their elbows on the glossy wood as if listening. It struck Lydia that anything said on any subject was, in this large and busy room, an attraction for someone's ears.

As part of his neutrality, the clerk went out of his way to protect even the most innocent confidence. "If I was you, miss, I'd start at the Sanitary Commission headquarters. I think you'll find them more helpful than the Union army surgeons. Let me write the address for you—it ain't far." The iron nib of his pen scratched briefly as he murmured. "And they are kind, as well."

The Commission Building with its three stories of Greek front would, before she saw the Willard, have intimidated Lydia. But now she was too weary and impatient to allow her lack of worldliness to impede her. Along the boardwalk, an iron picket fence guarded a deep well where a row of large windows brought light to basement rooms. Spanning this moat, six broad marble steps led up to the first floor. A sign proclaimed the headquarters of the United States Sanitary Commission, listed its purposes, and bore the engraving of a national shield with thirteen stripes resting on a fasces and spear.

"Yes, miss?" A woman in a black mourning dress, equally black hair pulled tightly back from her high forehead, looked up from an ordinary table that served as her desk. It was filled with stacks of papers, a pile of freshly printed chapbooks entitled "The Soldier's Friend," and several examples of rolled bandages.

"I was told you might help me. I'm looking for a wounded soldier."

Her blank expression shifted to one that was almost weary, as if Lydia were but one more of so many women who had stood before her uttering the same words. "I truly hope we can help."

She copied down Lydia's recitation of Simon's complete name, Union or Confederate, birth date, regimental affiliation, wounded at or near what location, date of injury, severity of wound or illness if known, return address of any subsequent letters, any other information that might help, such as relatives in the army or the names of close acquaintances in his regiment. Many of the questions were unanswered, but when she had all that Lydia knew, she rose.

"Please sit down. I will consult our directory." She gestured toward a long wooden bench flanked by small tables at each end. The bench seat was littered with newspapers; the tables held Sanitary Commission pamphlets and pasteboard cards listing approved lodgings for soldiers' families. On a back corner of the farthest table, a discrete stack of handbills labeled *Thomas Holmes, Undertaker* offered the latest in the new science of embalming and cited rates for officers, $80, and enlisted men, $30. A wooden box was included in the price, zinc lining extra, shipping provided at special rates.

"Pray rest. I'll return directly." The woman paused before disappearing into an adjoining room. "The hospital's directory contains six hundred thousand names so far. It may take some time."

Setting her valise down, Lydia ladled a tin cup of cool water from a crock and drank thirstily before sinking onto the bench. Its wood was polished slick from all those who had preceded her, and the cool smoothness rested her back. She should have been shocked or worried by Mr. Holmes's handbills and the number of hospitalized soldiers, but she had grown too weary and disoriented to feel anything except sadness at how few questions about Simon's life she could answer. Rather, Mr. Holmes's notice of service seemed appropriate to this focus of illness, injury, and death, and was but part of the room's functional decorations. Despite trying to stay awake, the heat and quiet and weariness caused her eyes to close and she lost track of time. The touch of the woman's hand on her shoulder jerked her into the present.

"You are tired."

"Yes. I'm sorry. Did you find him?"

"No need to apologize, my dear. These are weary times. I found his billet: the Armory Square Hospital. It's on the Capitol Mall at B Street. Do you know how to get there?"

"He is alive then!"

The severely dressed woman's eyes blinked as she hesitated. "He was entered nine weeks ago and has not since been reported as transferred or deceased. But our directory is several days behind events—there are so many—"

Lydia felt her surge of joy ebb back into stifled apprehension. "I understand. The Mall?"

"It's a few blocks away. F Street will lead you there. Then turn toward the Capitol Dome. You will find the hospital four blocks up the Mall, just across from the Smithsonian Building."

"Thank you."

"Please—take this. It's a list of residences that offer reputable lodging at an honest price. If you are destitute, the Commission provides a lodging house that includes a breakfast and supper. You are invited to apply, and you may stay as long as your soldier is in a hospital or a rest home."

"I thank you again. I have funds."

"You are fortunate."

Something in the woman's voice cut through Lydia's focus on Simon. "Your commission is in need?"

"Of much. Nurses are always needed. Trained, competent, stable ones. Many women volunteer with visions of some grand service to the wounded and ill—or even finding a husband. But few of those know what will be demanded of them. And money is needed—money, always."

Lydia groped in her handbag for one of the Demand Notes that had paid for Star.

"No—you will need your money here. Keep what you have to tend your soldier until he is home. Then if you wish to contribute, you may mail a draft to any local office of the commission." She smiled. "I assure you, it will be well used. Perhaps to help a woman like you who seeks her husband or son."

"Nonetheless, please let this help one of the destitute!" She held out the carefully folded note.

The woman took it but did not look at it as she dropped it into a small drawer under the tabletop. "Some mother or wife will thank you. As I do."

Lydia once more toted her valise across dusty and busy Pennsylvania Avenue. As she plodded through the heat, she passed a building whose three stories dominated shorter buildings on each side. The tall arches of the ground floor supported two rows of oversized windows each capped by a wide Doric triangle. A poster board at eye level said "Ford Theater" and listed the evening's entertainment.

Reaching the Mall, she turned toward the distant capital. Before the war, the Mall had been a long pasture with copses of trees, meandering sandy lanes, and scattered piles of marble blocks for the buildings and monuments under construction. Now, a city within the city, it held single-story clapboard barracks clustered in squares and echelons, tent camps filled with soldiers, row upon row of massed cannon waiting transport, squadrons of hospital wagons in rows awaiting call, and numerous horse corrals. A tangle of railroad tracks leading to the Potomac River crossed between buildings and storage yards. Near the massive stub of what someday would become the monument to General Washington, dust and thirsty bawling rose from pens where army cattle were held prior to slaughter. The Armory Square Hospital was one of the clusters of pavilions and tents near a noisome canal that carried sewage to the Potomac. She directed her weary legs toward the flagpole in front of one of the flimsy-looking clapboard buildings. The flag, she had been told, always marked a headquarters.

"A captain?" The young man had thinning straight hair that swept down from a white part in the middle of his head to become curly over his ears. He did not raise his eyes to meet hers, but he did open a drawer filled with papers. "Morse. Fifty-First New York—we have officers from that regiment."

Lydia tried to breathe naturally.

"Morse, Simon, you say?"

"Captain Simon Morse, yes."

"Aha!" His finger slid down a paper. "Simon Morse, Captain, Fifty-First New York." His dark brown eyes followed the finger that slowly scanned all the way to the last line on the paper. Lydia felt her fingernails bite into her palms as she waited. "He's not been transferred to the dead house, anyway. Pavilion H, it says here. That's over behind the chapel." He finally looked up and studied Lydia's plain dress, unimposing in its lack of petticoats and dust-powdered from travel. "But you can't see him yet. Army regulations got to be followed, you understand? Today's not a visiting day. You'll have to wait until Sunday."

"That's four days off!"

"It's army regulations, is what it is. Visiting day is Sundays."

"But I have traveled so far—"

"Well, we just can't have folks wandering around the hospital any time at all!"

Lydia, her back twinging with pain, stifled the wave of anger that swept her vision toward blackness. After a moment, she could smile at the young man's expressionless, uplifted face. "Of course not." Some men, it seemed, turned from human to machine when they donned an army suit, and this would not be the first soldier she had lied to. "Can you give me directions for when I do return on visiting day? Next Sunday."

"Certainly!" His arm gestured. "It's just beyond the chapel, yonder. Pavilion H—four down. You won't miss it." He called after her. "You're welcome on Sunday!"

Lydia's "thank you'" hung in the air behind her as she held her feet to an unhurried pace until she was out of his sight. At the corner of the headquarters building, a raked gravel path led past the chapel, a whitewashed structure five windows long whose roof, rather than being peaked like the pavilions, was a semicircular curve. A stubby spire topped by an onion-shaped dome rose over the main door. A brick chimney stuck up beside that. Beyond the chapel, white-washed clapboard pavilions with their own chimneys formed a long row. A one-legged soldier with a beard half-way down his chest swung toward her on crutches.

"Sir—can you direct me to Pavilion H?"

"Sho' ma'am—right over yere." He aimed a crutch at the next barracks. "Got kin yere?"

"Thank you—yes—thank you!"

"Sho'" He swiveled on the crutches to watch her haste.

A single doorstep lifted to a floor of thick planks laid with inch-wide gaps for dirt and blood and scrub water to drop through. She peered down the long room. The ceiling was a series of trestles that braced the roof runners and re-vealed the undersides of the shingles. The walls, unpainted inside, were framed by upright studs to which the outside boards were nailed in overlapping fashion. Every third pan-el between the studs held a glassless window, its shutters open for air. At the far end another door stood open for what breeze might come by. Three rows of cots filled the room. One row lined each wall, the foot of the cots toward the center; the third row was cramped into the middle, leaving two narrow aisles. Men sat on their beds, lay asleep or stared at the ceiling, smoked or read or talked with visitors beside their cots. For a terrifying moment as heads turned toward her, they all looked alike in their narrow pain and suffering, and Lydia, not recognizing Simon among them, feared that she would no longer know his face.

"Who ye looking fer, miss?" A youth whose mustache scarcely darkened his upper lip limped toward her on a cane. A forage cap with a Jaeger horn emblem sat on the back of his head. "It ain't visiting day, ye know."

"Captain Morse. Simon Morse. Fifty-First New York infantry."

"Morse. A captain, ye say?"

"Yes!" She tried to study each face down the long rows of beds.

The youth's hand, palm up, wagged gently before her. "Why, I think I recognize that name. I think so, anyway." The palm wagged again.

Suddenly, Lydia understood and fumbled in her purse for a coin. "Where?"

The youth glanced at the silver ten-cent piece and slipped it in his pocket. "Well, I said I recognized the name. I didn't say he was here."

"Then where is he?"

"Well, he was moved out, I know that much. As to where—I guess I need to think some more." The now-empty hand wagged again.

"Here. Please think!"

"A quarter—now that stirs my memory, ma'am, it sure does. Soldier's home. That's where he went—the soldier's home across over on C Street. Day before yesterday." He touched a forefinger near his eyebrow. "Them that ain't well enough to report to their regiments but ain't sick enough to take up space here and don't have a home to go to, they get sent to the soldier's home for a few days."

"C Street, you say?"

He angled the cane toward the wall. "That way. C Street Soldiers' Home."

Not sick enough to take up space. Not well enough to report back to his regiment. The phrases gave strength to her limbs and urgency to her stride. No home to go to. Not sick enough to take up space...No home to go to...sent there for a few days...She forced herself to walk even faster, dodging between horses and wagons as she plunged across the crowded streets. Sent there for a few days...moved day before yesterday...no home to go to.

The large brick building was north of the Capitol Building. Its ground floor reached out to the sidewalk. And above that were stacked three deep porches supported by white wooden columns. The now-familiar shield of the Sanitary Commission hung beside the entry, and Lydia, fighting against the fear that Simon had already been transferred again, knocked on one of the Doric pilasters that flanked the door leading to a small hallway. Another bearded soldier on crutches leaned through the nearest door in the hallway. "Ma'am?"

"I'm seeking Captain Simon Morse. I was told he arrived two days ago from the Armory Street Hospital.

"Yes, ma'am. You want to sit in the visitor's parlor? I'll see if he's still here." He motioned to another open doorway across the hall.

Lydia went into a small room crowded with half-a-dozen plain wooden chairs. It smelled faintly of harsh soap and damp wood. Though she set the valise down, she did not sit. She did not feel the weariness. She scarcely dared to think and instead stood rigidly and listened intently for the sound of boots or a voice, but heard nothing.

Finally, a man with sunken eyes above gaunt cheekbones and a full beard streaked with gray stepped slowly into the room.

"Lydia?" His hoarse voice quavered. "Is it truly you?"

Chapter 27

It was night by the time she left the Soldiers' Home to find her lodging. Noting the names of ill-lit cross streets, she threaded her way under gleaming square lamps. Pennsylvania Avenue was even busier with evening crowds. Gentlemen in their finest coats mingled among soldiers in dark uniform jackets with sparks of polished brass; descending from carriages and cabs that filled the avenue, women displayed evening dresses ballooning with at least six petticoats, their bertha necklines modestly covered by light scarves. But all the excitement and gaiety were nothing compared to the joy in Lydia's heart. Simon was alive! He was weak, he moved cautiously and winced when that caution was ignored. He had lost much weight and looked so tired and frail that she doubted at first it was he. But it was, and he was alive, and—at least in spirit—he was the same! Tomorrow, they would go to the Sanitation Commission's Back-Pay Agency to complete the applications for Simon's records and then take the afternoon train in time to make their connection at Annapolis Junction.

At first, they had spoken little, content to drink in each other's face with their gaze. Even as her look caressed him, the stiff, tense creases at the corners of his eyes seemed to soften. Deep and large from his illness, his eyes gained warmth and a smile.

Finally, breaking a long mutual silence, he asked about her health, about Marshfield, Gretchen, Dan the horse, the crops.

She asked about his wounds and their progress, about his doctors, his convalescent duties. She did not know enough about soldiering to ask about the battlefield events that led to his wounds, and Simon did not speak of them.

"The colonel expects me to join the regiment in Kentucky. Veteran officers will be needed when the summer campaigns begin."

"But will your wounds be healed?"

"Near enough. Especially since my care has so improved in the last hour."

Lydia, studying her hands, could not help but say, "Then I have very mixed feelings about providing it, that you may leave again so soon."

Gingerly, he leaned forward to place his hand over hers. "I don't report back until May third. We have over thirty days. Remember, I had earned leave before it was canceled."

"I remember." She remembered, too, the undertakers' handbills.

"As for any regret you may have about being here, I can't fully express my wonder and gratitude at seeing you, Lydia. I never expected it. It gives me such joy."

"I've been so worried—so frightened. Learning that you were wounded and not knowing where you were, or if alive—receiving no answer to my letters—"

"I wrote! Or rather a visitor wrote for me. He came to the hospital once a week, until I was able to hold pen and paper."

"I received nothing."

"But Mr. Whitman sent the letters. He even provided the postage."

"They never arrived."

"I'm sorry, Lydia. I wrote—I dictated, at least—every week. I apologize for your suffering, my Lydia. The letters are probably shoved away in some corner of the postal service."

"It's unimportant now, Simon. I have found you alive."

He tugged at a streak of gray whiskers on his chin. "I have your letters under my pillow," he offered. "They're worn with much reading. And your gift box, which was so thoughtful and comforting."

She drew a long breath and tried to sound happy, "I'm glad. And I'm glad we will have that many days together."

❧❧❧

It wasn't until she awoke to the steady roll of the *Lydia* that the effort of the railroad journey and the tumult of impressions from Washington began to fade. The return trains had been almost as crowded as those arriving. Many of the soldiers had been pale, sick, and wounded. Most traveled on their own, a few were accompanied by weary sun-darkened men going home with them on leave. Women in fresh black, some with children, traveled in silence, accompanying the bodies of their husbands in the baggage cars; other women sat beside sorely wounded husbands or sons and struggled against their own exhaustion to tend their patients. Many drunk soldiers whose contracts had expired were bidding goodbye to army life some loudly, some bitterly, most simply staring out the window with unvoiced thoughts.

Across the boat's cabin and within arm's reach, Simon slept on the small wooden bunk. The heat and rough jolting of the train used much of his strength, and almost as soon as Roger steered the *Lydia* clear of the harbor, he fell asleep to the cool bay air and the gentle motion of the water. Now the boat heeled under a strong March breeze and Lydia braced her shoulders against the low roof as she tugged the quilt high on the gaunt figure. Rest and food—plenty of both. She could do that for him.

Quietly and bent over, she made her way up the short

steps to the cockpit where Roger cradled the tiller under his
arm and sat with his back to the wind.

"He sleeping still?"

"Yes. He's weaker than he admits."

Roger nodded, eyes going to the horizon on each side of
the bow before coming back to hers. "I'm right glad you
told me it wasn't his fault the soldier hit me. It's easier to
ask the Lord to make him whole."

"I appreciate your prayers, Roger."

"Yes'm.

She, too, gazed out across the rough water toward a
shoreline that was but a misty shadow in the late afternoon
sun. "He will grow healthy. He will!"

"Yes'm."

Roger held the craft steady under a wind that sharpened
from the stern quarter. Waves began to spray over the side-
boards and he suggested she go below to stay warm.

"I'm well enough, thank you, Roger. Do you want me to
spell you at the tiller while it's still light?"

"I'm well enough, too."

As dusk spread across the choppy water, Roger furled
the aftsail and lowered the foresail to half-mast. It slowed
the boat but also made it less visible in the gray light. Once,
he nodded silently toward a bump on the ill-defined horizon
and Lydia squinted into the evening sky to make out a trail
of black smoke that narrowed to the stack of a steam ship
whose hull was out of sight.

"Patroller. Union, most likely."

"We have a Union soldier aboard."

"Might be they'd care," he said mildly as he angled the
tiller away from the dark streak.

The light faded, but somehow Roger knew where they
were.

"Another hour or so, we'll reach Smith Island," his
shadow said. "Where my boat is. You'll have to follow me
to Marshfield from there."

"All right."

She had to haul up the keel board as they approached the darker smudge of the island. With night, the wind lessened, and Roger threaded through channels of low-tide mud banks into the small inlet where his boat rested. Quickly, and without mooring, he came alongside his craft and—as the *Lydia* nudged against the smaller open canoe—handed her the tiller and swung over the side.

His motion rocked the boats and drifted them apart. He quickly hauled up his anchor. Its chain sounded like a muffled growl over the bow. "Wait until I got some headway, then come about and follow me. Turn where I do."

"Yes."

With a rattle of dry canvas, Roger hoisted his sail. Then his boat glided through the dark, and Lydia, sculling the rudder to make the foresail boom cross over and catch the breeze, clumsily turned after the pale triangle of sail that led into the dark waters.

❧❦❧

A late-rising half-moon provided a path of rippling light down the channel as Lydia followed Roger's sail into Fowler Creek's estuary. Beside her, Simon, wrapped in the quilt against the cool night breeze, sighed deeply.

"It's a vision of beauty and peace, Lydia."

She listened as frogs began to sing after the passage of Roger's boat and then abruptly fell silent again as her own sail frightened them. They were almost home. The word surprised her with its emotion, as if this patch of marsh and sandy soil and the isolated house that sat on it had, in her absence, gained a sensibility that now welcomed her back. "Would that the world shared such peace."

"Amen." After a moment, he added, "Yet perhaps without such suffering we wouldn't rise to our true humanity. Perhaps God tests us to remind us that we are brothers and sisters all, and subject to a will greater than our own."

The thought of God expending Simon's life as a lesson

to her brought a tart phrase—"perhaps the dead share our gratitude"—to her lips. But she stifled it.

Which he noted. "You're silent, my Lydia. Is it disagreement? Well, it does seem eminently selfish that God should kill thousands so the remainder of us may suffer and find Him, doesn't it?" After a pause, he sighed. "Sometimes at night, when the wounded and dying in front of our lines groaned and cried for water, I asked myself what kind of God would demand such suffering to prove his authority. It's hard to imagine it would be a God of love." For a long moment he watched the ripple of the moon on the still, black water of the slough. "Mr. Whitman, the man who wrote many of my letters, sometimes spoke of the compensations of suffering."

"What could he possibly find to say, Simon?"

"That we suffer so we can understand the suffering of others. So we can join them in spiritual unity."

"I will have to think on that."

"As I've tried to do—not very successfully," he murmured. "Mr. Whitman's brother, George, was an officer with me in the fifty-first. He was wounded at Fredericksburg, too, and taken prisoner by the Rebels. He's since been paroled and sent home. Mr. Whitman came down to nurse him and vowed to stay in Washington as long as other wounded needed his services. I think his faith comes from his own experience: he came seeking his wounded brother, and now he's made brothers of all the wounded."

"He must be a great man."

"No. Just a civil clerk in a government office. And a member of the Christian Commission. But the times have raised in him a dedication to others and a faith in God's will."

"May his faith not be too long tested!"

He surprised her with a faint chuckle. "I say 'amen' to that, my Lydia."

In silence, they glided on the trembling silver path. Ahead, Roger dropped his sail and quickly tied up to the far side of the pier. Then he stood, a dim figure on the moonlit planks, and waited for the *Lydia* to coast gently into the pilings. Simon dropped the fenders over the side and, against Lydia's urging not to—"But I feel wonderful, Lydia. Better than I have in weeks"—tossed the bowline to Roger.

When they had secured and unloaded the *Lydia*, Roger dropped into his boat.

"You're most welcome to stay, Roger. At least let me fix supper for you."

"No'm. But thank you."

"When will we see you again?"

"I'll be by." He asked, "Is Gretchen looking after your place?"

"No—she's at home yet. Her mother."

He nodded. Then, "Right pleased you're feeling good, Mr. Morse."

"Thank you, Mr. Bradshaw, for doing so much for Mrs. Sensabaugh. She has told me of it. Know that I am your friend forever, and if you need anything at any time, please don't hesitate to ask. Good luck to you, sir."

Roger shoved the bow away from the dock and the light breeze pushed against the sail. "Good luck to you, too, Mr. Morse."

The moon glow whitened the sail as they watched it glide around a point of cordgrass. Then Lydia took the supply hamper and Simon the quilt and valises. As they went down the dock toward the shadow of the house, the uneasy boards creaked and groaned softly.

"I've neglected to keep my dock in repair," murmured Lydia.

"It will give me pleasure to work on it again."

"Your pleasure must be to gather your strength."

"But that's the kind of healthy work I crave. A quiet, sun-filled, constructive labor instead of the dark labors of war."

"We are more likely to have April showers, and you must avoid chills."

"Ssst!"

"Simon, did you hear something?"

But Simon was already moving. Quietly dropping the valises and quilt, he seemed to almost float in an animal crouch across the moon-silvered lawn toward the house. He angled for the darkest corner where a lilac bush made a ragged shadow. Lydia tried to follow his movement but the blackness swallowed his blurry figure. A moment later two silhouettes burst running from the dark corner, one chasing the other, the second lunging at the first as both became a dark writhing tangle on the moonlit grass.

"Simon! Simon, are you hurt?"

"No—" But his voice gasped. "All right, sirrah, up! Get up!"

"Miz Sensbaw—Miz Sensbaw—it's me!"

"Zekial? Is that you, Zekial?"

"Yes'm it's me—please tell this white man it's me!"

"Why, Zekial—what—"

"I been waiting around and waiting around ever since. Oh, laws, please tell this white man, Miz Sensbaw!"

"It's all right, Simon. It's Zekial—the boy I hired to look after the stock."

"Oh, Miz Sensbaw—I'm so glad you home!"

"Zekial, what's happened? Are you all right?"

The two figures untangled, Simon grunting slightly as he straightened against the sharp twist of his wounded shoulder.

"Men come late day before yesterday and took them little barrels from the barn. They talked about coming back to burn down your house—I been waiting and waiting to warn you."

"Yankee soldiers?"

"No'm. Just men."

"Do you mean Rebel irregulars?" asked Simon.

"I don't know if they regular or not. Two come on horseback and two come on a boat. I was coming down the path from Jack Town to take care of the animals and seen the two of them ahead of me setting off there in the trees looking at your place for the longest time. Then a little before sunset, they rode on in and one of them knocked on your door and then tried the latch while the other one went into the barn. Then both mens rolled the barrels out and rolled them down to the dock and while they was rolling, a little sloop come up the slough and tied up and they put all the barrels on it. Then the sloop left and the two mens come back to get their horses.

"They took nothing else?"

"No'm. Just your barrels. By then, it was getting on dark and your cow was calling for to be milked, so I moved close to hear and one talked about burning down your house. Said it was what you deserved. But the other said they wasn't told to do that. Said they could always come back and do that if that's what he wanted."

"'He'?"

"That's just what he said: 'If that's what he wants.'"

"They said nothing else?"

"Just the other one kind of laughed. Said something like, 'you know he'll want a barn for a barn, so we might's well.' And the other one said 'No, not without him saying so' and they left."

"A barn for a barn."

"Yes'm."

"Does that mean something, Lydia?"

"It means Parnell Carswell." She unlocked the front door and led Simon and Zekial in.

Simon set the valises near the stairs while Lydia groped for the wall sconce and its match holder. Absently rubbing his aching shoulder, he said, "I remember him. Your neighbor to the south—owns a large plantation, doesn't he?"

She replaced the glass around the candle. "He promised me trouble."

"What was in the barrels?"

"Fertilizer for my husband's Great Agricultural Experiment."

"In barrels?"

"In fifty-pound kegs. It was Franklin's dream and favorite topic of conversation. It was also, I'm afraid, something of a joke among the neighbors." She peered into the food safe. "Zekial, would you care for some bread and cheese? It's all I have right now."

"Yes'm, I can allus eat. But I better get home, too, before momma gets to worrying."

"Well, here—you can eat this on the way. And take Dan. I'm sure he needs exercise."

"Yes'm, well, maybe not—"

"Why?"

"Well, I kind of been riding him some already. Just a little—back and forth since them mens was here. I didn't want to leave him alone. You know, because they might come back and steal him or burn down the barn with him in it."

"Of course. That was very smart of you. Use him now and bring him back in the morning. And here," she handed him a silver quarter. "An extra quarter for telling me about those men. And don't forget to take your chicken."

"Yes'm!"

With a bit of a flourish, the boy demonstrated his ability to mount Dan, and trotted into the night, a ruffled and angry chicken tied on his lap. The faint clop of hoofs could be heard after their shadows blended into the moonlit tree line.

"Does your shoulder hurt, Simon? You must have stressed your wound."

"It's merely stiff." Absently, he picked up a scrap of cheese with his fingertip. "Why do you think Carswell wanted that fertilizer?"

"I don't know. Unless he intends to enrich his crops." Then Lydia shook her head as if to reject that idea. "But he had the kegs put aboard a boat."

"Meaning?"

"His plantation doesn't have a landing. If he planned to use it himself, he would have used a wagon. But why send fertilizer to the mainland when so much cropland there is being destroyed by the Yankees?"

Simon listened for a long moment to the night sounds: crickets, a whippoorwill, the soft call of an owl. Much of the Confederacy was now dominated by Union troops: the Long Valley of the Shenandoah, the plantations of the Virginia Peninsula and around Fredericksburg. Those along the Mississippi, in the valleys of Tennessee, and into northern Georgia were all under Union domination and had been burned to deny their produce to the Rebels. Why, indeed, send fertilizer to the Mainland? "What kind of chemical mixture was it?"

She recalled her husband's litany of its contents. "Nitrogen, phosphorous, and potash. Where we used it judiciously, we had greenness and rapid growth. But too much killed the plants. Franklin kept very good records of—"

"Gunpowder!"

Lydia blinked. "Gunpowder?"

"The old recipe for gunpowder: potassium nitrate, sulfur, and charcoal dust. That makes black powder. We read of it at the Academy. And the Eleutherian Mills have been converted into a gunpowder manufactury. Easy to do, since the chemicals they use for fertilizer are much the same as gunpowder."

"But there's neither sulfur nor charcoal—"

"They can be added, and they're plentiful. The key physic in the recipe is the nitrate—potassium nitrate—saltpeter. The ancient mix for black powder is six parts saltpeter to one of sulfur and one of charcoal dust. Compact and ignite in a musket, and boom—off goes the ball!" He nodded more to himself than to Lydia. "It won't be very powerful by itself, because of the other chemicals. But it can be mixed with regular strength powder to double or triple the amount on hand. And at close range it will work to satisfaction. How many kegs did you have?" he asked.

"I think thirty-five remained."

"Almost a ton. A goodly amount. Carswell's done his country a service, and at your expense, Lydia."

೧つe୨

While Simon, taking Franklin's shotgun, walked around the barn and grounds—a "security tour" he called it—Lydia washed the dishes. But her mind was elsewhere and, after wringing out the dishrag, she took a deep breath. Then, lips firm, she carried both valises upstairs to her room and unpacked them. When Simon returned to assure her that all was quiet, she led the way to the parlor and poured them each a glass of apple brandy. They toasted each other's health and sipped, their glances touching through the lamplight of the room. A long silence emphasized the house's stillness and grew increasingly tense with unspoken thoughts. Finally, a sense of propriety demanded some kind of conversation. "I have no proof to bring Carswell into court," she said abruptly. "Zekial is the only witness to what was said, and the testimony of a Negro won't be accepted."

Simon agreed hastily, "Nor was Carswell named. We would need one of the thieves to name his employer."

But the self-evident character of his comment embarrassed him and, he feared, revealed that his thoughts had not been focused on Carswell. Nor had Lydia said what she was really thinking.

But as another silence lengthened awkwardly, words of some kind were called for to mask the thought that rose like a fever in her breast. "And we don't know the thieves."

"No. We don't," he agreed.

"No."

Another long silence. Lydia took a very large sip of her apple brandy and felt its warmth spread from her stomach. "You must be quite tired, Simon." She hoped he did not hear the quiver in her voice.

"No, no. Being at Marshfield is a curative."

"Oh." Another large sip and a deep breath. "That's good. Nonetheless—I—have made up—our bed."

"Oh." Simon studied the woman whose dark eyes gazed

at him in a silence that rang with the meaning of that pronoun. He felt himself trying to mask the stir of his flesh. "Yes. I do feel some weariness."

Wordless, Lydia stood and took the lamp and turned to ascend the stairs, her head bowed and tense.

Simon followed her. As she went up each step, her dress made a gentle sway that spoke of the woman beneath. The shadow of her figure rippled along the wall. She led past the closed doors of what had been Gretchen's room and Lucy's across the hall, and at the end of the passage opened that to her room. Setting the lamp on the bedside table, she stood with her back to him, almost quivering and unable to turn or speak.

Simon stepped close behind her and his fingers, by their own will, reached to caress the cloth of her sleeves.

As he touched her, she gasped.

"I'm sorry," he said quickly.

"No!" She turned, eyes wide and deep. "I—I unpacked your valise. Your clothes are there in the chest." She cleared her throat. "Beside mine."

After a long moment, Simon's arms wrapped about her and he felt her arms slide up his back to suddenly clutch hard and he lost himself in the rich thickness of her hair, the fragrance of her powder, the taste of her lips.

Chapter 28

The sun's heat, unusually harsh even for late May in this year of 1864, wilted the leaves of Lydia's kitchen garden and made her labors heavy with perspiration. Instead of cooling with sundown, the air felt like damp wool until well after midnight. Tossing between sheets, restless with the weight of the humid warmth and worry for Simon, she returned time after time to the open window to stare into the night. It seemed that the mold of Nature itself, as she remembered King Lear's lament, was cracked by the deeds of humanity. Her eyes followed the gliding, winking dots of fireflies moving across the dark of the unmown lawn and the pier Simon had worked so hard on more than a year ago. Equally dim heat lightning—much too soon for the season—flickered nervously beyond the ragged silhouette of treetops. It seemed as if the guns that sought Simon's death showed their teeth against the night sky—as if the explosions he had faced last September in the terrible battle of Chickamauga, and could be facing even while she stood and yearned, threw their hateful glare as near as her bedroom windows.

The war dragged on and on and on, and every "final" battle led only to another. Her life, dull and featureless since Simon had returned to the army, dragged with equally blind doggedness, for her mind and her heart were no longer at

Marshfield. How much more could humanity absorb? How many more would be slain? How much effort could human will assert against the horridness of the lengthening lists of dead and wounded? How long, Oh lord, how long? Even Simon, in his letters, wondered at the determination that kept Rebel soldiers in the field against always increasing Union arms and always ebbing Confederate supplies. His last letter, dated May fourth, had come two weeks ago, addressed—like the others he had sent since returning—to his Dearest Wife Lydia. He had whispered the word "wife" that morning following their first night together. And on the day he left to return to his regiment, he had held her and murmured it over and over in her ear. And she had replied "husband," not because she felt it was needed to condone their union but because, as his eyes testified, it made him happy.

9 *May, 1864*
Near Jamestown, Virginia
I send my fondest wishes and most endearing words—you already have my heart. It will be forever with you, regardless what the coming days bring. We left Tennessee for Virginia and are encamped near Germanna ford on the Rapidan to make ready for the summer campaign. Genl Grant proposes to cross into the Wilderness and force Lee to bring his army in to the open where our numbers may provide a speedy end to this war. But your countrymen have proven resilient, and so we will see. Because of Genl Grant and his success at Vicksburg, almost our entire company have re-enlisted IW—In for the War, as they say. Only a surprising few did not return from their thirty day leave and they bear no opprobrium for that. As one who left said, I have no wish to monopolize patriotism and am happy to share it with others. The men are fine soldiers who know what they face and are determined to do their duty. I am very proud of them and

comforted by their hard won skills at war. So should you be, for their abilities help insure that we will be together once more when these dark days end. I rec'd yours of the sixteen of April in Kentucky and am delighted to learn that the chickens are now laying well and that you have had no troubles from The Squire Who Covets Marshfield. Perhaps my visit to his plantation last May had an effect on his behavior. Certainly he understood very clearly that Capt Gaines will be strict to protect the property and lives of threatened citizens. He also understands that any harm to you will be laid directly at his door by Captain Gaines and myself. Rest easy and be comforted, my Lydia, and dream as I do of the days and nights we shared and of those we will share in the future. My health, so you will not worry, is fine and I have no pain or fever from my wounds, all of which is directly attributable to your care and love. I thank God that you, too, are healthy and caution you to labor lightly at your work. When I return home—and I think of any place where my wife resides as home—we will bring fruition to our dreams.

Lydia, having read the page daily for three weeks, could recite it from memory, as well as the following half-page that recalled the warmth and beauty of their too-brief nights of love. Even as she scanned Simon's words once more, memories of those swift days and nights returned, and she felt an animal heat in her flesh that almost embarrassed her. It also made her wonder again at the differences between the passion that Simon raised in her and the passiveness of Franklin's effect. Perhaps it was not all Franklin's lack. Unlike the girl who had married him, she was now a mature woman who was no longer timid about admitting—to herself at least—that a conjugal duty could also be a pleasure. Indeed, and she almost blushed, had become increasingly pleasurable until it was a magnificent and soul-wrenching convulsion of giving and union. In all but law, she was married to Simon. In her flesh, her heart, and her mind, she was his wife and he her husband. She did thank God that, unlike poor Lucy, she was not with child. There had been three frightening weeks after he left when her regularity failed, but even then she had not regretted her act. Should she bear his child, she knew that when this long war finally ended, they would solemnify their marriage before the law as—she assuredly felt—it was already solemnified before God.

She turned from the window to light one of the scarce candles. More than a year had passed since Simon left, yet she lived more intensely in that past than in this present. Instead of flowing in seamless days, time now leapt only occasionally.

Between those rare leaps the days seemed repetitions of meaninglessness. It was a twisting of time that Simon had pondered, lying beside her in the dark, both of them sated with love and discovering that their minds were as entwined as their bodies had been. For him, months in the camps seemed routine and dull prefaces to the intensity of one day or even one hour of war.

She had not then fully understood; but now she shared this new measure of time. It was not that time really slowed or sped, but an intensity made a few hours memorable while the rest were at best dull and at worst irrelevant. It was as if one lived only in brief moments and found the remainder of life to be unwanted space between. It left a sad sense of waste and was, the analogy surprised her, akin to the sad feeling she had when she massaged the wrinkled, shiny scars of Simon's wounds.

This odd perception of time also seemed evident in the weary tone of Bonnie's three-month old letter that had come with Simon's latest. Indeed, her sister seemed to sense it even more strongly than Lydia, perhaps because the most trivial and ordinary detail of life now called for such a heavy effort of mind and flesh that it was another burden for her.

February 22, 1864
Mangrum Plantation
Charlton County, Georgia, CSA
My Dear Sister,

This may or may not reach you. The world is so distant from us and our suffering that I often despair that any soul knows of us or even cares. Our brave soldiers fight on, living in some manner to defend our soil from the invaders. Thank God for General Lee!! We manage as best we can. Fortunately, the plantation provides food enough for our needs and even a little extra to send to our soldiers, though a number of the field hands have sneaked away into the swamps where the few patrollers can't find them and where for all I care they can drown. Or become bait for snakes and gators. Uncle Louis and Aunt Julie have been kind masters to them—perhaps too kind—but that is the gratitude they show. Perhaps it is only to be expected from those so recently raised from the level of savages.

My children are my solace now. My husband has been at sea constantly for the last year with no opportunity to visit even for Christmas which disappointed me and the children bitterly. I do not know if he is alive. His last letter came two months past from Charleston port and nothing since. I pray constantly that I receive a letter from him but that prayer has yet to be answered. Perhaps we have been forgotten by God Himself. I pray to receive a letter from you as well.

I wish I had something good to write of but it is difficult to think of anything good. Or, indeed, of much at all except scraping together another breakfast, dinner, supper. Sometimes I feel I am deep in a root cellar where days pass but there is no life. Life is somewhere outside the cellar, and I wonder if I am going mad.

This is a somber letter, Sister Lydia. I am sorry. It is difficult to be happy, it is difficult to organize my thoughts or my words. But you are in my thoughts, what thoughts I have. Surely this war must end sometime! I pray for that day, too, if God listens. I love you and hope all is well with you. Your Sister Bonnie.

When she had read her sister's letter at the Sundries Store, Lydia, eyes damp, had been moved to sit in the rocking chair of the Ladies' Parlor to write an immediate answer. Mr. Henderson, shaking his head at the address on the envelope, could not promise its delivery. The anaconda, he said, was even tighter and communications of all kinds were more difficult now and much more expensive. The best he could do was try. Lydia had to accept that.

Now, as a stray breeze swayed the candle flame and threw shadows across the stiff piece of wallpaper, Lydia tried to remember the last time she had seen Bonnie in Norfolk City. But that image would not come. Instead her mind kept returning to Simon: his joy in the work of replacing the broken planks and braces of the pier, her joy in his growing strength and appetite as his torn and weakened body healed, that soft evening aboard the *Lydia* when, letting the boat drift as it would, they repaired to the cabin and, later, he teased her by describing the energetic swings the mast must have made.

She could not share those memories with Bonnie, nor could she share with her sister her fear and yearning for the man she loved. She could not even mention Simon's name.

Lydia saved his letters in her secretary: the first telling of his tour of Provost duty in Kentucky after the fall of Vicksburg and Jackson; a later one lamenting that he would not receive his regimental veterans' leave in the spring; finally his joy to learn that the Fifty-First was to rejoin the Army of the Potomac and how glad he would be to see Annapolis because together they had passed through that place, and how hard to be so near yet unable to visit because the regiment was constantly moving. But last week she had read in *The Salisbury Union Trumpet* early reports about the conflict faced by the Army of the Potomac at the Spotsylvania Court House.

Too tense to sleep, she blew out the candle and sat beside the window in the cooler dark, her mind jumping from thought to thought. Life at Marshfield had gone on, no matter how stale that going seemed. Lights occasionally flickered in the marsh, but Lydia knew whose they were and was cautious enough to ignore them.

Once on a following morning she had ridden Dan over to the point of land where she and Roger had discovered that faint track leading to the water's edge. Now it was a well-worn path to a muddy bank where sailing canoes nudged ashore to be loaded.

Lucy's baby, according to Gretchen, looked just like Allen Rafer, which made Lucy's father hate the baby all the more—"Not like it was that little baby's fault!" snapped Gretchen. Lucy responded to her father's anger by refusing to speak to him. "I reckon being a mother's given Lucy some spunk, which she can certainly use." Gretchen herself seldom visited Marshfield. Her mother's wasting illness lingered so that the poor woman thought constantly of going to heaven as relief from pain. But she did not want to escape before Humphrey came home. "Pa needs me, too, ma'am. He's just as sorrowful as can be about Mama, and we ain't heard nothing from Humphrey in the longest time. He finds comfort that I'm there, and I reckon my brothers do, too."

"Of course, Gretchen! Your first duty is to your family!"

"Yes'm. But it can get, well, right close sometimes. Fletcher's going on sixteen and him and Pa's already fighting about him wanting to enlist. That would break Mama's heart for sure. I did ask Pa if I could spend a couple days to help you with plowing." She added with a slightly defensive note, "I figured being away a bit would give me strength when I go back."

"You may visit whenever you wish and stay as long as

you like. You're always welcome at Marshfield, Gretchen, and you need not pay your way with the plow."

"Yes'm, I thank you, but sometimes it just makes me feel better to work up a swea—ah—a perspiration. Oh, and I seen Roger Bradshaw when I was going home last time. He told me all about you two sailing over to the Federal City last year to bring home that captain. He sends his regards."

"Was he in good spirits, Gretchen?"

"Seemed to be. Talked more'n I ever heard him do before, leastways." She looked away across the corn field. "He ought to trim that beard some. But his nose don't look near as bad despite it's crooked. He still covers his mouth to laugh, though. The missing teeth, you know. He did say he's doing right good at fishing and sells everything he catches."

❧❧❧

Lydia remembered, too, a visit from Mr. Talbot on a day in February when the sun glared whitely but the still air was cold enough to frost his breath: "That soldier-boy of your'n around, Miz Sensabaugh?"

"No," she said with a sense of caution. "But he's due for leave. He may visit soon."

"Well, right soon ain't right now, and I'm right glad." The black beard parted to show grinning teeth. "I'd sure hate for him to think I was courting his woman. Specially after he offered to horse whip the squire should something happen to you or your'n."

"Mr. Carswell would have nothing to fear if he had stayed out of my barn!"

"Oh, he ain't afeard—I'm not sure what he is, because I don't see him that much anymore, except on business. But don't think of him as afeard to do what's best for Parnell Carswell when the time is ripe, and damn the rest of the world." His dark eyes lost all hint of humor. "Don't make that mistake, ma'am, Yankee soldier-boy or no."

"I appreciate your concern, Mr. Talbot."

He shrugged away her sarcasm. "And just so's you'll know: I wasn't here when they took that fertilizer or whatever out of your barn. Squire made a right good profit out of that, since his cost was so low." The laugh came and went. "But Squire won't bother you right now. He don't want the Yankees stirred up to patrol the slough."

"I've seen the lights."

His black eyes seemed to glitter. "I hope you ain't told nobody about that."

"I haven't."

"That's good—that's mighty good for all concerned." The man turned the brim of his hat in his hands and then looked up. "Well, I come to tell you there's going to be a lot more lights soon, and it's best you don't pay attention to them, neither." A small twist of his mouth under the ragged mustache. "I'm in the import business now, and work's picking up smartly, since about every harbor along the Atlantic's cut off. We're seeing more and more blockade-runners around this neck of the woods. I'm here to tell you that Squire's willing to leave you be if you leave us be."

"I will not accept terms from Parnell Carswell."

"Yes'm that's fine. But I also tell you he won't care about killing a Yankee if that Yankee finds out about those lights. So you're to let Squire know when your Yankee comes to visit, so that won't have to happen."

She had not considered that her defiance of Carswell would place Simon's life in danger. "He would not!"

"Oh, he would. Yes'm. He might even do that one himself. He had his nose twisted hard by your soldier-boy and he ain't one to forgive that."

"I don't know when Simon may visit. He may not come at all!"

Talbot bobbed his head in agreement. "True. Lots of hard fighting going on right now. It's just that if he does come, you best let Squire know." He held out a square of red kerchief. "Just hang this out...let's see..." His eyes narrowed. "How about one of your bedroom windows? They're easy to see from the trees. Just hang this out your bedroom if he does. Somebody will see it and know to leave you to your privacy." His black eyes caught at her wide ones. "And if he don't happen to come back from the war, I hope you will remember my offer. You were good looking to start with, and exercise has brung improvement. Good day, ma'am."

She had not thrown away that red kerchief. Well, yes, she had, immediately, as if it embodied not only the threat from Parnell Carswell but the filth of Mr. Talbot's mind. But then she had gone out to the trash pile beyond the pigsty and taken it back and washed the ashes of burned trash from it. She might not use it—but, then, she might. To throw away any opportunity to protect Simon when he returned to Marshfield would taunt fate, and she would not allow her injured sense of honor or her contempt for those men to endanger Simon's life.

Chapter 29

The lights appeared a number of times, but in late June Lydia's thoughts were focused more on newspaper reports of the terrible fighting in the Wilderness Campaign. Simon's regiment, along with Grant's army, had fought day after day against Lee, but only now were details of that savage fight coming out: seventeen-thousand Union casualties, eight-thousand Secesh killed and wounded. Horrible stories of forest fires that burned to death those too injured to escape. Grant was written of as a "killer arithmetician" willing to expend two of his soldiers for one Rebel, knowing that Union losses could be replaced but the Confederate's could not. And he earned a disquieting sobriquet: "The Butcher."

In the welcome relief from summer's heat provided by the Sundries Store's Ladies Parlor, Lydia sat looking at a thick envelope addressed in Simon's hand and wrinkled with travel and rain. She did not open it immediately but tried to calm her apprehension of what it might say by caressing the scuffed paper as if her fingers could touch the fingers that had sealed it, as if they could tell whether the letter held good news or bad.

"Mrs. Sensabaugh?" Mrs. Henderson, her hands wiping inside her apron and eyes widely staring, came slowly from the back of the store. "I must speak with you. I must."

"Of course, Mrs. Henderson." The flesh around the woman's mouth was drawn taut and her words struggled to break the stiff mask that was her face.

"I must tell you that you are no longer welcome in this parlor."

Startled, Lydia started to ask why. But her surprise flashed into anger and stifled the question. She deliberately gathered together Simon's letter, her newspapers and emotions, her shopping list, her reticule, her sunbonnet, her pride, and stood. Shock, anger, and hurt sealed her lips. Mrs. Henderson's eyes bulged with rage as they watched every move. Lydia sensed the woman holding herself tightly against an explosion.

"I trust the porch bench is available to me?"

The woman's gray hair, tied into a heavy bun at the back of her neck, jerked down and up once. "That's Mr. Henderson's. The Ladies Parlor is mine! And you are not welcome in it."

Lydia, too, nodded once and went stiffly into the heat of the open porch and its plank bench. The long, thick board was carved and pitted by idle knives and smoothed by years of use. Vague dark streaks marked the wall behind it where perspiring backs and greasy heads rested. At each end and halfway down, chipped porcelain chamber pots half filled with sand served as spittoons. The porch boards around them showed the results of poor marksmanship. She sat at the end farthest from the open door and tried to calm her breathing. Lydia would not ask that woman's reason; if that woman could not civilly explain her attitude and give Lydia the opportunity to reply, certainly Lydia was not going to beg her to.

But she felt both resentment at being insulted and the bitter knowledge that there was no other store where she might buy supplies or receive mail. A swirl of dust from the road made her blink and wafted the odor of the nearest spittoon. She edged away from the smell, clutching the letter in an angry grip and unwilling to open it to that stench. Somewhere beyond the church a dog barked listlessly in the thick heat. Dan, tied to the rail, munched softly at the grain in his feedbag, an occasional deep breath indicating his contentment. Inside the store, the slow thump of distant heels moved along the aisles, paused, moved again. Finally the sound came closer, hesitated, then came to the doorway. "Mrs. Sensabaugh? What are you doing sitting out here in the heat, ma'am?"

"Your wife ordered me out of her parlor."

"Ann—" The man blinked. Then his lips pursed in a silent whistle and he dragged his spatulate fingers across the bristles of his chin. "Well, I'm sorry for that. I'll speak to her."

"Please do not. It is her parlor, she told me, and she told me that I am unwelcome there. I have absolutely no desire to return."

"I see." He stared down at the dusty boards of the porch. "Her youngest brother was killed. Over at Cold Harbor— she heard about it yesterday. She ain't—she's hurting awful, is what it is, ma'am."

"But what have I to do with that? I'm sorry for her loss—deeply—I can understand how she feels. But why does she hate me for it?"

"Well, I reckon it's your Yankee soldier she hates. The one sends you the letters." His head indicated the envelope in her hand. "Squire Carswell's told us about him. It don't bother me," he said hastily. "I got one Union uncle and one Secesh. And a lot of cousins on either side, and some that's been on both. But Mrs. Henderson, her family lives over near Fairfax, and they all went with Virginia." He paused to think. "Lived. They lived near Fairfax. But both Bull Run battles went across their farm and they've lost everything they had—house, stock, slaves. And now her brother who was her favorite."

Slowly, Lydia felt the anger drain from her. "I am sorry, Mr. Henderson. It's a terrible war and so many are suffering so much. I am truly sorry."

"Yes'm. I appreciate that. And Mrs. Henderson will, too, in time. I just thought you should know why she said what she did, is all." He sighed deeply. "I'll load your wagon."

℘℘℘

The towering oak tree that marked the Williams farm was almost blue in the heat that shimmered from the white road and the baking fields on each side. Through her cotton print dress, the sun burned Lydia's shoulders and drew perspiration from beneath her sunbonnet to tickle down her neck. The letter lay still unopened in her reticule; she had not wanted to open it in the atmosphere of Mrs. Henderson's hatred and now did not want to open it under the burden of the sun and its painful glare. Instead, she huddled in the small circle of shade from the parasol she held in her free hand as she willed the tree to draw nearer, bringing its refuge of shade for the plodding horse and water for both of them.

Twice, groups of Yankee soldiers, not bothering to ask for her pass, cantered by in a haze of dust that hung above the sun-bleached road. Instead of the ballooning red pants of the Zouaves, these wore the more familiar pale blue trousers and sweat-stained, dark blue coats. Their forage caps lacked the Zouaves' kerchief to shelter their napes, but many had unbuttoned their collars and tied bandannas of various colors about their necks for protection from sun and dust. The listless guidon of the first group was notched at the rear and had two circles of white stars, one within the other, in a blue field above the red and white stripes of the bottom of the pennant. Lydia did not know what regiment the symbols stood for, but she had read that the army was beginning to send war-weary soldiers to more peaceful occupation duties as a rest between battles. A few men from each group eyed her as they went by, some with only a glance, others with a long stare that felt like the lick of a hot tongue. But most of them just seemed wearily numb, as if they rode in a dream and she was not part of what filled their minds.

Lydia, her throat sticky with thirst, turned Dan into the Williams' farmyard. Their dog, Jenny, lay quiet in the shade under the porch, tail thumping once or twice in recognition and too hot to bark. At the smell of the water trough beside the pump, the sweating horse picked up his pace. She let him drink deeply before leading him into the tree shade to stamp and swing his tail against the flies. Then she rapped on the frame of the open door.

"Mrs. Sensabaugh—it's been ages! Come in, dear!"

The coolest room in the farmhouse was the porch off the kitchen, shaded by another oak tree that spread its relief over a corner of the barnyard as well. As they sipped tea cooled in a crock wrapped with a wetted cloth and set in an open window to catch any breeze, Lydia told the woman about Mrs. Henderson's brother. From the wilting fields, insects creaked and buzzed listlessly, and even the chickens, beaks gaping from heat, sprawled their wings in shaded sand to find comfort.

"It do be unnatural hot." Mrs. Williams waved a palm-leaf fan in front of her face.

"'Sometimes too hot the eye of heaven shines,'" quoted Lydia, adding, "and this is certainly one of those times."

"Now where's that from? Who said that?"

"Shakespeare—in his sonnet 'Shall I compare Thee.'"

"I never read the Bard—Pa wouldn't have frivolous writings in his house, and since I have been married, there just don't seem to be much time for reading. But maybe it would provide comfort in times like these." She went on hastily as if to ward off bad luck: "Not like the Bible, certain! That's the true source of comfort, and I do read that when I can. But maybe some of the times when the Bible's not too clear..."

"Wise words can come from many sources," Lydia mused. "I used to think real wisdom was to say clearly what our heart had already told us. But this war is so beyond anything my heart has ever considered that it's as if I'm in a reality still undefined. I don't know that words can encompass so much pain and loss."

Mrs. Williams did not quite follow her guest's thought, but she nodded anyway and went back to the previous topic. "Well, while I don't take to Mrs. Henderson throwing you out like that, I can't help but feel sorry for her loss."

"Nor I."

Another silence where words did not stretch far enough to cover pain.

"I thank the good Lord that I had all girls and that they're married and mothers themselves, now." She wagged her head, "If I had to worry about a son in all this, and it coming closer every day, I don't know what I'd do."

"Closer? What have you heard?"

"There's a lot of sea fighting betwixt us and the mainland—Mr. Williams said there's been prizes seized near as Point Lookout." Her voice dropped as though her words could carry that far. "And he said the Atlantic side's busy, too. Some blockade-runners were using Wachapreak Inlet a lot, so some Chincoteaguers piloted a Yankee frigate down that way to catch them. And, I reckon, to get their share of the prize money as well."

"I passed two Union patrols between here and New Church. They weren't the Zouaves—they wore regular uniforms."

"That must've been some of the New Jersey men Mr. Williams heard about—part of a cavalry regiment sent here to rest up from fighting." She stared out the window a moment. "The Zouaves been sent over to the Western Shore. Mr. Williams heard they wasn't too happy about that—said they didn't sign up to be cannon fodder for U. S. Grant."

"A lot of these soldiers seemed...very distant."

"Mr. Williams heard the New Jersey men seen an awful lot of fighting from First Bull Run on. Said there's only about forty of them left out of more'n three hundred. Said they're real hard men who wouldn't think twice about shooting any Rebel who looked at them cross-eyed."

Lydia sipped her tea and gazed across the quivering fields. Absently, her hand stroked her reticule with the letter within, and she now hungered to read its words and to hear his voice lift from the page. She was rested and calm at last, thanks to Mrs. Williams's hospitality, and the sun was lower, lessening its heat. With the revival of her mind from the stultifying heat and the shock of what happened at the Sundries Store, she felt a growing eagerness to be back at Marshfield where she could at last open Simon's letter in a place where they had shared happiness.

Chapter 30

*P*etersburg, Virginia
June 19, 1864
My Dearest Wife Lydia,

Please excuse this disordered letter. I have been writing it since May ninth but we have been moving so much, and this is the first time the postal sergeant has collected mail. I'm almost out of writing paper as well. Our baggage and commissary did not keep up and our pay is four months in arrears, so I must send this as poor as it is. We have finally dug in, as they say. The men have dug with a will, since Petersburg is well-fortified and enemy shot comes hot and fast when anyones head shows above an entrenchment. We all hope that US Grant will not try to take Petersburg with direct assault. We learnt our lesson at Cold Harbor last month and do not need a repeat. I love you, my Lydia and I miss you so very much. Though I send this in haste I promise to write again soon but want to get this to the postal sergeant before he goes. I love you now, and regardless what may happen, I love you always. Simon.

The torn strip of paper ended. The next leaf was dated almost six weeks earlier, May ninth, near Piney Branch Church, and held a series of fragmented entries.

My Dearest Wife,

The Wilderness lives up to its name. We hoped to catch Old Lee by surprise but when we crossed the Rapidan, we heard considerable fighting and saw many brush fires that night. Fighting began again at dawn but we could see none of it for the thickness of the forest. The wounded and stragglers told of much woe at the hands of an enemy who knows this Wilderness better than we do. Around noon our corps was called forward through woods so thick that no enemy could be seen until they fired not fifty feet away. By late afternoon we built a breastwork and the enemy came at us behind burning woods whose fire and smoke threatened to do what enemy bullets and cannon had not. But we held and as darkness came none could see to shoot and the men were so worn that when I inspected the line, I could not distinguish between those who slept to wake and those who would wake no more. Today, except for a few shots and cannonading off in the woods, we rest, foe and friend alike exhausted, and I take this moment to assure you of my wellbeing and love.

The Wilderness
May fourteenth
My Dearest Lydia, despite weariness and loss our spirits are high. We had thought that after our losses these last days our army would retreat as Genls Pope and Hooker have done before us. But instead of returning to the Rapidan, we turned south toward Spotsylvania. When the men realized the direction they were taking, they cheered as US Grant rode past. That cheer though losing much of its early strength has remained to see us through days of fighting since. We lost Uncle John Sedgwick the beloved genl of VI Corps who was killed just after he told his men that Rebel marksmen could not hit an elephant at this distance. Our IX Corps attacked a strongly defended

bend called the Horseshoe Salient at 4.30 in the morning of May tenth. The fighting was so close that men were bayoneted through a parapet of logs with us on one side and our foe on the other. We fought hard but we could not break their lines and many brave men died on both sides. Our flag bearer, Sgt. Jos. Willey among them. It is said that more than 12,000 men fell in one square mile. We hoped for a rest but US Grant does not allow us or more importantly our opponent that luxury and we are marching again—still to the South! I hear a runner calling officers together and must continue this later, but not without a hasty I Love You.

31 May on Topotomoy Creek
My Dearest Lydia
My mind is numb with constant marching and skirmishing. We exchanged pleasantries with Lee at the North Anna river, moved into line along the Pamunkey river on May twenty-sixth to twenty-eighth, and night before last moved here to drive our enemy away from the creek so the army might camp safe from sharp shooters. At present we rest and do laundry—well, do stockings and scrub our hands and faces, anyway, and cook some hot beef, since we finally have enough water for other than drinking and horses. It is pleasant to sit for this while in cool shade and recall the peace of Marshfield and the face of its dear mistress, and to dream on what you may be doing this very instant. Despite the weariness our men are elated at the movement southward. We are truly On to Richmond with promise of making it before summer is over. Would it not be a wonder, my Lydia, to have all this ended and come home to you!!

June fifth Cold Harbor
My Dearest Wife,

It has been hot work at Cold Harbor. And bloody work, too. Our regt was beaten back from Rebel lines time and again on the first, second, and third of June. Their entrenchments are constructed in a very clever manner so when one trench is taken the attackers are under enfilade fire from yet another. It is a kind of fighting not seen before in history, and is a mark of the determination and ingenuity of our opponent. On that last day in a matter of just ten minutes our army lost 7,000 men. The ground in front of the entrenchments was so covered with the fallen that no grass could be seen. Before the attack some wag said it was going to be a lottery and a lot would win a capital prize, and so it proved. No one in the Fifty-First believes that more than a few men can return from assaulting such fortifications. But the Fifty-First will attack when ordered of course. It is a bravery and determination that awes me, My Lydia, yet it is matched by those we face who fight so fiercely. I feel love for the men under my command regardless that many of them drink heavily, curse amazingly, and gamble on anything. Surely if there is a God, he must have room in heaven for sinners who are so brave. Some of the newspapers point out we are where Genl McClellan was two years ago but this time it cost us over 50,000 men dead and wounded to get here. Almost half our army's strength. Our opponents have lost half as much dead, wounded, and captured. But when called, we will attack because to a man we want this war over, and no man wants that outcome more than I for reasons you well know.

James River
June thirteenth
My Dearest Wife Lydia,
Our genl has broken off from Lee and left him in his entrenchments at Cold Harbor. Our immediate

goal is Petersburg whence we will be able to follow
the rail road lines north to Richmond. Many—I
among them—are vastly relieved not to be charging
those fortifications. They held tenaciously and took
very many brave souls. Lieutenant Rice announced to
his company that he would give his right arm to swing
a sword at Lee and when a Minnie Ball took it off it
occasioned much humor amongst the men. Jokes and
stories now have a grim note and men who once
would have lifted their hats to pray over a lost soul
will now readily use his body for protection against
enemy bullets and think nothing of it. The only thing
that fills our mind is to end this.

Petersburg
18 June
My Dearest Lydia,
To be so near to the end and yet see the Stars and
Bars still flying stubbornly over his entrenchments!
Genl Smiths XVIII Corps attacked on the fifteen instant and took the larger part of the fortifications
from the Rebel who started it all, Genl Beauregard.
But rather than press his attack, he waited for reinforcements. When they did arrive, Smith still did not
attack. Everyone including the Drummer Boys knew
he should attack and Genl Hancocks soldiers cried
tears of rage when no orders came and some even
threatened to go forward without orders if Smith
would not send his order. But no order came. That
gave Beauregard time to rebuild his lines and Lees
army time to arrive from Cold Harbor. These entrenchments make a veritable city underground. Log
redoubts covered with earth that cannonading cannot
break are connected by miles of walled trenches that
reinforce each other. It is Cold Harbor made worse.
Taking those that remain will be a very costly waste
of life, since Genl Smith did not do his duty. Our bag-

gage train has finally reached us and we are settling into bivouac life surrounding Petersburg. When opportunity arises I will send this collection of letters to you with my love. I hope that your letters will soon be brought forward, my wife, for I cannot tell you how much they mean to me and how much comfort it is to read your words. Lydia my wife. I cannot say those words enough.

Chapter 31

Blown by a winter gale off the bay, icy rain rattled the windows. Lydia and Gretchen closed the door to the dining room against drafts and pulled their chairs close to the heat of the kitchen stove. They sipped fragrant, hot tea made of dried rose hips gathered in the autumn. Blackstrap molasses took the place of brown sugar, now expensive and often not available at the Sundries Store.

Grateful for the warmth, Gretchen dried out from her ride to Marshfield as Lydia summarized Captain Morse's letters. "Humphrey's at Petersburg, too," Gretchen said. "A letter come last week, through Maryland Mr. Henderson said. Humphrey says all he's doing is sitting in the diggings with mud up to his chin and hunger down to his toes. He says since the big mine explosion last summer they spend half their time listening for Yankees digging underneath their lines and the other half trying to dodge mortar shells coming from above, and the other half crawling through mud at night around the enemy entrenchments."

"That's three halves, Gretchen."

"Yes'm. Humphrey ain't strong on arithmetic. He said he don't hate Yankees any more but he will keep trying to kill them and they will keep trying to kill him. Says the Yankees got a lot better chance at that since now they got repeating rifles that can fire eight bullets to his one."

Gretchen sighed and added another dollop of molasses to her tea. "Said he spent some time talking with Yankee pickets in a trench not too far from his'n, and they even crawled out one night and traded tobacco for soap and real coffee. He said they're just as tired of war as he is. They call him Johnny despite he tells them his name's Humphrey, so he calls them all Billy."

As she listened, Lydia noted the lines marking Gretchen's face. The softness of girlhood was drying into the more defined and heavier face of a woman, a result, Lydia surmised, not only of her increasing years but of the worry and burden of her mother's illness and her brother's absence.

"I do hope he comes home soon. I don't know how much longer Ma can hold on, she's just skin and bones now."

"Is Doctor Dawson able to help her at all?"

"He's give her some laudanum. It helps some with the pain. But it makes her sleep a lot, too, and she don't eat more'n a smidgen of her meals." Another sigh. "The laudanum dries up her innards, you know. I do hope Humphrey comes soon."

There seemed to Lydia an invisible, massive weight pressing down all over the Confederacy and felt even in this occupied fragment of Virginia. Perhaps her sense of burden was intensified by the months that had passed since receiving Simon's last letter in September. But that feeling had also been strong in Bonnie's letter which told of the displaced citizens of destroyed Atlanta drifting hungry and exhausted past Mangrum Plantation, and of the devil Sherman burning, looting, killing, and worse as he cut his way toward the sea: *The world that I once knew is gone forever, and in its place nothing but desolation, ruin, and the death of loved ones. Oh, that my husband is alive and well! If I knew that, I could smile even in the face of this Hell. But I do not know and that is a greater Hell in itself.*

"Mr. Henderson tells of fights in the Atlantic near Wachapreak inlet. Picket boats going after blockade-runners," Gretchen said. "And they say over at Reason

Creek a Yankee steam boat was set afire by some Home
Guard men after it run aground." She frowned and wagged
her head. "It seems this war's getting closer and closer, despite we've been lucky to be out of it so far. I never in my
life thought I'd say that about being occupied by the Yankees." A small smile softened her face. "I got a letter a
while back from Joshua Hines. He wrote it just before he
was killed."

"I was so saddened to find his name listed."

"Yes'm. Me too. Despite him being a Yankee and all."
Gretchen stared out the kitchen window at the wet night.
"He wanted to marry me after the war. Said if I said I would,
he'd come down when he was mustered out and ask my
folks for my hand."

"Ah—"

"Well, I wrote him I would. But he didn't get my letter
in time."

"I'm so sorry."

"Well."

A surge in the gale trembled the house. The flames in the
hot stove gave a muffled, flannel-like rattle.

"I reckon I better not go looking for any more beaux, not
if I don't want them killed off."

The weak humor hid the girl's tears. Lydia murmured as
much to herself as to Gretchen, "This war must end soon.
Life will be better then."

"Yes'm. But the war does seem to be moving closer."

❡❦❡

Two weeks later, on a clear and icy February night, the
war came to Lydia's door with a soft but insistent tapping
that pulled her out of sleep. She shrugged quickly into a
quilted dressing gown and, with a candle-lamp, lit her way
downstairs. The tapping came again from the front door and
Lydia stared at it for a long minute before peeking out the

parlor window. In the wash of cold moonlight across the porch, she made out a pair of booted legs. The figure above them was lost in the blackness of the porch.

"Simon?" Her breath caught as she asked.

No answer.

"Who's there?"

"Is this the Sensabaugh farm? Mrs. Lydia Sensabaugh?"

"Yes. Who are you?"

"A kinsman. One who needs your help."

She slid the bolt and opened the door a crack. "Who are you?"

A bearded face, breathing heavily, leaned to the opening to murmur, "Andrew—Bonnie's husband. Are you alone, Sister Lydia?"

"Good lord!" She opened the door and stepped back as the man glanced over his shoulder and moved quickly to close the door behind him. "Are you alone?"

"Yes." She stared wide-eyed at the man's face where dried blood ran from a swollen knot over one eye and down into a muddy beard. "You are injured!" The face staring back was only slightly familiar, but it was Andrew—so changed.

"Only lightly. Please blow out the candle. I think I lost them, but a light will catch their eyes."

"What—How—"

In the moon glow from the window he held a finger to his lips. "Shhh. Voices carry at night," he whispered. "I'll explain all, but let's be silent for now. Water—might I trouble you for a drink of water?"

"Come," she whispered back as she blew out the candle.

He removed his muddy boots and followed to the kitchen where the pump made wheezing, squealing noises that seemed inordinately loud. Andrew gulped several glasses of water and then, shivering with cold, settled wearily on a kitchen chair. Lydia brought him a quilt and held her questions as they listened to the night. Once, came the deep bay of a hound from somewhere.

A short time later they heard the thud of hooves.

"Quickly," said Lydia. "Upstairs." She led him to her cedar closet and shoved her dresses and petticoats aside. "Hide here."

He wasted no words but burrowed into the darkness, muddy boots in hand. A few moments later, knocking sounded at her front door.

Lydia counted to twenty. The knocking came again, louder. She groped down the stairs to the candle lantern and lit it with a phosphorous match before going to the door. "Who is it?"

"United States Army. Open up."

"What do you want?"

"To ask some questions. Open up."

"It's late! I don't want to open my door!"

"Corporal, get around to the barn. Search it good. If necessary, burn it. You two: go down and look in that boat. Make sure he's not hiding there. Now, you in there, by God open this door, or I'll kick the dum thing down!"

"Wait—I'm unlocking!"

She rattled the bolt and opened the door part way. The wavering light from the candle lamp fell on an angry bearded face, on buttons glittering against a dark uniform, on an oily-looking pistol in his fist. "What do you want?"

"We're looking for a man. Followed him to your lane. Anybody here with you?"

Behind the sergeant's shoulder, three or four figures held muskets and stared curiously at her. "No. I'm alone."

The sergeant peered past her into the dark parlor. "There's mud on your porch. Wet mud. Did you take that man in? He's a Rebel blockade runner—taking him in means you're aiding and abetting an enemy of the United States."

Lydia stared at the man's bloodshot eyes. "I haven't been on my porch. If there's mud there, it must be yours."

"Not likely. Step aside. We'll search the house."

"You can't! You can't barge in like this!"

The sergeant pushed the door back and her with it. "Baker, take the candle and search upstairs; Sassi, you go through the downstairs rooms, Dougherty, with me."

She watched the sergeant stride toward the kitchen, bumping loudly against a dining room chair and cursing as it clattered against the sideboard. He opened the back door to trot toward the barn. Lydia's breath caught as she listened to boots go from room to room overhead. Behind her, the remaining soldier used his musket barrel to probe into dark corners. Then he called up the stairs, "Find anything, Henry?"

A voice came down, followed by the man's loud boots, "Naw."

Across the moonlit lawn, a rattle of heels came from the dock. The sergeant's voice called out of the barn, "Muster here, people. Son of a bitch is around here somewhere."

Lydia felt her chest heave with deep breaths as figures gathered in front of the barn and then broke into three groups to move swiftly in different directions. She waited until the faint sound of hooves had died, then went upstairs.

"Andrew? They're gone—Andrew?"

A murmur came from the cedar-lined closet. "Blow out the candle, Lydia. They may have left someone to watch the house."

"Oh! Of course."

Andrew materialized, a dim shape against the window. The floorboards creaked under his weight but his stocking feet made no other sound. He stood in shadow beside the window to study the night. "Best we assume there's someone out there. If you allow me, Lydia, I'll stay out of sight in the house and leave tomorrow night."

"Of course—stay as long as necessary."

"Thank you. I'm not sure they would have been content just to take me prisoner. Not after your neighbor told them I was a spy."

"My neighbor?"

"Your neighbor." Andrew snorted, "And my trusted agent ashore."

"I don't understand."

"Carswell. He was supposed to guide the *Juno* to a landing inside Matomkin Island. But a Yankee steamboat met us instead." Andrew's whisper grew bitter. "They knew the signal lights—they signaled that the coast was clear and we sailed in under their guns. We didn't have a chance—it was over the side and swim for shore or be captured," he growled. "And the Yankees aren't paroling captured men any more—it's prison, now, and the rope for spies."

"Mr. Carswell told the Yankees you were coming?"

"Yes, damn him."

"But why? He's been running contraband the whole war—why would he turn you over to the enemy?"

"Because there's no place left where he can market goods. Almost all roads and rail lines to Petersburg have been cut. Can't get to Richmond. Atlanta's burned to the ground. This way he gets a share of prize money for telling the Yankees about the *Juno*." Andrew pressed his fingers to his forehead and squeezed his eyes closed. "I'm sorry, Sister Lydia, but I am almost ill with fatigue."

"Let me get you something to eat."

"No—I thank you, but no. What I need most is sleep."

"In here." She led him to Gretchen's vacated room and piled woolen blankets on the bare mattress. Within five minutes, she heard his snoring through the closed door.

⊱⊰⊱

"You said Mr. Carswell told the Yankees you were a spy?"

Andrew emptied an enormous dish of scrambled eggs, grits, ham, and biscuits. He sat in a corner of the warm kitchen out of sight of the windows. Both were alert for any sounds coming down the lane or across the fields.

Mouth full, he nodded. The egg-sized bruise on his forehead had darkened, but he had washed away its dried blood. Morning light showed dark circles beneath his eyes, and she noted streaks of gray in the clipped whiskers covering his chin.

He had aged so that even now Lydia had difficulty recognizing her sister's husband of before the war. His eyes were watery and he sniffled from the results of running through the cold in wet clothing.

Lydia poured another hot cup of rose hip tea for him. The last heavy clothes she could find in Franklin's trunk—a knit sweater and a woolen topcoat—served to keep Andrew snug.

"I crawled out of the marsh north of Modest Town and headed for his plantation. But the soldiers had pickets on the Newton road and chased me into the woods." His fingers gingerly touched the lump on his forehead. "Almost got me, too—ricochet. Couldn't see anything but stars for five minutes. After some time, I reached Carswell's plantation. A mounted patrol had stirred up his dogs so they didn't wind me. Carswell was talking to them from the porch. Said he hadn't seen anybody from the *Juno* but if he did, he'd turn them over. The sergeant said 'Sure you will' and Carswell said 'You ask Captain Delaney. He'll tell you it was me reported the *Juno*. I have told you I do not protect Secesh spies, and if you harm me or mine, by Jesus Captain Delaney will have you up on charges before the Provost Marshall himself!'"

Andrew shook his head and dabbed a square of soft cloth at a sore, red nose. "So I eased out of there. I knew Marshfield lay over this way and tried to make it through the woods. But they saw me in the lane before I could get here."

"Carswell betrayed you!"

"Figured his skin or mine, I suppose. A lot of people are peeling off their gray to show true-blue Union colors, now."

"Thank God they didn't find you upstairs last night!"

"I would have surrendered. I will not bring bloodshed into your home, Lydia. And I must leave tonight. They could well come back."

"Where will you go?"

He had been thinking of that. "Mangrum Plantation. To Bonnie and the children." He stared at the tabletop. "My war's over now. Without the *Juno,* my war's over, and it's time to go home and take care of my family."

"The papers say Sherman has cut Georgia in two. How can you get through?"

"It's worse than that. He's left Savannah and moved into South Carolina. He's taking vengeance on that state for starting the war, and no army exists to stop him." The bitterness erupted again. "When General Lee invaded Pennsylvania, he would not let his soldiers take so much as a fence rail for firewood. But Sherman! He treats unarmed civilians—women, children!—like enemy soldiers!"

"Then how will you manage?"

He shook his head. "I must, that's all. I must get to Bonnie and the children."

"Take the *Lydia.*"

He looked at her for a long moment and then blinked away the hope. "It's too dangerous—with me aboard, she could be claimed as a prize. I can't deprive you of your boat."

"And I could never face my sister or your children if I didn't do all in my power to help you. Wear those clothes, pretend you're a fisherman. You're a civilian, you carry no contraband. She's a good inshore boat, and you can get her at least as far as Norfolk."

His chest rose and fell on a long breath. Then he nodded. "Farther! I can sail the *Lydia* to Jacksonville, if need be." He took both of her hands in his. "Bonnie and I will be forever in your debt!"

⌒⌒⌒

Andrew went before the late quarter-moon rose, taking

as much food as she could spare and promising to return the *Lydia* whenever possible. After learning who the "Simon" was she had named when he knocked at her door, he gave his blessing on their union and a wish for Simon's safety. "I am grateful some good has come out of this war," he said. "And your sister will share that feeling."

Lydia was not so sure of that, but she was certain she had done the right thing. Though Andrew's chances were slender, they were better than if he had to walk through enemy-held territory past armed and vigilant pickets. Even if blockade boats searched the vessel, they would find nothing but fishing gear. She had done the right thing, she told herself again. But though she had given the boat willingly, the emptiness beside her pier, like the vacancies caused by the disappearances of Roger, then of Willy and Gretchen, and especially of Simon made her feel how much Marshfield was diminished.

Chapter 32

Madam, I do not care what Union officer you claim to be friends with or what you aim to tell him. My duty is to find out where your boat is, and you won't say where it's at!" The one-armed captain, suffering a grippe whose results were evident in the gummy hairs of the mustache beneath his nose, rattled the piece of paper at her.

"I've told you I don't know. It was taken at night."

"And here you tell your sister in Georgia that it was her husband took it!"

"You have no right to my personal correspondence!"

Behind the officer's shoulder, Parnell Carswell smiled at Lydia. "Come now, Mrs. Sensabaugh. You have corresponded with the enemy. This letter is evidence of your collusion in Captain Parker's escape. It's a very serious issue and you're well advised to cooperate." He nodded at the one-armed officer. "Captain Delaney will tell you that under the laws of Union occupation, your property is subject to confiscation by the United States Army for aiding and abetting the escape of an enemy of our nation. And," he said, shaking his head sadly, "a dangerous and daring spy, at that."

"You told Sergeant Durgin your sister's husband wasn't here. That right?"

"That is so. And you have no proof he was."

In wordless reply, Captain Delaney shook the paper again.

"The sergeant's men searched my house and my barn. They found no one."

"Then he come later and you give him your boat!"

"I loaned it to him. I did not know he was the hunted man. Sergeant Durgin told me nothing of the man they sought, so I did not know it was my brother-in-law he hunted." There was nothing, she thought, in her letter to Bonnie that would contradict that statement.

Carswell shook his head. "You know full well he's a blockade runner!"

"He told me he was on parole. That he had been captured over by Matomkin Island and paroled. That someone, Mr. Carswell, had betrayed him to the Union Navy." Her eyes held Carswell's. "Someone who wanted prize money for the capture of him and his ship."

"And I suppose he didn't tell you he was a spy, either," Carswell said

"We did not discuss the war. We discussed family matters. Nor did we discuss the theft of goods from my barn last summer."

"All right," Captain Delaney said, "all right. Now where'd he go? Where'd he sail off to?"

"He told me he was going to the mainland. That he would return the boat in one or two weeks. That's all."

"You say in this letter here that his wife should be seeing him real soon. 'Dear Bonnie such joyous news. I have seen Andrew and he is safe and on his way to you.'"

"He told me he intended to go home. I wrote to put her mind at ease and to give her some hope."

"Perhaps you're being less than honest, Mrs. Sensabaugh?"

"It is certainly honest, Mr. Carswell, when I express my contempt for you!"

The man held his smile, but his cheeks darkened with a flush of anger. "You are on thin ice, madam. Very thin. And there's not one thing your Union paramour can do about it, so don't rely on him. Cooperate—give Captain Delaney the truth about Parker. Do that and Colonel Merritt, the Provost Marshall, might not confiscate your farm."

"I have told all that I know."

The captain deftly folded the letter with his one hand and tucked it into his breast pocket, quick fingers buttoning the flap. "He wouldn't have landed above Norfolk, not with Grant's whole army between there and Petersburg. Probably coasting south, trying to get behind Sherman. We'll tele-graph Norfolk, Wilmington, Charleston, Savannah—alert the picket boats. He can't have got much beyond Wilming-ton by this time. Name of the boat's the *Lydia?*" he asked Carswell.

"Yes," he said, not taking his hard glare from her face. "That boat will be located, madam."

↭

Petersburg, Virginia
February 21, 1864
My Dearest Lydia,
This letter will be brief. It is to explain my failure in correspondence and tell you that I have been re-deemed from Andersonville Prison in a general ex-change of officers and men and I am now back with the Fifty-First NYSV. Our reg't was captured almost entire at the end of September before Petersburg when the forces on our right flank gave way under an enemy charge. In the confusion the Secesh hemmed us in and captured nearly all 280 of us. Lt. Frank Butler fell mortally wounded in the groin, but fortunately other casualties were light and only three of my com-pany were wounded. Nonetheless we were forced to lay down our arms as we were under their muzzles. I remember writing after our withdrawal at Turkey Hill

that this would never happen to a unit under my command. The fates saw fit to humble the pride of that claim. We were taken to Richmond then Danville and then Andersonville. I will not dwell on the conditions we found there. Suffice to say the experience of that place has generated in every one of us a deep anger to finish this war and bring home our suffering comrades from that hole of starvation and brutality. And bring to justice those responsible for the inhumane treatment of our soldiers. Once again facing Petersburg, we are eager to repay their hospitality.

Petersburg
April 1, 1865
My Dearest Lydia,
The question is not if but when the Confederacy will be defeated. Genl Sheridan is rumored to have cut the last rail road link to Petersburg. What is not rumor is that we attack tomorrow. The men are ready and eager to swim out of this sea of mud and dullness and sickness that costs more even than gunfire. The story goes that one soldier with mud up to his hips was asked if he had been through Virginia and he replied Yes, I have been through it in a number of places. Despite weariness, cold, mud, sickness, and a foe that will not quit, spirits are high. Some men speak of their fear of being the last Union soldier killed in the war, and some when they are angry over some issue wish that upon their opponent. I must confess that thought is in our minds, but we will keep driving Genl Lee, for when he is defeated, the Confederacy will end and so will this terrible war. Then we can be together, My Wife, and have a life of peace and thankfulness for what we have been given. I think of you constantly and of the pleasure and peace of Marshfield, and with this letter I send you my love. Should I not survive tomorrows attack, I can not ask you not to

*mourn, but I do ask you to know truly that I feel I
have lived my life to its fullness in knowing your love.*

In shock from the first letter, in fear from the second,
Lydia sat on the scarred bench in front of the Sundries Store
and clutched the few sheets of paper. Though she stared out
over the street muddy with April rain, her mind was on the
Western Shore where the attack had taken place. But its results were unknown to her.

Circles from small raindrops shivered the puddles, and
the air—damp and cold—worked under the shawl she had
wrapped about her shoulders. Mr. Henderson tried to have
her sit in the Ladies Parlor near the stove, but with calm finality rather than anger she reminded him she was no longer
welcome there.

Simon's second letter had been posted on the first of the
month. The Salisbury newspaper, from Friday, April sev-
enth, told of the fall of Petersburg five days earlier, which
would have been the attack he wrote of. She prayed that he
had survived and was whole and healthy. But by now he
could be facing more danger in so many places: one head-
line said Richmond had fallen on the third of April in fire
and looting by its own drunken citizenry while Rebel irregulars shot at Union troops in the streets. Another report
asserted that Lee would join Johnston in Tennessee, with
Grant—and Simon—chasing after him over quickly repaired railroads. Another said that six thousand Rebel soldiers had surrendered at Saylor's Creek after a hard battle
but as yet no casualty lists were available. And a reporter in
the field told of General Sheridan's race to get ahead of Lee
at Lynchburg. It was, she thought, as if a massive chess
match drew to a slow and painful close with armies marching and counter-marching in a weary end game. But the
game's moves still cost lives, and one of those might well
be Simon's.

The weekly *Tribune* stated that Union soldiers were tired
but eager to see the famous Last Ditch that the Rebels had

been talking so long about defending. And that led Lydia to another prayer that in his eagerness to see the end of this war, Simon would not be careless or foolishly brave.

With its light rain and trees whose new leaves greened against a gray sky, this April day spread silently around her. A crow called from somewhere in a misty field at the edge of town; past that, out of a distant tree line, came the trill of an oriole. Lydia tried to remember when she had last listened to that music, but could recall only that it was long ago.

Gradually, the soft thump of hooves on soggy earth worked into her thoughts and she looked to see two riders coming south from Maryland past the church and toward the Sundries Store. As they drew nearer, she recognized Captain Delaney, and he looked sharply at her. The second rider wore a corporal's chevrons, but Lydia did not know his face. They halted in front of the porch and the captain dismounted. The corporal, remaining in his saddle, nodded at something the captain murmured and took the reins of the officer's horse.

"Mrs. Sensabaugh—afternoon." The one-armed man touched a finger to his hat brim. "This saves me a long ride out to your place." His thumb and finger flipped open the breast pocket of his coat and pulled out a folded paper. Without opening it, he held it out to her. "For using your property to store supplies to aid and abet the enemies of the United States, and for using your property to aid and abet the escape of a fugitive from military justice, the United States Army seizes your property under the Articles of War. You are herewith evicted."

She stared at the man, his words not fully registering in her mind.

Captain Delaney's rough hand grasped her limp fingers and pressed the paper into her palm. "Provost's Orders, dated today, April fourteenth, 1865: you got three days to vacate, and this is one of them."

His boot heels thudded down the two board steps into the

mud, and he swung into his saddle. "Two days from today a patrol will be billeted in your house. You will be gone by that time, or you will be arrested, tried, and hanged for treason against the United States of America."

❧❧❧

The oak tree in front of the Williams home loomed against the sky, its rain-blackened branches dotted by the fragile green of leaf buds. Lydia stared at the landmark as her body shook in tense spasms. As if in sleep, she had unhitched Dan from the Sundries Store rail and let him plod his way back to Marshfield. As if removed from the earth, she had drifted above the wagon seat seeing nothing, knowing only that the loss of all that she owned could not be true but it was true. Now she felt the cold as the rain drifted under the gum cape she at some time wrapped around herself. But it was not the cold that made her skin quiver and jump. It was some nervous action of her flesh as if the underside of her skin itched with fleeting attacks across her body. It could not be true that she was losing Marshfield. She would awake from this nightmare and know it to be false. She would awake and know that Simon would return to her and Marshfield.

Yet she knew she would not wake to anything different. As true as the tree she gazed at, as factual as the hard wagon seat she perched on, there would be no waking from it: in two days Marshfield would no longer be hers. And then where would she go? How would Simon find her? She would not believe that God was punishing her for lying with Simon—that act was sanctified by their intent to marry and by the love that filled her heart. But—the dark thought spread from a perverse corner of her mind—would Simon still want her if she were a pauper without Marshfield for a dowry? Had she not, long ago, discovered that Franklin married her as much, if not more, for her dowry than for herself? Had she not told Gretchen that a dowry was a large consideration for many men—and could not that include Simon?

Dan slowed and glanced back as they neared the familiar turn that led to the Williams farmhouse. Lydia touched the reins to guide him and he headed willingly through the two posts that marked their gate.

"Why, Mrs. Sensabaugh—come in out of this wet! Why, what on earth—!"

Lydia fell against the older woman, clutching her thick body tightly with a hunger to feel the warmth of a fellow human. Suddenly she was crying. Heavy sobs twisted her chest into hoarse, stinging gasps, and her words were unintelligible even to herself.

"Here! Here, now. Here—come now."

Lydia felt herself led from the porch and her oilcloth folded from her.

"Here—sit here, now. You drink this. Shhhh—just drink this. You're shaking like you got the ague!"

Gradually her breathing slowed to an occasional shaky hiccough, but Mrs. Williams would not let her say anything until finally Lydia, sipping hot tea that had a medicinal sting, could sink back against the chair and her trembles gradually subsided.

"Now, dear, tell me what this is about. Shhh—slowly. Just say whatever you got to say quietly so's I can understand. There's no rush. Just tell me, now, dear."

The words finally came in comprehensible fashion.

"Take Marshfield? The Yankees are taking your farm?"

Lydia nodded. "Because of the fertilizer Franklin stored there. But Parnell Carswell stole it and sold it to the army for gunpowder, so they accuse me of aiding the rebellion."

"But you didn't send it to the army!"

"It was in my barn. As well as other contraband Carswell stored there. And I helped my brother-in-law escape."

"And that was because Squire Carswell told the Yankees where his ship was coming in?"

"Yes."

"That man's behind this, believe you me. That man's hand is in this somewhere." She was silent a moment. "Thank the good Lord this news wasn't what I was afeared it was!" She drew a determined, deep breath. "Well, Mr. Williams isn't here—that man uses any excuse he can to go off somewhere—so I can't ask him. But I bet he'd say you could challenge this act in a court of law."

"It's military law, the captain said—an Article of War. I don't know what rights I would have, and if I don't vacate in two days he said they'll hang me for a traitor."

"That's not going to happen! Nobody around here is going to let that happen! Those Yankees think they been in a war, they'll find out what one really is, they go around hanging women, and innocent ones at that!"

Lydia smiled wearily. The tea, the warmth of the kitchen, above all sharing with someone else the burden of Marshfield's fate and her fear for Simon, had drained both the rigidity and the strength from her. Despite knowing the emptiness of Mrs. Williams's threat, Lydia could now begin to understand and accept the truth of what had happened to her.

"Tomorrow is tomorrow, and you're not going all the way to Marshfield this evening. One more cup of tea and then you stay here for the night. No—I know what's best right now, and that's for you to get a good night's sleep. Mr. Williams can go out tomorrow morning and feed your critters—won't hurt them to go without for one night. Here, drink this tea—another dollop of Frazier's Cordial will help you. It's good. It's got laudanum and alcohol, and that'll help you rest."

௸௸

Lydia had been surprised at the calmness of her mind when she awoke in the Williams's guest room. Mr. Williams returned home after she had gone dizzily to bed, and the next morning she repeated to him what had happened. Beside her, Mrs. Williams' nodding head verified Lydia's words. Outside the kitchen windows, a bright morning sun began to dry the land.

Mr. Williams, twice as broad as his wife but equally short, mulled over her comments about martial law and the articles of war. "I ain't a lawyer, but I reckon if Lincoln could use the martial law to suspend the habeas corpus and arrest the whole Maryland legislature, then the army can do pretty much what it wants whether or not there's any smidgen of truth to what they say you done. That's what happens when anybody, even a president, starts stretching laws—they stretch further and further." His thick white eyebrows, like two hairy caterpillars, lifted against a wrinkled forehead and he asked Lydia if any of the charges were true.

"I did let Mr. Carswell store contraband in my barn before he forwarded it to the Western Shore."

"Um. Well then. There's a skunk in the woodworks, for sure."

"My very thought, Mr. Williams, and I reckon we know who that skunk is!"

"I believe we do, Mrs. Williams. Well, first things first. We don't want you to get arrested and hanged, so I'll go with you to collect your goods and stock and you can move back here until we get all this straightened out. You got a roof over your head for as long's you need it, Mrs. Sensabaugh, and a place where your soldier can find you when he comes home. And we got plenty room for your animals and goods, too, and no, you don't have to thank us—we're neighbors. Then we'll see what a real lawyer can tell us. This war's just about over, I do believe, and so is secession. Then we'll see how Squire Carswell fares under the Articles of Peace."

Chapter 33

The war stumbled to an end. First the rapid thud of hooves paused in front of the Williams farm and a voice shouted of Lee's surrender. Then newspapers blared accounts of Lee's surrender to Grant at Appomattox Court House, followed a week later by gigantic headlines announcing Lincoln's assassination on Good Friday, and detailing the ferocious hunt for his murderers. Buried beneath those headlines were other stories of Generals Sherman and Johnston negotiating terms of surrender at a farmhouse in North Carolina, and of other Rebel units escaping and vowing to fight on.

The news—stirring, shocking—served for a time to take Lydia's mind off her own loss. As days passed and she began to form thoughts of a future of some kind, she refused to allow herself any plans that included Simon. She had heard nothing from him since his letter preceding the attack on Petersburg, and, she forced herself to admit as unemotionally and factually as possible, he could now be dead. In fact, some dark corner of her mind kept teasing her with the image of a letter announcing that he had been one of the last to die, heroically—and ironically—falling even as the war ended. But even if he lived, her new condition might change his affection for her. Though his professions of love had not been based on her ownership of Marshfield, he had often written of it as "home," had dwelt on the peace and comfort the farm held for him. Those phrases which once warmed her heart now hinted at an entirely different meaning: she knew enough of men to realize that a plain woman with a dowry was more attractive than a handsome woman without one. No, any plans she formulated had to be for herself; any future she might have with Simon was out of her hands and would depend upon his actions when he discovered that she was destitute.

The small purse of coins and greenbacks beneath her mattress upstairs was enough to pay her way to Norfolk where her sister and uncles might help her survive. But it could also pay her way to Washington and provide support for several weeks while she sought employment. From what she had seen in the Federal City, she could probably work there as one of the new women office clerks that the government hired. Or perhaps she could become a tutor to the children of government officials in a city that had, at best, poor schools and few of those.

If the Yankees had not already seized the *Lydia,* Andrew could sell it and provide additional cash. Dan would have to be sold, of course—but only to a gentle owner—and Mrs. Williams already said she could use another milk cow as good as Tessie.

April's raw damp eased into the softer air of May. In the Williams' front yard, seemingly overnight, the oak tree filled with dark leaves, and the sandy fields beyond the barn and animal pens greened with rising crops. Lydia and Mrs. Williams were in the chicken pen selecting eggs for the brood hens to sit when a woman's voice called from beside the house, "Heyo, Mrs. Williams—Mrs. Sensabaugh!"

"Gretchen Druer," Mrs. Williams called back, "is that you?"

"Yes'm. I was coming down this way, so I brought this letter for Mrs. Sensabaugh. It's from your Yankee." The girl grinned at the expression on Lydia's face. "I reckon you been waiting for it."

"Yes!" Without opening the envelope, she studied the address. The familiar extra loop at the top of the capital L told her that the hand was Simon's. "He is alive!"

Gretchen caught her breath and looked away; Mrs. Williams patted Lydia on the shoulder. "Of course he is, dear. You go inside and read your letter. Gretchen and I have a lot to catch up on." They watched Lydia, still staring at the envelope as if reading its travels, walk swiftly toward the house. Then they followed more slowly. "It's been a coon's age, Gretchen—how's your mother?"

"I don't reckon she'll ever be the same, ma'am. But she's a bunch better now that Humphrey's home. He come a week ago, and it's a blessing to see Mama smile so. She ain't quit smiling for the whole week. It's a wonder her cheeks don't ache."

"That's wonderful! How is he?"

Gretchen frowned, dropping into a chair at the kitchen table while Mrs. Williams stirred up the fire to heat water for tea. "Changed. Lost a lot of weight and grown a lot taller. I heard him in his sleep first night he was home yelling something." She wagged her head. "But some ways, he's the same old Humphrey—at first, he said all he wanted to do was walk around the farm and tend to the animals. But then like he's always done, he got tired of that pretty quick and started going down to New Church and about the county like a dog sniffing old smells."

"Well that's healthy, I suppose."

"Yes'm. We think so too, so Pa ain't said nothing to him." The young woman glanced toward the open door that led to the dining room and parlor, and her voice dropped. "She okay? Mrs. Sensabaugh?"

"She lost everything she couldn't load in a wagon or have walk behind it. That, and not getting any letters has worn on her a lot."

"We heard about Marshfield. She done a lot less than some others hereabouts. It don't seem fair."

"No, it's not fair. But maybe with this war over, the army'll give her back her place. Mr. Williams thinks it's possible, leastways."

"I thank the good Lord that Yankee of hers is still alive and finally wrote her."

The older woman nodded. "He can speak with the army about Marshfield, too, and if he cares for her as much as she believes, then he will." The kettle began to steam and she poured a little hot water on the tea leaves to start the flavor. "How have you been, dear? Lord, I can't remember when I saw you last."

"No'm, me neither. I been busy, you know, helping Pa, and all."

"You're a good daughter, Gretchen. Your parents can be very proud of you."

"Well." She looked again toward the doorway then raised her voice loud enough to be heard in the next room. "I do have some news, though." She waited. "I said I do have some news. I'd like to share it with you and Mrs. Sensabaugh."

A rustle of paper and Lydia, face pale, came into the kitchen. She carefully folded her letter into its envelope. "News to share, Gretchen?"

Mrs. Williams spoke first. "Is he all right? Your gentleman friend?"

A deep breath lifted Lydia's bosom. "He doesn't know when he'll be discharged, but he's alive and well. He has lived through it."

"Lord be praised," said the older woman.

"Amen," said Gretchen.

"You have news, Gretchen?"

"Yes'm. Roger Bradshaw done asked me to marry him."

"Roger?"

Pressing her lips together, Gretchen nodded and tried to read Lydia's face.

"That's wonderful!"

Her lips relaxed into a tiny smile. "You really think so, ma'am?"

"I know he's had feelings for you, but I always thought he was too shy to express them."

"Well, he expressed them—kind of, anyway." She blushed. "He's been coming over to our place now and then to help out."

"What are your feelings toward him?"

"I reckon I like him better than I used to. When we argued all the time, you know. We still do some, but mostly we talk through it, now."

Many marriages had started with less. "Roger will make a wonderful provider."

"Well, he is handy on a farm. For a waterman, I mean."

"He's also a gentle and kind man, Gretchen."

"Yes'm, that too." Her voice became animated. "And he don't drink nor look too bad when he's cleaned up some. He does that, you know: cleans up before he comes to call—trims his beard, and all. And his eyes is the same—he laughs with them." She brushed her hand across her pale hair. "He even got him some false teeth that clips in with a silver wire. And he said he thought I was right pretty."

"You are, Gretchen. You're lovely!"

"Well."

"When's the happy day?"

"I ain't told him yes, yet. Ain't told him no, neither. I sort of wanted to hear what you thought about it. You and Mrs. Williams."

"I believe we both think it's wonderful."

"Sure do!"

"Well, then, we'll see. Might as well do two at once't"

"How's that, Gretchen?"

"Humphrey. He's seeing Lucy Brown. Says he don't mind that she had Allen Rafer's baby because Allen was a friend of his'n and they was standing side by side when he was killed, so it just seems kind of right."

"Lord be praised!" Mrs. Williams' feet made a shuffling step that was almost a seated dance.

"Yes'm. Well, that's my news."

"And such wonderful news it is, Gretchen! I can't tell you how overjoyed I am. I wish you and Roger all happiness—and Humphrey and Lucy, too!"

"Yes'm. Thank you." Pink of face, Gretchen hid behind her cup of tea. Mrs. Williams bustled toward the kitchen cabinet and rattled out a squat bottle.

"This calls for a round of Mr. Williams's prize brandy!"

"Oh, we couldn't."

"If we don't, he'll be mad we didn't. And I wager he'll have one himself when he hears about it." She poured a hefty splash in three teacups, and raised hers. "A toast to the brides, to the grooms, and to the happiness to follow!"

"I second that," said Lydia.

The sting of the strong liquor brought laughter and Mrs. Williams poured another round as the women began to talk all together. Each thread of conversation wove among the others to create a fabric of words that, to Lydia, held the almost-lost spirit of music. She had forgotten how women's voices could nest together to create a world of warmth and comfort and joy that pushed aside all the pain and suffering and worry of war and injury and death. Finally, at one of those transient silences when the women collectively paused for thought and breath, Mrs. Williams asked Lydia what her gentleman friend had to say in his letter.

Glowing from the brandy, Lydia unfolded it from its envelope. "I'll read it to you. Some of it.

"'I write to tell you what you are sure to already know: it is over! Lee has accepted Genl Grants generous terms of surrender and our regiment witnessed the historic moment. The defeated filed past our ranks to lay down their arms, but not before they burned their banners and flags to prevent them from falling into our hands. We might have stopped that but orders were not to and our artillery was ordered not to fire in celebration. I believe those orders were right. The antagonist, your compatriots my Lydia, was brave and stubborn and fought in full belief of their cause as we did—'"

Gretchen scoffed. "Well, that's Humphrey, all right—that stubborn part."

"'The stillness of our troops witnessing the laying down of arms was far more eloquent and dignified than any cheers or trumpets, and many of the men had tears in their eyes at the thought of what this day has cost—'"

"Amen," Mrs. Williams agreed.

"'The idea now is to go home and heal the wounds of this fratricidal war—'"

"Yes, yes!" Gretchen replied.

"'Home. To me, home is Marshfield and you. Home to my Lydia. Home to my wife. I do not know exactly when that will be. There is caution about reducing the army whilst some out west have not yet surrendered. And we are told of a Grand Review of the entire army to take place in Washington in May and another for the regiment in New York following. Until then, the Fifty-First will be stationed at Alexandria where much must be done. There is talk of leave for those who did not enjoy it when the regiment was in Tennessee, and I could be included in that group. I pray so, but we will see. The Fifty-First left New York in 1861 with 890 officers and men, and replacements over the years of war brought the total names on its rolls to over 3,050. It returns from war with but 93 of the original members and only 250 veterans—myself included—who enrolled latterly. Two of the original officers are left, the rest being promoted, honorably discharged for disability, or killed. Many of the dead were my friends.'" Lydia stopped there and folded the letter.

Gretchen stared at her. "Why, I didn't know you was married to him!"

Lydia's cheeks grew hot, and not just from the brandy. "In spirit—and in promise."

"I see." Mrs. Williams's eyes sparkled. "Well, you're too young and pretty to remain a widder, so I hope it was a real spirited promise—hee!"

ₑↄₑↄ

In the warmth of the June evening, Lydia, in the kitchen helping Mrs. Williams prepare supper, did not hear the knock. But Mr. Williams—an odd, expectant look on his unshaved face—leaned in through the dining room doorway. "Mrs. Sensabaugh, you got a gentleman caller. He's in the parlor."

For a moment, Lydia simply stared. "Oh!" She tugged at the apron, tangling the strings so that Mrs. Williams—"Wait, dear. Let me do it"—had to undo the knots.

"My hair!"

"You look lovely! Here, let me." Mrs. Williams straightened Lydia's collar and then tugged at the back of her blouse to draw the cloth tight across Lydia's breasts. "You look beautiful!"

Which is what Simon thought when he saw her in the doorway. Awkward, eager, almost numb that it could really be happening, they gazed at each other with a mixture of hunger and strangeness, a mixture of question and hope. When he held her and her arms tightened fiercely across his back, the question was gone and the hope fulfilled.

The Williamses gave them time. After an uncertain while, Lydia became aware of little domestic noises from the kitchen.

"You must meet Mr. and Mrs. Williams."

"I met mister—he met me. At the door." His lips spoke through the sweet tickle of her hair.

"Oh, yes. Of course." Though he was wearing a suit rather than a uniform, Simon still smelled of salt air, sun, man-sweat. The aromas made her flesh clutch hungrily. "They—they have been very kind to me. They have given me shelter."

"Then they are forever my friends." The tightness of his arms punctuated his words.

She waited, but he said nothing about her loss of Marshfield. Perhaps he had not received her letter. But the sad words that would inform him could not pass the dryness of her throat. The only thing she could say was, "Ah, Simon."

"My wife."

A discreet knocking sounded at the kitchen door, followed by Mrs. William's voice, "I have set a place for your gentleman. I hope he'll stay to supper."

"Yes, ma'am. I certainly will."

Although the meal was a quiet one, a sense of joy bound them in warmth around the table. Mr. Williams said grace, giving thanks for the return of loved ones from places of peril. Mrs. Williams would not let Lydia rise to help serve the meal. Simon, trying to be attentive to his host's questions about the war, could not keep his eyes away from Lydia. Finally, the meal ended with rhubarb pie hot from the oven and doused in clotted cream. Mr. Williams, squeaking the cork in his brandy bottle, asked, "Do you know, Captain, why Mrs. Sensabaugh is staying here with us?"

Simon, blinking, drew his eyes from the curves and warmth of Lydia's face, the glory of her hair with its sunstreaks of light brown, and the softness of eyes that suddenly seemed worried. "I do know, sir. I found soldiers quartered at Marshfield. They directed me here."

"It's a sad state of affairs. But now that the war's over, maybe the army will return Mrs. Sensabaugh's property to her."

Simon thought briefly of not answering with the truth. But best to have it all out—best not to give Lydia a false hope that would have to be crushed all the more painfully tomorrow. And no bad news could overcome the pleasure and fullness of being once more with each other.

"It's no longer the army's property. The soldiers told me that the Provost Marshall has sold it to Mr. Carswell."

Lydia gasped, "Sold it?"

His heart stumbled at her shocked expression and he said quickly, "Perhaps the sale can be nullified." He did not add that many loud voices in Washington sought revenge on the

Confederacy for causing the war and on Virginia especially for President Lincoln's assassination by one of her sons. The most vulnerable victims of retribution would be those who could not defend themselves. "But should the worst come about, my Lydia, recall that you and I have triumphed over even harder circumstances. And now we are finally together, much to my joy."

A rising pallor drew the color from Lydia's cheeks. "I'm grateful, Simon, for our blessings. But to lose all that I own—to lose the home I believed we might share—to lose it so unfairly, and to someone like—like—"

"I'll visit Mr. Carswell tomorrow. Maybe I can convince him to withdraw his purchase."

Mr. Williams nodded. "I'll come along. As witness. Might help Squire remember his manners."

⌒⌒⌒

Mrs. Williams looked up from the open door of the iron oven where shimmers of heat carried the aroma of baking biscuits. "I reckon you needed your rest this morning."

Lydia tried very hard to keep her face and voice from showing any embarrassment. But she wasn't entirely successful. "Is Simon about?"

"He and Mr. Williams left already for Oak Hall to talk to the squire about Marshfield."

"Gone? Without telling me?"

"He'll be back. He wanted you to sleep—didn't say why, of course. But I must say, noises do carry in the night." The lobes of Mrs. Williams's ears quivered with her silent laughter.

The men had not returned by mid-afternoon, but the sound of slow hooves drew both women to the front door as a buggy with two riders rocked toward the house and sat for a few minutes studying the farm.

"That's Mr. Talbot," said Lydia.

"Who's that with him?"

"I don't know."

Mr. Talbot stepped down from the vehicle to walk up the steps of the porch and knock on the doorframe. The other man, fully bearded and wearing a tall hat, removed some papers from a carpetbag beside his feet and followed.

"Howdy, Mrs. Williams—Mrs. Sensabaugh." Talbot lifted his wide brimmed hat to nod at both women. "Is Mr. Williams to home?"

"He will be." Mrs. Williams wiped her hands on her apron. "What can I do for you, Mr. Talbot?"

Without answering, the man shifted his black eyes to Lydia and studied her face. "I hear your soldier's come back."

"Captain Morse. Yes."

He gave a short nod. "He's lucky. On two counts."

Lydia understood. "Yes," she said firmly.

"Well." He turned his attention back to Mrs. Williams. "Let me get to business." He gestured a thumb at the taller man beside him. "This here's Mr. Alonzo Willis. He's a district superintendent for the Freedman's Bureau. Wants to know how many slaves you owned."

The bearded man tipped his hat and held a pencil over one of the papers. "Your name, ma'am?"

"Williams. But we don't have slaves. Never did." She looked at Mr. Talbot. "You know that. I reckon you know more about slaves in Accomack County than anybody."

"Yes'm. That's why Mr. Willis hired me. But my word won't do—he's got to have a affidavit from prior slave owners saying they set theirs free."

"Yes, ma'am. War Department regulations. If you'll just sign here." He held out the pencil.

"What's this?"

"Affidavit swearing that you have manumitted your slaves. You can sign for your husband, it's all right."

"I don't know that I want to sign anything for Mr. Williams without him reading it."

"If you have manumitted your slaves, you got nothing to be afeard of. It's them that still have slaves and say they don't that will get their property seized."

"We never owned slaves. I already told you that."

"Yes ma'am. So just sign here that you freed them."

"We didn't free any. We never had any."

"I understand, ma'am. But this paper don't have a place for that. The War Department wants sworn compliance with the emancipation from all citizens of the late rebellious states. So you got to sign. If you don't you will be subject to judgment by the War Department through the Freedman's Court."

"I don't know about any War Department or Freedman's Court. I do know that the laws of the Commonwealth of Virginia do not allow for me to sign a legal document in my husband's name. You want his name on that, you come back when he is here."

Above the curling brown hair of his full beard, the man's cheeks tightened. "The Commonwealth's laws are suspended. All the states that were in the Confederacy are now under the governance of the War Department as surrendered territories." He wagged his head. "In your case, since you never owned slaves, this is just a formality, but it's got to be done—War Department regulations, and them regulations say you can sign as representative of the property owner. Now, I can come back, and I will if I have to, but you could save me a lot of time by just signing now."

Mrs. Williams shook her head. "I reckon you'll have to come back and explain to Mr. Williams why he's got to sign a letter about something he never did in the first place. And you, Mr. Talbot, have you driven this man over to Oak Hall for the Squire to sign that he's freed his people?"

"I did yesterday. Squire's already told them they were free to clear off his property. Told them that want to stay in their cabins that they're free to pay rent, now—cash, day labor, or sharecropping." Talbot wagged his head. "Used to be Squire just freed the old ones that couldn't work no more—turned them over to the county poor laws, so to speak, so they wouldn't burden his purse. Now he's a regular abolitionist." He grinned and tipped his hat good-bye. "Squire knows how to make a profit out of anything, I reckon. Even Marshfield Farm."

They watched the buggy turn and go out the lane to the high road.

"It is a different world now, Mrs. Sensabaugh. But that Carswell and his overseer is still the same."

                              ♥‿♥‿♥

It was almost sunset when Simon and Mr. Williams returned, stiff legged from the long ride. Both men were grim, but Mr. Williams said, before he and Simon headed out to take care of the livestock for the evening, that discussing business was less important than having a calm meal. Their news could wait until after supper. Finally, after the dishes were done, Lydia and Mrs. Williams joined them in the little-used parlor.

Mr. Williams looked at Lydia. "The long and the short of it is, Squire says Marshfield's his now, and that he aims to keep it."

Lydia was surprised at the feeling in her breast. She had told herself again and again not to place any hope on Simon's success. But nonetheless hope had lurked in her heart's recesses and now it ran out with a painful collapse.

Simon frowned. "We could file suit, Lydia. But it would be expensive in both money and time, and there's no guarantee we would win. The law—on an issue like this—with the new courts…"

"So Marshfield is gone?"

"It could take years for the suit to be settled. And no guarantee it would be in our favor."

"I see." Numbly, she rose and walked to the front porch. Her mind was blank and she stared at but did not see the silhouetted oak tree with, high in its crown, the chatter of birds settling for the night. Even as she cautioned herself not to have hope, her last hope for Marshfield and the dowry that it was had ridden with Simon. Now there was nothing. She brought nothing, and that opened the door for the worst to happen.

"Lydia." Simon's arm rested against her back and she felt his breath at her ear. "It's not the end of our world, Lydia. Remember, we've faced worse."

Almost woodenly, she said without turning, "You are free of any obligation, Simon."

"I'm what?"

"Free of any obligation to me. I no longer have a dowry. You are free."

His long silence gradually brought her back from an icy distance to the Williams's front porch. "Do you understand, Simon?"

A heavy sigh was his answer. "What I don't understand is if I should be angry at your supposition about my motives, or proud of your honesty and practicality. I think I will simply conclude that you are acting like a damned fool."

"Captain Morse!"

"Lydia, you will miss Marshfield. We both will. But it's not Marshfield I wish to marry—it's you. And by my intent and my light, we are already married. So your precious dowry is irrelevant. Our future is together, with or without Marshfield." His voice grew softer. "This war brought much loss for many people, Lydia: homes, fortunes, lives—gone. We are among the lucky. We still have each other. If our future together is not at Marshfield, well, it's a great and grand country. The new homestead law promises a bright future out west. I've saved enough of my pay to stake a claim in the territories, and in time you may find that you like the western lands as much as I do."

Lydia gazed into his eyes for a long moment. "Simon," she said softly, "does your nose itch?"

His eyebrows rose in query. "I don't understand."

"My mother used to say that when your nose itches, it means you're going to kiss a fool."

Chapter 34

Sheriff Hope leaned back in the chair as its rattan complained in tiny, muffled shrieks. "It will take me four or five days to get back to Oak Hall and Mr. Carswell."

Simon nodded. "That's all we need, Sheriff. We appreciate it."

Mr. Williams wasn't quite as pleased. "Sheriff, you know and I know that Squire didn't get as bad as he deserves. But the captain, here, said he'd seen enough killing, and that was Squire's good fortune, I tell you that!" he added with a laugh. "Though maybe not his wife's, being still married to that man instead of being his widder."

"I'm grateful Captain Morse didn't go that far. My job would be a lot harder right now, if he did." Sheriff Hope's large head wagged once. "Don't know that the law can do much to Carswell, either. One thing I've learned in this job is the difference between law and justice. And a lot of the law's up in the air, right now, what with military regulations and the Freedman Bureau's rules. But Carswell will remember you, Captain, for the rest of his life. Every time he washes his face, in fact."

"Simon, you didn't tell us about this!" Lydia was still trying to fit together the full account of Simon's and Mr. Williams's recent visit to Oak Hall, and the reason for Sheriff Hope's visit to the Williams farm this afternoon.

"The story wasn't fit for your ears. Or for Mrs. Williams's."

The older woman grinned. "It fits my ears right good! I only wish't I'd been there to see it."

"But what happened? What caused it?"

Mr. Williams snorted. "The man couldn't keep a civil tongue in his head. Captain Morse, here, spoke polite and I reckon Squire took his manners for weakness—he begun saying things about—um—his neighbors that was both ugly and downright lies."

"What things? About whom?"

"Never mind," said Simon.

"Broke down and cried, he did," Mr. Williams said. "Begged the captain to quit whupping him. So the captain just dropped him there like a dirty rag and walked off, wiping his hands." Mr. Williams paused. "Odd—his wife and his tenants, as he calls them now, just stood and watched. Nary a one tried to stop it nor said nothing against it. And when we left, they just stood there and watched him cry."

The sheriff shifted his bulk with a grunt. "Well, I must say he looked pretty used up when he came into my office. He went to the Provost Marshall first, but Colonel Merritt said it didn't involve the Articles of War. Said Carswell should go through the civil authorities." The black beard twitched in what might have been a smile. "That's me. And now he wants me to do his fighting for him, and do it quick."

He had arrived in mid-afternoon bearing an arrest warrant for Simon based on a criminal charge of assault and battery. The plaintiff, Parnell Carswell, Esquire, brought the complaint as the result of a severe beating inflicted by said Morse on the person of the plaintiff and on the premises of his, plaintiff's, own home, and in view of his, plaintiff's, own wife, as well as in the presence of Mr. Williams of Accomack County and other witnesses to be named. In addition to criminal charges, Carswell told the sheriff he intended to file civil charges of slander of title and slander per se, resulting in damage to material claims and to personal reputation by words spoken in the presence of said Mr. Williams and others to be named.

"I shouldn't have lost my temper."

Mr. Williams shook his head. "I'm glad you lost your'n before I lost mine—I'm too old to do as good a job as you done."

"Was he badly injured?"

"Mostly in the pride." Mr. Williams grinned. "But he will carry a few good scars. And be right colorful around the eyes and nose for a couple weeks."

Sheriff Hope heaved himself to his feet, the chair ticking with relief. Folding the warrant, he tucked the papers into the coat he wore, despite the heat of the June afternoon. "Like I say, I won't have time to serve these papers for a few more days. Got a lot of business what with all these new freedmen running about, getting into mischief, or being assaulted by those who don't like the emancipation."

Simon nodded. "We'll be gone by then, Sheriff. Thank you."

He and Lydia walked Sheriff Hope to his horse. The big man hauled himself into the creaking saddle as the large animal shuffled and braced under the weight.

"I wish the both of you good fortune and a safe journey wherever you go." He touched a finger to his wide-brimmed hat. "As long as it's not in my jurisdiction."

They watched the tall horse canter out to the highroad and turn south and out of sight. The sky reddened with the setting sun. In her mind's eye, Lydia envisioned the still, slow waters of Fowler Inlet reflecting the ruddy cloud glow. It was a glow that would outline the masts and hull of the *Lydia*, if the boat had been there. But it wasn't. She had not heard from Bonnie since Andrew had sailed away, and now, like the *Lydia*, Marshfield Farm was gone into a distance that was more than space. Simon was right—she would miss Marshfield deeply, and she would miss sailing the *Lyd-*

ia on evenings such as this more than she could explain to him. But he had spoken of the Colorado Territory, of prairies that stretched like the sea itself from horizon to horizon, of mountains that rose abruptly from the plains into snow that lasted through the heat of summer, of wide, high valleys with gentle streams and sweeping vistas of trees that turned gold in autumn, and of air that tasted like sweet wine.

ᴄᴐᴄᴐ

March 12, 1867
New Marshfield Farm
Boulder County
Colorado Territory
My Dearest Sister Bonnie,
Your letter of January twentieth has just arrived. I reply immediately, so the weekly post rider may take this with him on his return. A longer letter will follow. I am grateful for your family's health and for your good wishes. Simon and I congratulate you and Andrew on your newest son and he must, indeed, be a beautiful baby, having such remarkably handsome parents. I agree that we must pray that his world will be free of the sufferings of ours and that he may never know the bitterness of war. I would add that we must never pass on to our children the burdens of our lives, but face our children into the light of hope and the promise of their own futures. Perhaps my sense of optimism springs from the openness of this land, the sense of promise that seems to fill the very air, and the blessings we have already received from it. More likely it is the fact, my Dear Sister, that Simon and I expect our firstborn in June! I cannot express the happiness that fills our days as Simon, especially, labors long hours to turn our half section of prairie into a home for our child. I do confess to home sickness

when our September fogs lie on the prairie as they used to do over the water at Old Marshfield. But the compensations of New Marshfield are many, not the least of which is the beauty of those snow covered mountains that rise just west. Yes, the same ones that so awed and even frightened me when I first arrived and which I have now come to love not only for their coolness in summers, their gold flanks in autumn, but—ever practical me—for the snow that covers their tops year round and fills our new irrigation ditch with water that is valued even more than the silver mined up in Central City. Most of our apple saplings have survived and have new buds, long arrows of geese pass overhead and sing loudly of coming Spring, and Simon has joined our neighbors in a petition to the rail road for a spur to carry the fruit of our plowed acres to Denver City which is to be the territorial capital. As you once wrote when you learned of our wedding, Providence has its own plan. We must accept that and be grateful for what happiness comes our way. When I think on the tumultuous years just passed, I wonder at so much death and loss and can only believe that each of us is destined in our own manner to follow the Biblical examples of suffering and growth in order to learn Patience, Faith, and Charity. To help my State repel the Invader, I aided a fellow Virginian. But that Virginian turned out to be my worst enemy. And my State defended an Institution I did not believe in but did not object to. To survive, I was forced to deceive and to lie. Yet without those sins I would never have truly understood the effects of slavery on the soul of both master and servant. And the man I first thought of as the Enemy turned out to be the Partner of my soul and the Father of my child. Truly, Sister Bonnie, God does work in mysterious ways. As Simon has said on occasion (the occasion being the loss of a calf or an unexpected expense)—

*Even on a long march, the sky can be beautiful, flow-
ers may bloom, and rest will be sweeter. And so it is.
Like him, I am learning to put one foot in front of the
other, to enjoy the blessings of the journey, to trust in
the Lord for the remainder, and to be grateful for the
beauty and peace that is New Marshfield. To which I
would add only, let us be generous to all others who
march as blindly as we do.*

I remain your loving Sister,

Lydia

*P.s.—Gretchen Bradshaw has written that Old
Marshfield was taken from Mr. Carswell and given to
some of his ex-slaves as part of the Freedman Bureau's compensatory ruling. She and her husband
Roger are doing well on their farm and she says their
twins are already walking and thinks that one will be
a farmer and the other a waterman.*

L.

Author's Note

Cut off from the rest of Virginia at the outset of the Civil War, the Eastern Shore Peninsula was riven by issues of secession and abolition. The sheriff of Accomack County was an abolitionist, and the town of Chincoteague voted overwhelmingly to remain in the Union. The secessionist volunteers who fled the Union-occupied Eastern Shore to fight for Virginia called themselves "The Fugitives." A branch of the Underground Railroad, traveled by Harriet Tubman, ran up the peninsula through Maryland and Delaware to freedom. Sister-vessels of the "Lydia" were used to smuggle goods through the Union Blockade, and may be seen in "Chesapeake Bay Log Canoes and Bugeyes," by M.V. Brewington as well as at the Chesapeake Bay Maritime Museum. "Newton," Maryland—now Pocomoke City—and New Church, Virginia, are thriving communities, though much of the farm land surrounding them has become residential. The coastal marshes remain beautiful. In short, though names and specific locations in the novel are fictional, this story is set on the land and in the Civil War history of Accomack County, Virginia.

About the Author

Rex Burns is the author of numerous books, articles, reviews, and stories. The first in his series of police procedurals, *The Alvarez Journal*, won an Edgar for Best First Mystery and introduced the hard-boiled Denver homicide detective, Gabriel Villanueva Wager. Another, *The Avenging Angel*, was made into a feature movie starring Charles Bronson (retitled *Messenger of Death*, 1988). With *Suicide Season*, Burns introduced the Devlin Kirk series, a Denver private detective specializing in industrial security. Novels featuring the father/daughter detective team of James Raiford and Julie Campbell are published by Mysterious Press/Open Road.

Burns's books are published in hardback, paperback, E-format, and audio, and have been translated into a number of foreign languages. He is also co-editor, with Mary Rose Sullivan, of an anthology of detective stories entitled *Crime Classics*, and has published under the pen name "Tom Sehler." His short stories appear in several periodicals and anthologies, and his "Leonard Smith" series of Aboriginal police stories can be found in *Alfred Hitchcock's Mystery Magazine*. *The Better Part of Valour*, an absurdist adventure novel set in Latin America, was published in E-format by Tirgearr Publishing of Ireland.

For several years Burns wrote a monthly mystery book review column for the *Rocky Mountain News*. Other of his reviews have appeared there and in the *Denver Post*, the

Miami Herald, and the *Washington Post*. A number of his essays on craft have been published in *The Writer* and elsewhere. He was a contributor to *Scribner's Mystery* and *Suspense Writers*, and an advisor and contributor to the *Oxford Companion to Mystery*.

He received his AB from Stanford University, and, after serving in the Marine Corps, his MA and Ph.D. from the University of Minnesota. He has published articles on American literature and culture, and a study of nineteenth century values entitled, *Success in America: The Yeoman Dream and the Industrial Revolution*. Retired from the University of Colorado, he lives and writes in Denver, Colorado.

CPSIA information can be obtained
at www.ICGtesting.com
Printed in the USA
LVOW05s2256220817
546022LV00011B/136/P